Praise for

KATHY LETTE

'Funny, loud and uninhibited'
DAILY TELEGRAPH

'A delight'
COSMOPOLITAN

'Utterly outrageous, irreverent and screamingly funny'
JILLY COOPER

'Disarmingly perceptive'
SUNDAY TIMES

'Zippy, smart-mouthed… plenty of laughs'
EVENING STANDARD

'Funny, irreverent, smart'
GUARDIAN

'Kathy Lette can turn from raunchy farce to the most tender emotion in a trice'
STEPHEN FRY

'No one has a turn of phrase like Kathy Lette'
DEBORAH FRANCIS WHITE

'Kathy Lette is hysterical'
ERIC IDLE

'Deliciously rude and darkly funny'
NICOLE KIDMAN

'With her renowned clever wit and masterful (mistress-ful) wordplay, Lette delights us all yet again. Read this and know you are in the hands of a wise feminist who makes you laugh out loud!'
SUZIE MILLER

'In a moment when women's voices matter more than ever, Kathy's wit and clarity feel timely and necessary'
ISLA FISHER

'Hilariously unruly. I loved every fierce, frothy line of feminist inspiration'
TINA BROWN

'Breaking a taboo on every page, these are funny feisty women and I love them'
CAROL VORDERMAN

'This is Kathy Lette at her finest – every line is perfectly crafted and it had me laughing out loud from page one'
ADAM HILLS

'An absolute riot! Proper escapist fun that I thoroughly enjoyed'
JANE FALLON

'Funny, super sharp and bang on message – Kathy Lette knocks it out of the park, again!'
ARABELLA WEIR

the SISTERHOOD RULES

ALSO BY KATHY LETTE

Puberty Blues
Girls' Night Out
Hit and Ms
The Llama Parlour
Foetal Attraction
Mad Cows
Altar Ego
Nip 'n' Tuck
Dead Sexy
How to Kill Your Husband (And Other Handy Household Hints)
To Love, Honour and Betray
Men: A User's Guide
The Boy Who Fell to Earth
Love is Blind (But Marriage is a Real Eye-Opener)
Courting Trouble
Best Laid Plans
After the Blues
HRT: Husband Replacement Therapy
Till Death, Or A Little Light Maiming, Do Us Part
The Revenge Club

KATHY LETTE
the SISTERHOOD RULES

An Aria Book

First published in the UK in 2026 by Head of Zeus,
part of Bloomsbury Publishing Plc

Copyright © Kathy Lette, 2026

The moral right of Kathy Lette to be identified
as the author of this work has been asserted in accordance with
the Copyright, Designs and Patents Act of 1988.

All rights reserved. No part of this publication may be: i) reproduced
or transmitted in any form, electronic or mechanical, including photocopying,
recording or by means of any information storage or retrieval system without prior
permission in writing from the publishers; or ii) used or reproduced in any way for
the training, development or operation of artificial intelligence (AI) technologies,
including generative AI technologies. The rights holders expressly reserve
this publication from the text and data mining exception as per Article 4(3)
of the Digital Single Market Directive (EU) 2019/790.

This is a work of fiction. All characters, organizations,
and events portrayed in this novel are either products of the author's
imagination or are used fictitiously.

9 7 5 3 1 2 4 6 8

A catalogue record for this book is available from the British Library.

ISBN (HB): 9781035901326; ISBN (XTPB): 9781035901548
ISBN (ePub): 9781035901340

Cover design: Simon Michele
Printed and bound in Great Britain by
Clays Ltd, Elcograf S.p.A

Bloomsbury Publishing Plc
50 Bedford Square, London, WC1B 3DP, UK
Bloomsbury Publishing Ireland Limited,
29 Earlsfort Terrace, Dublin 2, D02 AY28, Ireland

HEAD OF ZEUS LTD
5–8 Hardwick Street
London, EC1R 4RG

To find out more about our authors and books
visit www.headofzeus.com
For product safety related questions contact productsafety@bloomsbury.com

For my beloved maestro, Brian O'Doherty. Anam cara.
And with undying love to my own three sensational
sisters, Jen, Liz and Cara.

THE SISTERHOOD RULES

1. **SUPPORTIVE.** Be a human Wonderbra – uplifting, supportive and making her look bigger and better.
2. **PROTECTIVE.** Think of yourself as a big pair of knickers: you've got her arse covered.
3. **EMPOWERING.** Remind her to think big. She doesn't need a man's seat on the bus; she needs his seat on the board.
4. **ALWAYS TAKE HER SIDE AT WORK.** If sacked by a bad boss, say something along the lines of 'He clearly took an IQ test… and failed', possibly followed by 'Hey, why not start our own company?'
5. **MASSAGE HER EGO.** 'No, your bum does *not* look big in that…' The only important thing about a backside is that you don't talk out of it.
6. **NEVER BE JEALOUS.** The colour green suits no female complexion.
7. **NEVER LET A PENIS COME BETWEEN US.** It's forbidden to go after a sister or girlfriend's hubby or crush. Men come and go, but the sisterhood stays faithful forever.
8. **HONESTY.** Tell her if she's being cheated on; if a partner's gone straight from puberty to adultery, she should know.
9. **ALWAYS TAKE HER SIDE IN A BREAK-UP.** Try saying something along the lines of 'Your ex is

as useful as a solar-powered vibrator on a rainy day.' Or 'How do you get rid of cockroaches? Tell them you want a long-term relationship.'
10. **COCKTAILS.** Two sisters walk past a cocktail bar – well, it could happen! If she needs to cut loose and get drunk, be her wingwoman.
11. **WINGWOMAN.** Never leave her when she's drunk too much. Don't let her dance naked on a table top either. Nor do the school run topless. And don't ever, ever let her drive when tipsy. No police officer will understand that she needs her car with her at all times just to make sure it doesn't leave her for a younger owner.
12. **BE THE WIND BENEATH HER BINGO WINGS.** Women suffer from facial prejudice; we get judged on our looks in a way that men don't. No wonder ageing to women is like kryptonite to Superman. But don't let her go under the knife. A woman should never pick her nose – especially from a catalogue. Remind her that she wouldn't want a bloke who only wants her because she's silicone from tonsils to toenails. He should read between her lines – her facial lines, that is.
13. **LOCKED LIPS.** Be her confidante and keep her secrets forever.
14. **LLL.** Love, Loyalty and Laughter: this is the sisterhood creed. Stick to each other like a nylon dress in a heatwave.
15. **THE SISTERHOOD IS POWERFUL.** If you aren't lucky enough to have biological sisters, don't forget you do have the Sisterhood – a network of fun and fabulous girlfriends. But a sisterhood of sisters? There's nothing more powerful. So go right now and thank your dear mum for giving you the best gift imaginable.

PART ONE

Sisterhood Rule
*Love, loyalty and sisterly solidarity.
Be a human Wonderbra – uplifting, supportive and
making her look bigger and better.*

ONE

'Mum's missing.'

My blood ran cold, like some heroine in a Dracula movie. It was the first time I'd heard my sister's voice in five years.

'I should have guessed it was you. The sky went dark and all the neighbourhood pets are running around in circles.'

Since Verity's betrayal I had become fucktose intolerant – the condition of being completely unable to tolerate other people's fuckwittery. Especially my twin sister's. It was the phrase I now lived by, and not just because it was needlepointed onto my throw pillows.

'I wouldn't have rung if it wasn't an emergency.' My sister's voice rose half an octave, losing much of its polished intonation in the process. 'Mum didn't turn up for dinner last night. I've rung the neighbours. Nobody's seen her for a week.'

My heart flopped like a hooked fish. 'Did you call Melissa?'

'Of course I did, Isabella,' Verity rebuked, her voice brittle. 'Mum cancelled rehearsals at the last minute and Mel had to get a replacement in for the Birmingham gig.'

The deadening weight of anxiety settled on my guts. Our workaholic mother cancelled a concert? And without consulting her manager? Unheard of. I'd once seen her conducting Mahler's Fifth Symphony with her leg in plaster. A single mum at twenty, Nicole raised us alone, against all the odds. ('What do you call someone who uses the rhythm method?... Mother!' was her quip de jour.) As kids, we got used to trailing her from one concert hall to the next: an endless architectural itinerary of huge, sooty, cocoa-coloured Victorian mausoleums or brutalist, futuristic buildings, first in Australia and then all around Great Britain and Europe.

We were often babysat backstage by tipsy bassoonists or left to sleep in the orchestra pit. Too busy to cook, Mum only ever served leftovers. The original meal has never been found. She was always about ten years behind with the ironing too. By the time she got around to pressing our clothes, we'd grown out of them. Mum used to say that behind every successful career woman was a laundry of dirty washing and crinkled school uniforms.

'Actually, Mum didn't turn up for our book club this week either,' I blurted. 'I tried calling but no answer. I just presumed rehearsals ran late. You know what a perfectionist she is. Plus it usually takes her a few days to get back, so I wasn't worried.'

'I just wanted to check that you hadn't heard from her before heading over there,' Verity interrupted crisply, poised to hang up.

'I'll go. I'm closer.'

'Maybe geographically... but not in any other way.'

My stomach bungee-jumped. 'That's crap, Verity! Mum and I are incredibly close.'

'It broke her heart, you know. Giving up a music scholarship to join a rock band.'

My guts clenched even tighter. When I told my mother I was forfeiting my scholarship to music college and moving out to live with a drummer, she was appalled. 'You're giving up your degree for an illiterate yobbo?'

'Mum, Johnny graduated from the University of Life.'

'Yes, with no grades.'

Turned out she was right.

The tree limbs outside the window of my tiny, pocket handkerchief Kilburn garden were necklaced with freshly spun spiderwebs. I felt as trapped as the small insect I could see struggling there.

'And you think what you did didn't break her heart, Verity?' I retaliated.

I thought back to the baroque, grotesque drama of it. Mum and I were hollowed out by the magnitude of my sister's betrayal. I'd produced industrial amounts of tears and snot. I cried so uncontrollably I was almost declared a protected wetland habitat.

'It may have escaped your notice, Isabella, but our mother conducts operas. She understands grand passion.'

If my eyes could have shot out fatal rays like the ones in comic books they would have zapped right through the phone and incinerated her on the spot.

It was hard to believe that Verity and I had come out of the same mother, and at the same time. Even before Verity's unforgivable treachery, we were the classic odd couple. Verity, a serious, intellectual child, went on to a successful career as a musicologist lecturer at King's College and a renowned critic with an internationally bestselling book on style to her name. The woman's so pernickety, she'd put paper down under a rocking horse. I, on the other hand, am your classic shambolic bohemian. Verity always says that my clothes don't look bought – but donated; as though I walked through a charity shop covered in superglue. While I regularly eat tuna straight from the can like a cat, she has an olive oil sommelier. She Instagrams about work–life balance, gut microbiome, ice baths and hot yoga workouts. These days my idea of burning calories is when my toast catches fire.

'Isabella?'

If I had to endure her voice a moment longer, I feared I would self-destruct in one big, howling implosion. Slamming the handset back into its cradle, I snatched up my car keys and wrenched open the front door.

Even though it was mid-June, London lay damp, cold and grey as a graveyard before me. I'd just prised open the door of my battered old Volkswagen with a butter knife – my car is held together by hope, rust, parking tickets and string – when I remembered that I had a pupil in the music room.

Leaving the car door flapping, I dashed back inside to find the student whose name I could never pronounce wrestling a diminished arpeggio into submission.

'Sorry... Shit. Um, Fear... cray... Far... quoir... Friggin'-Whatever-Your-Unpronounceable-Name-Is, today's lesson's cancelled. No charge, obviously.'

The tall, rangy bloke I'd been teaching for the last year and a half every Saturday morning at 9 a.m., looked up from his guitar fretboard, frowning. His strawberry-blond hair sat atop his head like a cumulus cloud. 'It's Fiachra,' he corrected.

'My mother's missing.' As I articulated the words, fright slammed through me. 'I have to go find her... Which means seeing my sister... For the first time in five years... Which is why I'm doubly flustered.'

'And why's that now?' my perplexed pupil asked, in a soft Irish burr.

'The woman's a vile, duplicitous, despicable worm,' I elaborated.

The cumulus cloud trembled as he ran his hand through it. 'So, um, don't hold back. Tell me what you really think of your woman.'

'God. Shit. Sorry... You probably think I'm bitter, cynical and twisted – and well, you're abso-bloody-lutely right.'

He laid the guitar across his lap. 'My six sisters are always at each other. I'm sure it's not as bad as you think.' He swept a straggle of buttery hair behind his ears, the strawberry strands like a smudge of jam across his forehead. 'So, what's the craic? Why are you so dark on her?'

Why was I confiding in a nerdy geek with an unproduceable Gaelic name who wore ironed jeans, white trainers and a beige cardigan? I could feel my heartbeat in my throat. I managed to fish out the terrible words from somewhere between my tongue and my toenails. 'Because... she stole my husband.'

TWO

I turned into my mother's Hampstead driveway so fast, the car wheels threw up noisy gravel, before slamming the brakes hard. Verity had commandeered the driveway, of course, her black Mercedes gleaming smugly by the rhododendrons behind my mum's beloved old Citroën. I reversed, cursing, and headed on up the hill, finally managing to squeeze my pockmarked rust-bucket between a huge, hybrid 4 × 4 and an electric car about a half a day's trek from my mother's house.

I jogged back down the road, dug the spare key out of my pocket and speared it into the lock. The front door gave a familiar squeak as it yielded. The warm, comforting scent of Mum greeted me. Kicking off wet shoes, I took in the scratched antique wooden furniture in the hall, the paint-clogged Georgian woodwork and flowery ceiling decorations with their whipped cream plaster confections.

'Mum!?' Bounding up the stairs, two at a time, I steeled myself. What if her body was lying prone on the carpet? But bathroom, spare room, bedroom – all proved reassuringly empty. Her light pink, fluffy slippers, lying askew on the bedroom rug, looked startled – proof that she'd left in a hurry.

Concluding this disconcerting reconnoitre, I barrelled back downstairs to see Verity making her way up into the kitchen from the basement.

Seeing me, my sister stood still. She looked like an exclamation mark – tall and svelte, in pencil skirt and high heels, her smooth dark hair falling neatly around her unlined face. Decades of academia had given her the expressionless expression of the English intelligentsia. My sister's exterior was so flinty she made an Easter Island statue look animated.

'What on earth are you wearing, Isabella? You look like a babushka setting off across the tundra to find a single twig for her feeble fire.'

I glanced down at my patchwork skirt, trainers and puffer jacket, which my Aussie mum calls a Tasmanian tuxedo. 'Any sign of Mum?' My heart was beating so loudly, I felt as though it was coming through stereo speakers.

'She's not in the house.'

'But her car's outside.'

We circled each other like wrestlers.

'Should we call the police?' My stomach churned sourly.

My sister's eyebrows took the moral high ground. The only thing you really need to know about my twin is that her two favourite sentences are 'Call yourself an adult?' and 'Pull yourself together.'

'Pull yourself together,' she ordered now, a champagne-coloured silk scarf frothing at her throat in a complicated bow. 'There's no need to involve anyone else just yet.'

As she rummaged through a pile of mail on the kitchen counter I was assailed by a flutter-click snapshot of memories. First was Johnny walking out with the words 'It's over' – his declaration had a dull final sound to it, like a lead door closing; a submarine hatch, with me, marooned outside, scrabbling, pounding to be let back in and not cast adrift. Then me, snatching up a family photo of us all together in one big hug – Mum, Verity, Johnny, Chrissie, me – and throwing it against the wall, screaming as the glass shattered. Actually, the range of sound effects available to me as a human that day were totally inadequate. I wanted to be a lioness, so I could roar; a hippo so I could bellow; a dingo so I could tilt my head and howl at the moon.

As Verity continued her forensic search for evidence of our mother's whereabouts, I took her in. Although twins, the differences between us were stark. While my own eyebrows remained big and Frida Kahlo bushy, hers were plucked into sceptical arches. Her flawless skin was stretched tautly over prominent cheekbones. Whereas my beauty regime involved whacking on some Boots No7 occasionally, Verity believed in all the rejuvenation mumbo jumbo and voodoo magic of expensive lotions and potions. Growing up, her shelf in our shared bathroom cabinet was lined with vials of unguents – eye of newt, puréed sloth, minced nuts of Norwegian fluke fish – she was a sucker for it all. Okay, her skin did look luminous, while mine was a damp grey canvas, but we weren't that far apart, wrinkle-wise. Were we?

I glanced at my reflection in the mirror above the kitchen table. Who was I kidding? I looked at least five years older than her. Verity wasn't getting older, she was just getting tighter. Was it botox and fillers… or a happy romance? My blood curdled at that thought.

I next appraised her smooth, auburn, well-trained hair with its neat parting and flat, straight fringe. Eyes darting back to the mirror, I confronted my own unruly nest. I looked like a vegan, creative dance instructor who fired things in a home-made kiln for a hobby.

Maybe if I'd got more of our mystery father's genes, I'd have lovely tame locks like my sister and less of my mother's thick, curly, salted caramel–coloured hair which sprang from our craniums as though we'd had a million brainwaves simultaneously.

My sister noticed my scrutiny. Reading my mind, she then bitched, 'So, remind me, Izzy. What does your hairdresser do for a living again?' She smiled as she delivered the barb; the smile of an iceberg, if an iceberg could smile.

I felt the heat of anger flare up my neck and across my face. My grief and fury were like tinnitus – constantly there on the edge of my consciousness. The worst thing was, I'd thought Johnny and I were happy… and then suddenly, there I was, tumbling through space like Alice, shoved down the rabbit hole by my own sister.

Determined not to react, I stuck my head in the fridge to cool off… and came face to face with a bowl of greenish hummus, growing fuzz.

Verity pushed past me to examine the milk carton. 'Expired,' she pronounced, which pretty much summed up our relationship. She poked her pinkie into a bowl of cream, the skin of which had wrinkled. She'd no doubt soon offer it some advice on how to 'roll back time and make the most of itself'.

Tutting, Verity steamed across the kitchen to the table as though motorised. She folded up a *Guardian* newspaper, dated, I noted, a week earlier. Beneath the paper lay a scattered assortment of brochures, which I recognised as glossy NHS handouts. I snatched one up and read the title out loud. 'Pancreatic cancer.' My eye raced down the page, picking up key phrases about life expectancy and pain management. I drew my hand back from the pamphlet as if it was a live socket.

'Oh my God.' My sister handed me another leaflet – for a Dignitas clinic in Switzerland. 'To ease your exit' read the tag line. Anxiety grabbed me in a rib-cracking squeeze.

'Our mother has pancreatic cancer?' I gasped. We locked eyes, forgetting all animosity for a moment. 'It can't be true. I mean, why wouldn't she have told me?'

'Because assisting someone to take her own life risks prosecution for murder or manslaughter.'

'Take her own life?! Not Mum. She's a life force!'

'…which would make living with a painful, degenerative, terminal disease all the more unbearable.'

'But Mum tells me everything.'

'Ah, clearly not.' Verity's voice dripped condescension. 'Especially when it could lead to a jail sentence of up to fourteen years. Why do you think that so many Brits travel to Switzerland every year without their skis or hiking boots?'

A throb started in my temples – urgent, painful. 'There must be some mistake. We need to check her computer.'

A swivel on her Prada pumps and Verity was gone.

I followed, quailing inwardly. By the time I reached Mum's study, my sister was already seated at the desk and tapping out various trial passwords into Mum's computer. As I picked my way through a room crammed with scores, instruments and music stands, I paused to look at the trophies and awards marching across the mantelpiece.

I absorbed the framed photos on the walls – Nicole in front of various orchestras, baton raised, smiling assuredly. Our mother gave off a warm, confident glow that made the mere mortals around her seem faded. It was impossible for me to imagine her crippled with disease, diminished, in agony... And nor, it would seem, could she.

By the time I turned back towards the antique oak desk below the big, bay window, Verity had cracked Mum's code. 'It's a mash-up of our names: Izzity.'

'Note that my name comes first.' It was an appallingly petty utterance under the terrifying circumstances but it made me feel fleetingly better. I'd always believed that I was top of Mum's speed dial, because, just like her, I too was a single mother, to my now seventeen-year-old daughter, Chrissie. The love of a mother for her child was an emotion Verity could never understand, having sacrificed her desire for children in exchange for my husband, who didn't want another.

'We're twins, Isabella,' Verity retaliated, scrolling through our mother's search history. 'Mum loves us equally and identically.'

'But we're not identical, are we? Not in looks nor in personality... I mean, I'm an honest, kind, loyal person... while you're a selfish, two-faced bitch.'

Verity's eyes narrowed. 'Actually, the reason Mum loves me the most is because I'm rational and unemotional, like her. We're both cool-headed academics, unlike...' Her voice tailed off. The cursor was pulsing over two entries on our mother's most recent history: a search for flights to Switzerland and a hotel near Lucerne. As I peered over my sister's shoulder, a volt of panic zigzagged through me, twisting, writhing, squeezing at my heart so hard I couldn't draw breath.

'Emails,' I muttered. 'Check her emails.'

Outside, the summer storm had picked up, turning the trees in Mum's manicured garden into one big snarl of limbs and leaves.

The email search revealed a flight to Geneva. One way. Plus a reservation at some kind of mountain glamping site.

'Do you... do you think that glamping place is part of... of a Dignitas clinic?' While fright licked like flames all over me, the perfect skin on Verity's smooth cheek merely ticced once or twice.

'I believe they do have places where clients go to be, you know... prepared,' she said, ashen-faced.

The pounding in my chest and head now shook my whole body. I heard a low painful moan, a kind of keening. It took me a while to realise that this strange disembodied animal sound was coming from my own mouth.

While I stabbed at my mother's number on my mobile for the hundredth time that day, Verity rang the glamping site, but of course, they would not give out any information.

We stared at each other, dumbfounded. I felt translucent, like a hand held over a flashlight or one of those jellyfish you see on a David Attenborough documentary, floating in the sea.

My sister was the first to snap out of her stupor. She sprang to her feet. 'Let's get going.'

'Where?'

'To Switzerland. To save our mother's life.'

THREE

'So, are you here for business or pleasure?' the train conductor asked politely as we sped around Switzerland's shimmering lakes in a dark green, double-decker express train.

'Hmmm...' I replied, sarcastically. 'Your mother trying to kill herself... That kind of thing can really put a damper on your vacation plans.'

My sister shot me a censorious look. 'A bit of both.' She was back in charge again, her smile as controlled as her Spanx, her smile as lacquered as her hair.

'Don't ever go to Madam Tussauds, Verity. They may melt you down.'

Stretching my mouth wide, I threw in a fistful of the vacuum-packed peanuts I'd bought at the back of the plane – Verity, of course, was up front in business – and started chewing ferociously. Seeing my sister again had time-warped me back to when Johnny walked out. My body had become a bumpy, sickening carnival ride: palpitations, sweats, nausea, hysterical laughter, uncontrollable sobbing, carpet-writhing, hand-wringing... and I was starting to feel the need to strap myself in for another nail-gnawing, roller-coaster torment.

'Isabella, this is a delicate situation which requires diplomacy.' My sister's voice oozed patronising sympathy, like a veterinary nurse about to euthanise a pet dog. 'I understand Mum best. So, when we get there, let me do the talking, okay?'

I ground what was left of my teeth. This was the last place on earth I wanted to be. For the last five years I'd gone out of my way to avoid my sister, only to realise I'd merely been bungee-jumping with our umbilical cord. What irked me the most was that Verity had never said sorry. The only person my sister has ever apologised to is a composer she'd maligned in print – and even that was court ordered. 'Well I'm sorry, but I don't ever apologise' was her sarcastic motto.

'Mum and I have much more in common,' I seethed.

'Don't make me laugh. You are a pale reflection of our mother.'

'Hey, at least I have a reflection... How's that stake through the heart working out for you, Verity, by the way?'

My sister wedged in her ear pods in a huff. I gazed out of the big wide window. With the sun dancing on the pale blue lake, and the sun-drenched, ancient vineyards cascading down sloping hillsides to the sparkling shoreline, it was like being in an animated postcard. It wouldn't surprise me to learn that even the mountain goats, ibexes and chamois in Switzerland hold PhDs in tourism; only taking a break from their glacier treks and wood frolics to read some Nietzsche or brush up on Einstein's mathematical theories.

We hurtled on through the lush, pristine countryside in silence, both of us broadcasting a buzz of hostility.

When the train sighed its way to a stop in a picturesque village of flower pots and red-roofed chalets, my sister motioned for me to get up. Moments later, we were aboard a sleek catamaran and gliding across the glassy water.

I looked around in awe. The view was a holiday brochure writer's perfect mix of snow-dappled mountain tops and glittering lakes whose waters lapped, cat-like, at the foot of steep fir forests.

Disembarking at a small beach, a funicular then whisked us up, up, up to the *Dr. No*-type underbelly of a lavish spa hotel. The approach could not have been more cinematic and dramatic. Elbowing our way through startled guests, we slalomed across the shiny limestone floors of the grand foyer. An impeccably groomed receptionist was chatting casually to a tour guide.

I put my elbows on the desk and glanced pointedly at my watch; couldn't she see that we were on a deadline? Literally.

'Glamping ground?' I blurted, urgently.

The aloof administrator coolly pointed the way. My sister and I pushed through the heavy glass doors and careered off down a dirt path through the woods. It must have been raining for the last few days as we soon found ourselves squelching through mud, thick as clotted cream. All around us there was an odd percolating sound – mud, drying in the sun. Fungus shone like blisters on the trunks of trees. The dark forest finally opened onto a shaded glen of ten or so tepees.

'Mum!?' I called out, before slipping on leaf mulch and landing spread-eagled on the wet grass.

'A natural outdoors woman,' commented my sister, sarcastically.

'The outdoors is why God invented hotels,' I shot back, wiping mulchy hands on the back of my jeans as I lurched upright again.

'Shhh. Listen.' Verity cocked her head, ears pricked. I heard it then too. The faint thud of drums and low bellow of horns. My brain scrambled. I could see from my sister's face that we'd both had the same thought: some kind of end-of-life, death-welcoming ritual?

'Christ. I hope we're in time!'

Verity's words impacted like a blow to the chest. I shook all over. I was like a distressed damsel in need of whisky nips and smelling salts. Any minute, a St Bernard dog would come bounding up with a reviving barrel of schnapps around its neck. What shocked me the most was that I'd had no idea. Nothing. Not an inkling of my mother's ordeal. What kind of selfish, neglectful daughter was I? The music was wafting up through the woods. A winding path off to the right obviously led to the terraces below but the quickest route involved a steep, downward pitch into forbidding forest. My sister made for the path, but with guilt and fear fuelling my feet, I just smashed and crashed down through the trees towards the drums, which throbbed like blood, louder and louder and louder.

When I emerged, panting, into a clearing, skin lacerated and hair festooned with brambles, the light was fading, which made the vision before my eyes a little indistinct. I seemed to be looking at a single, blurry, writhing blob. It took me a moment to realise it was a group of naked people dancing around an open fire. Amid them was my mother, limbs locked around a naked man half her age.

My mother's cheeks were pink and healthy, like an ad for alpine yoghurt; all four of her cheeks that is. I hadn't seen my mother naked since we were kids. Her nipples were party girl pink; her bush resplendent. Forget a lady shaver. Or even a lawnmower. Bringing that bush under control could only be achieved by several months of strategic bombing with napalm. In fact, were there any Viet Cong in there?

My sister now burst into the clearing from the path and took shocked stock of the group of starkers musicians lined up by the fir trees, bellowing out a tune into the crisp, Alpine air through long, ornately carved horns. There were six or so other couples, dancing and singing and sweating happily in the nude democracy of this pagan ritual. As the music crescendoed, there was an impish, unhinged joy in their leaping and cavorting.

My mother – imperious, proud, strong, no-nonsense – had always seemed destined to end up on a postage stamp. Gyrating naked around a fire pit with a toy boy is not the way I had ever pictured her.

My mother's lover broke free and wheeled in our direction, the fleshy metronome of his massive appendage swinging rhythmically. It was cold up here in the mountain air, the kind of day where most men have nothing to be proud of. Well, this man's genitals could have been coming straight to us from a beach in Barbados.

'Welcome,' he smiled, thumping his suit-of-armour six pack, 'to the Alpine Horn Festival.'

'Horn being the operative word,' I sotto-voce-ed to my startled sister, before remembering that we weren't on speaking terms.

As my bare-arsed, chest-beating mother let out an exuberant yodel, there was one thought on my mind: if I got beamed up into some spaceship right at this moment, I'd treat it as a rescue mission rather than an abduction – because nobody could be more alien to me right now than my own family.

I stared at my mother, agog, for what I estimate was about, oh, a decade, before I finally located my voice box. 'Mum?!'

FOUR

I tried to lever my eyebrows down from my forehead but they seemed to be stuck there. 'Jeesus, Mum. What the hell's going on?'

'Izzy?!" my materfamilias exclaimed, equally agog.

'Mum, are you okay?'

'Never better, darling.' Her curly, honeycomb, silver-flecked hair, usually pulled sharply back, was splayed out across her shoulders and looked, well, bouncy. Her blue eyes, normally hidden behind the thick, black frames of her glasses, smiled back at me, fluorescent in the firelight.

Verity's Stonehenge countenance now cracked. 'Mother! What in God's name are you doing out here?'

'I could ask the same of you, Verity.' She looked from one daughter to the other, amazed. 'The two of you, together! Oh, darlings, you couldn't have made me happier.'

My sister whipped off the beanie of a passing dancer to shield my mother's lady garden. I shrugged off my puffer jacket and also moved towards her. The grass seemed to billow under my feet like a water bed.

The muscular young man ceased prancing, picked up an alpine horn and joined the musicians. The thirteen-foot horn, carved from one piece of tree trunk, was like the European version of a didgeridoo. As he wrestled one end to his lips it looked as though the instrument was playing him, rather than the other way round.

'Mum, are you sick?' I took hold of her hand, consolingly.

'Yes.' I steeled myself for the body blow. 'Love sick.' Then she giggled. Giggled. Our earnest, erudite matriarch? 'I've learnt something from Gawain this week. Women don't give up sex when we get old... We get old when we give up sex!'

'Gawain?' My sister sent a snide glance my way. 'His name is Gawain? What is he? Some kind of knight?'

'A one-knight stand, hopefully,' I said, making a feeble attempt at humour.

'Shall we go somewhere a bit more private, darlings?' My mother shrugged on a most uncharacteristic leopard-skin-print kaftan and led us back up the path towards the glamping ground. She then plonked down on a log, gesturing for us to flank her. We sat either side, taking a hand each, just as we did when we were children.

'Mother, I can't believe you didn't you tell me you were sick,' Verity reprimanded.

'Sick of working? Yes. Yes, I am.'

'We saw the brochures, Mum,' I said, gently. 'Pancreatic cancer.' My mother has a deep, dark, velvety voice. If you had to orchestrate it, it'd be a cello; if you gave it a colour – burgundy. Beside hers, my own anxious voice sounded pale and weedy, like an out-of-tune oboe.

'What? Oh! No. That wasn't me. That was Helen. My dearest Helen got the diagnosis three months ago. Terminal. She planned to come here, then on to the Dignitas clinic, but had a brain aneurism last week and died immediately.' Her voice tightened in grief.

'And who exactly is this Helen?' My sister's voice had taken on a stern BBC wartime broadcaster's tone.

'My lover for the last three years.'

There was a beat while we both took this in.

'Your lover?... You've had a lover for three years?' My synapses were zinging and pinging like an overactive pinball machine.

'And your lover is... was... a woman?' my sister echoed.

'Yes, a bit of late onset lesbianism. It's quite common, you know,' Mum explained, calmly.

'I'm sorry. But where is my real mother?' I asked, confused.

'And who the hell are you?' Verity queried, equally perplexed.

'We were Pilates pals... So sympatico. Then we got drunk one night and it just happened. It was so cosy and comforting.'

'Why the hell didn't you tell me?' Verity demanded, briskly.

'Or me,' I added, proprietorially. I tried not to feel six years old; I tried to feel at least seven or eight.

'I couldn't tell you because Helen is... was married. Very churchy. They'd have been scandalised. So we decided not to tell anyone. Not even you two.'

I listened in rapt astonishment as Mum described the way Helen had suddenly got thin, her clothes hanging on her frame like flags in dead calm. Apparently, my mother's lover was diagnosed with pancreatic cancer, a blush of wild cells diffusing, and then a month later a tumour fastened in her brain like a burr, crowding her thoughts to one side.

'And then she was just in bed all the time in a turban, her skin peeling,' Mum said quietly, 'and we had to face the fact that she was dying, fast...'

'I'm so sorry, Mum.' I tried to squeeze her hand but she balled it up into a fist.

'She'd booked to come to the Dignitas clinic, alone... But then she died. Moments like that, well, your life changes.'

'Deepest condolences on your loss, Mother,' Verity sympathised.

Mum wiped away some tears. 'Helen's death taught me that we are all suffering from a terminal illness... It's called "life".'

She then went on to explain that Helen had a bucket list and her dying words were for our mother to fulfil it, starting with this alpine horn festival. 'So, I came here on her behalf.'

'But why didn't you tell me you'd be away?' Verity bounced up onto her feet, brushing leaves and moss off the back of her designer pantsuit.

'Or me...'

'I did. Didn't you get my emails saying I'd be off-grid for a while?'

'No!' Verity removed a twig from her hair and snapped it in irritation.

Mum ducked into a tepee, flipping open her laptop as she returned.

'Oh look, they're in drafts! I'd planned to send each of you an email from the airport when it would be too late to talk me out of it. But in all my grief, I forgot to hit send. Sorry, darlings. Didn't mean to worry you. It's been so discombobulating – Helen's death. But then I met Gawain and started living! Oh girls, listen to that beautiful music…'

My sister and I strained our ears to hear the throaty rumble of a traditional folkloric piece in several deep pitches echoing up the mountain. 'The alpine horn?' Verity imbued the words with utter contempt. 'I'd rather shred my eardrums on a cheese grater.'

'No… the bees buzzing their requiem. I want a lot more of that!'

I swapped a bewildered glance with my estranged sister. Our mother was a musical sorcerer. She could coax the sweetest melodies from her musicians, conjure the most nuanced rhythms and phrases from her soloists and milk the strongest emotions from an enraptured audience… and here she was rhapsodising about insects? I tried to absorb all she had just told me but felt waterlogged with information.

'Mum, be honest,' I picked at the mud which clung to my trainers like melted marshmallow, 'have you been taking hallucinogenic substances? I saw lots of mushrooms in those woods. And, I mean, you are wearing a kaftan.'

'Yes, and it's leopard-skin print,' my sister winced, 'the ultimate proof that controlled substances are in widespread use.'

'Darlings, I've never been more sane. Love at first sight! I always thought it was a myth, but my connection with Gawain was instant. I'm giving up work so we can go travelling.'

'For God's sake, Mother, how old is he?' Verity demanded in a prodding, metallic tone.

'Thirty-eight.'

'But you've just celebrated your sixty-ninth birthday!' Verity gasped.

Our mother gave a deep, painful sigh. 'When Helen was diagnosed, do you know what she said? That she wished she'd let herself be happier. Happiness is a choice, girls. People think, "Oh, I'll be happy when I get a designer house or a handbag" or whatever... But you'll be happy when you're laughing with a friend or having an orgasm... or ten!'

I thought back to my 'happy marriage'. In my experience, happiness is that lovely, warm, toasty feeling you get... just before you fall flat on your face. 'So, um, I take it you're no longer a lesbian then?'

The chilly wind at the glamping site had made a comedy of my sister's carefully constructed coiffure. She took a moment now to pat it into submission. 'I just can't believe you've been a lesbian for three years and I didn't know!'

'Why are you making it into such a big deal, Verity? Didn't you try lesbianism at school?'

'Don't be ridiculous, Mother!'

Mum now looked my way. 'Izzy?'

'Um... no, Mum, I did not... It's not like trying lacrosse. Or, I dunno, hopscotch.'

'Really? I thought all young women went through a period of experimentation.'

'Blusher. I experimented with blusher and false eyelashes,' I elaborated.

'I experimented with the Second Viennese School and Stravinsky,' Verity added, haughtily.

Our mother gave a sanguine shrug. Helen had been very clear about her commitment to organ donation, she now told us, describing how the transplant coordinator had ticked off Helen's organs on her clipboard. The active cancer meant she couldn't donate her heart, lungs, liver or kidneys but was she happy for her corneas to be taken? Her skin tissue?

'It sounds macabre, I know,' Mum clarified, 'but Helen found the whole ritual oddly calming. The official then gave her a keyring engraved with the slogan "The Gift of Life". It was a pathetic swap, I thought – a small metal disc in exchange for this warm, witty, gentle woman. But when I found that disc in my pocket the day Helen died, it became my most prized possession.' Mum pulled a chain up from under her kaftan and kissed the small round pendant. 'So, that's what I'm doing, girls. Giving myself the gift of life.'

'With a naked alpine horn player half your age?' Verity's collagen-enhanced lip curled.

'Why are you two policing me? I reached the age of consent 100,000 consents ago... Oh no. Wait... make that 100,001... Who could forget about last night!' Mum gave another giggle. It was a most incongruous noise coming from my mother's sensible lips.

'Well, it didn't take you long to forget about Helen,' Verity added, crisply. 'Clearly you're having some kind of breakdown, Mother.'

'Helen was my dear friend. Our love was cerebral. A warm cuddle in a cold world. But this... this, well, girls, I've had a sexual epiphany. I'm doing things in bed that I can't even pronounce!'

'Mother, puh-lease. Stop embarrassing yourself,' Verity said, prissily.

Mum grabbed hold of our hands once more, tugging Verity back down onto the log. She lectured us then on the importance of not living life as if you have another spare life in the vault, like those women who save outfits for 'best' – then never wear them. 'Because this is best!' she enthused. 'My advice? Enjoy yourself, girls. It's later than you think.' Once more, I didn't recognise my mother's voice. Her tone was normally sonorous, resonant, commanding – not this impish little purr. 'Everyone's obsessed with the length of life but I want to live the width and the depth of life as well. I want a life in 3D!'

'With a one-dimensional boyfriend,' Verity retorted, sharply, prising free Mum's fingers.

What was left of my mind boggled. I attempted one last time to make sense of it all. 'So, just to get this straight, so to speak...' I punned. 'You came out... and now you're going back in again?'

My mother sighed. 'You see? This is another reason why I didn't tell you about Helen. You young people are just so judgemental.'

I smiled at Verity, forgetting our animosity for a fleeting moment. 'I love the fact that she thinks we're young.'

My sister raised a condescending brow. 'Well, I am. I can't say the same for you.'

'Wow. One twin turns forty-nine while the other remains a perky forty! It's a medical miracle!'

'It's not my fault you've let yourself go, Isabella.'

'Clearly the reason you can lie convincingly about your age, Verity, is that at your age, you can't always bloody well remember it!'

'Girls! Girls!' My mother raised her hand as if silencing an orchestra. 'Why is the world so obsessed with women's ages? Every interview I do references it. "Nicole Nightingale, sixty-nine, is riding a horse aged eighteen, past a tree aged two hundred and ten." Do they want to chop me down and count the rings? Ageing is just another word for living, girls... And impending seventieth birthdays are nature's way of telling a woman to drink more champers and do more horizontal tango. Gawain has just anointed me with magic.'

'It's called sperm, Mother,' Verity countered, tersely.

Mum became suddenly sombre and dabbed at her eyes. 'When some people leave the planet you feel it's emptier. Helen left me empty and heartbroken, but since meeting Gawain, well, I feel as though I've escaped from an open prison... Just been snatched away, darlings, via a rope ladder and a waiting car, into a beautiful world of colour, spontaneity and joy,' she reflected. 'Helen secretly transferred two million pounds into my account before she died. A gift from her mother. She didn't want her horrible, misogynistic husband to get his grubby hands on it. Her dying wish? That I spend it all, ticking off her travel wish list.'

My sister and I exchanged another tacit took of alarmed bamboozlement.

'And so tell me, Mother dear, does Gawain, by any chance, know about this fortuitous financial windfall?'

Whereas I might have tiptoed through this psychological minefield in ballet pumps, my confident sister stomped ahead in steel-capped boots.

'Of course. That's how I'm funding our trips.'

I looked up at the branches of the trees rustling in the wind, every leaf sharpened to a glass-clear edge by my heightened sense of astonishment.

Verity's lipstick was emergency-beacon red and the words coming out of her mouth were a clear SOS. 'Mother, seriously. You can't go gallivanting around the globe with a man you've only just met.'

'Verity's right, Mum. And that's not a sentence I use often... But I've got condiments in my pantry that have been around longer than he has.'

Verity took our mother by the shoulders. 'You know nothing about him! He could be a conman! A murderer!'

My mother scoffed. 'Single women my age aren't dating but "carbon dating". The only men who want to sleep with us are ten, twenty, thirty years older.'

'What about that bookish don from Oxford?' my sister mused. 'He was nice...'

'Yes, but his back went out more often than we did. He required advance warning about when to schedule an erection too... He practically needed building permission from the council... Erect the scaffolding!'

'I get it, Mum, I do.' I stood to face her. 'You don't want to be a nurse... but isn't it just as bad to be a purse?'

My mother raised a combative eyebrow. 'What are you, Izzy? A social worker? You'd better start listening to Enya and eating bloody lentils.'

My head ached from where I'd whacked it on a tree branch on the mad dash down the mountain to save my mother's life and I could feel a bump and a bruise building. 'But Mum, this is all just so out of character.'

'Look, as you two keep helpfully pointing out – seventy looms! And I don't want to become one of those sanctimonious, pinched-faced, withered, Ozempic bores who exist on one cup of skimmed air a week… I want to live! And Gawain worships me. He says I'm in my Enchantress Phase – liberated from the parenting and career trenches and ready to embrace my prime.'

Mum gushed away for a bit then about what soulmates they were. 'Gawain's a composer. We've connected not just artistically, but also spiritually, emotionally and physically. Oh, so, so physically!' she drooled.

I'd read in the guide book that Einstein lived nearby in the labyrinthine, cobbled streets of the baroque city of Berne. I clearly needed to make an emergency trip there, to try to understand his theory of relativity – as in, what the hell was going on with my relatives? Late onset lesbianism, organ donations, pagan naked fire-leaping, a composer conman, sexual symphonies…

'The really terrifying thing about middle age, darlings, is that you grow out of it. Look, you girls are the greatest love of my life. When the midwives placed you in my arms, our eyes locked and that was it – bonded forever. But,' she postscripted, 'a woman cannot live by vibrator alone!'

This comment hit a nerve and I glared at my treacherous sister. 'Why is it that whenever a woman starts having great sex, her IQ goes down?' I asked, pointedly.

'Why don't you start having great sex and find out?' my mother suggested. 'Just get yourself a man and—'

'The reason I can't get a man,' I interrupted, tetchily, 'is because she's got them all.' I gestured at my twin. 'Or have you forgotten that my sister stole my husband?'

'I didn't steal Johnny! He fled… because he just couldn't stand living with you any longer.'

'Girls! Girls! Stop it.' My mother's stoicism faltered. 'My best and most beloved friend in the world has just died. But through that trauma, somehow, miraculously, it has brought my darling daughters back together.' She pulled us both into an embrace.

'I comprehend the situation, Mother,' Verity said, through a mouthful of leopard-skin-print kaftan. 'Life is full of unexpected tragedies but—'

'Exactly.' Our mother then seized our hands and forced them together. 'So don't wait until your deathbed to tell people how you feel."

'Yeah, best to just tell them to fuck off now,' I shot out in Verity's direction, wriggling free of the familial embrace.

The inky gauze of the evening had settled upon the hills in the distance. I shivered, suddenly cold, and longed for a thermal dirndl. We stood in awkward silence for a moment before my mother spoke again.

'I suggest you both put that trauma behind you and start to enjoy life. Only three things improve with age – cheese, George Clooney and vino.'

'Well, I agree with you on that score, Mum.' I nodded. 'Wine really does improve with age; the older I get, the more I love it. Speaking of which,' I tapped my wristwatch, 'it's wine o'clock. I don't know about you two, but I don't think I've ever needed a drink more.'

'Excellent! I'll ask Gawain to join us. Once you meet him properly, all your fears will evaporate! You girls are going to absolutely adore him!'

This seemed as likely as Hannibal Lecter opening a vegetarian restaurant.

My disaffected sister was wearing a sucked-on-lemon expression. So, that would go nicely with our gin and tonics then.

'We can drink to not ageing gracefully, but playfully!' My mother winked.

'Or to chronic self-delusion,' I stage-whispered to my long-lost sister.

FIVE

We'd just ordered emergency cocktails when Gawain, thankfully clothed this time, came gliding towards us across the hotel's elegant herringbone oak parquet floors, which gleamed expensively beneath sparkling chandeliers.

Judging by his linen shirt, chinos and man bun, Gawain was the kind of guy who had danced in full body paint at feminist festivals all over the world, then flitted off to workshops on the phallus-centricity of twentieth-century architecture, before rounding out the day with some *ayahuasca* surrounded by musical friends in a flowery bower by a fjord. Even his unblemished, buffed complexion was like a shade from a fancy paint shop – Albatross Aura or Snow Leopard Breath or something similarly pretentious.

Our mother beamed up at him. He flashed piercing blue eyes our way – eyes topped with curved dark lashes – and bent to kiss her full on the lips, accompanied by a little moan of gratitude. No, it was more than gratitude. It was reverence. He then cupped my mother's chin in his manicured hands and gazed into her besotted face.

'The best view in Switzerland,' Gawain gushed, before turning to gesture through the panoramic windows at the snow-capped mountains bathed in a sunset glow. 'Which, in this beautiful country of mine, is really saying something.'

Our mother laughed so intensely I thought she must have snorted cocaine. She stroked the skin on his face, as creamy as expensive Swiss chocolate.

My estranged sister and I played a quick game of eye tennis.

Gawain sat down at our table, then ordered a hot chocolate for himself, cocktails for us and a plate of local cheeses.

'My love for your mother grows each day,' he told us, 'just as an oyster makes a pearl, grain by grain, into a jewel from the sand.'

I'd presumed all dining experiences in Switzerland would be basically fondue with a view but hadn't expected the conversations to be equally cheesy. Cheesy? Who was I kidding? Gawain's conversation wasn't just cheesy. It was deep-fried Brie in a béchamel sauce on a bed of melted cheddar.

While Verity made do with a small, elegant moue of disgust, I'm pretty sure I threw up a little into my own mouth.

After another bout of eye tennis, my sister, the Navratilova of the back-handed compliment, replied coldly, 'It's so nice, Gawain, so generous really, that you don't notice the age difference.'

'Fruit tastes even more delicious when it's ripe,' our mother's Swiss swain elaborated with a sugared smile.

'Unless there's a worm,' my sister added, tersely. 'Ripe means its season is ending... No offence, Mother.'

'Ah, but autumn is just as beautiful as spring,' Gawain volleyed, smoothly. 'So much has been written and sung about beautiful young women, but why doesn't anyone write sonnets and symphonies about the beauty of older women? *No spring nor summer beauty hath such grace as I have seen in one autumnal face...*'

'John Donne,' my mother sighed, appreciatively. 'My favourite poet.'

'Such a perceptive wordsmith,' Gawain added, gazing into her eyes so penetratingly I wondered if he was checking for cataracts.

When they then ate each other's faces off in a carnivorous kiss, my sister and I became grand slam champions of ocular Wimbledon.

'Of course, as a musician, I've admired your brilliant mother from afar for so long,' Gawain said, coming up for air, 'but to meet her, serendipitously, then discover that she is even more beautiful in the flesh...' he added in a sighing staccato. 'What can I say? I just fell heels over head!'

'It's head over heels, darling, unless you're describing our bedroom antics!'

They both dissolved into laughter once more. My mother laughed at everything he said, making many extravagant, comical gestures with her arms, as though conducting a modern symphony. She then pinched his rosy cheek. 'And I am very, very fond of you too, darling.'

'Thank God, Nicky...'

I baulked. Nicky? Nobody was ever allowed to shorten our mother's name.

'...as I was beginning to think all of that sex was for nothing!' And they both roared with hilarity once more.

This time it took all my control not to projectile vomit. In the brasserie mirror above the bar, my sister and I looked as pale and grave as our mother was flushed and jovial. Our glumness added to the brasserie's *fin-de-siècle* atmosphere. The waiter delivered plates and drinks. I loaded up a wedge of Gruyère onto a big piece of fresh bread and stuffed it into my mouth so that I wouldn't say anything I regretted.

Gawain readjusted the Bono-like tinted shades on the bridge of his long, narrow, aristocratic nose, then turned to us with a glittering smile. 'It's just so wonderful to meet the famous daughters I've heard so much about.'

He looked from one of us to the other. Verity, all snappy power suit, salon-perfect hair, blood-red nails and drop-dead beauty; and then me, the plain twin, who'd clearly thrown on some clothes – and missed.

When Verity remained tight-lipped, I reluctantly extended my hand. 'Oh yes, sorry, I'm Isabella and this is Verity, my twin... Although she's much younger than me, apparently. We don't know by how many years because a camel ate the Dead Sea Scrolls where my birth is recorded.'

Verity snatched the cheese-laden piece of bread from my hand. 'You too could look this good, Isabella, if you took better care of yourself.'

'Verity's secret to staying young,' I explained to my mother's alpine Adonis, 'is to eat plenty of vegetables, limit herself to one chocolate a week, exercise daily, abstain from cake, biscuits, salted nuts and crisps... oh, and lie constantly about her age.'

'Ah, but you see in Europe, age means nothing,' Gawain philosophised. 'It's how old you feel that counts.'

'And trust me,' my mother tittered, 'the best way not to feel old... is to feel a man thirty years your junior every night.' With a lascivious look, she grabbed Gawain's shoulders and pulled him towards her for another long, succulent kiss – the kind of kiss that required a lifeguard.

I felt totally bewildered. We didn't do this sort of emotional display in our family; we did temper and sarcasm. Nicole was renowned for her no-bullshit brio and punchy charm, not for this kind of gooey sentimentality.

'Isn't he adorable?' she chirped, before glancing our way for an acknowledgement of this observation.

But our reflections in the mirror behind her begged to differ. Verity had the demeanour and attitude of a North Korean checkpoint-guard who suspects espionage. And I was glowering at Gawain as though he was carrying a concealed weapon and possibly packing a few hand grenades.

'You lucky girls will always stay young-looking because you picked your mother very carefully,' Gawain schmoozed, delicately layering a slice of Brie onto a cracker.

Verity responded with granite indifference. Oblivious to her disdain, Gawain now fed the cheese-topped cracker he'd prepared to our mother, who devoured it in one big bite.

'Besides,' he added, creamily, 'your mother's wrinkles are the medals she's won in the battle of life. The truth is, the older you get, the better you get.'

'Unless you're a vegetable in the crisper,' I amended. 'Or, I dunno, a banana.'

'Age is nothing more than a number; a state of mind,' he added, tritely.

'Yeah? Tell that to my bingo wings!' I shook the fleshy maracas of my biceps. 'I have enough wingspan to land at Heathrow.'

Gawain gave me an earnest look. 'Life isn't measured by how many breaths we take, but by how many moments take our breath away. And your mother does that to me, all day, every day.'

He picked up his hot chocolate and blew off the halo of steam, accentuating his look of boyish innocence.

'Isn't he something?' My mother melted towards him, drawn into his embrace as though magnetised.

While they lost themselves in another deep passionate pash, I mimed sticking my fingers down my throat. Verity nodded, reheating the remains of Gawain's chocolate with a scalding glare.

When the alpine horn player resurfaced, he turned his icy eyes on us. 'It's my exceptional good fortune to have met your mother.'

'With the emphasis on the word "fortune",' Verity said, tersely.

Gawain gave a toss of his blond head and smiled. 'Ah, you are so like your mother, Verity. A straight talker. That's one of the attributes I love most about you, Nicky…'

I baulked again at the abbreviation of my mother's name.

'…the way you shoot from the hip.'

'Albeit titanium,' Verity fired back.

My mother gave Gawain a conspiratorial look then 'why-me'd' her eyes heavenwards. 'Now come along, girls. Behave. Nothing intensifies life like death,' she reminded us. 'Life is for living.' She then leant over the table and held both our hands. 'I'm touched that you were so worried; worried enough to put the past behind you and join forces to find me. But as you can see, I'm fine. Better than fine! I've won life's lottery! In fact, I've never been happier. I've booked us all into the hotel for the night. Put dinner and anything else you'd like on your rooms. My dear Helen's paid for everything... But Gawain and I need to retire now, as we're leaving early in the morning for Geneva.'

'That ejaculatory fountain will give me ideas, my Enchantress.' Gawain winked at our mother, who erupted into another unnerving gaggle of giggles. 'I'm Swiss... but have never been to Geneva, can you believe it?'

'Out of range of your parole ankle bracelet, is it?' I said, through a fake smile, as if joking.

When my mother's lothario then showed me a screenshot from his camera roll of the Mont Blanc suite that awaited them, I ruminated on the fact that Switzerland is approximately 60 per cent mountains, which is clearly what makes its men so adept at social climbing and put my mother in the mood to mount his Matterhorn.

'Stunning, yes? I grew up in an orphanage so am not used to this kind of luxury.'

'Yep. That suite looks like a perfect haunt for a James Bond villain,' I said, facetiously.

'Speaking of vocations,' my sister added, with equal flippancy, 'what do you actually do for a living, Gawain?'

Mum's alpine inamorato turned his azure eyes upon us. They were clear and cold and hard as candies. 'I could tell you, but then I'd have to kill you,' he 007-ed.

Gawain's words sent a chill down my spine. Unfazed, my sister carried on her slit-eyed interrogation.

'But you're able to just drop everything, at a moment's notice? No work? No family to consider?'

I glanced at his left hand, looking for tell-tale signs of a tan line from hasty wedding ring removal.

'As I mentioned earlier, Gawain's a composer. Freelance. A total autodidact,' my mother gushed.

'Clearly, it's a word he taught himself,' I muttered, suspiciously. Gawain's tan may be real, but his résumé must surely be fake.

Unconcerned, Mum rose, kissed us both on the forehead, then beamed euphorically. 'See you in London, darlings. Not sure when.' The air around her seemed lit up with love, or possibly lunacy. 'I'll keep you posted. I'm sure you've both got a lot of catching-up to do.'

And then they walked off together, arm in arm, Gawain wearing a cat-that-got-the-canary look of smug self-satisfaction.

I downed my cocktail in one gulp. My sister followed suit. Then we looked at each other.

'What the actual fuck?' she said finally.

And for the first time in a long time, I wholeheartedly agreed with her.

SIX

'Flabbergasted. That's the only word for it. I'm totally fucking flabbergasted. What about you? Are you okay?' my sister asked.

'Yeah, fine... I always claw my face off like this.'

We'd moved into the rustic grill restaurant, where we ordered salmon so fresh it had clearly leapt straight out of the stream and onto our plates. But we merely toyed with our food, preferring to make a meal of the wine instead. Both of us seemed to be refilling our glasses to the brim every five minutes.

'Can you believe that our mother had a three-year lesbian affair she kept secret? And now she's some kind of femme fatale cougar?'

I glugged down a hefty slug. 'Did you see his chin? The bloke has fuzz. Not even stubble. Just fuzzy down.'

'Do you think he'd be hanging around if she hadn't told him about her two-million-pound windfall?'

I glanced out of the high, wide windows. The moon hung low now among the bones of the trees and the mountains looked like jagged teeth. 'Monied women Mum's age need an anti-shark device to deter male predators. I glimpsed her glamping bill when she checked us in to the hotel. It looked more like England's entire defence budget.'

'Well then, let's go to war. We have to stop her before she loses everything,' Verity decreed, tightly.

'Oh yes, how, exactly? I think she's a little too old, legally, to be grounded and sent to her room.'

'Join forces.'

'Yeah right,' I scoffed. 'Hey, the UN headquarters is in Geneva, right? Maybe we should just pop by and explain that our mother's human rights are being exploited in a clear case of financial Granicide.'

'I'm serious, Izzy. Let's call a truce and fight this scam artist together.'

Verity's grave expression pulled me up short. She was actually in earnest. I looked at my nemesis. 'A truce? Are you kidding? What you did to me is unforgivable. Even Satan would take out a restraining order on you.'

'Oh, Isabella. It was so long ago. Can't you just get over it?'

'Oh yes, I'm so over it... Any slight niggle of resentment I might occasionally feel is easily soothed by simply standing in the shower for a few hours and screaming and screaming and screaming.' I slurped so angrily at my wine that it spilled down my chin.

My sister emitted a sad sigh. 'We used to be so happy, Izzy... We dressed alike, we walked alike, we talked alike...'

'...and liked men alike... apparently.'

'Think back to when we were girls. You were my sidecar...'

'Yeah, until you crashed the bike.'

Verity waved her hand back and forth like a windscreen

wiper to clear away the debris of the past. 'This is an emergency, Izzy. Can't we go back to normal?'

'Normal is history.' I thought about Johnny then – the back rubs, the foot rubs, the little private pleasures only the two of us knew how to broker. I still missed him every day. I missed us: Johnny, Chrissie and me, against the world.

When my sister stole my husband, she'd written me letters which I burnt without reading. She'd left long phone messages too, excusing, explaining and justifying her appalling behaviour for, oh, three or four hours per call. But it was just a wall of words. And no words could ever work. I might get closure after a slow agonising death – hers, obviously. Verity had broken the Sisterhood Rule of love, loyalty and sisterly solidarity. And there could be no coming back from that.

'When Johnny and I met, well, it was like a centripetal force pulling us together.'

'Yeah, while causing everyone else to fly off into space.'

'I pushed down the attraction for so long, but then, after Chrissie was born, you two drifted apart...'

'We did not drift apart! I was busy being a mother!'

Much to Johnny's surprise and despite his initial reluctance, he loved being a father. But he resented the humdrum mundanity of domesticity. Nor did he like being with the other parents, all those quinoa-munching yummy mummies sharing strong opinions about bin collection schedules with their spreadsheet-addicted, croc-wearing hubbies. A night owl, I'd had to drag him to Chrissie's school events. You're coming to the nativity play, Johnny – whether you need the sleep or not...

And there, waiting in the wings, was stylish, exciting

Verity, offering glamour, gourmet meals, Rolling Stones and Springsteen concerts, first-class travel, escape... Five years later I still woke in the night, the past growling like a jungle beast waiting to pounce. My sister's betrayal was always there, in the rear-view mirror of my mind. How could I ever forgive her?

'Now that I know Mum's not terminally ill, I'm booking the next flight home.'

'She may not be terminally ill, but she's not in her right mind! Our mother is threatening to abandon her career.'

I shook my head in shock. 'It's surreal. Conducting, for Mum, is not so much a profession as a religion.'

'Exactly. Which is why we have to work together to save her.'

'The only thing we do together is fight, Verity.'

'A truce. That's all I'm asking. To save our mother from this charlatan. As you keep pointing out, next year we turn fifty. A rapprochement would be the best gift imaginable.'

I scrutinised my sister then. Her face, bathed golden in the candlelight, looked so angelic. For a moment I telescoped back in time and saw us sprawled on our single beds, dreaming, scheming, plotting, planning, lusting after various boys, bitching about others, trading secrets, laughing, guffawing, sobbing occasionally, bolstering each other up, braiding each other's hair... I remembered the psychological shorthand, the ocular semaphore, the lingo, the slang, the codes, the patois, the in-jokes, the outtakes. Those cherished, secret, sisterly moments lingered in my body, even now. Part of me longed to fling myself back in time, to hover above our shared bedroom, the vinyl records spread out across the carpet – Kate Bush, Fleetwood Mac, David Bowie and the piles of CDs – Prince, Madonna, Michael Jackson, Whitney Houston, INXS, the Eurythmics...

But then her betrayals chalked themselves up in my mind again like a gruesome grocery list.

I got to my feet, my food untouched. 'The best fiftieth birthday gift imaginable would be to have my husband and my old life back, gift-wrapped – oh, and to never, ever see you again.'

SEVEN

After booking my flight back to London, I took a dip in the infinity pool. 'Where will it all end?' I mused as the steam rose up into the crisp, evening air. Forearms resting on the pool edge, I gazed at the vertiginous plunge into the shimmering lake below and thought about my sister.

My twin and I had always been different. While she liked truffles and oysters and seagull eggs harvested from cliff walls by abseiling gourmands, I loved a burger and chips. Thanks to her olive oil sommelier, my sister can explain the difference between Picual Spanish and Koroneiki Greek varieties, while all I know about olives is how much I like them in a martini. Verity is an expert cook too – especially adept at exotic cakes... The last time I baked was when I fell asleep on the beach. Not that she eats them. My sister is always either on the Gluten-Free Goddess diet or micro-dosing with Mounjaro. Whereas she makes her own kimchi, I could live for a day on the half a Mars bar I found down the back of the couch... A couch I'd sourced at a charity shop in a colour and texture that always horrified her. Verity doesn't have boring three-piece sofas; she has statement chairs and pops of colour.

Once, as kids, when we were staying in a hotel in Manchester mid tour with Mum, Verity had come down for breakfast in the morning and said, 'I have to go back to bed. I can't stand the colour of that carpet.' And it wasn't a joke; she actually meant it.

When we were teenagers, Verity would swan off for the day with nothing but a lipstick in a designer purse; whereas I never left the house without enough in my backpack to establish a comfortable wilderness homestead. Of course, this was pre-heartbreak, when I was active and sporty.

Although Mum made sure both of us were studying an instrument – violin for Verity, classical guitar for me – while I preferred a jam with musos at our local pub, my sister attended lectures at the Guildhall on 'Meeting Yesterday's Artistic Challenges Tomorrow'.

She knew all about vintage wines too. While I was 99 per cent craft beer, if you cut my sister, she'd bleed champagne. Another of Verity's life mottos was to never scrimp on wine, sushi or cosmetic surgery. My lean twin, with her trampoline-taut tummy, has the androgynous deportment of a department store mannequin, while I'm as curvy as the guitar I cradle on a daily basis. My eyebrows are the colour of caramel toffee. Hers – jet black. Whereas she has the softest sofa-cushion lips – lips a man might lie down on – mine are always pulled wide into a sarcastic grin or poised to make a sardonic crack. The only thing we share is the same nose; I know her nose well because I've spent such a great deal of my adult life with her looking down it, at me.

Where I hero-worship jazz giants, Verity can listen to piano and violin sonatas and know exactly who's playing. A cryptic crossword ninja, she uses words like 'perspicacity' and 'mellifluous' in everyday conversation. She speaks three languages fluently, one of them dead. 'Why resuscitate it, if it's carked it? Leave it to rot,' I'd say, much to her disdain. Where she reads leather-bound books from foreign publishers, with impenetrable plots, I like fast and frothy tales that give me quip-lash – *Gentlemen Prefer Blondes, Love in a Cold Climate, Travels with My Aunt, Breakfast at Tiffany's, PG Wodehouse* – Verity prefers George Eliot to Jane Austen, although she takes pride in her prejudice and is never unsure of her literary opinions.

At school, she was an aesthete; me – an athlete. I played touch football and tennis and cycled everywhere in summer; activities I stopped after Johnny knocked the stuffing out of me. Verity doesn't play sport, unless you count Scrabble as a sport. If she had to play one, it'd probably be croquet. The closest she ever gets to an accelerated heartbeat is when there's a Caravaggio retrospective with limited ticket sales or a reported reduction in caviar stocks. She keeps slim and supple with Bikram yoga. While my sister posts photos of herself doing advanced Cobra, Locust, Camel and Eagle poses in a sauna situation, these days I'm just thrilled if I can get my leg up on the bathtub for a shave.

She runs her life and home like a military base. She books her Ocado Christmas delivery in June. She checks the ingredients on all food packaging for glucose spikers and individually dries her organic lettuce leaves. Her diary is full, her time allotted and apportioned, whereas my life is about as orderly as my underwear drawer. Speaking of which – silky lingerie for her; white cotton knickers for me.

We were the classic Cathy and Patty Duke twins. 'What a wild duet!'

Basically, my twin sister and I may look out of the same window but we don't see the same view.

And yet, I mused, backstroking my way back up the infinity pool, despite our many differences, we had once been so close. When we moved from sunny, funny Sydney to rough, tough London aged eleven – getting our heads flushed down the school loo because we didn't know which football team to barrack for – we clung to each other like life rafts. A twin sister is the ultimate safety net, made of giggles, secrets and shared memories. Our laughter was the soundtrack of my childhood. The late-night snacks, the pillow fights, the crazy dances, the silly confessions of boy crushes… A twin is half your DNA but triple the fun. Growing up with a twin sister is basically having a built-in bestie for every 'brilliant idea' – that gets you put on detention. We could communicate by facial expression alone. She could hear me smiling in the dark and vice versa. A sister, especially a twin, is a therapist you can drink with and not have to pay by the hour.

I hung over the edge of the pool once more and looked down at the black calligraphy of trees by the dark, glittering lake and thought about my sophisticated sis. Even as we matured into two quite opposite characters, Verity had still been the chocolate in my cookie; my big plate of fabulous, covered in whipped cream with a cherry of sass, cheer and camaraderie on top.

Whereas I have tomboy tendencies, my elegant sister is jaw-droppingly beautiful. I spent so many days as an awkward tweenager trying to be as pretty and cool as her.

When you look up to a stylish, confident, stunning sibling, you have to find your own version of non-conformity. Mine was to give up my music scholarship and join a rock band with the sexiest man I'd ever met, disappointing my mother forever. Our band, Panache, modelled itself on Fleetwood Mac with a glam-rock twist. When young, Verity had been my fashion icon, so naturally became my band stylist, dressing me in vintage Mary Quant and snakeskin skirts and regulation Stevie Nicks ensembles of long, floaty, sheer chiffon dresses with ruffled skirts and handkerchief hems worn over witchy boots.

I made no fashion statement without consulting her. Yes, we'd loved each other once. Intensely. At night I use to drive Johnny mad because I hadn't talked to Verity for at least, oh, two hours. Not talking to her for more than a day did my head in.

Ah, Johnny. I felt the usual pang of pain in my chest at the thought of him. Stroking my way up and down the suspended hotel pool, memories engulfed me like octopus tentacles. I pictured him, on our first encounter. A friend had dragged me along to a pub in Camden where local musos gathered to jam on a Sunday evening. Johnny was standing, one foot on a bar stool, like a conquistador.

Of course, as a classical musician, I had nothing but disdain for these leather-jacket-clad, biker-booted lanky rockers with bone structure, smoky breath, trouser bulges, cocksure swaggers and hot and cold running groupies... But not quite enough disdain not to bed one of them, who became my husband.

A splash of water in my face brought me back to the present. I dodged a loud group of aquatic Eurotrash as they pretentiously breaststroked past me in full bling jewellery and designer sunglasses, despite the inky night sky. They were trying and failing to look hot and seductive, whereas my Johnny's every gesture shimmered so effortlessly with sex appeal. His velvety voice, raspy with wear and tear and dripping with longing and hunger, combined with his Michael Hutchence, Jim Morrison, early Mick Jagger swagger, aroused dark appetites in every woman he encountered.

That fateful night we met in the Camden pub, I, of course, wasn't even on his radar... Until I picked up an electric guitar and played my mock Paganini riff, that is. Johnny's attention had turned to me then like a sunflower to the sun. He straddled the drum kit and laid down a groove. I improvised over it as he drove the pulse forward. We segued into some Van Morrison and both sang without restraint, a great vocal blaze of light. Two songs in, we didn't know each other's names, but our eyes were making love across the stage.

When the set ended, he slugged down a beer. I watched him dry his wet hands on his back pockets. Oh, lucky jeans, I thought, to hug a peachy posterior like that. This was the kind of man who could make a girl's nipples tingle with a single look.

Johnny sidled closer, slid his arms around me and growled hotly into my neck, 'Your G-string broke on that final solo... You look as though you need consoling,'

Later that night I was back at his flat. Unsnapping my jeans he said, 'I won't stop until your legs are shakin' and the neighbours know my name.'

Oh, okay then. If you insist.

Put it this way, Johnny Cox knew how to make a woman wake up laughing. Getting vertical ever again, let alone walking, might be difficult, but laughing? Easy-peasy.

It was a jacuzzi of joy, those first few months, a froth of hedonistic happiness. It was a non-stop sexual gymkhana, too, during which he occasionally left on his cowboy boots. I'm talking the kind of sex which leaves a gal begging for physiotherapy.

When I gave up my classical music scholarship, my mother was appalled. 'Really? That's your idea of a career? A CV in which thrashing an electric guitar in a pub band is the high point?'

But after I joined Panache, the band took off. Our sound became fat and hot and tangy. Musically, Johnny and I gelled. Together, we were like the gleeful riff of a sure-fire hit. As the last note of a song hung in the air, I'd watch the faces of the audiences emerging from their dreams back into the raw reality of some grimy pub. Applause would erupt and I'd drink it in. It was like diving into a warm bath. Johnny would catch my eye and we'd share a secret smile. Oh, how he loved it, the first rough licks of fame's tigerish tongue.

He loved it; and I loved him – heart and soul and all the bits in between. I kept expecting him to tell me he'd fallen for some supermodel or indie movie actress, but then one night after a knockout gig, he got down on one knee and said, 'With this bottle top ring pull, I thee wed.'

'A family heirloom?' I'd replied, insouciantly, to disguise my elation.

Yes, my sister had always been the beauty in the family but I was beautiful at last. When Johnny fell in love with me, I was no longer a loser; no longer second fiddle; no longer second best. It was positively Hans Christian Andersen-esque; the ugly duckling turned swan-like, suddenly.

My teens were spent preparing for music grades and performing for adjudicators. Johnny set me free. Think Sandra Dee before she gets Travolta-ed; Kylie pre Hutchence. This rock god had the knack of finding the fun in everything. Creative, wild, free-spirited and with a jazz-hands energy, he made me laugh all the time. And then there was his enormous hinterland; a place where size truly does count. There was nothing he didn't know about bluegrass and flatpicking, jazz, bebop, rockabilly, soul... He'd broadened my musical horizons. I felt a pang of loss once more, like a knife cutting into an old wound. The truth was, I missed the woman I was when I was with him – carefree and sensual. I missed improvising with him, musically as much as sexually. I also missed being cherished and adored by a man all other women wanted.

When we did actually get married it was on a whim in Las Vegas, mid tour. We tied the knot in a themed Elvis chapel, high on life, fun and, in his case, a tab of ecstasy. Vegas is chock-a-block with gambling dens – not just the casinos but also the wedding chapels. But I was convinced that Johnny was a safe bet.

At first we lived a loose, lovely existence, free and easy, spontaneous and anarchic, with endless applause. We had one album under our belt and a new bigger and better recording contract to keep us buoyant. Everything was perfect – until I fell pregnant. Parenthood was something we'd never discussed or even considered.

I was thirty-two and Johnny thirty-four. He presumed I'd terminate but I didn't want to be one of those weeping pop art women I'd seen on T-shirts, sloganed 'Oops, I forgot to have children'.

Johnny was behaving like all nascent rock stars: paaaartying hard, with no thought of tomorrow. In Ireland, he once climbed over the gates of Bono's mansion at midnight to gatecrash a party and charmed U2 into letting him stay. After a night of Hollywood carousing, he'd strip naked and perform daredevil dives into his host's pool, then go rustle up a big fry-up for breakfast. On stage, he combined charisma with an easy, devil-may-care charm and knockabout demeanour that effortlessly bonded him with audiences. At the end of every gig, he'd leap out from behind his drum kit, strike some statutory rock god poses, then rip off his shirt to stage dive.

So no, he was not ready for fatherhood but I went ahead anyway. Although vehemently against the idea, it was love at first cuddle. And, until Chrissie started pre-school, I kept right on touring. But one day we were driving to a festival and got stuck in traffic and she got car sick. I had to leave her crying in the arms of the roadie. As I was running, distraught, towards the stage, Johnny had to remind me to put down the bag of vomit before I went on. Clearly we couldn't go on like this.

Shortly afterwards, when Chrissie turned four, I decided to settle down. I gave up the band and Johnny gave up me.

As a successful music critic, Verity was always afforded a special, backstage, Access All Areas pass – and that's exactly what she did: access all areas of my husband. An award-winning travel writer, music and restaurant critic, she was soon whisking him away for secret trysts in lavish five-star country spa hotels; those subtly chic, mellow-staffed havens with four-poster beds and couples' massages – far from the banality of Aquatots and Tippy Toes Ballet. Exclusive Wagner Bayreuth festivals or Maldivian diving holidays, nothing was too good for him, and all of it bake sale and Little Princess Party Fingerpainting classes–free. Of course, I only found this out much, much later.

While all I'd ever offered Johnny was a camping trip on a wet weekend in Wales, Verity could spoil him on all four corners of the earth.

About the time Chrissie turned nine, Johnny suddenly started composing a lot more love songs. He'd sit at the keyboard for hours – cigarette dripping from his lips – his lying lips, as it turned out, because the love songs were not for me.

When Johnny finally told me the truth, just after Chrissie's twelfth birthday, I didn't recognise my voice. It was high-pitched and wheedling. 'My sister!?' I said, over and over again. Finally followed by, 'Don't leave me!'

But he brushed me away as if I were a moth. I could see him now, sauntering casually out the door like a gunslinger; his wife lying there, in a metaphorical pool of blood. He just left me, flat as roadkill. I crawled into our bed fully clothed, and lay there as cold as a corpse, the bedsprings mourning beneath me, for days on end.

Minus our musical alchemy, the band stalled, recording contracts fizzled out – and I fizzled out too. I took up guitar teaching and raised my darling daughter all alone. I just sank beneath the waves – scuttled.

I felt myself sinking now from the weight of all these sad memories and swam to the steps of the infinity pool. Climbing out, I wrapped myself in a robe and made for the sauna to warm up.

I had just stretched out on the aromatic slab and begun to slowly poach in the herbal-scented mist when the door suctioned open and Gawain walked in. Naked.

'Hello,' he said, nakedly.

'Hello,' I said in a falsetto that was new to me. His appendage was truly eye-wateringly proportioned, like those oversized pepper pots Italian waiters whip out and grind over your lasagne. Willing the steam to hurry up and congeal, I averted my eyes. But he moved to the bucket to pour water on the coals – an activity which required a full bend from the waist, his rosy cheeks in my face. I turned my head the other way only to see Gawain again spreading out on the slab below me – to see too much of Gawain; enough to know that he'd had the full Tom Cruise, back, sack and crack wax. Leaning up on one elbow, he offered me an enamel pill pot of weed gummies before topping himself up with a micro-dosing pipette.

'Would you like some, Isabella?'

'I don't do drugs,' I said, primly, squeezing my eyes tightly shut.

'That's what your mother said, only a week ago!' the crafty Casanova laughed. 'Ah, meeting your mother! It's been a week of Swiss bliss. And now she's going to take a sabbatical and we're off to tour the world. Although I do have big plans to collaborate on the world's first alpine horn concerto. Your mother said she would drop everything to do it. Imagine this great conductor, debuting a piece by an unknown composer. The thrill!'

My eyes boinged open and I swivelled to scrutinise the stranger more closely. I'd had a lot to absorb today – lesbianism, bisexuality, organ donation, drug-taking... but career sabotage proved the most astonishing. Actually, astonishment was a feeble word for what I felt. I was poleaxed. Sideswiped. Winded. The world's first alpine horn concerto? From a totally unknown and untried composer, oh, who just happened to be bonking the conductor? Nicole Nightingale worked with the world's most renowned artists, from pianists of the calibre of Martha Argerich to sopranos of Cecilia Bartoli's exceptional standard to virtuosic violinists like Joshua Bell. Gawain's debut would make her the butt of every joke, a total laughing stock.

'So,' he chit-chatted. 'Do you like my country?'

'Well, your flag is a big plus,' I prattled, to cover up my discombobulation. 'I like the snow-capped mountains too, although I'm a bit suspicious of the way your glaciers go creeping about. That's not normal...' Who needs drugs, I thought desperately, when you can be a gibbering idiot of your own accord?

Luckily the steam was thickening up again like soup. But the thicker the steam, the clearer the situation. This con-artist had dosed my grieving mother up on drugs, seduced and enchanted her, and was now set to fleece her financially and then launch his musical career by trashing hers. My mother is such a wonder woman she should really wear some kind of sequinned cape. How else had she succeeded in juggling single motherhood with a stellar, international career without dropping anything? Until now, that is, when she was throwing it all away for a lederhosened lothario with a metronomic appendage. There was something I deeply distrusted about the man. I couldn't quite put my finger on it – but if I did, I'd be sure to disinfect it, pronto.

I had to save her! But that would mean calling a truce

with my vile twin sister. The type of person you go out with says a lot about you – and going out with your own sister's husband, for example, clearly states to the world that you're a two-faced, lying toad. Still, growing up, we had been each other's human Wonderbras: uplifting, supportive and making each other look bigger and better.

Blaming heat exhaustion, I fled the sauna, turbaned my wet hair, stuffed my arms into a fluffy white hotel robe, shoved on the over-sized complimentary terry-towelling slippers and shuffled off to find Verity. Through the hotel's huge plate-glass windows, I could see the moon – lopsided and yellowish now with a pale greasy ring about it like a badly fried egg. It only added to my queasiness.

The chic, contemporary twin bedroom my mother had booked for us came with a built-in fire pit, flickering beside a sunken jacuzzi – and that's where Verity was now luxuriating, sipping chilled bubbles in the hot bubbles, while gazing at the most spectacular moonlit panorama.

'Okay,' I acquiesced. 'A ceasefire.'

Verity looked up at me, astounded. 'Really?'

'It's not the end of the war, okay. Just a momentary suspension of hostilities.'

Yes, I loathed my sister. Yes, she'd ruined my life. But this was one of those 'Fold your tray table back up, ensure that all luggage is secured safely in the overhead lockers and brace for turbulence' moments. We needed to buckle up – together.

'So, what changed your mind?' she asked.

'Gawain says Mum's going to drop everything to conduct his debut alpine horn concerto.'

My sister flailed about then, swallowing half the bath

water. 'Are you fucking kidding me?' she said, once she'd stopped spluttering. 'The alpine horn is the missing link between music and noise."

'Well, he's playing Mum, that's for sure.'

I poured myself a glass of champagne from the ice bucket. 'It's time for a Gawain-ectomy.'

Verity raised her own glass in a toast to us. 'A truce. Two heads are better than one; unless they're on the same body, of course.'

'Yes, I suppose it could be worse; we could be Siamese twins... Imagine, we'd have to keep going to Europe, just so the other could get a turn driving.'

As we snorted with overwrought, irreverent laughter, champagne spluttering down our chins, we even forgot for a moment that we were mortal enemies.

PART TWO

Sisterhood Rule
Loyalty.
Stick to each other like a nylon dress in a heatwave.

EIGHT

Looking back over the last year, I realise what a big orchestral piece I found myself playing in. A symphony is made up of several movements of often complex, elaborate themes. The mad dash to Switzerland, well, that was like an overture, and of course the crescendos and scherzo are imminent. But before that, there needs to be a slower movement – the fugal part of the score, where themes are realised and intertwined. Themes, in this case of MILFs, GILFs, hornbags and hotties; love, lust, betrayal, sisterly solidarity; and its opposite.

But first, the adagio...

'Your mother seems to have gone a little bit bonkers,' were Melissa's opening words when she flounced into my living room two nights later.

'A little bonkers?' I snorted. 'That's like saying that Kim Jong Un is only a little demonic.'

My mother's blonde glamazonian agent threw herself down onto the couch, her floral dress riding up over long, brown legs, wedge shoes kicked off, zodiac toe-ring glinting, a hand flung across her forehead like a swooning southern belle in desperate need of a mint julep and a hand fan.

'She's just cancelled all her performances for the rest of the year. Apparently, she's "travelling".' She said the word as though it was riddled with ricin. 'Do you have any idea how few female conductors make it in a man's world?'

I drew breath to answer but Melissa powered on.

'You can count the female principal conductors in top-tier orchestras and opera houses on one bloody hand. And now, just when your mother is at the peak of her creative powers, she's throwing it all away. Giving up a prestigious residency with the British Symphony Orchestra – well, that was a huge bloody risk. But since going freelance, offers are pouring in. And I've accepted the most lucrative. So, what the hell am I supposed to do now? I mean, why is she self-sabotaging?'

'Yes, it's a mystery,' I replied, facetiously. 'Lonely, grieving, workaholic woman and effervescent, energetic, spicy younger man… I just can't work it out.'

Melissa leapt up and started pacing. 'What is it about you super straight cis women? Why are you constantly falling for these kind of male bullshit artists… Thank God I'm bi.' She adjusted her knickers with a thumb and a wiggle of her curvy backside.

'Are you honestly saying you've never been taken hostage by your hormones, Mel?'

'Maybe in my teens, but not now. Who has time? I've represented your mother since I was thirty. That's nine long, hard years. And you wouldn't believe the sexism she's endured.' My mother's agent paused to suck on the huge flask of water she carried with her at all times, suck-suck-sucking on it like a giant teat. I sometimes wondered if it was secretly full of vodka. Either way, it was a relief to know that she hadn't perished from thirst between her car and my living room.

'A conductor's body language must be energetic and authoritative. Right? Wrong. Nicole was endlessly criticised: her gestures were too overbearing; her facial expressions too fierce – the very qualities that would be regarded as assets in a male conductor.' Melissa picked up the remains of my croque-monsieur from a plate on the table and crunched into a brittle, noisy triangle of toast. 'One stale, pale, male music critic told her that she should "smile a bit more". I wonder if anyone ever said that to Furtwängler or Celibidache.'

'Who?' asked a bewildered voice.

I wheeled around with delight to see my darling daughter throwing down her backpack. Chrissie's honey-blonde hair was pulled back into a ponytail, which boinged up and down cheerfully as she bounded towards me for a hug. Her legs were tanned after a week at a musical festival and her face freckled.

'Only two of the greatest male conductors in history... The greatest, most sombre male conductors. Hello, cupcake.' Melissa slapped Chrissie on the backside as she made her way into my embrace.

'Darling!' I drew my daughter into a fierce hug. 'You're back early. How bad were the portaloos?' I attempted an ABBA song parody – '*Portaloo, couldn't escape if I wanted to*' – but it had been so long since I'd sung, my rusty voice sounded like a buffalo giving birth in a swamp.

'Ugh. Off the grunge-ometer.' My daughter broke free and plonked herself down on to the piano stool. One skinny leg wrapped itself like a snake around the other about seven times. Her elbow descended to her knee and a face landed in the upturned palm. Then, with a look of exhilarated intrigue she gushed, 'So, Gran went lezza?'

'You got my voicemail then... I'd always presumed Mum thought an "outing" referred to a family day at the beach... but apparently no.'

'And now she's hooked up with some cute male hottie?'

'If you think a man bun is cute, then yes...'

'Did you know Granny went lezza, Melly?' my daughter asked cheerfully.

'No. But what's the big deal if she did?'

'Exactly. Lesbian sex is just like straight sex... except one person doesn't have to fake an orgasm,' I quipped.

Melissa snorted. 'Well said, Izzy. I just don't understand why you don't come party with us at Pussy Liquor.' She'd often tried to get me along to her favourite lesbian club at Bethnal Green Working Men's Club, featuring gay cabaret and a lot of glitter.

'Type shit! Way to go, Gran!!' My daughter pumped the air.

'Oh, Chrissie, I'm all for your grandma having some fun and adventures and hitting life's ski slopes... But this is way off-piste.' That was putting it mildly. My mother had gone straight from the nursery slopes to a Schumacher-annihilating black ski run.

'I'm spitting chips!' Melissa was pacing again. 'Years I've spent building up Nicole's reputation. The critics who review her concerts now? Well, superlatives gush like a treacle fountain after every performance. Viva la Diva! And now, just when we're earning the big bucks at the big gigs, she goes AWOL with a... with a—'

'Soooo fine stud muffin! Good for you, Gran.'

'—with a Swiss conman who is sabotaging her career, Chrissie. This is a family emergency... Which is why your Aunt Verity will be arriving any minute now.'

My daughter's eyes widened in astonishment. 'It really must be an emergency if you're letting your sister into our house, Mum!'

'But no need to be nice to her, okay? And absolutely no hugging. Ever. On pain of death. Your Aunt Verity might be coming over occasionally now but she still doesn't deserve to have you in her life.'

'Totally. Gran's asked me to housesit, anyway. But right now, I'm gonna take a bath, okay? Call me when the sulphurous smoke has cleared. And try not to be too chalant,' she advised me.

'Chalant – it's the opposite of nonchalant, apparently,' I decoded for Melissa. 'But I mustn't attempt to use her slang because that's just "dog water".'

'Dog water?' Chrissie winced. 'Oh, Mum, that's so, like, 2020. I might have said it when I young, but it's cringe now.'

'Oh, how mortifying! 2020! Forgive me. I might as well be speaking Sanskrit.'

Chrissie had only just bolted upstairs when an Uber rattled to a halt outside and a door slammed.

'Great. She's here. I'll make snacks,' Melissa said, striding off into the kitchen in her capable way, clutching some grocery bags.

I looked out of the window onto the hot, wet, windy street. In fuchsia Armani, my sister was arriving. She stood on the pavement, subduing a billowing designer raincoat, but not before I caught the disparaging glance she gave her surroundings. Thanks to the Blitz bombardment of this part of London, elegant, Georgian houses now fraternise with grim, grey tower blocks, which sprouted up from the holes blasted there by doodlebugs.

When I opened the front door, Verity's words of greeting were, 'Christ. I imagine your babysitter demands medical benefits before daring to set foot here.'

'Chrissie is seventeen, Verity. She does the babysitting now,' I corrected, wondering if my sister could hear me above the sound of the disintegrating enamel of my grinding teeth.

'How is Chrissie?' Verity looked around, hopefully, her voice suddenly tender and tentative. 'It's hard to believe I haven't seen her since she was twelve.'

My sister stepped gingerly inside, as if ready to hand her coat to the nearest mouse who would hang it up on a peg somewhere. A dormouse, literally. Verity lives in Primrose Hill, in a pastel-coloured four-storey terrace. Whereas vermin would be too intimidated to enter her hallowed halls, Kilburn mice don't just scuttle under a counter when you flick on the kitchen light; they pick up your entire refrigerator and lumber from the room, chortling.

My sister glided past me and looked around at my mismatched furniture. 'Gosh, that church jumble sale certainly did well out of you, Izzy, didn't it.'

I suddenly saw my cosy little home through her judgemental eyes. My house is as jowly as a nonagenarian's saggy jawline. It bulges with books and bikes and unhung paintings and instruments. My walls are painted various shades of pink and I have a yellow kitchen and purple bathroom. My sister prefers a colour palette of greys. To my mind, only school jumpers should be grey. Or cooking pots. Or prison porridge. She'd recently written a piece in the Sunday papers about how 'out-of-date home furnishings make your home look tired' and I'd mentally ticked them all off: curtain pelmets, beanbags, crocheted throw rugs, fake chandeliers and big, bulky, chunky wall radiators, two of which dominated my sitting room.

'Have you thought about underfloor heating?' she asked, as if reading my mind.

'Where would I dry my knickers?' I said, through a clenched smile. 'Give me your scorn, but I like a warmed cotton gusset.' After all, nothing else was warming me there, I seethed silently. My heart stuttered as memories of Johnny ambushed me – the throaty richness of his voice, like dark, tart chocolate; the way he called out my name in bed. Even though I was furious with him, the memories of his touch could unravel me in an instant. He made love like a wild pirate, his black hair falling around my face. He was perfect and he was mine and then... he was gone. To her.

Verity excused herself to use the bathroom and I crossed to the drinks cabinet to get glasses and a bottle of red. I was going to need a lot of alcoholic fortification to get through this. A few minutes later, my sister returned, grim-faced.

'What? Don't tell me I have a crinoline toilet roll holder? Or is it that my loo doesn't flush Evian water?!'

'Your toilet paper! It could be used to deflect machine-gun fire.'

I was very restrained – I didn't stuff the toilet brush up her nose. Instead I poured us both a tumbler of wine. She looked as if I'd just handed her a magnum of syphilitic blood.

'Sorry, I would have brought something drinkable, but I've just come straight from work,' she condescended.

The temptation to add a splash of strychnine to her glass was overwhelming. It was Tuesday evening, three days after we'd discovered our mother was being scammed by a smooth-talking swindler. I'd been teaching guitar all day to pampered private school girls in Hampstead; students more interested in their fake nails than their scales. But this 'peri' (peripatetic teaching job) meant that I hadn't had time to shop on the way home.

'So, what's our plan?' Verity took a tentative sip of wine and crinkled up her nose. 'We need to find out what this Gawain creep is up to.'

'Yeah, sure… So, did you bring a Ouija board?'

'Look, let's both just drop the sarcasm, shall we? We're on the same side, after all. So, let's recap. What do we know so far?'

'Ah… that on Gawain's tax return he lists his occupation as Older, Lonely Woman Fleecer?'

'Let's consult Dr Google.' Verity sat at the table and extracted her iPad from a designer bag.

'You should be excellent at sniffing out his fraudulent and duplicitous behaviour, Verity, being equally fraudulent and duplicitous.' The words were out of my mouth before I could catch them.

Verity then started in on a very complicated sentence about love and fate and how '...the heart wants what the heart wants—'

'Dress it up however you want, V, but you're a traitor,' I interrupted. 'If I'd had a radio in World War Two, you would have turned me in to the Nazis for a loaf of bread... Though of course, I forgot, you don't eat carbs.'

'Hmmm? What's that smell? Oh yes. The scent of lumber being cut for your bloody cross... I can't really explain what happened, Isabella, except that it was a *coup de foudre*... a bolt of lightning,' she decoded. 'A grand passion. If you'd ever bothered to read any of my hundreds of letters or answered any of my millions of phone messages, but no. Nothing but a deafening silence. You were far too busy turning all of our friends and family against me. The brutal truth is that Johnny was out of love with you and our attraction became too passionate to resist... A passion that's lasted. The proof's in the pudding. I mean, it's five years and he's stayed with me.'

'Let the air out of his tyres regularly, do you?'

'I didn't mean for it to happen, Izzy. But Johnny's the love of my life. He's my Don Juan, Lord Byron and Franz Liszt – all the charismatic romantics in one. Do you remember the men I used to date? All those pretentious prigs called Eustace, Ignatius or Aloysius. And then suddenly I'm dancing to the drum solo in Iron Butterfly's 'In-A-Gadda-Da-Vida' by moonlight on a beach in Ibiza. Johnny made me realise I'd been holding the map upside down. I was so uptight. He turned me on to life.'

'Turned you on? What are you? An electrical appliance? You should have said no! You broke the sisterhood rules, the most important of which is – loyalty. Sisters are supposed to stick to each other like a nylon dress in a heatwave.' I loomed over her. 'Look, this truce thing? It's not gonna work. You should go. It's Mum's life. Let her live it the way she wants. God knows you showed no restraint when you wanted to live your life, your way. So why should she?'

'But she's throwing away our inheritance.'

'What do you care? You've got plenty of money... Ironic that you made your fortune writing an internationally bestselling book on style, only to do the least stylish thing possible – stealing your sister's husband.'

'Yes, sure, I have enough money – unless I need to buy something. Like food. Or, I don't know, heating.'

'What are you talking about?'

'The truth is—'

'A foreign concept to you, surely?'

'—Johnny has lost all our savings. On Bitcoin. I've been counting on Mum helping us out... Hence the urgency of this situation. Urgent for you too. I know Chrissie's been offered a Guildhall scholarship but it will still be expensive... Mother always promised to finance her music studies, as you let her down so badly on that score.'

White-hot outrage shot through me. 'Well I had hoped Chrissie's father would help her out... Aren't you furious with him?'

'Johnny's intentions were good. He wanted to buy me a Jaguar sports car. A Shaguar, he calls it... That boy was destined for the big time. If you'd stayed in the band, who knows where you'd both be? But as you know, once you left, they flatlined.'

That much was true. After I quit Panache, the band quickly descended into B-list gigs in pubs or the odd warm-up act for bands who used to warm up audiences for us. Appropriate, really, as they now played so many covers I'd suggested they change their name to 'Duvet'. The album they made without me was so bad, it should only have been released on parole.

'And now he's felled the money tree.' Verity gestured to herself. 'Timber!'

I crossed to the cabinet, snatched up the whisky bottle and poured two hefty slugs. We both took a swig, chanting, in unison, 'Disgusting habit.'

It was something we used to say, before our break-up. The informality and intimacy of this verbal tradition caught us both off guard. As I savoured the warmth of the whisky, a huge wave of sadness washed through me. As twins, we used to finish each other's homework and sentences, loving, laughing, defending. We'd shared clothes, make-up, allergies, desserts – and then, finally, unforgivably, a husband. Pain and anger zigzagged through me once more. My sister and I stood staring at each other, unsure of how to move on.

Melissa now pushed open the kitchen door and strode back into the living room carrying a tray piled high with sandwiches, hummus, crudités and other savoury snacks.

'I brought supplies,' she explained. This was Melissa all over – kind, competent, organised. Mel fought for smoking bans and cycling lanes and endangered moths and caterpillars. She went to bed with an eye mask and a sleepy tea, listening to a mindfulness app, and ran to meetings with her iPhone strapped to her bicep. She also gave herself, body and soul, to her clients, of whom my mother was the most esteemed. 'Well, I must say, it's very nice seeing you two working things out.'

'And that's exactly what we're here to do – work,' Verity said, brusquely.

'Agreed.' Melissa placed the tray on the coffee table. 'Nicole wants me to cancel her reunion gig with the BSO at the Royal Festival Hall. Have you any idea how mean-spirited that will look? We have to save her from professional suicide. The clock is ticking and the race is on.'

'We need to discredit Gawain. But how?' I asked, biting into a dainty, crustless, egg-and-cress sandwich. 'Verity, did you find anything online?'

'Nothing. No digital footprint. Which is super suspicious in itself. We could hire a private eye, I suppose?'

Melissa banged a tetchy teaspoon around her china cup. 'And where on earth do we find one of those? Let alone afford one.'

Verity studiously eschewed the nuts, crisps and sandwiches. She ignored the hummus too but waved around a stick of celery in her bejewelled claw, as though conducting an orchestra. 'If only we knew someone from the underworld. Surely, in this neighbourhood…?' She was clearly still recovering from her bracing glimpse of the Kilburn underclass.

'Not really the kind of info people impart in the cake shop queue, Verity.'

'But you must have heard something. The houses here are so cheek by jowl and the walls so flimsy...'

'Yeah, true,' I snarked. 'When my neighbours are bonking, I have the orgasm... If the couple on the other side start shagging too, then it's multiple orgasms for me! You really are such a snob.'

'I am not! I don't care what other people think – well, only the ones who count.'

'Gosh, V! How on earth are you ever going to get the whiff of Kilburn commoners out of your linen pantsuit?'

'Speaking of outfits, who dressed you, by the way, Isabella? Stevie Wonder in a dark room? A crocheted bolero? Really?'

'It's retro chic,' I said, defensively.

'Ladies, ladies, please.' Melissa clapped her hands. 'Focus. Can't you think of anyone who can help us? Anyone in the law? Or surveillance? Anyone with criminal contacts?'

We stared at each other blankly for a moment. Clearly we were a first-rate cabal of international masterminds. This was 'chalant dog water' if ever there was any. When a knock came at the door, our collective sigh of relief was audible.

'I'll go,' Mel said, desperate to escape our twin toxicity.

A moment later she popped her head back around the door.

'The male stripper's here.'

'What?'

'Did you order a male stripper? He's asking for you.'

'Ah, no... it's not exactly a hen night.'

'Really? There's an awful lot of pecking going on,' my sister said sharply.

'He must have the wrong address.' I sauntered out into the corridor to see the pupil I'd been teaching for over a year, and whose name I could never pronounce, standing on the doorstep in a police uniform.

Mostly life has terrible timing. But occasionally, just occasionally, the fate fairy comes good, waves her magic wand and the planets align.

NINE

'Fear-car! Farquoir…? F… F… Friggin' whatever your name is. What are you doing here?' I asked, surprised.

'It's Fiachra. My lesson? The one you cut short?' He gestured at the guitar flung nonchalantly over one shoulder. 'You texted me to come after work tonight.'

'Oh shit. Sorry. I completely forgot. Family dramas. I didn't know you're a police officer.'

'You never asked. Actually, I'm a dog handler,' he clarified.

I opened the door wider and he stepped inside. His aftershave invaded the hall before he did. The smell was of lemon and lime. But his companion didn't smell so sweet. A big barrel-bodied dog with lolling tongue and ribbons of saliva shoved its snout around the doorframe.

'Ah… you can come in, but not that.'

'It's far too hot to leave him in the car. Come on now, it's just a wee dog. He'll be grand.'

'Can't you crack open a window?'

The man with the unpronounceable name looked at me as though I'd suggested some recreational cannibalism. 'You don't like dogs?' he asked, bending down to ruffle the fur of the big beast, which stared lovingly up at him. 'This boy's in training.'

'The only reason I'd like to get a dog is so I can call it "Peeve". My pet, Peeve... which is what dogs are.'

'His name's Cyril and he's very well behaved... He's just grand, aren't you, boy?'

'What is it about you Brits and your dogs? You treat them better than your kids. I've seen dogs leap up onto the dining table to polish off the roast lamb and nobody raises an eyebrow. Speaking as an Aussie, I don't think you should ever allow a dog to eat at the table, no matter how good his manners.'

The dog handler looked my way, green eyes blazing. 'Aye, well first of all, I'm not a Brit. I'm from Muff, in Donegal. But grew up in Derry. And second of all, I'd say his manners are a hell of a lot better than some humans I could mention.'

And with that, he walked into the living room, his furry friend padding happily after him.

'Hey!' I called out, to no avail.

'Well, well.' My sister looked up from her iPad and noted the canine companion. 'This is going to be an interesting act. What do you call it? Puppy Love?... Animal Magnetism?'

'Sorry to disappoint, but he's not a strippergram. This is a pupil of mine,' I explained. 'F... F... Far... Jesus. That name of yours. It can't be your real name; surely, you're simply breaking it in for a friend? I'm just going to call you the Derry Man, okay? I mean, Muff Man is funnier but could be misconstrued. This is my twin sister.'

'Your sister's a twin? You never told me that.'

I handed him a wine glass. 'Well, I'd prefer to go with some other, more descriptive category like, I dunno, Spawn of Satan.'

The Derry Man shrugged the guitar off his shoulder and turned to face my sister.

'Hello. I'm Verity.' She extended a manicured hand.

'Fiachra.' He gave her hand a firm but friendly shake. 'Fiachra O'Flaherty.'

'I'm sorry, Fiachra,' Verity purred, pronouncing his name perfectly. 'Would you actually like something in that glass? My sister never notices anything.'

'Yes, like my twin sleeping with my husband. Some men are so lazy,' I addressed my student, 'they'll just use any old thing that's lying around the home.'

Verity proffered both the wine and whisky bottles. 'She's insufferably rude, too. I don't know how you put up with her.'

'Being a lightning-fast shredder helps.' He smiled, politely refusing both bottles. 'Combined with her classical guitar technique, well, that makes her the ultimate axewoman.'

Melissa, who was making her way back from the bathroom, jolted as if cattle-prodded. 'Wait. You're actually a real-life police officer?'

'Aye. Sorry to disappoint. Last time I checked, my uniform didn't have Velcro seams down the sides. I actually train police dogs but—'

'Can you help us uncover a conman?'

The Derry Man ran his hand through his hair. 'Conmen are hard to track down. They slip into other names and disappear without trace. It's hard to unearth the truth, ya know?'

'All men are liars, that's the truth,' I replied, tartly.

'Not all men.' The Dog Handler's large bright eyes blazed my way again.

'Yeah, I've seen that bullshit hashtag, too,' I said, sardonically. 'In truth, all men are guilty till proven innocent.'

'And she wonders why she's single.' Melissa waggled her brows. 'So, officer, are you tech savvy?'

'Well, I don't think you have to worry about me sparking a computer-generated international missile exchange with a foreign power, but otherwise, aye, I'm pretty competent. Why?' He looked us over with an amused eye. 'I take it you girls survived the information explosion unscathed?'

But Melissa was not in a playful mood. She put her hands on her hips. 'We need to dig the dirt on a Swiss alpine horn player. Nicole, my client, is sixty-nine and this conman, late thirties, has inveigled his way into her affections.'

The dog handler scratched his head. 'Is it just the age gap you're worrying about? Surely that's simply revenge for centuries of it working the other way around: older man, younger woman, blah blah?'

'Gawain is deeply in love, all right – with our mother's cash. She just inherited two million pounds,' Verity expounded.

The Derry Man shrugged. 'I'm sure your ma is old enough and wise enough to take care of herself.'

'Let me put it in terms a dog handler can understand...' I condescended. 'He's a Rescue Boyfriend. Something she picked up from the pound. With Rottweiler tendencies. He's going to take out her jugular when the time is right, mauling all of us in the process.'

The Derry Man picked up his guitar. 'Aye, well, it's a sackable offence to use official police databanks. Look, maybe we should take another rain check, Isabella?'

'Free lessons,' I said, impulsively. 'In exchange for a little light sleuthing.'

The man with the unpronounceable name put his guitar back down and gave a rueful half-smile. 'So, what's the fella's name and what does he look like?'

Verity pulled up some photos she'd taken on her phone. 'Oh my.' She shuddered. 'Did you see the trousers he was wearing? With that shirt? And socks with loafers. Puh-lease!'

'Aye. Civilisation is clearly in serious trouble.' The Derry Man smirked.

'His name is Gawain Frei. Grew up in an orphanage,' Verity said sternly. 'That's all we know. And that he speaks impeccable English.'

'No harm in doing some unofficial back channel sleuthing using open source intel.' My pupil jackhammered his thumbs against his phone screen, firing off texts, google searches and requests at two hundred miles an hour. 'I also have a few Swiss contacts. Lemme see what I can dig up… But only if you're nice to my wee dog there.'

I gave the big, drooly, panting beast a tentative pat on its horrible head. The dog then began licking himself in a disgusting area.

'Typical male,' I muttered.

It was clear to all of us that this was the start of a formidable fighting task force.

TEN

Your mother taking up with a gold-digger is the ultimate laxative.

According to Melissa, complaining about anxiety levels is 'so last year.' Declaring that gut health is the new mental health, she took to openly discussing her digestion troubles triggered by Mum's erratic behaviour. My sister calmed the butterflies in her stomach by mainlining fermented foods and kimchi shots. I, on the other hand, just numbed the little buggers with alcohol.

All through July, while Mum was busy ticking off Helen's bucket list by gallivanting around the world with Gawain, the Derry Man got busy digging; or 'daisy chaining' as he called it – where one bit of info leads to another until you build up a 'POL' – Pattern of Life.

His first discovery was that the 'target' turned out not to be an orphan at all. The Derry Man broke this unsurprising news to us at my kitchen table one warm summer's day.

'Shock! Horror!!' I said, drolly. 'That whole raised-in-an-orphanage-running-into-burning-buildings-to-save-puppies is trope number one in the conman's "How To" textbook, am I right?'

'No record of the target at any Swiss orphanage or in foster care either – which is when I dug a little deeper to uncover your man's real identity.'

Verity, who was normally only impressed by people who made mozzarella from scratch, hand carved their own cedar clothes airers or could perfectly trill the coloratura flourish of Mozart's 'Queen of the Night', raised an appreciative brow. 'Gosh. How?' she asked, adding another slice of lemon to her gin and soda – tonic being too fattening. (While I'm afraid of heights, my sister is afraid of widths.)

'Facial recognition software. As you may have deduced, Gawain Frei is not the fella's real name.'

'Well, no surprises there. "Gawain" sounds about as Swiss as a calorie-free, vegan, sugarless carob bar.' I grimaced.

'Aye. My Swiss police contact tells me that Frei means "free man" in the feudal system, which is probably why he chose it – so he could start again.'

'But why?' Verity drummed her varnished nails on my dining-room table.

'Aye, well, that's the question, the million-dollar, no, sorry, the two-million-pound question. Your man actually hails from your typical Swiss middle-class family in Berne.'

Verity whipped out her iPhone to check our mother's whereabouts on Instagram. She was currently ziplining in Brazil. Eager to unmask Gawain as a villainous liar, she hit Mum's number. As soon as her smiling face popped up on the screen, Verity blurted out our discovery.

'Oh yes.' Mum breezily waved away Verity's revelation. 'Apparently Gawain's parents were terribly right wing, so he ditched the name Urs Bodmer and reinvented himself. Totally understandable. We all want to be the hero of our own narrative, right? And girls, believe me, all that subterfuge comes in so handy for sexual improv. The other night we pretended not to know each other and he picked me up in a bar!'

'But you don't know each other!' I interjected.

But Mum was already enthusing about her new favourite position. 'A sixty-niner, darlings. I haven't done that since the seventies. We're both biting off more than we can chew!' And then she was gone, proving that, for now, this was the only type of 'face time' our mother was interested in. From zipline to sixty-nine; forget the gin and tonic, I needed something much, much stronger. An induced coma, perhaps.

ELEVEN

A day or so later Melissa barrelled into my house to play a maddening message Mum had left on her voicemail. Mel had been trying to cajole her top client into agreeing to conduct the London Philharmonic Orchestra at the Proms, deputising for an American conductor taken ill. The Proms were offering an eye-watering whack of money.

Mel pressed play. 'When is the "Last Night of the Proms" going to actually mean that? Promises, promises!' My mother laughed. 'The answer's no. All my adult life I've done nothing but work. I worked hard to avoid all temptation but have now realised that temptation was avoiding me. Hence my new motto, "Don't put off till tomorrow anyone you could be doing today." You should also take that advice to heart, Mel, darling. Toodles.'

'Toodles?' Mel threw her phone across the room. 'Your mother may be having her jollies, but she doesn't seem to jolly well care about how her behaviour is impacting on my income and reputation!'

I tried to console her but had worries of my own. Chrissie had made a demo of a song she'd written. It was so good, I'd sent it to her father, without her permission. We'd named our daughter after the pioneering rock goddess Chrissie Hynde, and she'd turned out to have the same kind of voice – velvety but edgy with silky, seductive phrasing, coupled with a solid guitar technique. My darling daughter shared Hydne's lanky, lean physique too, with a sartorial predilection for rail-thin jeans, silver boots, tank tops, leather jackets, chipped red nail polish and lashings of black eyeliner. But she was also a laughing, quicksilver girl, with a ready smile and sun-kissed hair. My darling daughter was a one-woman task force for world happiness – except when it came to her father.

Johnny had been a devoted dad before our bust-up. When Chrissie was little, he sang her nursery rhymes at night and took her to Legoland by day. He built her huge Lego forts and even refrained from swearing when regularly crushing his instep on missing pieces. By the time she was ten, he was giving her drumming lessons and by eleven, spending hours playing those boring video games with abundantly bearded baddies of indeterminate nationality.

But when Johnny blew up our family and everyone was embedded with shrapnel, Chrissie took it upon herself to become my human shield. I developed insomnia and went to see the doctor, who diagnosed PTSD. I gave up touch football and cycling. I stopped seeing friends, despite their offers to put Johnny's face on a dart board and cut up his clothes. I'd sobbed and sulked for, well, far too long before I 'pulled myself together', to use Verity's favourite phrase. It had taken many boxes of pralines, but after two troubled years, I could be in the same room with him again; only Chrissie wouldn't let him inside the house. She stopped using his surname, Cox, and became a Nightingale girl. Chrissie Nightingale was the grenade, now. Whenever her father came to pick her up for dinner or a movie, I'd put my hands over my ears waiting for her to explode. I'd spent the last three years trying to minimise casualties by defusing my dear daughter. To no avail.

'So, when is that two-timing mongrel coming to collect me?' she'd say.

'You could just say "Dad". What time is Dad coming?'

She'd stomp out to his car, narrow hips swishing, her shoulder so cold it was bristling with invisible stalagmites.

Annihilated, he'd tried to find the funny. 'Darlin', you can't give me up for adoption. I'm just a bit too old to be left at the orphanage with a note pinned to my PJs.'

At his every utterance, she'd roll her eyes so far into the top of her head I felt pretty sure she could see her eyebrows growing.

'Sweetheart, your dad leaving doesn't mean you'll grow up to write the sequel to *Angela's Ashes*,' I'd gently pointed out to her recently. 'Even Mowgli survived, you know?'

'I'm okay, Mum. I can just never forgive him for hurting you.'

My guilt gland throbbed. If I'd handled the whole break-up better, she wouldn't be so angry with him. It was my job to build bridges… and it was the clever bridges in her songs that might just do it. And so, I'd secretly sent Chrissie's demo tape to her dad. Johnny had called immediately to say that he was on his way over.

TWELVE

Hearing the throaty growl of Johnny's motorbike made my stomach turn over. And then there he was, striding up the steps, dark, handsome, moody; Heathcliff in a leather jacket. His topaz ginger eyes jumped to my face. 'Bella.' He said my name as though biting into a ripe mango. He was also the only person who called me that. His voice still made my heart surge in a very peculiar way.

I felt an instinctive gravitational pull and was suddenly in his embrace. There was a new spicy scent to his skin, above the musky tang of leather and sweat; a caress of some exotic aftershave no doubt called 'Thrust' or 'Alpha' or 'Jizz' or something similarly macho. The man was effortlessly charming; he actually wore charm like an aftershave. What the hell was I doing here, pressed up against his chest? This was the worst place for me to be. I was like one of those baby ducklings who imprint the first person they see upon hatching, except I'd done it with the first man I loved.

'Lookin' good, Bella,' he bass-baritoned, holding me at arm's length. His eyes seemed to smoke their way into me.

'Wish I could say the same for you. You have a face that only a mother could love... a mother who is blind in one eye and has glaucoma in the other.'

This was a lie, obviously, as Johnny, although now in his early fifties, is still gorgeous. The man's a tenured professor in the Department of Sexiness. Johnny has always had an irreverent, insouciant, devil-may-care outlook on life. When we met, he was half man, half mattress. We made love all day and night. And the rest of the time, we made music. Raw, raunchy, punchy, fabulous rock'n'roll that blew the roofs off pubs and clubs. It was heady, happy, heartachingly joyous. Which is why, after all these years, the signals he broadcast still had the ability on some level to make me hum like a studio amplifier.

Johnny sidled into the living room and shrugged off his jacket. 'House looks good. Just the same, actually. As do you.' He glanced around, his gaze coming to rest on my face. Seeing him here again, in our old home, after five long years, was totally disorientating. 'Christ, I'm wrecked. I've been workin' so hard all day. Haven't stopped since I got up!'

'Want some breakfast?' I knew my lazy ex-husband so well. He'd no doubt rolled out of bed at noon.

He chuckled, then turned as Chrissie entered the living room. She stopped abruptly and leant up against the wall, one foot turned out like a dancer. 'What are you doing here? I told you never to come inside our house.'

'Don't be mad with me, darlin'. I forgot... You know I suffer from attention deficit dis...' he joked.

I laughed, willing Chrissie with a widening of my eyes to do the same. She tried to smile, but it was a flimsy effort. I kissed the soft knob of her nose. 'I asked your dad here to talk about your fabulous demo, darling.'

'Mum! You had no right to do that!'

'I'm sorry, sweetheart, but your father knows so much

more about your kind of music than me these days.'

'Yeah, I do and it's bloody good, Chrissie. I love that song so much I wish it could become a person so I could take it out and buy it ice cream. So, what do you wanna be when you grow up?'

'Why? Are you looking for ideas?' Chrissie blew a strand of fair hair from her eyes.

I saw his shoulders slacken, but he pressed on, ignoring her sarcasm. 'Because I reckon you're good enough to go pro. Like your old dad.'

'And like Mum,' she said, defensively. 'Mum's a brilliant musician.'

'Yeah, yeah, of course, your mum too. You've got the double genetic whammy, kiddo... A case of designer genes. So, wanna go out back and jam?' He gestured towards the music room. Johnny's drumsticks were tucked into the back pocket of his jeans. He wore them the way that other men wear Purple Hearts or a Victoria Cross. 'And then maybe you could come hear Panache playin' next Sat'dee night. In a club in Brixton. We're a warm-up act for some failed Eurovision contest geezer called Giovanni Groppoli. Ever heard of him? Exactly. Ya see? Dreams really can come true!' He gave a world-weary, self-deprecating laugh.

Chrissie crinkled her nose with disdain. 'Ah, you probably don't remember, because of your attention deficit dis...' she parroted, sarcastically, 'but I'm only seventeen.'

Johnny produced a fake ID from his back pocket and handed it to her with a flourish. Chrissie examined it, exclaiming, 'Type shit! That's soooo cool.'

'Yeah well, I bet you say that to all the dudes who enable your underage drinkin'.'

'No drinking!' I said in stern, responsible Mother Mode. 'Music only.'

Chrissie was beaming at her fake ID but then looked to me for approval. Yes, it was a teeny bit illegal, but hadn't I done the same? A thin tank top revealed her delicate shoulder. My heart gave a wrench of protest. If I allowed Johnny any influence over her, she was in danger of becoming a shoplifting, glue-sniffing termagant. But then again, how often I wished I knew my own father. During my school years Mum had pushed me hard. She wouldn't accept any excuses for missed music practice – well, nothing short of cholera, decapitation or abduction by aliens. And look how drastically I'd rebelled. My rebellion was standing in front of me right now, tossing his bike keys into the air and catching them with insouciant ease like some kind of Brat Pack movie star.

'Okay,' I said, warily, cross-hatched with doubts. Every inhalation seemed to echo in my chest as if I was scuba diving.

Yes, I wanted to hold on to my darling girl forever. I longed to make time stand still. But she was on the move and the training wheels were coming off. My only job was to get the hell out of her way without getting squashed.

THIRTEEN

The following Saturday afternoon, I was sitting at the kitchen table with the Derry Man, jigsawing together pieces of incriminating evidence about my mum's dodgy lover, when Johnny breezed by to pick up Chrissie.

As she opened the front door, I moved into the hall to gauge her emotional temperature. Johnny, grinning broadly, handed her a big, pink box. 'Verity baked her favourite niece her favourite cake.'

'Her only niece,' Chrissie amended, coolly. But lifting the lid on the layered strawberry and chocolate-whipped-cream concoction, she couldn't help emitting an appreciative 'Oh wow! My favourite...' She pivoted in my direction. 'I know Aunt Verity's just aura-harvesting...'

'Currying favour,' I deciphered for Johnny's bemused benefit.

'...but that's the best cake I've ever seen.'

Entering the lounge, they both dived straight in. As they oohed and aahed in lip-smacking delight, I examined my hands. I looked for the pale line on my finger where my wedding ring used to be, to find it completely faded. But seeing Johnny here again, after all this time, laughing along with our daughter, was a totally discombobulating time-warp. I tried to avoid looking at him, but my head seemed to have its own automatic satnav system, swivelling in his direction every time he spoke.

'Totally yum but we'd better get going. Just let me get my guitar,' Chrissie said, heading for the music room behind the kitchen.

It wasn't till Johnny started to follow that I remembered my ad hoc undercover cop was seated at the kitchen table.

'Oh, sorry. This is…'

'…Fiachra,' my guitar pupil volunteered in his soft Irish lilt, rising to his feet and outstretching his hand. Johnny pulled him into a manly hug, which the Derry Man clearly found as welcome as a hiccup mid-vasectomy.

The two men facing each other could not have been more opposite. Johnny, louche and laid-back, could make a soufflé look tense. The Derry Man stood so straight and still, he looked like a groom cake-topper figurine.

'Jeez, where'd you buy those jeans, man – 1972?' Johnny joked.

I think it's fair to say that the Derry Man was not a slave to the capricious whims of fashion and today he'd outdone himself in brand new, light blue, ironed denims, a white V-necked T-shirt, pristine trainers and green bomber jacket. I noticed for the first time the curly tufts emerging from the open V of his T-shirt. He'd clearly been sired by some kind of yak.

Johnny gave a hearty laugh, then tousled Chrissie's hair as she reappeared from the music room, clutching her guitar.

'We'd better get goin', princess. Car's outside.' He pointed to the shiny, tail-finned Buick my sister had bought for his fiftieth birthday.

'No drinking and driving,' I warned.

'For Chrissake.' Johnny eye-rolled.

'The Derry Man here is actually with the police.' I decided to leave out the bit about him only being a dog handler who possessed the killer instincts of a chihuahua. 'If any harm comes to my darling daughter, I'll have you arrested. You'll be sharing a prison bunk bed with a morbidly obese heavy metal fan who's hard of hearing before you can say "burst eardrum".'

I hugged Chrissie to me, holding on for too long.

'Jesus Christ. She's not emigratin'! She's goin' to a gig, for fuck's sake. Enough with the goodbyes, already.' Johnny shouldered his daughter's guitar, then steered her towards the hall, giving a disinterested salute to the Dog Handler en route.

My super-sleuth looked at me then. 'Do you think you should let the fella know that Brian Cox rang to break the news that the universe doesn't revolve around him?'

'Yep and that the sun doesn't shine out of his arse. Want one?' I poured myself a hefty glass of wine.

The Derry Man shook his head. 'Naw. I'm grand.'

'I have a genetic condition where my body doesn't produce its own alcohol so I have to take supplements. Cheers!' I took a restorative slug, then started banging cooking utensils down onto the countertop, fetching flour, milk, eggs…

The Derry Man took in the chaotic mess. 'So, um, a wee question… what's the actual plan here?'

'I'm baking a cake, obviously,' I snapped. 'Verity's not the only one who can create a warm fucking family atmosphere!' I noticed that breadcrumbs had gathered around the toaster like the debris from a tiny landslide and started frantically sweeping them into my palm. The more I thought about Verity's spotless kitchen the more manically I tidied.

The Derry Man got the dustpan and brush to help. 'Chrissie's a good wee girl. You need to trust her. She knows more than you think.'

'I'm not worried about what she knows... I'm worried about how she found out! And by the way, it's him I don't trust. Not her. But,' I sighed, 'he is her dad. And I wish I knew mine. From Mum's DNA, I got curly hair, a dimple, a tendency to sneeze cacophonously, an allergy to pineapple, oh, and an inability to cook cakes... From Dad's side, I don't know.'

The Derry Man leant up against the counter, arms folded. 'I could run a background check, no bother, but you'd have to fill me in first.'

Disarmed by the emotion of the day, I suddenly found myself blurting out my story. Why did this nerdy guy who favoured stone-washed jeans, brogue shoes and, on one occasion, a sleeveless knitted vest; a man who listened to Coldplay without irony; a dog handler who no doubt got all his news from the *Woofington Post* – why did he have the knack of getting me to spill my guts? Before I could ponder this conundrum, my mouth was in gear and I heard myself explaining how Nicole had come to London from Australia aged eighteen to study conducting at the Royal Academy of Music, then met a man playing Celtic rebel songs at a pub near Marylebone called Diddy's.

'Diddy's?' he queried.

'Yes. Apparently the pub was full of old-timers who kept falling off the perch. Every time a regular walked in, the bartender would mention someone who'd just died and the regulars would shout out "Did he?"'

The Derry Man chuckled. 'Oh, and by the way, when baking, Izzy, I think the main rule is that there should be more flour in the cake than in your hair.' He took the sieve from my hand and neatly took over the task.

'Anyway, a night of passion resulted in us; our father's whereabouts, unknown. After Mum graduated, she took us home to Sydney into the bosom of her big, boisterous family. But when we were eleven, she was offered a dream job conducting the London Symphonia, which is how we ended up in a school in Camden, a school so rough it had its own Accident and Emergency ward.'

'Yeah? My school was so tough the teachers took to asking, "So, what do you want to be *if* you grow up?"'

It was my turn to laugh now. 'Okay, you win. I just kept my head down and worked hard at music. Got a scholarship to the Guildhall, but then threw it in to join a rock band. Fell in love, had Chrissie – and then Johnny left me. End of story. Have you ever been in love, Derry Man? There's nothing worse than being cheated on.'

'Apart from a pandemic, world war or asteroid shower annihilation, yeah, sure…'

'Oh, so you're saying I'm not keeping this in perspective?'

'I just don't get why that's the end of your story. Why put your life on hold? I've only known you, what? A year and a half now. But it seems to me that you are your own worst enemy.'

'Ha! Not while my sister's alive.'

'I grew up in the Troubles, but I've learnt to let it go.'

I turned to face him. 'It's awful what you went through. I can't imagine how horrible it was. But my sister put a hole in my life, a wound through which all my hope and joy seeped out. My singing voice just seized up when Johnny left me. I had to start teaching to support my kid. Still, I did learn something in this time too – not to trust men. I got caught with my synapses down. Never again.'

The Derry Man took the egg whisk from my hand and started to beat and fold the cake mixture together. 'You can't judge all men by the behaviour of one big eejit. You say you don't like dogs, but trauma victims like you gain a lot from a support animal.' On cue, the big Alsatian nuzzled up to his leg, tail wagging. 'Maybe you should borrow Cyril for a bit?'

'I gain a lot from my support vibrator, actually. It's top of the range and can do everything imaginable… apart from cake cooking.'

I'd wanted to shock him, to trick him into thinking I was a feisty, independent, mouthy broad who took no prisoners, but he didn't look remotely ruffled.

'Humans can learn a lot from dogs – like loyalty, living in the moment, having fun…' he said, gently.

'And… licking your own genitals, apparently.'

I pointed to Cyril, who was once again licking his private parts with the zeal of a wanker banker snorting up a line of cocaine.

'Just hurry up and put that cake in the oven so I won't be tempted to shove my head in there, à la Sylvia Plath.' I looked from Verity's perfect pink confection to my own pathetic culinary effort. Oh, how I hated my sister then – for having her cake and eating it too. Or rather, for having her beefcake and eating him too. The tectonic plates of sisterly love had been smashed. Irreparably broken. And, unlike the Derry Man and his Troubled Past, there was no way I could ever just 'let it go'. And no amount of 'aura-harvesting' could help me either. It was one of the Sisterhood Rules not to be jealous – the colour green suits no female complexion. And yet, despite knowing this, in a fit of pique, I chucked my own culinary effort into the bin.

'A mercy killing,' I told the Derry Man.

'It's the humane thing to do.' He smiled.

Then I gouged out a big slab of Verity's cake with my fingers and shoved it into my mouth in one big, crumb-spraying, icing-smearing, gluttonous, furious bite.

FOURTEEN

All through August, in exchange for me perfecting the Derry Man's tremolo (an extremely tricky technique which involves a continuous melody repeated rapidly with the right-hand fingers), he homed in on Gawain with the nocturnal accuracy of a bat. His next discovery was that Gawain, as Urs Bodmer, had declared bankruptcy. And this vampire was now sucking the lifeblood out of our mother; the financial lifeblood, that is.

After I repaid the Derry Man with an extra lesson or two on *rasqueado*, an intense flamenco-type strumming which is incredibly hard to master, he left to train Cyril in the park.

I immediately summoned Verity, who was soon striding into the situation room, i.e. my kitchen, eyes ablaze. Today she was featuring 'statement shoulders' in a strapless top that put her clavicles and coxal bones centre stage. Her hair was sculpted into a casual asymmetric, sloping chignon. I was wearing trackies and a misshapen T-shirt which set off my bird-nest hair beautifully.

'Clearly *Vogue* will be on the phone any minute now,' was her appraisal of my outfit. On autopilot, she then made me a cup of tea just the way I like it – dunking the teabag five times, turning the cup for luck and adding just the right amount of milk. At the times I was most cross with her, she'd do something thoughtful and suddenly I was sliding on the comfortable slippers of our old relationship once more. It was baffling and soothing, all at once.

Verity then ran her eyes over the evidence the Derry Man had unearthed. 'Good God. Gawain is clearly laughing all the way to the bank – our mother's bank.'

Melissa had also cycled straight over from her office in tight, designer sportswear, her muscular, shapely calves on display, her blonde, Valkyrie hair in tight plaits. Mum was not communicating with her so she was hoping to get to her client by piggybacking onto one of our calls.

Although a practical businesswoman, Melissa is also tuned in to the woo-woo world. She loves mantras, manifesting and angel numbers, whatever the hell they are. Mood boards and vision boards are also on her radar. These are a way of 'willing your goals into being, with positive thought visualisation', apparently. Shucking off her backpack, she extracted, then lit, a manifestation candle called 'Abundance'. Evidently, its floral aroma with citrussy top notes would enhance her persuasive powers, assuring success with our wayward mum. Verity and I preferred the persuasive powers of a gin bottle, from which we now drank liberally.

After fortifying ourselves alcoholically, we located our materfamilias – she was on a scuba in Cuba – and reported our latest findings. But Nicole just shrugged off Gawain's big bankruptcy revelation.

'A youthful indiscretion,' she said coolly, sipping a colourful cocktail, the sun dancing on the water behind her. 'Gawain's already told me all about it. It's part of the reason the darling boy changed his name. And why are you snooping into his affairs, anyway! It's none of your business.'

She was much more interested in updating us on her carnal repertoire, doing so in such explicit detail that three minutes into the conversation, I started to feel the urgent need for a dip of my own – into a jacuzzi of penicillin.

'...So the G spot... Are those magical nerve endings the internal extension of the clitoris? What do you think, girls?'

'Ummm...' I retorted, with Dorothy Parker panache.

'Mother,' Verity peered more closely at the screen, 'what are you wearing? That costume's so ancient you look as though you're about to swim the English Channel.'

'Oh, it doesn't matter, darlings. We prefer the nudist beach.'

There was a beat while my sister and I took this in.

'Mother, you are far too old to go naked in public!' Verity reprimanded. 'You're nearly seventy. Look at your hands. They're covered in liver spots!'

'They're not liver spots... they're just erratic bits of tan.'

I was in awe of my mother's self-assurance. My confidence level was so minuscule it would take an X-ray to locate it. The only way I'd allow anyone to see me naked in public would be at the morgue with a tag on my toe.

'For some wonderful reason, Gawain just worships the water I walk on.' She gave a rich chuckle, her laughter vibrant with pleasure.

'That's because you house and feed him like some expensive pet.' Verity took another big slug of gin.

Mum had just started in on some more anatomical musings, when my sister interrupted with the severity of a headmistress; a headmistress trained by the SAS. 'Mother, we're extremely worried about our inheritance.'

'Sorry, darling...' Mum paused her R-rated repertoire. 'What did you say?'

'I said "inheritance"? You know, big amount of money, destined as a legacy to your beloved children...'

'I understood, Verity, just wondered why you wanted to know about that? I helped both of you buy your first houses and of course you are the beneficiaries of my will, so...?'

'Blessed are the young, as they will inherit the tax burden bequeathed to them when their mother's disreputable lover spends all her money, remortgages her home and goes into debt ...' my sister warned, bluntly.

'What's the problem, Verity, darling? You made plenty of money from your bestselling book.'

Verity sank into an uncharacteristic silence.

'Mum, remember that big nest egg you worked so hard to build up when we were kids?... Well, Verity needs to hatch it.'

'Hatch the nest egg? Why? After all your success?'

Verity, crestfallen, glanced up at me with a look of such mortified dismay that I leapt into the conversational breach once more. 'You know how Verity gave Johnny an unlimited budget? Well, he exceeded it.'

'He's lost all our money on Bitcoin,' my sister finally blurted.

Johnny had always been a gambler who played for high stakes – emotionally and professionally. I, too, had taken a bet on him, and lost, in a completely different way, of course.

My mother's eyes now narrowed into laser beams. 'Well, you clearly need to choose the men in your life more carefully... Both of you,' she added, pointedly.

I was suddenly winded. The memory of my sister's betrayal could still hit me square in the chest when I least expected it. And here I was, flummoxed and floored all over again. Verity always acted as though stealing Johnny from me was accidental, like stubbing her toe. But I was the one howling in pain. 'Mum,' I amended, trying to hold it together, 'honestly, you're entitled to spend your money however you want...'

'Then stop making me feel as though I'm some kind of a welfare case!'

'...just not on this scam artist,' I concluded.

My mother sighed and removed the umbrella from her exotically coloured cocktail. 'Yes, I worked hard raising my daughters single-handedly. Motherhood is the toughest on-the-job training scheme imaginable, which is why, at my age, I deserve some fun. Why can't women have a sensational second act? Haven't you heard of *je ne sais quoi*?'

'Mum, "je ne sais quoi" is just French for a weak pelvic floor and strong bank balance.' I didn't want to hurt her, but it was true.

In response my mother just gave a mischievous grin. 'I want to behave, girls, I really do, but there are just too many other options... My plan is to die young, as late as possible.'

'It's your dying career I'm worried about,' I told her. 'I gave up my career and I regret it...'

'Get back on stage then, Isabella. Stop hiding away. You need to borrow my Gift of Life pendant.' She yanked Helen's organ donor disc up from around her neck and kissed it. 'You need something to perk yourself up, darling. You look exhausted.'

Melissa, who'd been waiting out of sight, now commandeered the iPad. 'Nicole, I have another fabulous offer for you. The Gewandhausorchester needs a conductor, urgently. They've offered you the gig. Beethoven's Third! A week in Leipzig. You simply cannot turn this down!'

'When are you coming back, Mother?' Verity demanded. 'Lately, you're never off a plane.'

'That's because I have frequent-flier age points. Time to cash in!'

And with that, we were left talking to her slipstream, words fizzling out in our mouths.

I'm partial to collective nouns and often pass the time between pupils thinking up new ones. A queue of Brits, a condescension of critics, a shortage of jockeys, a password of IT guys, a percentage of agents... Only not in Mel's case right now; I was 100 per cent sure about that.

Melissa, Verity and I just stared at the empty screen for a moment, frustrated and tetchy. With nowhere to put our ire, we took it out on each other.

My sister blew out Melissa's manifestation candle in one angry burst of air. 'Mother is right. You do look tired, Isabella. You could so with some tweakments. We are twins, after all. Your ageing is ageing me.'

My sister is so averse to wrinkles, she even remakes the beds after the cleaner has left so that there's no hint of a crinkle in her Egyptian cotton sheets.

'Yeah, well, as Mum pointed out, single motherhood will do that to you. I'm so busy, some days I only have time to shave one leg... Mind you, at least that way, when I'm sleeping, I can pretend I'm still with my hairy-legged husband.' I sent a heated glare my sister's way as she paced the kitchen.

'Talking of legs, leg-over is all your mother can talk about.' Melissa threw herself back into the kitchen chair, making it groan. 'Can't she pull back on the sex, for just one concert?'

'...And talking of pulling back, maybe you should pull back on the face surgery, Verity. You're starting to look like a cross between a frilled-neck lizard and an alien.'

I saw my sister's eyes narrow as she registered the barb. 'Grooming is about self-respect – an alien concept to you, Isabella...' She scooped my unruly hair into her hands and swept it into a stylish updo, just as she did when we were girls. Once more, her automatic sisterly gesture was bamboozlingly at odds with her harsh words.

'I suppose you have to keep looking hot for your hot rock-star lover.' Envy ran molten through my veins once more. After what Johnny had done to me, I didn't want him, but didn't want her to have him either. 'Of course, they'll have to cremate you when you die, as you're no longer biodegradable.'

When we fought as girls, we'd pinch, kick, scratch and inflict Chinese burns. Now we just hurled verbal javelins.

'I'm actually much younger than my biological age. I mean, look at me,' Verity bragged, 'I don't even need glasses.'

'Just drink straight from the bottle, do you?' It was a weak shot, but I took it anyway.

Melissa scraped her chair back across the kitchen tiles with a screech. 'Christ, this is what puts me off having children.' She sucked from her huge water bottle as though just emerging from two months in the Gobi Desert. 'Mind you, motherhood can't be as tough as agenting.'

I could see her point. Managing my mother right now must be like trying to lasso jelly.

Melissa strapped on her bike helmet and headed for the door. 'Call me when you two brats stop this childish bickering and come up with a sensible plan.'

'You're not getting any younger either, Melissa,' Verity snapped back, snatching up her designer handbag. 'What are you now? Thirty-nine? Forty? If you are going to have kids, don't leave it much longer… Otherwise you'll put the baby down and forget where you left it. Mother Nature is a bitch that way.'

'Clearly why you know so much about her,' I fired back at my twin, unravelling the impromptu hairdo she'd given me.

As the door slammed, hard enough to make me worried about the front half of the house falling off, I wished I'd taken some tips from Mother Nature. In particular the black widow spider. She mates just the once, then eats him. Then I wouldn't have had to put up with Johnny's shady shenanigans – with my very own sister.

FIFTEEN

Chrissie was now gigging with her dad all over London. Even though we'd established a temporary truce, every time he took her off in his car I felt as though I was handing a Stradivarius to an orangutan. When he'd dropped by for a rehearsal recently, I'd had to tear strips off him for giving Chrissie vodka shots before she went on stage to play with Panache at the Half Moon pub in Putney.

'Yeah, but I didn't let her drive us home afterwards.'

'Oh, yes, the model parent.'

A moment later he was kicking his bike into clamorous life and speeding away. My fear was that he would soon be taking my daughter with him too, riding in his sidecar into career oblivion. And I wasn't wrong. A few weeks later Chrissie called me up to her bedroom to announce, her face vivid with excitement, that she had formed her own all-girl band called Femifesto.

Her exam results had come in – straight A's as expected – and her music scholarship was secured. 'But you're not giving up music college,' I said sternly. 'Right?'

'Why not? You did.' She looked polite but sullen, her eyes bright but unreadable beneath the rim of her sequinned baseball cap.

'Yes, and look where it got me?' I gestured around our ramshackle house. The paint was flaking off Chrissie's bedroom ceiling and the window sash had snapped. Whenever my sister came over, I had to pretend we'd just been burgled to explain the mess. 'Chrissie, you do not want a career in rock music. The grimy dressing rooms, the grim pubs, the communal toilets shared by hundreds of people with starkly different standards of hygiene...'

I looked at her guitar and amp. She'd babysat every Saturday night for two years to buy them. Same with the huge loudspeakers positioned like sentries either side of her bed. I glanced up at her eclectic posters – Chrissie Hynde, Lizzo, Janis Joplin, P!nk, Billie Eilish, Dua Lipa, Kate Bush... I couldn't bear her butterfly enthusiasms being pinned down, but it had to be done for her own good.

'You'll be paid in love and fava beans. And the terrible men you'll meet! Male rock musos insist on discussing their many wonderful qualities, general fame and fabulousness long after your own interest has waned. They all fake their working-class upbringings too – "Oh, you grew up on an estate, I was raised in a shoebox" – every one of them acting prolier-than-thou, when they're all actually middle-class boys from Tunbridge Wells... Then there's the creepy promoters...'

Given the abundance of lowlifes in the rock industry, Chrissie's father had seemed like a prince, I wanted to say, but refrained. Plus he hadn't feigned his inauspicious beginnings, hailing as he did from the mean streets of Walthamstow.

'And the venues! Those endless festivals where it always rains. Torrential storms will never miss the chance to pour down on canvas... Hurricanes will leap whole hemispheres just to make it to Glastonbury in time to drench the main act…'

But she might as well have been wearing headphones for all the impact my words had achieved. 'We've been working on about ten songs and I think they're good.' Chrissie tilted her face up towards me, smiling. There was hope all over her; she smelled of it. 'I played my newest song on stage with Dad the other night and wow. The reaction was immense! It was just so…!!' She lit up, momentarily lost for words.

I remembered that feeling. The audience a boiling kettle, heads bobbing up and down in time, your lyrics on their lips.

She passed me her headphones. 'Will you take a listen?' I could hear the *tss tss tss* of drum and bass.

I waved her away. 'You know I'm no judge of rock music any more, Chrissie.' Since leaving the band, I listened exclusively to classical, baroque, jazz…

'At least let me take a gap year to give it a go.'

'What?! An unemployed would-be muso on a gap year? Why can't you just be gay, like all the other kids?' I kissed the top of her head and inhaled her warm, familiar scent. 'Show me a daughter who wants to give up education to start a rock band and I'll show you an orphan… Honestly, Chrissie, that would just kill me. Please don't make the same mistakes as me.'

The next time her father was over I tried to get him to back me up. 'Chrissie, listen, it's okay to have a band as a hobby, but you must take up that scholarship. Right, Johnny?'

But my feckless ex just shrugged. 'I dunno. A classical muso plays four thousand chords to four people; a rock star plays four chords to four thousand. Do the maths, Bella, babe.'

'Says the man who is now the warm-up act for bands called "Satan's Balls" and "Jerk to Inflate".'

'You just didn't have the guts to stick life on the road... Just when we were on the brink of really makin' it big...'

'You, on the other hand, couldn't wait for success – so went ahead without it,' I snapped. 'Chrissie, darling,' I stroked the hair out of her eyes, 'you don't want to end up like us – your dad a recovering celebrity, your mum a peripatetic music teacher, trudging off to private schools, trying to bridge the yawning chasm between pampered little princesses and rhythm. Being self-employed, you can't even ring in sick, as you'll know you're lying...'

But Chrissie and her father were now in their own world, improvising a song about dissolute rock'n'rollers – 'One tequila, two tequila, three tequila, floor...'

As they harmonised away between laughs, I took a deep breath. One thing motherhood had taught me is that hamsters, goldfish and pet mice are more resilient than they may at first appear. And that the same is true of mothers. As for my own mother, well, I had to be resilient on her behalf because her big, beautiful brain had turned to mush. That's what happens when a woman gets laid by a bloke who lies like a cheap carpet – another home-grown homily to needlepoint onto a throw cushion. It was time to be vigilant. After all, I didn't want end up like my daughter's hamster: asleep at the wheel.

SIXTEEN

'Jail time?! Are you serious?'

The Derry Man opened his laptop. 'Aye. Two convictions for credit card fraud. Six months inside.'

My guitar student was so chuffed with his progress in *apoyando* (a complicated rest stroke manoeuvre used to bring out melodies with the right-hand fingers) that he'd put in some extra sleuthing on our behalf. With the help of his Swiss police pal, he'd secured Urs Bodmer's, aka Gawain Frei's, prison records. Keen for the latest low-down, Verity and I had dashed to meet him during his lunch break at the pub garden of the Dog and Duck in Chadwell Heath, east London.

'You really work around here?' Verity asked, turning up her nose at the surrounding grim tenements, grimed with existence. She pulled her scarf up over her mouth for some protection against the toxic breath of factories and car fumes which thickened the air.

'Aye. There's a dog training unit based here at HQ. I work at the kennels teaching the new dogs to track down drugs at airports and ferry terminals…'

'Like Sherlock Holmes, but with a bit more sniffing.'

'Aye.' He smiled at me. 'I have many curious incidents with my dogs in the night-time.'

'I think *you're* the one with the real nose for clues. Hungry?' I proffered the box of takeaway sushi I'd grabbed en route, tearing the ginger packet open with my teeth.

He gave the sushi a dubious look. 'Back home we'd call that bait. I'd use it to catch salmon in the Faughan.'

'Oh great. Another unpronounceable word. Fear-car... Far-quoir fishes in the F... f... h... h... hon.'

'Ohh-kaaaay.' My sister drummed her nails on the cracked linoleum tabletop, eager to get the hell out of here. 'As riveting as this feeble banter is proving to be, can we please get back to business? Basically, when Gawain calls himself "creative", he clearly means creative accounting,' she tut-tutted.

'And when he calls himself an "artist", he means "rap artist", as in, it goes with his sheet?' I ventured.

The Derry Man nodded, shucked up his sleeves, then turned his laptop our way.

'So, what now?' Verity sighed, after we'd finished reading our mother's lover's prison report – not a high point for any progeny.

'Um...' I contributed, with Hercule Poirot-like perspicacity. The raw prawns, lying uneaten on their beds of rice under a green slime of wasabi, wilted in the heat, much as we did.

'The plot sickens...' the Derry Man punned as his crackling police radio summoned him back to work.

My sister and I stared at each other despondently over lukewarm wine. Not only was my glass half empty... but it was cracked and chipped and I felt as though I'd just swallowed a jagged shard. The Derry Man may have gone off to train canines at the kennels but we were having our very own dog day afternoon.

SEVENTEEN

My dislike of Gawain was subtle at first; but as the dossier of his misdemeanours built up, I began to fantasise about tripping him down the stairs then 'accidentally' standing on his thorax while pretending to help him up. Especially when the Derry Man's next big revelation was that Gawain was married.

We were gathered at my place for a meeting. I'd taken to calling these weekly Saturday update sessions 'Breakfast at Epiphanies'. It was only mid September but there was a chill in the air. To warm up I'd made revitalising melted cheese toasties for Verity, Melissa and our super-sleuth.

'I'm so glad you took me at my word and didn't go to too much trouble.' Verity, a caviar queen who'd once reprimanded me in a restaurant for not knowing the difference between beluga and oscietra, had always been irked by my lack of culinary sophistication.

'Humble apologies, m'lady.' I served the toastie up to her with mock obsequiousness, bowing with the flamboyance of a French courtier. 'In truth, you'd eat a slug if I gave it a posh name – les sluggato slimeato.'

Melissa, who was normally busy working on either her inner child or outer thighs, was so distressed by our mother's behaviour that she forgot to ask if the cheese was organic before wolfing it down. She'd also gone cold on her infra-red heated Pilates class and cancelled it to stay longer.

'Not telling the woman you're bonking that you're married, well, that's clearly a red flag.' She crunched her teeth into her toastie. She'd already stood in front of the hall mirror to make her 'affirmations'. These turned out to be positive reinforcement mantras. 'Conscious breathing is my anchor,' she'd chanted to her own reflection, followed by, 'Step into freedom' and, 'The perfect moment is now.'

It was actually the opposite of a perfect moment because Melissa had brought along what she called a visualisation board. This huge bit of cardboard was now leaning up against my lounge-room wall. It was covered in images of what Mel wanted to manifest – a holiday home in the south of France, six Persian cats, a red sports car, a penthouse apartment on the river, a baby...

'A baby?' I asked, surprised.

'My clients are my babies. That photo just represents them all. And right now your mother is giving me postnatal depression!' She tapped a manicured nail on the picture of a British classical music award. 'Let's concentrate on making this happen. Come on. Close your eyes and picture your mother accepting this award at the Albert Hall in front of all her peers.'

As Mel began to chant, the Derry Man surreptitiously slipped away to make another pot of tea. I exchanged an exasperated look with my sister but reluctantly closed my eyes. Melissa's repetitive 'Ommmm' noises made me sleepy but I was dragged from my reverie by a blood-curdling growl.

As we'd been chanting, eyes closed, Cyril had stalked my feather duster, which he was now shaking with a violence and vigour that centuries of attack dog breeding told him should swiftly break its neck.

'Cyril!' I shouted, as coloured feathers flew about the room.

Cyril celebrated the defeat of the feather duster by then sniffing the bottom of Vikram, my newest music student, whom the Derry Man had let in while we were 'manifesting'. Looking closer, I now realised that the big dog also had the underwear I'd been drying on the radiator clamped between his foaming fangs – not my good underwear either, but a fraying grey bra and faded cottontails.

I rushed to placate my startled pupil and retrieve my spittle-flecked smalls before the Derry Man could take in the whole saggy elasticated horror. I then noticed that my sister's toasted sandwich was nowhere to be seen. Allergic to carbs, she'd no doubt taken it outside to be garrotted while I was mock meditating.

As I packed the Derry Man and Cyril out the door, I heard Melissa prattling on to Verity about her belief in numerology. 'Numbers, taken from your date of birth and the number of letters in your name, have a vibrational frequency, influencing fate,' she espoused.

I had no doubt that my numbers would predict total failure. Maybe I could legally change the spelling of my name to include a few more letters to get a better reading? But the only obscure numbers I knew were the songs I'd co-written with Johnny, back in the days when we were happy, Mum was sane, Chrissie was all set for music college, my sister was my best friend and nothing was savaging my household cleaning appliances, chewing on my undergarments or sniffing the nether regions of a startled new student. 'Manifest that, motherfucker!' I seethed at Mel's visualisation board.

EIGHTEEN

As our investigation proceeded, it quickly became clear that Gawain's motto was 'I'll double-cross that bridge when I come to it.'

The following Saturday, when the Derry Man cracked open his laptop on my kitchen table, we girded our loins for his latest discovery. Our lesson had run over time while he'd tried to master the delicacies of *campanella*, a complicated technique which involves crossing strings to create a bell-like, continuous sound, meaning that Verity had been hovering anxiously nearby for half an hour. And when I say hovering, I mean it literally: she refused to sit down because she'd seen a mouse.

'Are you sure it wasn't just a very small squatter?' I teased her. 'There are just so many undesirables in this area.'

'Aye, well,' the Derry Man interrupted, 'there's something much worse than a mouse... a rat.'

I stopped buttering my toast to scrutinise his face. 'Oh God. Do I need to book Mum a fumigator? What the hell have you uncovered now?'

'Well, I don't want to alarm you both, but it turns out that Gawain's wife met a very suspicious end. House fire.' The Derry Man's voice dropped a register into a guarded, more cautious tone. 'Any guesses who got the insurance money?'

My toes curled up like autumn leaves.

'Aye, and there's more,' the Derry Man said sombrely. 'Restraining order.'

'Come on, we're not that bad,' I joked.

'The dead ex-wife's family took out a restraining order against Gawain, three years ago.'

A pretty formidable silence ensued during which nobody could think of an appropriate follow-up sentence. In fact, all I could think about was that our mother's latest bucket list destination was Iceland, a country famous for ways in which you could die – earthquakes, volcanic eruptions, scalding hot springs, arctic waters and pitch-black winters, requiring you to walk by Braille past all these death traps...

Our only communication with Mum of late was a postcard from the world's biggest penis museum in Reykjavik. I handed the card to Verity for closer scrutiny.

'Wait. Does that mean the penis museum is the biggest in the world, or that it houses the world's biggest penis?' she enquired.

'That would be the blue whale,' the Derry Man informed us, matter-of-factly. 'I imagine the tip of that beast's mighty member would enter the female of the species at six p.m. and the base of the shaft about half past ten.'

I might have laughed, but too many questions were crowding my cranium, particularly if we should contact the Icelandic Phallological Society about a potential, priapic 'organ' donor currently milking the bank account of a sixty-nine-year-old classical conductor atop one of their glaciers.

But just when we were planning a call to Interpol, or possibly Hire-a-Hitman Inc., Mum texted to say she was on her way home for Helen's funeral. Due to travel arrangements for far-flung family (Helen's brother was a missionary in New Guinea), the ceremony had been delayed. A big memorial was also planned for January and our mother, in the role of Helen's 'best friend', was musical director.

With Mum back in London, now was our chance to discredit Gawain. Prison conviction, fraud, bankruptcy, using a false identity, lying about his childhood, a secret marriage, mysterious death of a spouse in a house fire, insurance payout, restraining order... We had a lot to talk to her about. But would she listen?

Verity and I decided to jump off that bridge when we came to it.

NINETEEN

'Darlings!' Mum greeted us, enthusiastically. 'Oh, how I've missed you!'

'It's so wonderful to see you, Mum!' I leant in for a kiss, hugging her around the neck, not wanting to let go.

We'd been summoned to a high-street nail bar, of all places. Mum, her hair bouffed up into a kind of auburn soufflé, was sitting in one of those vibrating pedicure thrones, her tootsies soaking in the foot spa, a manicurist bent over each hand.

My sister gingerly positioned her pert posterior on the huge throne on Mum's left and I sprawled across the throne to her right. This kind of beautifying was so out of character I found myself wondering if our mother had perhaps inhaled too much sulphur dioxide and hydrogen sulphide in the Nordic land of lava.

'Mother,' Verity pecked her cheek, 'thank God you're okay. We've been so worried.'

Mum barked out a laugh. 'Good God, why?'

'Okay, well for starters,' Verity said stonily, 'did you know that Gawain has done jail time?'

Mum's response was a cascade of laughter. 'That's so ironic, darlings, as we've just starting using handcuffs in our boudoir play. No wonder he prefers me to wear them!'

Needless to say, neither Verity nor I found this information quite so amusing.

'Mother.' Verity tapped her own perfectly manicured fingernails on the vibrating armrest with irritation. 'Aren't you vaguely perturbed by the fact that he didn't tell you he'd been in prison?'

'Oh, darlings, I'm trying to get to know everything about him but there's never enough time.'

'Unless you're serving it,' I muttered.

'The man's a felon, Mother.'

'But a long time ago, I'm sure. It was probably over that bankruptcy business you two snooped out.'

'Yes, you're right... probably way, way back when he was um, married. Did he happen to mention his matrimonial status?' Verity probed, through tight lips.

'Yes, darlings, I know all about that. The marriage was a youthful indiscretion. Gawain's clearly moved on, emotionally. As have I! I'm becoming the woman I always should have been.'

'What,' I suggested, 'a teenager? Except with wrinkles instead of pimples.'

'No, it's her boyfriend who's the teenager,' Verity corrected.

'Your hairstyle is actually older than he is, Mum.' A pulse of anxiety beat behind my ear.

Verity's facial muscles twitched, as though an invisible spider was crawling across her visage. 'You're supposed to be our tribal elder, Mother, offering words of advice.'

'Advice?' Mum's eyes were summery with laughter. 'Sure, I have some advice. Never grope through your toiletry bag in the dark in case you mistake the Deep Heat for the lube tube.' She threw her head back now and chortled. 'Burn, baby, burn!' she sang.

Who was this woman? My sister rallied first.

'Mother, when you began your conducting career, Gawain was still doing laps in amniotic fluid. No need to page Dr Freud. I think we can all diagnose the attraction,' my sister decreed. 'You're clearly his mother figure.'

'Oh, darling! I don't mother him! He's teaching me… Have you ever experimented with S&M?' she asked, conspiratorially, looking directly at me.

I glanced nervously around the nail bar but Mum was the only customer and the attendants were busy shouting over each other in rapid-fire Vietnamese. 'Ah, no. I've always presumed bondage is just an inventive way of keeping your partner from going home too early.'

'Dominance?'

Once more I shook my head. 'The only thing I've ever whipped is cream.'

'Orgies?'

I gulped again. The very thought of group sex makes me suffer from a performance anxiety I haven't felt since those hedonistic hours of enforced folk dancing in primary school. 'Surely, the only good thing about an orgy is that it does away with any angst about what to wear?' I hazarded.

Breathless and endorphin-sozzled, my mother confided, 'I'm never quite sure what to do with my knees!' She extracted her right hand from the drying machine and admired her hot-red nails. 'Gawain mentioned autoeroticism this morning… I don't even know what that is but can't wait to find out!'

'Mother,' Verity said sternly, 'I know Gawain keeps saying that age doesn't matter and money makes no difference, but I'm yet to meet a toy boy who falls in love with an older woman who's broke.'

Mum gave an insouciant shrug. 'Scientists report that sex with younger men is good for your heart...'

'Yeah, well, nine out of ten statisticians agree that statisticians make up statistics,' I countered.

'Sorry, did I say scientists? I meant middle-aged women!' Mum trilled. 'I'm too busy putting the sex into sexagenarian to worry about anything else! Gawain is the best thing that's ever happened to me. Meeting him, well, it's miraculous. I mean, look! He's even brought you two back together!'

A plate of complimentary doughnuts was sitting on the little table in front of us. As I reached for one Verity slapped my hand, hard. 'Why don't you just buy a bakery and cut out the middle-man?' She gave me a look of narrow-eyed reproach. 'Mind you, at least being seen with you these days is making me look so much slimmer!'

I snatched up the doughnut and gobbled it in one gulp, spraying Verity with crumbs. Oh, yes, we were definitely back together again, clearly closer than ever. Mum, busy appreciating the novelty of her brightly painted toenails, paid us no heed.

'And did he also tell you what happened to his wife?' Verity lectured. 'How she died, in a house fire.'

'Yes. Too horrible. Such a tragic accident. Do you know how he spent the insurance money? Commissioning a requiem, dedicated to Bettina's memory... And now that very same angel is dedicated to me. He says he wants to give generously to my sex appeal!' Her laugh was alarmingly coquettish for a sixty-nine-year-old retiree.

'Mother, you don't have sex appeal, but tax appeal.'

'Gawain may not have money but he's rich in every other way,' Mum said defensively. 'My man has the heart of a warrior.'

'What? The one he gouged out of his ex-wife with a corkscrew and now keeps in a jar under the bed?' I asked. 'Hey, what's that on your arm?' I leant in closer.

'What? This?' Mum rolled up her sleeve.

'Is that a... a... tattoo?' Verity picked up the word with invisible tweezers.

'Ah-huh.'

'What does it say?' my sister asked, aghast. 'It looks like L... T... D... S...'

'Life's Too Damn Short. As Helen's funeral tomorrow reminds us. So, make the most of it.'

'Mum, would you like me to come with you?' I asked, gently.

'Count me in too, Mother.'

'That would be lovely, girls. Thank you.' She squeezed our hands, genuinely touched.

As the three of us left the salon, my mother's words niggled at me. Of late I'd felt as though my destiny was on hold to one of those call centres in India – 'Your call is important to us but we've put you on hold for the rest of your natural life.' Maybe it was me who needed an LTDS tattoo...

TWENTY

The funeral was a High Anglican mass with candles, incense, chanted prayers and vestments. The service, held in an ancient church, perched high on a hill in Hampstead, was deeply solemn, highly ceremonial and awash with liturgical grandeur. The stone archways that swooped overhead echoed with musical lamentations. Mum, bookended by her daughters in a back row, cried quietly throughout the sermon.

It was a big turnout too; Helen had clearly been loved, although the congregation had no idea just how loved by my mother. And Mum had been right about Helen's family; they were more stuffy than a taxidermist's showroom.

When Helen's husband delivered his eulogy, he pursed the bitty sinews that passed for his lips, then, in a pinched voice, delivered the most parsimonious praise for his wife. He was powerful-looking in a compact way, like a bull terrier on steroids. I took Mum's hand, so glad that Helen had found some warmth and comfort in her loving arms.

After the coffin was sprinkled with holy water and mourners began to follow the procession to the family burial site, Mum suggested we peel away. As we walked back down the hill in the watery autumnal sunshine, she wove her arms through ours. Turning off the main street towards home, we passed a cosy little pub.

'Two perimenopausal women and their grieving mother were passing a wine bar… ' she began, adding cheekily, 'Well, it's not beyond the realm of imagination, is it?! Could I talk you both into a tipple?' Without waiting for an answer, she steered us towards the beer garden.

'Okay…' I jibed, 'but only a magnum or two.'

We'd just sat down with a bottle of Montrachet and toasted dear, departed Helen when Mel flumped down at our table. 'Nicole! You're up for a Classic Brit Award. For your *Symphonie Fantastique*. *A virtuosic tour de force from start to finish*, say the critics.'

'Mel!' My mother waved a chastening finger at us. 'Okay, which one of you girls told her where we are?'

'*Moi*,' Verity admitted. 'Mother, take pity! If you don't accept this award, Melissa may implode.'

'Actually it will be a posthumous award, because your agent will have killed you,' I advised. 'And surely one funeral is enough for the time being.'

Melissa made a slashing motion across her neck to underscore this fatal prediction. 'I manifested this award nomination and it came true!' she added. 'It's a sign.'

'Man-a-what?' my mother asked, perplexed, pouring Mel a glass of wine.

'Manifesting. You've stressed your agent out so much, she's gone all woo-woo-voodoo. The woman is meditating twenty-four seven.'

'Oh good. At least you're not sitting around doing fuck all, then, like most agents,' my mother joshed.

Mel extracted the press release from her bag. '*Nicole Nightingale brilliantly balances the string section, the winds and the brass of this taxing and vigorously colourful piece,*' she read aloud, '*...subtly illuminating the sense of foreboding required by Berlioz's semi-autobiographical drama of a suffering artist in love.*'

'Well, I am an artist in love... but my suffering is over, meaning no more tedious awards ceremonies. I've turned my back on all that. And have no regrets.'

'Do you really mean that, Mum? I have regrets, all the time,' I confessed. 'My main regret is that I'm not a different person... A successful career woman, for one. Like you.'

'What's so bad about wanting to recapture my youth?' Mum sighed.

'Easily done. Just lock him in your hotel bedroom,' I joshed.

My mother's smile is so bright, she could act as a personal beacon for sailors adrift in the ocean, and she lit up with full wattage now. 'I just want to snog the man until there's nothing left but his socks!'

When Mum popped to the loo, Melissa – a vegetarian who campaigned for animal rights, petitioned for more organic food in supermarkets and promoted the ancient Indian Vedic principles of doing no harm – punched a cushion and screamed.

And I knew just how she felt.

TWENTY-ONE

'The fucking Swiss!' Melissa squawked, the morning after my mother did not turn up to collect her British classical music award at the Royal Albert Hall, preferring to go salsa dancing instead with her twinkle-toed lothario. Mum had also told me they'd signed up for tango, boogie burn, pole-dancing-meets-party-vibe classes and Morning Gloryville, a sober rave in Shoreditch blending yoga and electronic beat, apparently.

Melissa tossed her bike helmet towards the couch, but missed. It was now rattling angrily around my wooden floorboards. 'Swiss people routinely get into fist fights over the correct time. And yet, while they were delicately dipping fondue, we were kicking Nazi butt!' said the peace-loving, counter-culturalist who'd only recently made us all partake in a sustainable lifestyle audit.

Verity, Fiachra, Melissa and I were having our usual Saturday morning strategy meeting – only we were all out of strategies. We'd been chipping away at Gawain's credibility for months and our efforts had proved as effective as trying to proofread promo pamphlets for an invisible-ink shop.

A rattling of footsteps on the wooden stairs and Chrissie came crashing into the living room wearing ripped jeans,

Doc Marten boots and a vinyl bustier. She leant into me for a kiss, then curled contentedly into the circle of my arms. I buried my face in her hair. She smelled like coconut – the girl was summer, personified. 'So, will you come hear Femifesto play, Mum?' She pulled away and gave a shy smile, lowering her eyes in an absurdly touching way that tore at my heart. 'We have a great gig lined up next Saturday night. At the Dublin Castle...' Registering my sister's presence, she then added, 'Oh, hello, Aunt Verity.'

For once my loquacious sister was struck dumb. As Chrissie had been housesitting for her grandma and Verity was only permitted into our home once a week for strategy meetings and Mum Updates, this was the first time they'd physically collided. Verity drank in her niece from top to toe. A sudden stabbing sweetness of love for my gentle, optimistic, kind and compassionate girl caught me off guard. Thank God bitterness isn't genetic, I thought, ruffling her hair.

'Please say you'll come, Mum. Dad's going to perform with us.'

I'd always encouraged Chrissie in everything she did. Oh, the endless school plays, concerts, tedious assemblies and freezing cold sporting matches I'd attended. It killed me to say the words I was about to utter. I leant forward, head down, as if assuming the crash position in an aeroplane, and braced for impact. 'I'm sorry, darling. I just can't let you become a paid-up member of Underachievers Anonymous. That's my job.'

My daughter gave me a look which said, 'Raising parents these days isn't always easy.' Then, with a disappointed sigh, she left for band rehearsal, giving the door a good, teenagery-type slam on the way out.

'What a fearless, feisty and totally fabulous girl! Are you really not going to her gig?' my sister interrogated. 'Maybe you and I should go, Mel? Aunt Verity to the rescue!'

I glared at my sibling. 'I'm sorry, but taking mothering lessons from you is like taking tap-dancing lessons from the Taliban... One of the few classes our mother hasn't signed up for,' I added, flippantly.

'I'll go hear Chrissie's band with you, Verity. Why the hell not?' Melissa took a sip from her thermos of turmeric oat milk latte. 'I can't believe you're not curious, Izzy. Having a gorgeous daughter like Chrissie could make even the most barren woman crave the pitter-patter of little feet.'

'Well, yes. Having a daughter definitely comes in handy for all those times you've left something upstairs... ah, the pitter-patter of little feet as your teenager fetches it for you,' I clowned.

'Well, if you do want a child of your own, you'd better get a move on, Melissa,' Verity said, briskly, '...while your mother's still young enough to take care of it. Another reason I'm glad to be childless. Being called "Grandma" is unbelievably ageing. Besides, ugh. Pregnancy. Life is hard enough without some random stranger kicking you from the inside.' She winced, queasily. 'Oh, and the weight gain! Izzy, you weren't eating for two. You were eating for you, the baby and Pavarotti.'

'Oh my God.' Fitness Freak Melissa shuddered. 'I couldn't stand that!' She checked the step count on her Fitbit. 'Besides, I already have something to ruin my carpets, sleep and sanity... a Persian cat. Plus gay people are very bad at maths. We don't naturally multiply,' she quipped. 'Not without help, anyway.'

I felt a hot flush coming on and fanned myself with a pamphlet about HRT – the closest women could get to the magical elixir during the current nationwide shortage. Would the government ever let Viagra stocks run this low? Stiff chance. I silently fumed, fanning furiously. 'You know what? As none of you have children, I don't think you can fully appreciate how disconcerting it is when your daughter reaches the age when she stops asking you where she came from and starts refusing to tell you where she's going.'

'Aye, but you know where she's going. The Dublin Castle. Next Saturday night. For her first big gig,' the Derry Man chipped in. 'A bit of rock rebellion's pretty low on the parental charge sheet, you know, Izzy. It's not like she's scrambling her brains with acid... or, God help us, voting Reform.'

I mopped my brow. I seemed to be having my own weather. 'I made my daughter take the suitability test and she just doesn't have a big enough ego to be a rock star. End of.'

'She's good, though,' the Derry Man confirmed. 'Having heard her rehearse, I reckon it's a case of "adore the wee girl now and avoid the stampede".'

I was now perspiring more than a woman in a pleather jumpsuit at a disco inferno in the middle of the Sahara.

'The girl's practically an adult,' Melissa observed. 'Soon you'll have as much say in her life as...' She groped for the right analogy.

'Monaco on world politics,' the Derry Man suggested.

'Or us, on our mother's love life,' Verity added, bleakly.

My face was now on fire. 'Look, zoologists find organisational structures right through nature,' I said, bristling.

'Lions form prides, whales form pods, sheep form flocks, cows form herds… and flesh-burrowing maggots form rock bands.'

'I'll come with you to the gig, Izzy. We'll take Cyril. It'll be grand.'

'No, no, no.' The dying process begins the moment we are born, but it certainly accelerates when your daughter threatens to give up her music scholarship to join a frigging rock band. 'Absolutely not.'

All six eyes scalded me. I sighed. Being a mother was much harder than being a proofreader at an invisible-ink shop. At least nobody could see those mistakes. Motherhood made you feel as popular as a cocktail waitress in an alcoholic rehab clinic yelling 'It's Happy Hour! Who wants a double shot?!'. My own mother was the only one who'd understand how I was feeling right now… and yet she had never felt further away.

TWENTY-TWO

The female of the species has three major guilt categories: weight, career, motherhood. Especially the latter. Exactly a week later, a rattling of footsteps on the wooden stairs and Chrissie came crashing into the living room. I looked her over. 'That outfit needs one accessory: a crack pipe.'

'I take that as a compliment, Mum!' My darling daughter laughed, readjusting her leather crop top and torn tights. 'Femifesto's got that gig tonight, remember? Dad's picking me up later.'

Johnny was no longer the 'two-timing mongrel', I noted, but just simply 'Dad'. While they'd become so much closer, a slightly awkward membrane had grown between my daughter and me. 'Well, let me feed you first, darling.' I turned towards my sister. 'I'd ask you to stay, Verity, but this meal will be so forgettable that you won't be able to photograph it for Instagram. The trauma could kill you.'

My sister's Instagram feed is full of, well, food: artisanal bakeries, Organic Heritage tomato fruit emporiums, succulent pit-cooked mechoui lamb and mint tea in a Marrakesh spice-lined souk… A baked chook with over-boiled veg just wouldn't cut the Instagrammable mustard.

I opened the front door to hasten Verity's departure. My sister left reluctantly, casting curious looks at her long-lost niece, her eyebrows taut as an archer's bow. 'See you at the gig, Chrissie. Mel and I will be there cheering you on,' she called out over her shoulder. 'Not that you need it. From what I hear, you'll have your own perfume, wine and lipstick line in no time!'

Chrissie glanced my way to ascertain if it was okay to react warmly to her aberrant auntie and when I nodded, she replied, 'Aw, shucks, thanks… And you, Mum? Are you coming?'

My heart was splintering into a billion pieces. I tried to devise a facial expression that would hide this fact, finally settling on the pretence that I was mentally calculating pi to eight billion places, so couldn't be distracted. I then made a mental list of mothers much, much worse than me – Medea, Joan Crawford in *Mommy Dearest*, *Hamlet*'s Queen Gertrude… With the door still ajar I glanced at the Derry Man. 'I imagine you're not that hungry?' I hinted.

'Starvin'.' He rubbed his hands together. 'That *rasqueado* can certainly take it out of a fella.' We'd spent a good part of the morning mastering that intense flamenco style.

'Flamenco's a bit beyond me,' Chrissie chatted, patting her sweet little Alhambra guitar.

'Aye. It's not easy. What do you like to play then?' he asked her.

In answer, Chrissie sat on the edge of the sofa, cradled the neck of her guitar in her hand and picked out one of her own compositions – a sweet, lilting ballad about love and longing. Her voice was honey, sieved through silk. Scallops of sunlight fell across her face as she played, only increasing her resemblance to an angel. When the last chord hovered in the air, her eyelids fluttered open.

'So, what do you think?' she asked tentatively.

'That's some tune,' the Derry Man said. 'Especially that chord sequence in the middle.'

'You really like it? You're not glazing me?'

'It's the dog's bollocks,' he said, which I took, from his big broad smile, to be a compliment.

A light of hope began to enter Chrissie's eyes like a timid guest. 'Mum?'

'What can I say, kiddo?' I kissed the top of her head. 'You obviously had a very good teacher.'

'Stay for dinner,' she asked my pupil-turned-private-eye. 'You can help talk Mum into coming to my gig.'

'That'd be grand. I could do with a feed.'

'It'll be grand' or 'you'll be grand' was his habitual invocation of fate. The man with the unpronounceable name was a country-bred, cocking-an-elbow-out-the-car-window type of guy, completely out of place in the urban jungle.

I'd just got the roast chicken out of the oven and started carving when Johnny breezed in. I glanced pointedly at my watch. I'd never known him to be early in his whole damn life. 'What's the matter? Did your mattress catch fire?'

He sat down, uninvited, and served himself up a huge helping. 'Drumstick for me, obvs!' he joshed, playing a drum roll with his cutlery on the table top.

'How's it goin'?' the Derry Man asked.

Johnny looked up from his plate, clocking my pupil for the first time. 'Good, mate, good... Christ! What used-car dealership dude died and left you his jacket?' he joshed.

Before he could reply, Johnny launched into a monologue about his latest compositions. As usual, he glittered and shone, commanding attention – especially mine. I could not get used to seeing him back in our house, sitting at our dining table, eating with our daughter. I felt my throat thicken with remembered emotion. By the time Johnny drew breath I'd stripped the chicken down to its carcass. It lay like a metaphor for my marriage, in a haemorrhage of gravy.

'Thanks for the feed, Bella babe. Gotta bolt.' Johnny pushed up from the table without offering to take his plate to the kitchen.

'The ability to clear the table and do the washing-up does not come pre-installed in the ovaries, by the way,' I mocked.

'Jeez, I'm a hopeless case. When your mum tried to teach me how to clean the kitchen, Chrissie, well, you'd have thought I was gettin' instructions on assembling a rocket launcher!' He gave a self-deprecating laugh. 'Music's the only thing I'm good at.'

'But of course, you have hot and cold running staff for all life's mundanities now.' I looked around for the ventriloquist who was uttering these harsh words when all I really wanted to say was 'We were so happy!' and, 'Why did you ruin it all, you idiot!?' And, 'Couldn't we give it another go?'

'Mum?' I swivelled to see Chrissie leaning in the hall doorway, one foot up behind her, like a flamingo. 'Please come hear me play.'

I would rather die than hurt her but never ever wanted my sweet girl to feel that her destiny, like mine, was on hold to some random call centre. 'Sorry, darling. As I keep telling you, I can't encourage you to make the same mistakes as your pathetic mum.'

Chrissie gave me a look I recalled from her childhood – the look of a kid who has just dropped her ice cream onto the hot pavement. 'You're not pathetic, Mum. You're the best.' And with that she gave a long, low exhalation before trudging off down the steps towards her dad's car. The guitar banging against her back looked twice as big as she was. The image twanged my heart strings.

When I entered the kitchen, the Derry Man left off his meticulous stacking of the dishwasher and turned his gaze on me, full beam. 'Do you want to talk about him?'

'What? Don't be ridiculous! My second-favourite pastime is talking about my ex-husband... My first being beating my head against the wall until I'm concussed.'

The Derry Man did not look convinced. 'Sure you don't need a twelve-step programme to break the ex-hubby habit? Romantics Anonymous?'

'Look, when I first met Johnny, he was just a head of hair with a cigarette stuck in it. I made that man. And now *she*...' sometimes I just couldn't bring myself to say my sister's name, 'gets the benefits of all my hard work... Plus, I gave him the best years of my arse, boobs and thighs.'

'Really? I'd say you have quite a few good years left in that department,' the Derry Man said to the aspidistra.

'Don't be ridiculous! My vibrator just requested a blindfold!'

The Derry Man put some elbow grease into the baking tray now, soapsuds splashing, then abruptly changed subject. 'So why won't you go hear your daughter's band? Just to find out what the craic is?'

'Rock music,' I confessed. 'It triggers me. Oh, for the days when "triggers" were just things in cowboy films, right?'

'Aye, I didn't know what "triggers" meant either, till my own wife held me up at emotional gunpoint.'

I looked at him, afresh. 'I didn't know you'd been married. So, you were similarly ambushed?'

'Aye. Well, my wife-to-be left me on our wedding day… for a guitarist.'

'Ah… that explains it. The lessons, I mean.' I didn't look his way, but busied myself putting condiments back into the fridge and filling up the compost bin, all the time wondering why I'd never asked him anything personal before. I knew he'd been studying with a teacher in Belfast before moving to London and coming to me for more advanced lessons. He was so diligent and serious about his study that, until Mum went missing, I'd always kept our interactions professional, crisp, no-nonsense. It wasn't hard. When it came to men, I'd surrounded myself in barbed wire barricades. I was an emotional no-man's-land.

'So, what's the plan? To learn to play guitar better than him and win her back?'

'Aye, something like that. I moved here to forget the past and work with these lovely fellas.' He leant down to scratch the scruff of his beloved canine. 'I get to bring them home, too, which is grand, isn't it, Cyril, there's a good boy.' He cupped the dog's chin and looked into its big brown eyes, attaching the lead in preparation to depart. 'Dogs, well, they never let you down.' The Derry Man's devotion was rewarded with a big, wet lick on his hand.

'Unrequited love – the only kind you can really count on. What's her name? Your ex?'

'Bridget,' he said, before, once again, quickly shifting conversational gear. 'Anyway, I'm changing jobs soon. Training guide dogs; that's what I really want to do.'

'Well, love is blind. If only there was a place you and I could train for that. Thanks for washing up, by the way.'

'Ah, no bother.'

We shared a melancholy glance. When it came to love, the Derry Man and I certainly had something in common – we were a total success at failing.

TWENTY-THREE

A few hours later the horn honking outside my house got so loud, I had to investigate the commotion. I checked my watch. It was nearly seven thirty.

'I've got a wee bit more info. Get in.'

'Really? Now?' I asked the Derry Man, casting a dubious glance at the dog hairs pinstriping the front seat of his van.

'Are you going to come quietly or do I need to put on my noise-cancelling headphones?' he joked.

'Oh, ha ha. What passes for police humour, I take it?'

My PJs and an episode of *Strictly Come Dancing* were calling but still, we'd been trying to save Mum for so long now and what had we achieved? Not only were our ducks not in a row, we didn't even have any damn ducks. And so I reluctantly heaved open the heavy van door and climbed up into the front seat, holding my nose to stave off pungent canine aromas. Twenty minutes later I was being bustled into a side door of a pub in Camden.

'What's this place got to do with helping my mother?' I asked, suspiciously.

'Well, it is about helping a mother – you.'

'What?! You bastard. This is a clear-cut case of entrapment.'

Then I heard my daughter's voice. It wafted across the room, melodious, mellifluous, minus vibrato, just clear and clean as a chiming bell. I looked towards the pub stage and there she was, her hair streaming back from her face, like a goddess at the prow of a Viking ship. I stood transfixed. Chrissie's normal shyness had evaporated and a confident, strong, proud young woman held the crowd in her spell. And no wonder. The girl had perfect pitch, a natural ease with improvisation, a big and dynamic vocal range and a virtuosic guitar technique. A spasm of love shot through me, from the tip of my head to the end of my toes. I twanged like a tuning fork. Chrissie clocked me and her face lit up. A moment of deep endearment passed between us and I suddenly felt less of a need to murder my music pupil.

The motley female musos my daughter had assembled around her seemed wary and furtive, like urban foxes on the scavenge, not to be approached. Their collective look was one of aloof insolence; a look they'd no doubt perfected to disguise stage fright. Their antithesis was Johnny, who played the drums as though being tasered, his chest rising and falling to the pumping rhythm. I descended, against my will, into vivid memories. Time telescoped and we were back, in our twenties, rocking out our raunchy, punchy songs before a similarly adoring crowd.

Under the soft stage lights Johnny looked the same as he did then – silver chains, a chunky bracelet, his dark luxuriant hair tumbling past his shoulders, muscles bulging in a tight T-shirt; the man might not be able to pack a dishwasher, but he sure could pack a six-pack. It wasn't rocket science to work out why I'd fallen for him way back then.

Chrissie now segued into a sassy, sizzling satirical number called 'Namaste Motherfuckers' about hipster losers who pray for immortality, yet don't know how to get through a drizzly Sunday afternoon. Her voice, which was honey made audible – sweet, strong and tangy – now shifted into a raspy, rocky, guttural growl, her guitar pealing out perky riffs.

Beside me, the Derry Man was clapping along, hooting with pleasure. I'd never seen anyone dance so badly. He danced as though looking for his phone – which pocket is it in? Did he drop it? His naff manoeuvres sent me into spasms of laughter.

The Derry Man laughed at me laughing at him. 'Jay-sus. Am I that bad?'

'You look like one of those whacky, waving, arm-flailing inflatable tube men outside a petrol station.'

He exaggerated his sky dancer moves for my added amusement.

I spotted Verity and Mel then, beneath the big bay windows. They were on their feet, swaying together, one arm around each other, chardonnay in hand, nodding along appreciatively.

To conclude, Chrissie launched into a satirical Eminem-type rap song about women's rights which she titled 'Feminem'. She then wrapped things up, literally, with a rap called 'Clingfilm', about a rapper who was too clingy. It was witty, wise, wicked and wonderful.

When the set ended my daughter was swept up in a noisy whirlpool of newly converted fans. Breaking free, she swam, salmon-like, upstream through the sea of cheering admirers towards me.

'What did you think?' She eyed me nervously, hair falling into her eyes like the mane of a shy pony.

I pulled her into my arms. Another spasm of love shot through me. All I could do was take a deep breath. I breathed in, breathed out, as though in labour, panting. She was taking leave of her childhood. I hugged her till the pain of losing her passed, replaced by the most profound pleasure.

She beamed up at me. 'Thanks for coming, Mum. It means the world.'

Johnny barrelled over then, lapping at a tumbler of Jack Daniel's. 'Not bad, eh? Our little rock star.' He played my arm like a keyboard. The thrill of it zapped through me, the remembered adrenaline rush of making music together up there in the spotlight. He pulled me into an embrace. I buried my head into the crook of his shoulder and inhaled his familiar musky, slightly sweaty scent and against all my better instincts, it stirred me.

He finally held me at arm's length and looked into my eyes. Some tenderness passed between us, a glowing of pride for our beautiful girl. I astonished myself then with an impulse to kiss my ex-husband. But, unlike my selfish sister, I didn't behave badly with another woman's bloke. Plus, I had also just seen his T-shirt slogan, which read 'It ain't gonna suck itself'.

'Really?' I queried, aghast, breaking free of his grasp. 'Why is it that rock musicians have the globally guaranteed immunity to sport sexist slogans on their clothing at all times?'

But he and Chrissie were then tugged back into the enthusiastic riptide. As the audience chanted for an encore,

I turned to look for the Derry Man. He was leaning up against the bar, watching us.

'Okay,' I said, walking towards him. 'I've decided not to press charges for holding me against my will. But don't ever dance in front of me again.'

'Yeah, well, I can't promise that,' he said flatly. 'What I've learnt about humans in this life is that humans learn nothing from life. We just keep repeating and repeating and...'

I looked at him quizzically. 'Are you talking about my daughter repeating the mistakes of her mother?'

'No. I'm talking about you. And your ex. Why do you act that way around him? If you were a dog you'd have sat on your hindquarters and hung your tongue out.'

'I did not behave like that!'

The Derry Man's look of disdain was so loud it could be heard by penguins sunbathing on their arctic ice floes. 'After the way he's treated you, well, it's mind-boggling. Why do women always go for bad boys?' He sighed. 'They're the ones I train my dogs to keep at bay. Ask the drummer to drive you home. I think I just need to use my body as a repository for Guinness for a while.'

And with that he was gone.

TWENTY-FOUR

'Alcohol!' Melissa's head emerged out of an enormous faux fur coat like a wombat coming out of its burrow. 'I don't care what kind. I just want a bucket of it.' She flopped down, spread-eagled on the park bench like a stranded starfish.

We were sitting at the top of Parliament Hill gazing down over the sweeping green slope to the jagged outline of the city. Canary Wharf towers twinkled in the sun and a jumble of white clouds scattered across the horizon like washing.

After his lesson, Fiachra had said he wanted to take Cyril up to the Heath for some training. Police dogs need to be taught not to react to squirrels, joggers, E-bikes, phone zombies, etc.

'Ha! If only I could be similarly desensitised to my mother's toy boy,' I'd sighed.

'Why don't you come along and clear your head?'

It was such a beautiful day, the air fresh and crisp from an early morning shower, and so I'd texted Verity and Mel to change our meeting place.

'Dare I ask...?' Verity poured a Bloody Mary mix from her flask into a glass and handed it to Melissa.

Melissa took a big slug, then vented. 'Okay, so I reluctantly accepted that your mother was taking some kind of six-month sabbatical. But she's now cancelling gigs for next year as well!'

No amount of visualisation boards, yoga, meditation, full-body massages, sensory-deprivation-tank therapy, sound baths, forest healing or breathwork classes could help Melissa now. She was in full implosion mode.

'After Helen's memorial, she's heading back to Europe, apparently, where they have a "more sophisticated approach to relationships".'

Verity sighed. 'Mum said as much to me. She said Europeans understand that women hit their sexual peak in their sixties and men at about, oh, thirty-six.'

'Jay-sus. I don't remember having a sexual peak in my thirties; I just remember grovelling and saying sorry a lot,' the Derry Man said, throwing the ball for Cyril.

'Well, do you know what? We're through with pussy-footing and apologising.' Verity slammed her hand down onto the park bench with such force that the flask of Bloody Marys jumped and fell onto the grass. 'We're like a shoal of petrified fish being circled by a killer whale. We need to go on the attack.'

'Oh yes, and where exactly do we buy a psychological chainmail suit?' I enquired, flippantly.

Melissa retrieved the flask and poured the remaining cocktail concoction into her giant water bottle. 'For the journey home,' she informed us, taking another restorative swig.

'Okay, Mother's only back in London till the memorial,' Verity said. Above us, aeroplanes were embroidering the blue sky with garlands of vapour, emphasising our mother's imminent departure. 'So we don't have long to prove that her lover plays the field.'

'Gawain doesn't just play the field... I suspect he plays the whole damn province.' I glugged down my own remaining cocktail in one big gulp.

'There's only one way to prove to our mother that Gawain's "love" for her is fictitious and transactional.' Verity cleared her throat. 'One of has to seduce him.'

Bloody Mary spurted out of my nostrils. 'What? Like a honeytrap?'

'Well, we are in a pretty sticky situation,' my sister elaborated.

'Well, clearly it will have to be you, Verity. After all, you're an expert at seducing other women's men,' I said, cattily, before calling out to the Derry Man, 'My sister loves men. Her two most popular types are a) single and b) married.'

'I am not flirting with my mother's paramour. That's a disgusting idea. Talking of disgusting...' The tomato juice I'd jettisoned made it look as though I'd had a nosebleed. Verity absent-mindedly patted my face dry with a tissue – a sisterly gesture I found as confounding as it was consoling.

'But you love to flirt, Verity. It's hard to think of any time when you would think flirting inappropriate. Perhaps during childbirth, in a police line-up, or at a friend's funeral. Otherwise, for you, there's no greater pastime.'

In the time-honoured sport of competitive flirting, my twin sister had always come first. One flick of her hips and any man was hers. All she had to do was cock her head to one side and languish at him through those long lashes and his member would be hydraulicking around in his trousers.

'Five minutes and he'll be all over you like a fake tan. Just get a tongue kiss out of him, which we'll film, and then you're out of there,' I insisted.

'Absolutely not. It's far too incestuous.'

The cloudy laundry overhead had thickened. 'Mel?' I said, turning to her, hopefully.

'No way!' Melissa wore the same expression of disgust you'd give an intestinal parasite. 'I'm gay, well about ninety-nine per cent gay... It'd be like dancing with no music.'

'No bodily fluid will be exchanged, Mel. Well, maybe just a teeny-weeny bit of saliva. It's the only way to convince Mum that Gawain's insincere,' I urged.

The Derry Man wrenched the soggy tennis ball from Cyril's salivating chompers. Melissa dry-retched, which I took as a firm no. 'You do it, Izzy,' she said, 'if you're so bloody keen!'

'Oh, ha ha. No way. I'm so out of practice! I haven't flirted for...' I thought back to the time I'd met Johnny, 'decades. I'm a hopeless flirt.'

I recalled how, as a teenager, I'd once tried to copy my sister's sashay across a bar towards a handsome bloke and merely succeeded in banging my hip into the wine waiter, sending an order of Harvey Wallbangers, Pink Panty Dropper punch and Red-headed Slut shots cascading into the handsome man's lap. I then made a joke about a wet patch and it was another six months' celibacy for me.

'No, it has to be you, Verity – you're the one who's good at seduction.' I added, pointedly, 'We all know no man can resist you.'

I saw my sister's facial muscles twitch, as if a smile was trying to break free. 'Do I get to wear a wire?' she asked, excitedly.

'Ah, we're not in *The Sopranos*,' the Derry Man drawled. 'But use the time to good advantage. The key qualities that go into extracting human intelligence – or "humint", as it's known in spycraft, are flattery and empathy. Have a wee bit of craic with him, draw him out... then pin him down. And I'll be filming it all.'

'Just call me Bond,' my sister preened, 'Jane Bond.'

PART THREE

Sisterhood Rule
*Think of yourself as a pair of big knickers:
you've got her ass covered.*

TWENTY-FIVE

'Listen carefully or a sexual perversion... five, two, four, four...' Gawain read the crossword clue aloud.

My mother peered at the newspaper spread out on her kitchen table, then whooped like a Californian aerobics instructor, clapping her hands together. 'Prick up your ears!'

They fist-bumped and high-fived, then collapsed into flirtatious giggles. I turned my back to them and looked out of the window so they wouldn't see me gagging with nausea. If only I had a paper bag handy, to gasp into.

'Mother, are you wearing contact lenses?' Verity quizzed.

'Yes. Do you like them?'

'And what have you done with your hair?'

'Straightened it. Gawain's decided he likes it best this way, don't you, darling? And guess where he took me last night. A karaoke bar!'

After all their exotic holidays, Gawain's face was now deep brown except for a white goggle stripe from his sunglasses. He was sitting in the lotus position on Mum's kitchen banquette like some kind of urban guru. 'Your mother was horrified that they didn't play any seventies music.'

'At first I was afraid...' Mum joked and they both fist-bumped, high-fived and fell about laughing once more.

Contact lenses, hair straightening, manicures, leopard-skin-print kaftans, a tattoo, karaoke – my sister and I looked at each other; the kind of glance you exchange under a storm at the sound of thunder.

'Oh, and by the way, girls, remember when I said I didn't know what "autoeroticism" is? Well, just to be clear, it does not mean making love in the back seat during the wax/dry cycle. I won't be going back to that carwash for a while!'

They both dissolved into giggles once more.

'It's so nice to be home,' Gawain said.

I swapped an indignant glance with my sister, bristling at the word 'home'.

'Although we really did have the most stunning time! A highlight was cold-water snorkelling in the Blue Lagoon to increase brain cell stimulation. Incredible, no? It cost a couple of thou, but so worth it.'

'A couple of thou?' my sister whispered to me. 'Did you hear that? The man's now on nickname terms with our inheritance! If our newly minted mother doesn't lend me some money pronto, I'll have to remortgage my house!' she lamented. 'Or sell a kidney... Or maybe harvest one of yours?!' She pointed a painted talon in my direction. It was as sharp as a scalpel.

But Mum didn't seem all that perturbed by the fact that, due to Johnny's budgeting problems, the light at the end of Verity's tunnel was currently turned off. She was far more preoccupied with bending Helen's strait-laced family to her musical will for the upcoming memorial. As soon as she left for choir rehearsals, Verity wasted no time in arranging a 'let me show you around London' cocktail with our mother's predatory paramour.

Once Gawain had agreed, it was all systems go. The next night Verity rang me on her car phone after work. 'I'm just going to pop home to slip into something that makes me look younger...'

'A Tardis time machine?' I teased.

Later, at the Café Royal in Piccadilly Circus, Melissa, the Derry Man and I surreptitiously stationed ourselves on the upper tier, phones at the ready. My sister made some final adjustments to her slinky outfit, then gave her reflection an approving ocular once-over in the mirrors that lined the walls.

'Well, Verity, there's a few familiar facelifts here tonight, meaning you'll be right at home!' I nudged her towards the stairs.

'I have not had a facelift,' Verity shot back over her shapely, bare shoulder. 'I'm just less lined from envy and bitterness.'

The Derry Man, beer in one hand, phone in the other, positioned himself up against the railing, the poor man's Cecil B. DeMille. 'So, this sibling rivalry routine... it's just a cover-up for a comedy double act, am I right? Next stop, the Edinburgh Fringe.'

'No. We really do detest each other. Although,' I grinned, 'I must admit that my twin has a formidable and fabulous sister.'

'Aye. So, what you're saying is, sure you'd pick her up after a fall... but only 'cause you tripped her in the first place.' He grinned back at me.

'Exactly.'

'Shhhh!' Melissa, half hidden behind a pillar, whipped out her opera glasses for closer viewing. I made do with peering through the palm fronds of a nearby pot plant. It wasn't exactly *Mission: Impossible*-level surveillance, but the best we could manage at short notice. We watched in silence as Verity draped herself seductively on a settee and ordered two martinis. Gawain arrived punctually at seven and sat opposite her with his back to us. We couldn't hear their conversation, but Verity was laughing and smiling and batting her eyelashes; her batting average would have rivalled Steve Smith and Joe Root.

Gawain remained rigid on a stiff-backed chair, holding on to its arms as though trying to squeeze blood from them. A Stasi interrogation would have looked more relaxing.

Verity played with her hair, threw back her head and gave a tinkling little laugh, then, in full geisha mode, leant across the table to caress his fingers. Gawain withdrew his hand as if electrocuted.

My twin is one of those people who go through life demanding to see the manager. She is used to getting her own way in all things. But not this time. Much to my astonishment, Gawain failed to succumb to my sister's infamous charms. Immune to her overtures, he left soon after, without the mandatory European double goodbye cheek-peck.

I billy-goated down the stairs ahead of Mel and the Derry Man. 'What the hell happened? Gawain was treating you like a cup of cold sick.'

'Apparently he did a deep dive on my music critiques. Turns out I reviewed an ensemble he once played in. I suggested that if readers wanted to recreate the sound of a glockenspiel and alpine horn duet in the comfort of their own homes, they should set fire to the tails of their cats.'

'Oh, well done, Verity… Employing your great generosity of spirit as usual, I see?'

'Okay, smart arse, if you think it's so easy, you try getting him to let down his Swiss guard.'

'Me? Don't be ridiculous. As I told you. I don't flirt. It'd be easier to, I dunno, make a U-turn across the central divide of a super highway…' It didn't sound arduous enough. 'Or perform an appendectomy, blindfolded…' No, still not hitting the right level of horror. 'Or tongue-kiss Nigel Farage.' Yep, that did it. A wave of repulsion rippled through us.

'Come off it, Izzy.' Melissa rapped her fingers on the small round tabletop. 'You were in a rock band – you know how to seduce an audience. It's the same thing.'

'What?! No! I'm totally out of practice. In the last five years, I've only had the odd, drunken one-night stand… with the emphasis on odd.'

I thought back to my dating years. After my sister took up recycling – as in, repurposing my husband for her own use – I was dumped in chilly succession by a yoga instructor, a polo player, a sand sculptor, a maths teacher and a pest controller – a grim streak that corroded what was left of my self-esteem. I gave up on men shortly after that.

'Fiachra,' Melissa suggested. 'Could you role-play with Izzy? Just run over the basic techniques so that she can work her seductive magic.'

The Derry Man took a sip of his of teak-coloured beer and looked over the rim of the glass at me. 'Izzy, um, are you okay? What the feck are you doing?'

'My sexy look.'

'Oh, I thought you had a bad case of trapped wind.'

'You see?' I sighed. 'It's hopeless. I can't do it.'

'Well, we don't have any other option.' Verity gave me a once-over. 'You'll need some other clothes though.'

I glanced down at my boot-cut jeans and polo neck jumper. 'Why? I'm dressed okay, aren't I?'

'Yes... for a dog walk, with you on the leash.' My sister examined my outfit with narrowed eyes. 'You're probably wearing a frayed, greyish bra under there and nana knickers big enough to double as a car cover, am I right?'

She was annoyingly right but her condescension infuriated me. I swigged down Gawain's untouched martini. 'Do you know what, Derry Man? Let's do a practice run. I'm going to flirt the bejeezus out of you. Pick me up tomorrow at seven.'

'Aye, okay... but what do you suggest I wear? Regular body armour or full riot gear?'

On the Tube home, I kicked myself. What was I thinking? How could I have agreed to something so incredibly stupid? I clearly needed to join my mother cold-water swimming in Iceland to increase brain cell stimulation. Okay, I may not emerge from the Blue Lagoon with an Einstein-level IQ, but I wouldn't be stupid enough to take flirting lessons to mock-seduce my mother's lover for undercover surveillance purposes.

Sisters are supposed to be like big knickers – they've got your arse covered. But my sister was like a pair of pants that gets twisted, crawls up your crack then cuts off all circulation. With my knickers in a twist over knickers, on an impulse, I got off the Tube at Bond Street and darted into a lingerie shop to buy something lacy. I riffled through the many styles on offer – briefs, bikini, boy leg, French silk scanties... Not only had I seen more silk on a worm but how would I launder such pricey delicates? Perhaps edible knickers were the solution as at least they'd do away with the need for expensive dry cleaning.

In the end I bought a pack of lacy G-strings in black, green and purple plus a fire engine red bra. If this didn't get me in a man-eating state of mind, nothing would. I wore one of the G-strings home. As I bent over to pick up my bag on the Tube, the flash of thong peeking over the top of my low-cut jeans felt empowering, emblematic of my new, liberated, flirtatious status – a little lacy badge of honour. Nobody noticed, except for a startled vicar who'd been nodding off over his Sudoku and who suddenly looked in urgent need of a holy water Mojito. But still, hey! It was time for a whole Sexy New Me.

TWENTY-SIX

The next night I was ready to re-enter the Flirt-o-sphere, preferably without burning up my heat shields. Still, I rationalised, digging out one of my ethereal, long, lacy, Stevie Nicks dresses from way back in my wardrobe, if the idiots on *Love Island* can master the art of flirtation, how hard can it be? I slipped on a black lacy G-string and ankle boots to put me in a more flirtatious mood. Houston. We have lift-off.

The plan was to go to the corner pub after the Derry Man's guitar lesson and there, conquer the art of coquetry.

After working through some Bach preludes, the Derry Man segued into a hypnotic twelve-bar blues progression which was loose and rough. I'd never given all that much thought to my pupil's musicianship before but now noticed just how much he'd progressed; there was an admirable muscularity and confidence to his playing which was deeply pleasing.

Trying to ignore the elasticated dental floss chewing at my nether regions, I picked up my guitar to harmonise. A velvety interleaving of our instruments ensued. We embroidered tunes for a good hour or so with very few pointers from me, then crossed the windswept square to the local boozer on the corner. The improvised tune was still warm in my ears, like a hat left in the sun.

A sharpening wind had risen during the evening, squalling in corners, rattling windows. As I darted over the road, a sudden gust snatched at my hem, lifting the skirt sky high. I scrabbled at the airborne material to pull it back into place.

'Well, that just gave a whole new meaning to "Air on a G-string".' The Derry Man's smile spread until it was almost too big for his face.

'Poor old Bach must be turning in his grave!' I gushed. Oh God, how I missed my more sturdy nana knickers. 'I'm buying, by the way,' I insisted, to reassert my authority over proceedings.

I stood at the bar marooned midst a group of glamorous young women in short skirts and stilettos, with flicky blonde hair, perfect teeth, trust funds and luxurious flats in nearby West Hampstead. I felt like a prefab council house amid a row of immaculate Georgian terraces.

Guinness in one hand, Lady Petrol in the other, I joined the Derry Man at a table beneath a window which looked out onto the bustling high street.

'So,' he asked, 'just how remedial are you? How long since you've been on a date?'

'What? Oh God. Years. You?'

'After Bridget left me, the lads, well, their girlfriends really, set me up all the time. Fair play to them but I just haven't met a girl I've really got on with.'

I took a good long look at my music pupil. The ironed jeans, his unruly strawberry-blond mop combed into submission with a severe side parting, the white trainers... he didn't remotely rate as babe-magnet material.

'My girlfriends set me up too. The mums from school plus the touch-footy gals. They also wrote me up a big checklist.'

'Aye? And what was on it?'

'Well, he had to be faithful, number one. And solvent. Capable and kind. Oh, plus tall, handsome and sexy with a high-flying career and great friends. He also had to prefer at least three different types of lettuce leaf in his salads… A few months of dating later and I was prepared to make do with a bloke who had his own hair and teeth.'

'That bad, eh?'

'Any male homosapien without a secret bondage bunker would do… He didn't even need to have a day job… That's when I decided to become self-sufficient. You don't have to flirt with a sex toy.'

'Um, maybe not your best opening conversational gambit on a date with a fella,' he suggested, wryly. 'No man can compete with a ten-speed, electric powered, rotating, thrusting, pulsating pleasure enhancer.'

'Christ. Could I *be* any worse at this?' I said in my best Chandler Bing voice. I checked the time on my phone, wondering how much longer before I could call it quits.

The Derry Man took a sip of his cold, creamy pint, extracted my phone from my hands and placed it face down on the table. 'Just relax.'

'I am relaxed!' I said through clenched teeth.

'Aye, like a sideboard.'

Taking a deep breath, I took another shot at it, crossing my legs in a slow, sensual way and letting my dress ride up a bit. I lowered my eyes and glanced up from beneath heavily mascaraed lashes, with what I thought was an adoring pout. I even threw in a giggle; a giggle so forced it sounded more like a mosquito caught in a food processor.

'This is not coming that naturally, is it?' The Derry Man couldn't disguise the amusement in his voice.

'Give me a chance! I'm just warming up!' For the next few minutes, I persevered in the eyelash-batting, pouting, hair-flicking routine; I persevered with all the grim determination of one of Cinderella's stepsisters trying to shove her huge clodhopper into the glass slipper.

The Derry Man put my phone up to his ear. 'Aye, she's right here... It's the Dalai Lama. He wants to ask you for some tips on celibacy,' he teased.

'Oh, ha bloody ha. You blokes are so bloody lucky. Nobody hassles you about being single and getting "left on the shelf", now, do they?... You never get told to smile more. "Let's see those dimples!"'

'Well, you do have nice dimples.'

'Fuck off! Christ, I wish I were a man. Getting paid more for no reason... Monologuing and mansplaining and dismissing every comment from a woman with the phrase "Calm down, dear. Don't act crazy..." It makes me so angry, I can't speak!'

The Derry Man smirked. 'Jay-sus, Izzy. I've never seen you that angry.'

I lifted my hand to give him a playful slap but mistimed the move and knocked the remains of his Guinness into his lap. As he frantically mopped at the mess, he deadpanned, 'Well, this is going well. Maybe you should just call your sister and admit defeat.'

My flagging spirits rallied immediately. 'No bloody way. Come on. If you're such an expert flirt, what are your top tips, then?'

'Seriously?'

I nodded. 'So tell me, how would Bridget flirt with you?'

'Okay, well, she'd probably start with a bit of small talk... something to show she was interested in my world.'

I thought for a moment. 'So – has Cyril mauled anyone of interest lately? Chewed the testicles off any gangland mobster monsters?'

'Arousing,' he said, sarcastically. 'Why don't you try to say something witty, then? Wit is charmingly disarming... '

'Gurppppffff,' I bantered.

The Derry Man gave a dispirited sigh. 'Okay, well, Bridget would probably then up the ante with a few innuendos, something flirty or dirty...'

'Dirty? My shower needs de-moulding... That kind of thing?'

'Jay-sus. Okay, well, if you can't think of anything to say, why don't you just try to laugh at all his jokes? That's a classic Bridget move.'

I giggled in a grisly simulation of simpering flirtation.

'Oh-kaaaay, let's forget laughing, too. What about physical contact? Bridget is fluent in body language... Try a light and tender arm-touch maybe...'

I obeyed his instruction.

'Or you could tuck his hair behind his ear in a casual way... That's what she'd do.'

Once more, I complied.

'Or... stroke his thigh, but almost by accident...'

'Like this?' On the pretext of reaching for my handbag, I touched his leg lightly, then awaited his verdict. When none was forthcoming, I asked, 'So, which of those moves do you think is more effective?'

'Hmmm... Results are inconclusive... I'm going to need

a lot more data.' He grinned mischievously.

I withdrew my hand as though he was maggot-infested. 'Christ. Are you actually flirting with me for real, Derry Man?'

'No, I'm only carrying on. Nothing more than an academic exercise.' A sly light had sidled in from the street through the grimy windows, making it hard to see his face. 'That is why we're here, isn't it?'

'Okay,' I said, matter-of-factly, 'do you have anything else for me?'

The Derry Man raised a suggestive brow and gave a cheeky, lopsided grin.

'Besides that,' I said. 'And ugh! By the way. That's disgusting.'

'Chill. It's all grand. I don't mean anything by it. I'm just demonstrating how you can imply something dirty... without talking about shower tiles.'

'Actually, I meant it about the shower tiles. Can you re-grout?'

'One of my many talents.' He smiled, lasciviously.

'There you go again. Stop it.'

'Ah, recap. This is the point of tonight's mission, right? A flirting lesson. If I were flirting with you, which I'm most definitely not, that's the way I'd get your interest aroused. My round,' he said, getting to his feet.

'Well, that's one thing my vibrator can't do – buy me a wine!' I must have spoken this a little too loudly, as other customers now swivelled my way, brows raised.

The Derry Man rolled his eyes. 'Go to the back of the class, Ms. Isabella Nightingale. I might have to put you on flirting detention.'

Manoeuvring around the table, he accidentally touched

me on the arm as he passed. It was only a brush but his touch glowed briefly like a firefly or a blown-out match. I was clearly suffering from an affection deficiency and it was affecting my judgement. When he returned from the bar I said, 'Can we forget about the flirting stuff now? It's just way too stressful. The only thing I'm good at flirting with is disaster.'

'Aye, that's like meself too.'

And so, relieved of our task, we now just sat back, companionably. Rain started to pitter-pat against the window. A fire crackled in the hearth. A warm sense of cosiness settled in around the old pub.

'So, now you've mastered the guitar, are you going to win her back? Bridget, I mean?'

'That's the plan.'

'And marry her?'

'Aye, if she'll have me... Although romance experts agree that your perfect match is the woman who comes on the market two weeks after you get hitched. So, let's just see, eh? What about you?'

'Marriage is a brutal, cruel experience that crushes your self-esteem and shreds your dreams... There's lots of downsides, too,' I added, flippantly.

The rain had made it even darker in this corner of the pub but the white crescent of his smile was visible. 'Being in love is grand though.'

'Being in love is like going to, I dunno, Cairo or India. You're glad you've gone once but don't need to go back again.'

The wine was kicking in and I felt deliciously loose all of a sudden. Clearly Dr Guinness was also working his magic, as the Derry Man began to open up.

'Do you know what Bridget's parting words were?'

'Ah... That she faked orgasm every time you had sex?'

His Guinness went down the wrong way and he coughed so long and loud he could have been in a Puccini opera. 'How did you know?' he finally stuttered, laughing.

'So, what did you say?'

'I said that I just couldn't believe she lied to me not once, but twice.'

I threw back my head and gave a hearty chortle. 'And she really left you at the altar?'

'Yep, for a guitarist. Apparently all women eventually leave their husbands for guitarists, I'm told.'

'I get that. The digital dexterity, the rhythm, the instinctive understanding of slow and fast movements, the importance of crescendos... Oh my god,' I suddenly thrilled. 'I'm flirting, aren't I?'

'But don't forget to smile more. Let's see those dimples!'

I laughed again, to which he responded, 'Calm down, dear... Don't act crazy.'

And then we both cracked up. I was actually having such a nice time that I even forgot the too-tight G-string which was attempting to floss my fallopian tubes.

'Fake flirting is so much more fun than real flirting... Oh... and another drawback of vibrators: they can't laugh at your jokes,' I recanted.

'Or grout those shower tiles.'

'Oh, shower tile grouting – foreplay for all females.'

And that's how we concluded our non-flirty, flirting tutorial – with a promise from the Derry Man to do a little light bathroom maintenance for me.

'And they say that romance is dead,' he said, flirtatiously.

TWENTY-SEVEN

'Why did you make me wear this stupid thing? I'm freezing my arse off. I can hear my b... b... boobs chat... chat... chattering.'

I looked down at the skimpy, strapless dress Verity had forced me into with its dangerously low neckline and perilous knee-to-groin split.

'Call me crazy but I doubt you'd be able to seduce him in your usual attire, the chief characteristic of which is to be flame retardant.'

'It's mid November! My flirtation may be slightly impaired by the fact that when I bat my eyes, my ice-laden lashes will snap off like the teeth of an old comb.'

'I'm trying to make you look less of a music nerd, Isabella. No man has ever stuck his hand into a woman's bra looking for a plectrum.' Verity pulled her sleek Mercedes into the kerb outside a Soho nightclub.

I glanced up at the neon sign that read 'cocktails'. It was flickering on and off like a dying fly. 'As nightclubs go, it's not exactly Weimar Republic level, is it?' I was clearly in for some sticky linoleum and a worryingly damp banquette.

'Yes but Fiachra knows the manager so can film you surreptitiously without hassle... Although,' she looked me up and down, 'I'm not holding out much hope. If only we lived in a world where perimenopausal rage, chronic insecurity and career failure made a woman more attractive to the opposite sex.'

My sister leant over to open my door. A cold blast of air caught me off guard. My lips were instantly novocained from the cold.

'My legs are my only asset; shame I'm going to have to amputate them from frostbite. Christ. I think I just broke a nipple.'

'Okay, time for your pep talk.'

'It's not very peppy so far!'

'Okay, as you know, I have an opera to review tonight, Mozart's *Don Giovanni*, appropriately, so Fiachra's in charge. He's already in position. All you have to do is remember the drill. Compliment Gawain's clothes, then his physique, mention Mum's age, a lot, then fish for a compliment yourself, adding in a little light body contact.'

Fuelled by a fierce desire to prove my dubious sister wrong, I tottered towards the bar door in her ridiculously high heels, remembering just in time to turn my awkward galumph into a sexy sashay. Commandeering the nearest booth, I sat down, feeling as though I was waiting for a job interview – for a job I didn't want. Five minutes later I saw Gawain gliding across the tiled floor towards me in a tightly tailored suit, man bun bobbing. How could anyone walk so smoothly? The man must have little wheels in his loafers.

'Great to see you,' I said through lips that didn't feel like my own, and leant up for a kiss. I lingered a little longer on his cheek than strictly speaking necessary. 'I've been dying to get to know you better.'

'You too, Isabella.' He smiled. 'Your mother adores you so.'

Okay, first job – a compliment. I ran my eyes over his pale blue jacket. 'That suit really goes with your eyes,' I said experimentally. The words tasted sour and insincere in my mouth.

Gawain's azure peepers, topped with curved, dark eyelashes, widened in surprise. 'Oh, well, thank you. Drink?'

While he went to the bar to fetch cocktails, I hoiked my breasts higher in their bra cups, fluffed up my hair, checked my breath in my palm and tried on a sultry smile. This whole sexy act was slightly impeded by the fact that the underwire from the strapless bra I'd borrowed from Verity had come loose and was spearing my left boob.

He returned, and, after taking a nerve-bolstering glug of margarita, I cooed, 'It's just so wonderful of you not to be put off by the age gap. I mean,' I took another great swig of alcohol and prepared to lie a little, 'just the other day' – cue fake laugh – 'I heard Mum say "oops-a-daisy" when she spilled the tea. Sweet! And every time she gets up out of a chair now it's like a live performance of Snap, Crackle and Pop – the Musical... in Creak Major and Back Crack flat. Nothing a squirt of WD-40 won't fix!' I was making my vibrant and dynamic mum sound as if she was one step away from a sticky bathmat and a shower rail, but I had to lay it on thick. 'Yes, I think it's safe to say Mum's beanbag days are over!' I trowelled away.

Gawain gave me a puzzled look, then replied, 'In Japan, reverence for older people is ingrained into the psyche. When the Japanese mend broken objects they fill in the cracks with gold because they believe that when something has suffered damage and has a history, it becomes even more beautiful.'

'Oh, right, yes. What a lovely sentiment... I suppose as long as Mum keeps taking her cod liver oil supplements she'll retain some flexibility.' I forced another smile.

'Your mother's heart is unwrinkled, that's the important thing.'

As was Gawain's complexion. It was as smooth as an imported Gouda cheese. 'If only more men shared your enlightened attitude.' I tried to fizz alluringly, but suspect it merely looked as though I'd blown a fuse. 'My sister says it might be time my face underwent a little light tweaking.' Cue pout and hair flick. 'What do you think?' I was fishing for a compliment, as instructed, but Gawain didn't take the bait.

'A facelift makes a woman look twenty years stupider,' he replied. 'A mind lift is better than a facelift. And that's what your mother gives me. We talk about everything from The Second Viennese School to Renaissance art to the origins of the Kama Sutra.'

'Oh, right,' I said in what I hoped was a sultry, breathy voice, while simultaneously attempting a moue of steamy seduction coupled with some silent but smouldering eye-sex.

Gawain looked at me as if wondering if epilepsy ran in the family. What was next on my flirtation to-do list? Oh yes, more compliments. 'Well, you have nothing to worry about. You have the most lovely skin. And what a physique! Another thing I like about that suit, it really shows off your musculature,' I purred with counterfeit, kittenish enthusiasm. 'You clearly work out every day. Do you mind if I squeeze your muscle?' Following my sister's instructions, I reached out to touch his bicep.

But Gawain leant back, out of range. 'Ah, some sexism reversal. We men deserve it. The acceptance of a female gaze, as in, a female tendency to objectify men, might just stop us from viewing ourselves as the unique consumers of sex... And force us to understand that desire is very much a two-way street.'

'Ah-huh...' I gave my most bewitching, enticing smile – but still nothing.

'If we see a movie where the male actor is the same age as the female actor, we find that odd. Insane, no?'

I tried to hold his ice-blue gaze – but my eyes dried out so badly from not blinking, I rubbed them, smudging eyeliner everywhere.

'It should be completely normalised that the age gap can switch. Women internalise patriarchy, and you need to free yourselves from that.'

'Ah-huh...' said the racoon sitting opposite him. I tried pouting once more, but it was just a waste of face muscles.

'Your mother's age doesn't matter; what matters is the way she lights up my life!'

For the next half an hour I wore a bolted-on expression of polite interest as Gawain rhapsodised about Nicole; sentiments with which I could only agree.

My mother rang then, and even though Gawain turned his head and started whispering, it was clear from his husky tone that they were talking dirty.

'Phone sex. That can give you a nasty ear infection, you know,' I pointed out, prudishly.

'Ha, yes, sorry about that. We just can't help ourselves.

Nicky's home and the jacuzzi's on. Let's do this again some time.'

'Wait? Mum's put in a jacuzzi?!'

But Gawain was already on the move, rolling out of sight on his invisible shoe coasters. I felt as though I'd been with a man who was wanted for counterfeiting – and who had just paid me in cash.

A few moments later, the Derry Man slid into the booth in Gawain's place. 'Well, clearly the fella's gay. If he didn't fancy the drawers off you in that outfit, well, he's queer as a bottle of chips.' He gave my shoulder an almost imperceptible squeeze before immediately whisking his hand away.

'Oh, thanks, Derry Man. You're very kind. But I clearly have the allure of a half-thawed rissole. Gawain's not gay. No. What he is, is just far too sophisticated for us. We are way, way out of our league.' I threw back the rest of my cocktail in one gulp. 'The only way we can possibly bring down this conman is with a high-powered sniper's rifle. If only I knew a police officer with access to firearms...'

'I have unlimited access to worming tablets if that helps,' he said, half smiling.

We stepped outside; my lungs filled with damp chill air and the thin smoke of my breath steamed. The cold wrapped me up in a rib-cracking squeeze like a boa constrictor. 'Where is a perimenopausal hot flush when I need one?' I shivered.

The Derry Man gave me his coat for the ride home. I took his scarf too, then, opening his van door, swiped a dog blanket off the front seat. I was now wrapped up in so many layers he practically had to hoist me into his van using a block and tackle rig.

'It's all going to be grand,' he said, placing his hands on my arse and shoving me upwards with such force that I whacked my head on the door frame.

'There is absolutely no evidence to support that theory,' I whimpered.

And he closed the door with a muffled little thud.

TWENTY-EIGHT

Gawain was a time bomb ticking beneath our lives. We were constantly on the lookout for a way to deactivate him and disable his influence. And so, when Mum asked us to play a duet at Helen's memorial service, Verity and I accepted with alacrity.

To mark the sad occasion, Mum arranged Bach's 'Arioso' for piano and guitar for us to play together. As I only had a keyboard and Verity a grand piano, there was no choice but to trek to her house on the edge of Primrose Hill.

It was five long, bitter years since I'd been inside her double-fronted Victorian villa with its pastel-coloured window frames, chic designer blinds and flower boxes now sprouting seasonal holly and Christmas bush. I'd come straight from a Christmas school concert, having coached a guitar quartet in a Telemann piece I'd arranged for them. It had been such a huge success even the supercilious headmaster had stopped strutting about the school grounds like the president of some South American dictatorship to tell me he was impressed. My grateful students had presented me with an excellent bottle of vintage port. Parking on a meter outside my sister's house, I took a long, bolstering swig. It was only four o'clock but already getting dark.

The headlights of a passing car cut twin funnels of light in the rain. Twins – that word I could never escape.

Mounting the steps, my post-concert confidence evaporated and I had to summon every skerrick of courage to lift the brass knocker. When the door sprang open moments later I waited for a typically barbed comment from my critical sister about my clothes, hair, shoes or lack of make-up, but a momentary smile flickered over her lips. 'Welcome,' she said, warily. Was my sibling acting half human? Why? I steeled myself. She no doubt had something diabolical in store.

The house was just as I remembered it – oversized Diptyque candles, a butler sink in the kitchen, huge Le Creuset casserole on the hob, an antique copper jelly mould above the pantry. The cupboard doors had been salvaged from an old Italian church, as had the stained-glass skylight above the piano. There was little sign of Johnny in these pristine and perfect, Instagrammable surroundings, apart from an electric Gibson guitar in the corner near the French doors that led onto the garden and a set of bongos by the Art Deco drinks cabinet.

'Get yourself a cup of tea. I've just got to take this call. It's my editor from *Style* magazine. Apparently my homewares critique wasn't critical enough.'

Not critical enough? I found this surprising from the woman who once said of Martha Stewart's range that she brought to every collection the 'whiff of an unpaid tax bill' and that if you'd missed her last homeware range, 'this was your chance to miss it again'.

While Verity disappeared into the conservatory, her phone welded to her ear, I pushed open the pantry door in search of teabags. Even her immaculate pantry had cachet. No split bag of quick-cook rice from last century spilling onto a sprouting potato at the back of a skanky cupboard for Verity Nightingale. No salt-and-vinegar chips, cheesy whatnots and other plebian snacks. No, my sister's boujie staples ranged from Bonilla Olive Oil and Sea Salt crisps (£32 a tin) to beluga caviar from the Fish Society (£139.10 per can). She regularly posted photos of her home-made bread, which she kept in unbleached cloth bags captioned with Gwyneth Paltrow-type homilies about 'infusing every moment with wonder'. No teabags either, just loose-leaf Darjeeling. Even her coffee beans were chosen by the altitude at which they'd been grown.

Casing her poncey fare, I quickly forgot my craving for tea; a vodka with a heroin chaser would have probably proved more beneficial right now.

I wandered, tealess, into the living room towards the piano. The Bechstein shone beetle-wing-black in the open-plan sitting room.

My sister and I may have declared a truce but neither of us were inclined to sit around exchanging pleasantries about the price of avocados and so, when she reappeared, we launched straight into rehearsal. Verity picked out the melody on the piano, while I took my guitar out of its case to accompany her. Verity's piano playing was sinuous and exact, while my phrasing was more fluid, but we complemented each other perfectly; both of us drawing on the shadowy, mysterious powers of our auditory memory from years of playing together as girls.

'That was lovely,' my sister said when the piece reached its satisfying major-chord conclusion and the final notes hung in the air like gossamer – a moment definitely infused with Gwyneth-approved wonder. 'I've so missed playing with you, Izz.' Verity swivelled towards me on the piano stool. Her luminous eyes fleetingly held mine. 'Izzy, you know, Christmas is nearly here and well, Mother would like to ask us all over for lunch.'

My brow took an aerobic leap towards my hairline. We hadn't had Christmas together for half a decade. Since the great betrayal, Mum had been sharing herself out between us: Christmas lunch with Chrissie and me, Christmas dinner at Verity's.

'The thing is, I so want to be close with my niece. I need to build a friendship.' My sister is an al dente person: hard to bite into. This soft sign of tenderness was so out of character. To disguise her vulnerability, she quickly postscripted, 'I mean, who else is going to smuggle alcohol into my nursing home?'

'Wait.' I leant my guitar up against the piano. 'I thought you didn't like children. You're the type who would eat her young.'

She took a beat – a long beat – a breve in musical terms. 'Just because Johnny didn't want any more children, didn't mean I felt the same way.' She said this gravely, like she'd just disclosed that she'd been a Russian spy all these years. 'The doctor said I was still fertile. That I had lots of eggs left. Or good "ovarian reserve" as he put it. But Johnny said that he already had a perfect child so didn't need another. He said that it took all his energy trying to "keep Chrissie sweet".' Suddenly, sadness devoured her. 'But I always thought I'd make a good mother.'

I was surprised by this revelation but also realistic. 'Having a kid and expecting to be a good parent is as logical as imagining that owning a violin will make you a virtuoso... I'd like to be a perfect mother, only I'm too exhausted from raising Chrissie single-handedly because... why? Oh yes! My sister stole my husband!'

Verity's bottom lip gave an unexpected tremble. She looked down at the manicured hands in her lap. I could almost feel the emptiness in her womb like it was a living, breathing thing. For the first time ever, I noticed a chip in her nail polish. And was that a gnawed nail on her left hand?

'When Mum moved us back to London from Australia in our teens, we only had each other. Our bond was so strong. Do you remember?' Verity reached over then and took my hand.

I wanted to shake her off but felt like a gymnast trying to balance on a beam.

'Can't we find our way back, Izzy? Peace on earth and goodwill to all sisters and all that?'

Pine-needle aroma from her exquisitely decorated Christmas tree wafted towards me. The bells on Santa's reindeers sleighing across her mantelpiece gave a little festive tinkle in the warm draught rising up from the crackling logs in her marble fireplace. A family Christmas? My heart fluttered – a little staccato percussion. How happy it would make my daughter. I felt wonky. For a moment I feared I was slipping into a hyperglycaemic coma when it dawned on me that it was simply an overdose of sugary Yuletide sentimentality. There were kids singing carols outside on the street. Their sweet voices seeped into the room; a festive oil spill, coating my ears with commercial syrupification. I snapped out of my stupor as though injected with an EpiPen.

'Gosh, yes, a family Christmas at Mum's. We can have a Secret Santa,' I said, sarcastically. 'I get a broken heart … and you get my husband.'

'Izzy, I can't explain what happened. Johnny and I always felt this smouldering attraction. It's so unlikely on paper, I know, he's so not my normal type. Architects, designers, masters of the universe… they were the men on my menu. But Johnny and I actually have so much in common – we both love food, travel, music, adventure. I took him to exotic locations but he took me out of my comfort zone. And made me laugh. He set me free in, well, in every way. Whenever we met we just couldn't stop talking and laughing and… We tried to avoid seeing each other, we really did, but family reunions made that impossible.'

I braced myself for more, each word a bitter bullet.

'He was like a siren calling me onto the rocks.'

My lips thinned to slits. 'Yeah, well, you should have tied yourself to the sisterhood mast, like Odysseus.'

'Johnny and I adore each other. Our devotion to each other is a testament to that love. But I've realised of late that I gave up too much for him. My desire to have a child. My niece. And my sister…' Her face was naked in its hope and love.

'I still need my twin sister too…' I added flippantly, 'but just for spare parts. I'll get back to you if I require a kidney.' With what relish I boomeranged back her recent jibe about harvesting my organs.

'If only you'd let me share in Chrissie's life…'

'You took Johnny because you could. I bet you took up more space in our mother's womb too. I was probably just squished somewhere up near her appendix. You're just totally selfish. You didn't think of me, or Chrissie. Not once. You broke our hearts. So did Johnny. And you both have to live with that.'

'I want to say sorry to Chrissie. And to you.'

I looked at her agog. 'Wait! Has there been an emergency weather report? Is hell frozen over? My perfect sister who is never wrong... apologising?'

'I'm profoundly sorry for hurting you, Isabella.'

Her voice ached with longing. Much to my amazement, I felt a pang of empathy in my gut. But it passed shortly, like acid reflux. A heaviness settled then, deep inside my bones. The ache came over me quickly like bad weather. Her treachery hurt every time I thought about it, like a nerve exposed to air.

'I don't blame you for hating me,' she added, quietly.

I was hit suddenly with exhaustion. I felt as if my brain was going to fall out of my head. 'Hate you? Oh no. Not really... Sometimes whole seconds elapse where I forget that you destroyed my life.'

We looked at each other in silence. Her betrayal lay between us, as solid as a geographical feature: a mountain, say, or an ice field.

'You're my sister and I love you,' she said, softly.

'Gosh, well, then, that's interesting... Obviously stealing your sister's husband proves that love can express itself in many curious ways.' My voice was drenched in irony. 'And don't make out Johnny seduced you. You're the predatory one! An apex predator.'

'Please, Izzy. It's Christmas. Let me make amends. For Mother's sake.'

'Sure. So, what would you like for Christmas, Verity? Hmm... what to give to the woman's who's had everyone? A gold-plated condom? A sex toy Advent calendar?'

'I'm begging you, Izz.'

But I could never forgive my sister, not even if we were marooned on a space station and all the other astronauts were dead. The woman was a vampire on a day pass. I'd been happily floating about on the Love Boat, which she'd totally *Titanic*-ed.

'Please,' begged the iceberg.

'Verity. There can be no justification for your double-cross. Our rift is irreparable. As soon as we've extracted Mum from this con artist's grasp, we will once more go our separate ways.'

That was when her phone buzzed – and her life changed forever.

PART FOUR

Sisterhood Rule
Be The Wind Beneath Her Bingo Wings.

TWENTY-NINE

As Verity read the text the only discernible movement was the swishing of her bob cut, like a curtain. As she turned her head away from the screen and then back again over and over, it moved with metronomic precision. After a minute or so, her eyebrows, fashionably plucked to sceptical arches, crawled up her forehead like anorexic caterpillars.

'Is it Mum?' My stomach suddenly felt like I'd swallowed barbed wire. Gawain's charge sheet ran through my mind once more: bankruptcy, fraud, incarceration, mysterious death of wife, insurance payout, restraining order... 'What's happened?'

My sister gave me a glazed look. I snatched the phone from her limp fingers. Scanning the message, I was so surprised at what I read, I took another pass at it, this time more slowly.

> Hi Verity. It's taken me over a week to find the balls to send you this message. I love you as my friend and have always been very fond of Johnny. So last weekend when going for brunch at Blenheim on my way back from Oxford, seeing Johnny was initially a nice surprise. I was going to say hello to him, but then realised he was with a young woman. They

> appeared very intimate, showing public displays of affection and obviously oblivious to anyone else in their surroundings. I watched them for a good 40 minutes so I definitely know it was Johnny. The woman looked in her mid 20's, slim, well dressed. They seemed very happy. He definitely did not see me. You've got this information to do what you want with. I don't want to get involved and I don't want you to feel uncomfortable when I see you next – so I'm not going to reveal my identity. This is a burner phone so no point in trying to ring back. I'm sorry. But if I was being betrayed I'd want to know.

My sister's eyes blinked and blinked like the frantic beating of a trapped insect's wing.

'Ring back,' I said.

On remote control, she followed my instruction. The phone rang and rang but there was no answer.

'Text.'

My sister just stared at me, numbly. I commandeered her phone and typed a reply.

> Sorry. But you have to tell me who you are! This is too weird a message to get out of the blue!

We waited, peering at the tiny screen, but a cacophonous silence ensued.

I crafted another urgent missive.

> Whoever you are, thanks for this act of friendship. But I do need clarification. What does 'public displays of affection' mean exactly?

I took a closer look at the burner phone message. 'Brunch time on a Saturday morning… at a small country hotel… that could mean he, or they, rather, stayed the night. Where was Johnny last Friday?'

'Let me think. He was checking out a potential gig. In Brighton.'

'Do you know that for sure?'

'Yes! Johnny would never betray me. He gave up everything for me, his marriage, his daughter, you. He's my rock. My safe harbour. He's the only man in the world I have complete faith in.'

'Yeah well, déjà-screw; that's what I thought, too.' She looked so stricken that I tempered my remark with humour. 'Look, if it's true, I'll just beat him senseless. Don't forget, I know where all his sports injuries are.'

Verity gave a forced laugh, but her eyes were dull, her face pinched and chilly. 'It's not true. I would trust Johnny with my life. It's clearly a prank. Let's get back to work on the Bach. The end needs finessing.'

Outside, a squall of dark birds wheeled down from Primrose Hill. They squawked a harsh accompaniment to our rehearsal. Verity turned back to the piano, but her playing had become mechanical. She fumbled some notes and lost her place twice. It was a relief when I heard the sound of a key in the lock. Johnny entered, tinsel hanging from his ears and fairy lights circling his handsome head.

'Sorry I'm late, sweetheart. Few Christmas pints with the boys… Just leave me decorated through the festive period and take me down after New Year's Eve,' he joked. When he clocked me, half hiding behind the wing of the grand piano, a shocked grin split open his face. 'Well, well, well, Bella. What a surprise to see you here.'

I glanced back at the sheet music, but his gaze was like the touch of a hand on my shoulder, making him hard to ignore. Most women marry Mr Right, then ten years later find out they're hitched to a beanbag that farts. But Johnny had lost none of his sex appeal. He'd become more attractive, if anything. Even with tinsel in his hair.

When he moved towards Verity for a kiss, she averted her head and thrust her phone at him instead. 'I just got the strangest message. Anonymous.'

Johnny's feet were planted ridiculously far apart, like they were trying to maintain their balance on the deck of a trawler in a heavy sea. He swayed a bit, but quickly sobered after scanning the text. 'What the hell? Obviously a hoax,' he concluded, handing the phone back to my sister.

'That's what I thought... But who would prank me like that?'

I had to agree. Who would dare prank the formidable Verity Nightingale? Even reality is too scared of her to bite... Well, perhaps until now. She looked from Johnny to me and back at her phone,

Johnny snorted. 'Are you kiddin', sweetheart? You're a critic. You have so many enemies.' He started to count off some of her more scathing remarks on his fingers. '*This symphony has beautiful moments, but awful hours... If an elephant could sing it would do a more convincing job of a seductress than this operatic Heffalump... The most melodic part of the performance was the sound of the bottom of a barrel being scraped...*'

Verity exhaled, a relieved smile curling her lips. 'That's so true. It really could be anybody, couldn't it.'

'You even once wrote an article about Chrissie's school concert,' I recalled. 'You said school concerts were "nature's way of promoting adoption." The kids were seven!'

'You see?' Johnny laughed. 'Even the parents of north London are out to get you. It's one of the things I most love about you, V, that you speak your mind and don't care.'

Johnny has powerfully built shoulders and muscular arms, which he likes to display by wearing short-sleeved T-shirts, even in winter. Shrugging off his leather jacket, he flexed his biceps and ran a hand through his turbulent hair, peeling away the strands of stray fairy lights.

'Face it, sweetheart, your list of the peeved and vindictive is pretty damn long,' he chuckled.

Peeved and Vindictive, I thought, it sounded like a law firm. The question was – did my sister need one? Johnny sat down, but even so, did not relax. He balanced himself on the edge of the chair, his knee jigging up and down in time to a rhythm in his head. Suddenly, his head spun to look at me. 'Even your own sister hates you.'

Verity's smile narrowed between twin brackets of disapproval and she looked my way, suspiciously.

'It's true, Bella. You've never got over me leavin' you. And always blamed your sister. Maybe bitterness has addled your brain?' He tsk'ed his tongue and added, half-jokingly, "Fess up. Are you the mystery malicious text sender?'

My heart gave a bang so loud it hurt my chest. 'Wait! What?' The shock of the accusation was like lifting the needle off a vinyl record too violently, making it screech. 'How could I have sent the message when I was right here when it came through?'

'I dunno... An accomplice? A clandestine text sent while on a trip to the loo?'

Something in my stomach churned and twisted. 'I think the real question is, where exactly you were last Friday night and Saturday morning?'

'Linin' up a gig. In Brighton. Not that it's any of your concern. We're divorced, remember?' Johnny threw me a cold glance. It sliced into my emotional scar tissue and I felt the pain of him leaving me, all over again. A long vine of plastic holly and ivy still lassoed his neck. It was a loose noose and I was tempted to pull it tight.

'Ask the boys in the band if you don't believe me.' Johnny nonchalantly handed his phone to my sister, while giving me another dismissive look.

'It's flat,' she said, handing the phone back.

'Let me charge it for you,' I volunteered, reaching into my bag for my portable battery pack.

'I'll do it,' he said, a little too quickly.

I raised a quizzical brow. 'Yeah, that should give you ample opportunity to erase anything incriminating.'

'It's all right, darling,' Verity said, 'I trust you implicitly. I would bet my life on your fidelity.'

'Yeah, I would have said that once too,' I muttered.

'Use your bloody battery pack then!' he said to me, belligerently.

I offered the battery to my sister, who waved it away. 'No. I have complete faith in you, darling. Of course I do. But you...' My sister looked at me with a vinegary expression.

'Not so much. You've always wanted to break us up.' The trace of poison Johnny had introduced was now branching through her being.

Fury seared my cheeks like a branding iron. 'I can't believe you could accuse me of something so base. I would never stoop so low… Unlike you two.'

'Maybe we should just take a look in your bag for a burner phone,' Johnny suggested with more than a hint of animosity.

Without another word I upended the contents of my handbag onto the living-room rug – a cascade of car keys, plectrums, sunglasses, half-eaten chocolate bars, musical scores, a battered iPhone…

'Hey, I was only teasin', Bella. No need for that,' Johnny lied.

But my sister's eyes were raking through the upended contents, distrustfully.

'Anyway, sweetheart, I'm sure it's just some disgruntled nut job. It's the height of fashion, ya know, V, to have a stalker,' Johnny joshed her.

My sister is on the board of things. She gets picked up by chauffeur-driven cars. She's been a guest on BBC Radio 4's *Desert Island Discs*. Now she could add 'stalker' to her long list of accreditations.

The room was suddenly too hot and stuffy. I got down on my hands and knees to regather my possessions. 'After all you've put me through, Johnny, you're now accusing me of backstabbing my own sister?' I scrambled to my feet. 'That's it. I'm done. Truce over. We'll just have to let Mum sort out her own life, because I just can't do this for a moment longer.'

Our phones rang simultaneously and Mum's face popped up on both our devices. There was static and echo on the video call because Verity and I were in the same room on two different phones but, through the burr and blur I heard Mum say, 'Wonderful news, darlings! Gawain's just proposed! We're getting married!!'

Gawain appeared on screen then behind her, which was when I realised they were calling from my mother's bedroom – and that they were naked, the sheet barely covering anything.

'Hey, girls. Just call me Dad! It's about time you had one!' My mother and her dodgy paramour cracked up laughing at this suggestion. And hey, it was kinda funny, considering he was ten years younger than us.

I looked at Verity. Then back at my mother's hopeful face. As much as I loathed my twin sister, I loathed Gawain even more. Our family tree could never be contaminated with this sap. I would just have to grit my teeth and bear it.

THIRTY

An extended truce was one thing, but a rapprochement quite another. A cosy family Yuletide was not on the Chrissy cards.

On Christmas Day, my normally chic mother breezed into my place with Gawain wearing matching reindeer-themed jumpers. While helping me serve up lunch in the kitchen, she tore a few hunks off the turkey and devoured them ravenously, banging on about urgently needing to replace all the electrolytes and salts she was losing from her surfeit of aerobic sexual antics.

'Mum, I get it. You're enjoying your fling but you can't be serious about marrying the guy? The thirty-year age gap may not seem like much now, but it will... And I'm not sure they'll allow a water bed and a sex swing in your residential care home... And what will be your foreplay? Hey, big boy, pass me my teeth and I'll give you a love bite! Let me put my hearing aid in, then shout dirty to me!'

'You're just jealous, darling.' Mum licked her fingers. 'Because you have no love life of your own.'

'Nor do I want one! It's all such fairy-tale nonsense. Cinderella could have lived a happy life singing with her animal pals rather than settling for some tosser who made her try on a shoe because he didn't recognise her without make-up.'

Milky fog pressed against the window and the bare, gnarled branches of trees twisted up against the pale sky. My mother wrapped her warm arms around me. 'My darling girl. I just want you to be happy. As happy as I am.'

'Look, Mum, I get it that you got a bit burnt out by your career and by losing your beloved Helen… But marrying so quickly is not the answer.'

'Maybe not,' she winked, 'but it raises so many interesting questions. Oh, to be in love! That feeling of symphonies ringing in the head and the heart!'

'Like I said, Mum, life is not a fairy tale. If you lose your shoe at midnight, it's a pretty good indication that you're drunk. How much have you had to drink today by the way?'

'Not nearly enough,' she sighed, wearily.

Over Christmas lunch, my mother made a toast to living life to the full and throwing caution to the winds. 'Remember,' she said, looking straight at me, 'there are no luggage racks on hearses; no pockets in shrouds.'

After lunch, I glimpsed Gawain and my mother disappearing into the downstairs bathroom. From behind the door came the indistinct murmur of laughter, exclusive and luxurious. Followed by a silence I did not want to interpret.

When they finally reappeared, Gawain pulled on the rubber gloves and attacked the washing-up.

'Look at him.' My mother smiled indulgently. 'Most men can't empty a dishwasher without hiring a skywriting plane to advertise the fact. Followed by a ticker tape parade and a Red Arrows fly-past.'

'Mum, the guy's just schmoozing you. Honestly, you need a schmooze alarm on your phone.'

'And you need a snooze alarm that wakes you up to life's possibilities. Speaking of which, aren't you going to open your present?'

I tore off the wrapping to find an array of sex toys. 'Ah, thanks, Mum,' I said, agog. 'But surely I'll need a licence to operate such heavy machinery?' I had no doubt that any attempt I made to wield one of those gadgets would end up in a totally humiliating trip to the Casualty Department. Mum seemed equally perplexed by my gift – an age-appropriate book on happy homecraft skills, from needlepoint and basket-weaving to origami and pottery.

After fuelling up on pudding, they left for dinner at my sister's place. Unable to keep their hands off each other, I had no doubt they'd be pulling into a rest stop en route to give a more literal meaning to 'lay-by' and 'sex drive'.

Over the next six days, potential New Year resolutions piled up in my addled mind. I toyed with the idea of subscribing to a podcast on positive thinking... but felt negative about the idea immediately. My next vow was to be more chilled out. I downloaded some relaxation apps of babbling brooks and rain pitter-patting down window panes. I lay on the bed, closed my eyes and concentrated on the sound of waves breaking on the beach... but immediately panicked about being trapped by the tide.

The morning of Helen's memorial, Mum called to remind us not to mention her lesbian liaison. 'Helen's extremely conservative family could never comprehend how a woman could conduct a graceful, sensual pivot from men to women in later life,' she explained. An easier pivot to understand than a midlife swivel towards an alpine horn fraudster, I thought, but bit my tongue.

After exchanging icy New Year felicitations, Verity and I moved to the front of the cavernous Highgate church. We took our seats, me in a plain black trouser suit, perched on a stool, and Verity in a floaty black chiffon designer dress at the piano. We looked towards our mother, who nodded then counted us in. Mum's beautiful arrangement of Bach's captivating 'Arioso' brought tears to the eyes of all the mourners, most notably our mother. Dabbing her face dry, Nicole picked up her baton and, for the first time in six months, proceeded to conjure the most sublime phrasing from her small chamber orchestra and then, from the church choir, singing a cappella. Watching my mother conducting was mesmerising. She just shone with interpretive intelligence; it glowed like an aura around her. The old, weather-worn church swelled like a throat with the sound of serene yet sombre threnodic singing.

This ancient place of worship with its pale, lichened stone wore its steep, gabled roof pulled over its ears like a low hat. The reception was being held under its brim, in the vestibule. While nibbling on mandatory limp cucumber sandwiches, my sister and I were busily plotting ways to at least get a pre-nup in place, when Verity's phone pinged. As she read the message, her face paled.

'What?'

She screwed up her eyes as if in pain, then handed me the phone. I scanned the anonymous text.

> Verity, sorry for yet another message out of the blue. I've felt very unsettled since my last text. I'm aware that I could be anyone feeding you damaging information that's not

true. I've been sitting on three photos that I took on the day, showing Johnny and this woman kissing, holding each other very closely and laughing together. I've been advised not to send these to you online, but to print them off and get them delivered to your house. We are away for a few days, so I'll get them to you when we get back. Once this is done I will delete the photos and this phone will be thrown away as I need closure on this matter as I'm sure you do too. Take care. Xx

Verity levelled me with a measuring, suspicious look.

'Come on! I haven't left your side for two hours. Besides, the message says "we".'

Verity clicked her teeth. 'Perhaps that's just a trick to put me off the scent?' She bit a nail and frowned. 'What message should I send back?'

Verity asking for my advice? It was clearly a Christmas miracle. 'We need to flush her, him or them out. If the photos are coming in the post, I'm a bit unnerved that they know where you live. Let's be diplomatic.' I dictated a message which she duly typed.

Dear Friend, thank you for your kindness. I know you have my best interests at heart. The photos are the evidence I need for Johnny to be straight with me. Thank you. No need to post. You can just send them via your phone. It's too much trouble for you otherwise and thank you, whoever you are, once more, for being so candid and caring. I just need to clarify this ordeal.

We fired the message off into the ether, then just stood gazing in bewildered astonishment at the blank screen.

'Girls!' We looked up to see Melissa striding towards us in a tailored navy pantsuit with white lapels. She was in full professional mode, not a whiff of New Age woo-woo about her.

'Okay, I've lined up another gig for your mum. You won't believe it. Kirill Petrenko is indisposed and they've asked Nicole to step in to conduct the Berlin Philharmonic! I've texted and rung your mother but no reply. I'm hoping to pin her down today with your help.' It was then she clocked my sister's stricken face. 'What the hell's happened?'

I took a deep breath of church air, languid with incense. 'Can I tell her?'

Verity bit her lip uncertainly.

'Look, if this is a prankster with a grudge, Mel knows everyone in the music world and may have some ideas about who hates you most. She could at least put some feelers out.'

Verity gave an abrupt nod and I explained the anonymous phone message situation.

'Christ.' Melissa steepled her hands in front of her like a judge about to deliver a verdict. 'If it's true, treat Johnny like toxic waste. In other words – dump him.'

'Johnny is not cheating on me!' Verity snapped, shrilly. 'Some vengeful creep is just torturing me for their own sadistic enjoyment. But who?'

My sister's suspicious eyes slid my way once more. I shook my head furiously, like a dog tormented by wasps. Melissa said she'd keep her ear to the ground, before striding off to find our mother. Johnny sauntered over now, handing Verity a cup of tea. He gave her a wide smile, the kind of smile that can open doors without knocking. Verity nursed her warm cup in both hands, close to her chest, as if trying to revive her heart. 'There's been another anonymous message,' she told him.

'Isabella,' Johnny looked at me, his tone bordering on surly, 'you've had your fun but these silly games must stop.'

My anger rose up like boiling milk. I tried to turn myself down to a simmer but fury spilled over, hissing and splashing onto my emotional hot plate. 'Your mind is wandering, Johnny – and it really is too small to be allowed out on its own.'

'If you are behind this, Izzy...' agitation made Verity's voice rise, not in steps like a scale, but in a slow glissando, 'I will kill you.'

I looked at my ex-husband, who'd sat down at one of the little spindly tables and was insouciantly realigning silverware against the peach tablecloth. He then made a casual study of the tan knobs in the sugar bowl – the result of too many wet teaspoons. His expression was tranquil, but then I noticed how his foot was jacking up and down, as if working an invisible pump. My mild suspicion morphed into something bigger but that train of thought was derailed by my mother's arrival.

'Oh, my darling girls! Thank you. That was sublime.' She opened her arms to us both.

'No, Mum, you were sublime. It was spellbinding seeing the way you coaxed those mellifluous phrases from the musicians,' I enthused, coming out of the hug.

Melissa, spotting Mum, elbowed mourners aside to make her way back to us. 'Nicole, such a joy to see you at work again.' She slapped her top client on the back. 'You cannot possibly give up your career. Especially for a...' she approached the word with sterilised tongs, 'man.'

'Well, you'll be pleased to know that I've actually missed wielding my baton... which is why I've decided that I am going to conduct again.'

There was a general chorus of 'Oh great's, 'Hooray's and 'What a relief's.

'Ah! You got my messages, then! The Berlin Philharmonic at the Philharmonie concert hall. Incredible acoustics. It doesn't get any more prestigious,' Melissa preened.

'Ah, no. Not that gig. I'm going to conduct the debut of Gawain's alpine horn concerto. It was commissioned by the EU as a cross-cultural exchange and already programmed by the Derry Guildhall.'

A collective whiplash afflicted her audience. The clammy odour rising up from the church crypt was like the breath of a dying dog.

'The... Derry... Guild... hall...?' Melissa stuttered. 'Where even is that?'

'I'm guessin' Derry,' Johnny contributed, sardonically.

'You can't be serious?' Melissa groaned. 'It's career suicide!'

'A guildhall in Derry is the Dignitas clinic for conductors, Mother!' Verity decried indignantly.

'Nicole, don't make yourself into a laughing stock. How can you turn down such a distinguished gig for the most obscure instrument in the most obscure venue, composed by the most obscure nobody?' Melissa pleaded.

'Mel's right, Mother. It's a case of Mistaken Non-entity,' Verity pointed out.

'The definition of a kind, thoughtful humanitarian is someone who knows how to play the alpine horn... but doesn't,' I wise-cracked.

Mum retrieved her phone from a trouser pocket. 'Take a listen first.' She pressed play, her bright eyes speculatively half closed.

We cringed at the atonal, cacophonous cascade that spewed forth. This mock-up score of Gawain's alpine horn concerto sounded like a cow in labour. Or rather, labour-hosen.

'Original, isn't it?' Mum said, pressing pause. 'What do you think?'

We were on pause too. It was a pause big enough to drive a tank through. Outside the church windows, a chorus of blackbirds, wrens & hedge sparrows sang their intricate phrases, over and over; the melodious contrast was stark.

Melissa gave a little hiss. 'Can I be honest with you, Nicole?'

'Good God no.' My mother laughed. 'Then I'd have to sack you.'

'You're a woman of a certain age in a male-dominated world. You beat classical music's big beasts to get to the top. But there are a lot of hungry, younger competitors biting at your high heels. If you don't get back in the game right now, I predict a future of bar mitzvahs and neurodivergent church choirs. Is that really what you want?'

'What I want is for you to take on Gawain as a client,' my mother replied. 'After his debut, he's bound to get more commissions as a composer.'

Melissa snorted. 'Calling him a composer is like calling me a discus tosser.'

'Well, you are a bit of a tosser, Melissa,' my mother replied, coolly. 'Izzy?' She turned her laser beam my way.

'Mum, I'm sorry. But having been bullied and friendless all through your school years is no reasonable justification for composing a contemporary alpine horn concerto.'

'Verity?'

'The only reason I occasionally listen to works by modern composers is to remind myself how much I adore Mozart,' my sister said simply.

'The alpine horn is all very well in its place – buried deep in the ice cave of a glacier,' I added.

'And it's not even a real venue. But a guildhall.' Melissa gave the shudder of a dowager duchess contemplating a visit to the hovel of one of her poorer tenants. She flopped, despondent, into a plastic chair and put her head in her hands.

'I am not given to lachrymosity as you know, Mother,' Verity said, dabbing away tears with a napkin, 'but the marriage announcement and now this. It's too, too much.'

What it really was? The awful icing on the angst pie of the terrible text messages, I thought to myself.

'This ridiculous concert will ruin your reputation. The critics will know it's nothing more than, well, nooky nepotism,' Verity continued.

'Don't you slightly suspect Gawain's motives?' Melissa enquired, tetchily. 'Isn't there just one niggling suspicion that he's using you for your contacts and kudos in the music world?'

'The seal of creative approval you can give him is priceless,' my sister echoed.

Mum shook her head and tch-tch-ed. 'Good God, you girls are like the Gestapo! Why don't you get an Anglepoise lamp and simply shine a light into his eyes?'

We fell silent then as the conman in question sidled

towards us in his fair-trade organic cotton trousers, hand-knitted Nordic jumper, a Burberry Trench crossbody bag and Bono-like tinted shades. He looked as though he'd come straight from scaling the cliff face of a composting seminar on recycling and sustainable waste. My mother smiled indulgently as he kissed her hand. Honestly, if he'd had a forelock he'd have tugged it.

'If he took off his Bono shades, he might just find what he's looking for,' I whispered to my sister.

'Oh, I think he's found that – our gullible mother!' she whispered back.

'Has your dear mama told you the great news?' His voice was a high tenor, confident, clear. 'I cannot believe she's doing me this great honour.'

'Great dishonour, more like it,' Melissa grumped.

Gawain gave his thick blond hair a toss, then smiled over at Nicole through a silky fringe, his limpid, high-voltage blue eyes set to stun. 'Oh, how I adore her. She's my kindred spirit. Our hearts speak the same language. Your magical mother and I are cut from the same cosmic cloth,' he added, grandly. 'And did she give you the other exciting news? We've also decided to tie the knot in the Emerald Isle.'

My mother's eyes sparkled as she looked at him. 'The day after the concert. Just a registry office ceremony. But of course, you're all invited.'

My sister and I reacted with another bout of frantic eye semaphore. We were getting so good at this secret communication we could have been deployed in the Second World War to signal seafarers about incoming Luftwaffe. We didn't need an Enigma machine to spell out our mission either. It was crystal clear. Operation Derail Gawain.

After Mum and her lunatic lover had wafted off to console Helen's stern-faced family, Melissa drew us into a huddle to make a pact. The concert and the wedding had to be stymied, whatever way possible.

I went home burdened with anxieties. I just had so much to worry about – my mother's impending marriage and my sister's imploding one. Was Johnny cheating on her? If he was having an affair, who could it be? I ran through a mental Rolodex of possibilities. Panache's manager, Chantelle? I pictured her in her trademark sequinned bomber jacket with that dirty laugh and free spirit, handing out ganja and gummy bears. Or what about his personal trainer, Suzie? Panther-like in stretch Lycra and beyond bendy? His tennis partner was a definite candidate, too. All flicky blonde hair and fake fingernails sharp enough to disembowel a ferret, plus an absent wanker-banker husband? And the woman who ran the recording studio was not above suspicion either. Sassy, tattooed, leather-trouser wearing and with a rumoured penchant for rough sex? Not to forget the groupies – women are drawn to rock bands like wasps to honey. Or honey to a wasp, in Johnny's case. The potential list was long and tempting. But would he risk his pampered, perfect life for a pathetic fling?

I had to get hold of his phone to find out. And if Johnny wasn't at fault, then who was waging this vile vendetta? One thing was for sure, I had to clear my own name, and fast, because right now, I felt like a doormat in a world of muddy galoshes.

THIRTY-ONE

Family politics can sometimes make one long for the peace and tranquillity of the Balkan states. A few days later Verity received another anonymous message, which she forwarded to me.

> Had time to reflect and decided not to send the photos as I feel they will be quite destructive to you. I've deleted them and this phone is now being decommissioned. I have hated myself for telling you, however as I said, I would have wanted to know if it ever happened to me. Your friend.

Was it a bluff? I had to know – one way or the other.

My plan was to administer a big enough dose of drugs mixed with alcohol to render my ex-husband utterly unable to perform even the most basic human activity – except for lending me his limp hand to unlock his phone with his fingerprint. When I explained this idea to the Derry Man, he laid his guitar across his lap and looked at me quizzically for a moment.

'I'm glad we met later in life, Izzy, because I don't think me ma would have let me play with you.'

Today's lesson was on a technique called *étouffée*, from the French *étouffer* meaning to stifle or to smother. The technique refers to the muting or damping down of a note immediately after being played. It seemed to suit the clandestine nature of my own proposal.

'…And I want you there as back-up in case something goes wrong.'

'What could possibly go wrong with this foolproof plan?' my pupil replied, ironically, damping down the strings and my enthusiasm simultaneously. 'In case it escaped your notice, I handle dogs for the police. I can't be involved with anything illegal.'

'It's not that bad. I'm just slipping a mickey into his drink. I checked with a nurse pal who plays goalie on my touch-footy team. All I need do is mix some diazepam, which is basically Valium, with something morphine-based like codeine. My doctor actually prescribed me something super strong when I got knocked off my bike a few years back. Oramorph, I think it's called. It's in liquid form but very fast-acting.'

'Jay-sus. Who are you, all of a sudden?… The Mushroom Poisoner? Remind me never to try your beef Wellington.'

'Hey, shiitake happens…'

He groaned as though already contaminated. 'Christ,' he said, 'that bad pun has been growing in the dark for way too long.'

A perfect poisoning opportunity arose the next weekend. Chrissie was away on an overnight gig with Femifesto in Portsmouth so I asked Johnny to drop by to discuss our daughter's musical future. When we want to, women have a way of finding out more information than a McKinsey efficiency expert but it all hinged on tricking him to stay long enough for the drugged cocktails to take effect.

Of late, Johnny was an in-and-out man. So, how to snare his attention? The man's brain is primitive. Perhaps if I tried to look less like a librarian-meets-metal-detectorist, the novelty might intrigue him enough to loiter a little longer? And so, abandoning all feminist philosophy, I squeezed into a tight black dress, a pair of black satin kitten heels and slapped on some make-up.

When I opened the door, he patted me on the shoulder like a dog he was once quite fond of. I half expected him to give me a kibbles treat. Almost imperceptibly, I saw his eyes flick to my cleavage and then on down to my legs. His hand moved to my waist. It was a familiar gesture, like walking into a house you once lived in and knowing where the light switch is. When performing in Panache, I could never cross a room or a stage without Johnny patting my arse. I remembered then the way we fitted so naturally together, his strong, muscley leg parting my thighs, my hands holding down his wrists. I fought the insubordinate fizz of exhilaration that shot through my veins uninvited.

'Blimey, Izzy, you scrub up well.'

I felt the yellow lozenges of his eyes sweep over me, up and down. Johnny, who'd just come back from a studio session playing drums on a B-movie soundtrack, was suited and booted. 'Ditto,' I said, coaxing my lips into a smile.

He flashed a neon grin back with effortless ease. 'I've often wondered what happened to that frisky, free-spirited girl I once loved. The one who dyed her pubes pink and yodelled during orgasm.'

Um… her heart was shredded in the insinkerator by the two people she loved most, I wanted to say, but gave an insouciant shrug instead. 'Oh, she's still around.'

I handed him the doctored cocktail I'd mixed earlier.

He looked my way as though sizing me up for a meal. 'Jeez, Bella. How great we were together. Smokin'! J'remember when we met?'

I almost gave a snort of derision. Over the years I'd returned again and again to that private mythology, enriching and embroidering the moment when we'd first connected.

'I can't say what brought us together, originally,' I taunted, 'but I seem to remember there was some kind of a satanic ritual involved.'

Johnny threw back his head and laughed. 'God, I've missed that dry wit of yours – it's drier than this cocktail. What's in it, by the way? Zingy flavour. Cheers!' He took an appreciative swig. 'God, we had so much potential, didn't we?'

'Yes, but potential has a shelf life.'

'Still, don't you ever wonder where we'd be if we'd kept the band together?'

I stared at the midriff button of my ex-husband's denim shirt while I lied to him. 'You'd be in the rock'n'roll Hall of Fame, for sure.'

'Yeah, I was good, wasn't I?' Johnny sprawled back on the couch and started to prat on about his drumming skills for approximately eternity. 'Noel Gallagher loved the band. J'remember? Even Liam said, "Your drummin's all right, mate." I met Mick Jagger once, ya know. Plus I got to see Ronnie Wood playin' along to "Brown Sugar" backstage because he'd forgotten how it went. Ray Davies, Paul Weller, even Mark Knopfler liked our shit... It was heady stuff...'

This kind of reminiscing would have been annoying

except for the fact that it enabled me to just keep topping up his drug-infused cocktail.

'So, what's it like on the road now? Still fighting off the groupies?' I fished, when he paused his egotistical monologue to drain his glass to the dregs.

'Hey, I could go there if I wanted. But as you know there's only ever been two women for me. Shame they turned out to be sisters... I've still got a tattoo of you on my body somewhere though, if you wanna look for it...' He winked. 'Which is why this anonymous text message bullshit is such crap... Chrrrist,' he swooned. 'Feel like my brain's bein' sodomised by a platoon of gorillas.' A moment later he was collapsing into a languid jelly. 'I drunk thunk much too,' slurred the jelly, wobbling sideways. He tried to take another sip but the cocktail glass never reached his mouth, making sticky contact with his ear instead, followed by his forehead. And then he just fell down across the sofa and passed out.

After propping his comatose head on a cushion, I fished out his phone from a pocket and held the keypad to his fingertip. There was nothing to see in his emails or messages – but his WhatsApp had about ten incoming from the last day alone. And they were blood-chillingly incriminating. The 'I love you', and 'I miss you' and 'my hot, tight pussy is wet and waiting for you' missives were from a woman going under the name of Minxy. And then I found the video.

I was just about to press play when I felt a hand on my shoulder and jumped, in alarm. A trope from every horror movie instantaneously played in my head: unconscious victim mysteriously resurrected from the grave to seek blood-soaked vengeance – so it was a relief to see the Derry

Man standing there and not a ropable, spittle-flecked ex.

'Bloody hell! Where on earth did you spring from? I thought this was all too illegal for you?'

'Aye, well, I like to be law-abiding at all times… but when things go tits up, I also know how to get rid of the body. The front door was on the latch. Clearly Johnny here was aiming for a quick getaway. Although,' he glanced at my horizontal ex, '…not any more…' He cast his eyes down at Johnny's phone in my hand. 'Izzy, are you sure you want to open this particular Pandora's box?'

Part of me dreaded seeing what was in the video, but I also had a gruesome desire to know the truth. My finger impulsively pressed play before getting the final green light from mission control. A slab of my ex-husband's flesh flashed across the screen. His shoulders heaved. His taut abdomen tensed. My heart gave a massive thump. Either there was a kangaroo in my chest or I was having a heart attack.

I tried to concentrate on the thread count of the sheets – Egyptian cotton by the look of it – anything but the thrusting going on before my eyes. The thrustee was filming so I couldn't see her face, but the volume of her orgasm made her knick-knacks, a collection of snow globes, quake precariously from their perch on the bedside bookcase. My ex-husband's grunting crescendoed as his pace increased. I focused once more on the brocade wallpaper and rococo furniture – the carved bedhead inlaid with mock gold leaf depicting ornate asymmetrical designs. I studied the elaborate carvings, gildings and motifs inspired by nature – a mix of shell-like curves and floral patterns, with a forensic attention to detail.

But catching accidental sight of Johnny's peachy, muscled posterior once more was like falling down a cold damp shaft, as I, too, descended into naked memories. As he reached the peak of his pleasure, every particle of skin on my body prickled with intense revulsion. It was the same feeling I'd experienced when treading barefoot on a slug in the garden.

As the video played on, my love for him started bleaching out, like an old sepia photograph, until nothing remained but a faded, jaded memory. The realisation hit me like a hammer between the eyes: I'd been in love with a fantasy for all these years.

'Christ. I used to think he was so damn hot,' I whimpered. 'Now I know that was because his name is Satan and he hails from Hades.'

In those few seconds my love for him inverted into loathing, like a rubber glove turned inside out. I felt the colour drain from my face. My legs went cold. Numb. As though it was my drink that had been spiked. Johnny's every gesture shimmered with sex appeal, but what I hadn't realised until now was that the shimmer was radioactive.

'Oh my God. I wonder how many other women he's cheated with. What an idiot I've been. Bloody hell, do you know how many years I've loved this man?'

'Aye, but sadly it was mutual – your man's only in love with himself. So, what are you going to do?'

'I'm going to show Verity, of course. Can you forward me this video and the WhatsApp messages in a way that he won't find out that you have?'

'No bother.' The Derry Man took Johnny's phone and worked his technological magic.

'Can you imagine how sweet that revenge will be? To give Verity a taste of her own bitter medicine?'

'Aye, but also destroying her life.'

'Yes! Just as she destroyed mine!'

'You've always blamed your sister for preying on your husband, but maybe it was the other way around?' he suggested, tentatively.

I'd never looked at it through that end of the telescope. What if Verity hadn't conquered him but he'd colonised her? The thought of my sister as an unexploited, innocent country with rich, untapped resources ripe for the picking was ludicrous. 'No way. Have you actually met my sister? She's always in control.'

'Until now.' He gestured at the video, which had automatically started to replay. 'But do you really want to put another woman through all that pain?'

And that's when I felt it – a pang of compassion for my poor, betrayed sibling. This situation was so flammable it needed a fire blanket and a hydrant.

I quickly scrawled down a note for Johnny saying he'd drunk a bit much and that I'd had to leave for an appointment. I left the note on the table by the couch, under his phone. Now he was out cold, as an act of pure rebellion, I put ABBA on Spotify. He hated ABBA. The fact that he'd wake, hungover, to the strains of 'Waterloo' was deeply satisfying.

'Thanks for the advice, Derry Man, but there's only one person I need to talk to right now.'

He planted an unexpected and totally awkward kiss near my ear. In my hair mostly. He left with a mouth full of conditioner – while I left to talk to my mother.

THIRTY-TWO

'I never understood what you saw in that man.' My mother threw my phone face down onto her sofa in disgust.

'Um… And I never understood why you didn't take my side when my sister stole him.'

'I don't like the word "stole", Izzy. That implies Johnny's innocent. Have you ever thought that perhaps he ensnared Verity? Just as he's now ensnared some other poor woman? So, what are you planning to do? I don't want to see my daughter get hurt.'

'Oh, really? What about how she hurt me?'

'I love my daughters equally and unconditionally.'

I looked out the through the French doors to see a butt-naked Gawain whipping himself with some kind of tree branch under a cold shower. He let out a whoop before leaping back into the boiling broth of bubbles now dominating my mother's once sedate and stylish, landscaped Hampstead garden.

'Really? So, you love us equally, but not enough to ditch your jacuzzi-dwelling gold-digger.'

I'd arrived fifteen minutes earlier to find the lights on but nobody home. And no, the symbolism was not lost on me. After ringing the bell and the landline, I'd let myself in, just in time to see my mother sliding into a newly installed garden hot tub to cavort with her naked beau. I'd opened the doors into the crisp February air, shielded my eyes and called out, 'Mum! It's an emergency.'

Five minutes later Mum was sitting, dripping on the sofa, her hair turbaned in a towel, her gown wrapped tightly around her.

'Gawain is not a gold-digger!' she replied, purse-lipped. 'And the jacuzzi was my idea. Your best friend dying teaches you about the brevity of life. I've just looked death in the face and I didn't like what I saw. Whenever a woman dies in the movies, it's always acceptingly, bravely and more or less painlessly, while her wardrobe gets increasingly exquisite in exotic linens. She is never ravaged by the disease. She never has to be lifted in and out of a bath or heaved off the loo, her hair held back while she spews her guts up. But that's the reality. My advice is to live every day as though it's your last. Which is why I've momentarily joined the SKI team – "Spend Kids' Inheritance".'

'Mum, you can spend your money how you want. You deserve all the joy in the world. But not with him! He's making a fool of you. You're the one who always told us to stand on our own two stilettos and stay career-focused.'

'Darling, no offence, but taking life advice from you is like taking flirting lessons from the Ayatollah. How long is it since you had a lover?'

'That's not the point.'

'Isn't it? How much time have you let slip past, unembraced? Giving up fun, flirtation and sex doesn't increase your longevity, Izzy – it just feels that way.'

'You're too old to sow wild oats, Mum. You should be growing a veggie patch, for God's sake.'

'Well, you definitely are... Between your legs. When I'm in my nineties, I want to be able to say that I've been things and seen places. Don't you?'

I hated to admit it, but her words were hitting home. In truth, if it weren't for bra fittings, riding my bike over cobblestones and peak hour on the Tube, I'd have no sex life at all. 'You seem to forget that I'm still raising my daughter,' I said defensively. 'On my own.'

'Izzy, darling, nobody's last words were ever "I wish I'd spent more time picking up after my kids, eating more kale and sitting at home knitting my own orgasms".'

'I'm perimenopausal, Mum. Do you remember what that's like? Why did the menopausal woman cross the road?... To kill the chicken.'

'So many women complain about the menopause but I see it as the only time in a woman's life when she can truly be herself.'

'Really? Well put on your hard hat, Mum. Next mood swing approaching, in, oh,' I checked my watch, '...about five minutes.'

'You used to be so much fun, Izzy. Now the most rebellious thing you do is to go for a day without flossing. In fact, you must be starting to have romantic thoughts about your electric toothbrush.' She gazed adoringly at her paramour through the big, glass garden doors and sighed. 'Being in love is sublime—'

'It's a case of hormonal hives, is what it is; curable only by a dose of common sense. Romance is love without reality attached – a foolish longing for life minus mortgages, lawn mowing, flu doses and dentists. What women need is equality, not romance.'

'Ah, but a man who treats you as an equal, well there's nothing more romantic than that.'

'Oh yes? And where exactly do you find one of those?'

'What about that guitar pupil of yours? The Irish bloke. He's clearly mad about you.'

'What?! The Derry Man? Don't make me laugh! That's ridiculous.'

'Darling, he's almost as good a player as you, but keeps coming for lessons. I wonder why...?'

'No way, Mum. He's besotted with some Irish girl. Frigid Bridget. Besides, he's such a nerd. Have you seen the way he dresses? Ironed jeans? I mean, puh-lease! He is so not my type.'

'Oh, what? And Johnny Cox is?'

Normally, the very mention of my ex's name would melt me in some way. But now I felt nothing. My love for him had receded, like a tide on a beach. All that was left was the emotional driftwood. I suddenly couldn't understand the weight and importance I'd given to the cargo I'd carried for so, so long.

'Let me be your role model.' Mum twisted her engagement ring so that it sparkled in the light, then gave a five-fingered flutter of a wave to Gawain as he beckoned her back into the hot tub. 'You need to find a bloke who wrecks your lipstick, not your eye makeup.'

'Mum, I'm sorry. But you as my role model? I don't think so. You had a one-night stand with a man who left you with twins and now you're throwing away your career cachet on some cashless Casanova... Some dodgy gigolo... Some talentless parasite.'

My mother bristled. 'Life, like music, is about taking risks, Isabella. And you're running the risk of turning into one of those prissy people who spends all day reading the labels on things before you eat them; worrying about every ache and googling medical symptoms... Being in love, well, it cushions you from the pain of ageing.'

'Did you actually read that on a throw cushion? It sure sounds like it.'

She shook her head. 'Mother Nature must look at us and think – oh what a glorious world I made for you; why didn't you take more pleasure in it? Date the Derry Man.'

'Did I mention that he irons his jeans?'

'Coco Chanel said that life gives you the face you have at twenty, life shapes the face you have at thirty but at fifty, you get the face you deserve. So—'

'One thing's for sure,' I interrupted. 'Wrinkles are hereditary; you get them from your mother.'

'I'm serious, Isabella. What kind of face are you going to turn to the world on your fiftieth birthday?'

'Right now I'm more concerned about whose face my ex-husband is currently sitting on and whether or not to tell my sister.'

'It will kill her, Izzy.'

'She had no qualms about killing me!' I couldn't let it go. The heartbreak and betrayal enclosed me like a coffin, all my hopes and dreams entombed.

'Do you want my advice? That's what you came for, isn't it?'

I nodded.

'Confront him. Tell Johnny that you know all about his sordid affair. And that you have the proof. Tell him that if he doesn't stop being a love-rat, immediately, you'll tell Verity to get a fumigation order.'

Walking back to my car, I passed a dress shop window on Hampstead High Street. A surly mannequin thrust her plastic pelvis in my direction, bare, waxed, smooth – just like the glimpsed bits of the mystery woman who was about to ruin my sister's life.

Verity deserved to know, goddamn it. What did the last text from the anonymous informers say? That if they were being cheated on, they'd like to know. But then I thought back to when Johnny left me. I'd been lost down a descending labyrinth of the mind, mauled by monsters. Did I really want any other woman to have to go through that agony?

I felt another pang of compassion for my sister, as unexpected as it was unnerving.

I veered into a minimarket to pick up some milk and bread only to find myself in a long, stagnant line, waiting for the till. There ought to be two queues in supermarkets: one for insane people, and one for everyone else, I thought, as a woman in front kept on asking the cashier if she had syphilis. 'Do you have syphilis or not?' she demanded of the poor, bewildered checkout operator. It took me a moment to realise that the agitated shopper was mispronouncing physalis – one of the nightshade fruits. But it pulled me up short. Maybe Verity's sexually incontinent husband was giving her an STD right this very moment? Or herpes – the gift that just keeps on giving.

I mulled over my options. I felt confident I'd reach the right conclusion. As a forty-nine-year-old mother of one, surely I was intelligent and sensitive enough to come up with the best solution... even if it took a year or two.

THIRTY-THREE

As I drove home from Hampstead, the wipers scraped bugs off the windscreen; bugs I wished were my ex-husband's brains. It was the kind of moment where, if I drank whisky, I'd have downed a bottle. Or two. That night in bed, as I tossed and turned, my nightie twisting up around my thighs, my mother's criticism rang in my head. Had I shut down? Was I closed off from life's joys?

All the next day, as I taught pouty poshies in a north London girls' school to pick out two-chord pop songs on their pricey classical guitars, I went over and over what my mother had said and concluded that she was right. Johnny's betrayal was like a shadow on the X-ray of my spirit. It had dimmed me somehow.

By the time I turned into my street that evening my nerves were frayed and my spirits limbo-low. The sun came out from behind a black cloud and shone briefly in my eyes before plunging back under cover, clearly disappointed by what it had seen.

Something about the fading light gave my little overgrown cottage a meek, defeated look. I pulled up outside to see the Derry Man waiting on the front doorstep, a guitar in one hand, a huge German Shepherd on a lead in the other. Oh no. I'd forgotten that he'd rescheduled his lesson.

'Oh shit. I'm sorry, I forgot you're working next Saturday. That's so hopeless of me! Brain fog. How long have you been waiting?' I said, fumbling for my key.

'Not long. Half an hour. Do you mind if I bring Maisie in? She's too nervous to leave in the car.'

'Maisie? Are you kidding? She looks like that dog that drags people into the underworld. In fact, where are her other two heads?'

In a sign of guilty goodwill, I reached out a hesitant hand to pet the creature, but it let out a blood-chilling growl and I shrank back, shrieking.

'Don't worry. A lot of people think a dog is being aggressive when it's just a wee bit frightened. The other thing people get wrong about dogs is assuming all of them want to be petted. Some may be anxious and not tolerate it. Especially this one. Got this wee mutt from Romania. The poor girl's just exhausted...'

'What? From swimming the English Channel? And where's Cyril?'

'All trained up and sniffing luggage at the airport. Nose to the grindstone... Maisie's a rescue dog. Needs love and attention. An animal charity found her fending for herself in a cemetery.'

'Appropriate, for a hound from Hades.'

Casting dubious looks at his growling rescue dog, I reluctantly opened the front door. The Derry Man led Maisie into the kitchen and tied her lead to a chair leg before fetching her a bowl of water. The dog crouched back on her haunches, eyes swivelling.

'Everything to her is a potential threat because of what she's survived. She has generations of street-dog hardwiring telling her to trust no one. She was terrified when she first came to me and wanted to live in the garden... Now, she's grand. Sleeps in my bed, snoring...'

'Do you both turn around three times before lying down?' I joshed. 'What a happily married couple. You'll be doing the sudoku together next.'

A bird flew past the window and Cerberus, sorry, Maisie, sprang into yapping action, straining at her lead.

'Shhh, there, there, girl... Some dogs have a high prey drive,' the Derry Man expounded. 'Basically, she's chronically stressed, never off duty, always risk-assessing; scanning the horizon, as if she's back on those dangerous streets.'

I knew just how she felt.

He bent down and patted her big, brutish head. 'My job is to be the buffer between her and the chaos of the human world. I'll sort you out, girl,' he told Maisie, gently. 'Don't you worry, darling. Love conquers all.'

Watching him soothing the fractious dog with firm, reassuring strokes, it struck me how much I longed for a buffer.

'I'm trying to teach her to "unlearn" some instinctive behaviours. It's hard work but worth it ... Jaysus, I'm going on, sorry...'

I noticed for the first time that his gap-toothed smile was quite affable. And the way his cheeks dimpled when he laughed was also disarmingly charming.

'That's our signature move. Mansplaining, I mean.' As he glided past me to pick up his guitar, I inhaled a spicy, salty, earthy aroma tinged with coffee and leather.

'Oh well, don't worry. I've realised lately that I know so little about men.' I asked Spotify to play Billie Holiday and let the smoky vocals of 'I'll be Seeing You' wash over me as I mixed a medicinal martini. 'Do you want to join me? Or get yourself a beer.'

'Thanks but I'm on call.' He opened the fridge and selected a non-alcoholic pale ale. 'You basically have to just sift through the flotsam and jetsam to try to find life's better angels. They're down there somewhere among the fairy dust.'

I scoffed. 'What a typically Irish thing to say! You Celts are so... so... whimsical. When you're not kneecapping each other, that is.'

'Aye, no, that's what we're like,' he agreed, patting me gingerly on the back as if I was a stray dog and might nip his fingers. But I didn't draw away. In fact, I felt a pulse throb behind my ear. Followed by a shimmer of excitement which shimmied down my stomach to my thighs, igniting all those secret nerves in between.

I necked my martini and looked him over. The light behind him seemed warmer somehow, alluring. It had never occurred to me before, but the Derry Man actually could fall into the Tall, Handsome Romantic Lead category. It was like waking up in your very familiar bedroom to find all the furniture rearranged. I had to reorient myself. I made another martini while drinking him in – his broad shoulders, strong forearms and twinkly eyes; his mutinous, mischievous smile – and decided then that I liked him. A lot. I necked my second drink and felt the heat of it flow through me like melting butter. I turned and shrugged myself into his embrace, close against his chest and inhaled his scent once more – a smoky, burnt coffee bean flavour, which entered my mouth somehow and made it water.

'Izzy... I... You...'

'You're going to need a Heimlich manoeuvre if you keep choking on your words like that.' I wrapped my arms tightly around him and squeezed. 'Well, aren't you going to kiss me, Derry Man?' The martinis had electrified my palate and loosened my tongue.

He took my face between his palms. I closed my eyes, anticipating the soft touch of his lips. When they brushed mine, lust did a fast fandango in my brain and my blood sprang to attention.

I floated for an instant in the open sky on the backs of my eyelids, free-falling, until raw lust rushed up to meet me like the earth. 'I want you,' I growled, hotly, into his neck and pressed my mouth onto his. It wasn't just a kiss; I basically ate his face. I rubbed my breasts up against his chest, then made a lunge for his nether regions.

He caught my hand and held it in mid-air. 'Slow down,' he urged. 'You're like a whirling dervish...'

In answer I attacked his mouth once more with a ferocity that surprised me. I practically chewed his lips off.

'What's the urgency?' he asked, coming up for air. 'You're snogging me like there's a firing squad waiting next door.'

I grabbed him tightly and ground my hips into his. 'Don't you like it when I hug you like this?'

'Hugging? It's more like a mugging. I feel like a village being pillaged by a Viking.'

'Isn't that what blokes want? Hot sex with no emotional attachment? No complications?'

My salivary glands shifted into overdrive. With cocktail-fuelled bravado, I unzipped my dress so that it dropped to the floor in one go and I was standing there in my new red bra and brand new, bright green G-string. (Luckily, I'd been making an effort to wear nicer underwear ever since the day Cyril used them as a chew toy.) I took his hand and placed it between my legs. I was just waking up to the urgency of my desire when he inexplicably pulled back away from me again.

'Don't... don't you fancy me?' I asked, offended.

'Aye, I do, but not like this.'

'I think your trousers are saying otherwise,' I said blithely.

I could feel him tightening up. He cleared his throat and dropped his head. 'Sex is between the ears, Izzy, not just the legs.' His Irish accent was so soft, each word wrapped in silk. 'For me, anyways.'

'Really? If I thought too much about letting another man into my life, my legs would slam shut. Why don't you just shut up and let your body do the talking?'

'That's... that's not the way I want it.'

'Oh, what? You want it with soaring violins and sequins and birds singing and rainbows flying out of your arse?'

'Aye. Aye, I suppose I do. I like you, Izzy. I've liked you for a long, long time. But I want it to be special.'

'Special? Um... that's a helicopter trip over Niagara Falls... Or a yak ride to Machu Picchu. What happens between a man and a woman, this so-called "love", is not "special". It's a chimera.'

'How would you know when you've only ever let one man in?' he asked, tenderly. He picked my dress up off the carpet and handed it to me.

I felt aghast then, aghast at the loneliness melting my insides. 'Why take the risk? As I told you once before, all men are guilty until proven innocent.'

'Yeah, well, that's not the way justice works.'

'Rough justice is the only justice women get in this patriarchal world. No wonder we're so lacking in confidence.'

I didn't know if you'd categorise my condition as chronic low self-esteem but I definitely had an inflated idea of my own irrelevance. I held the dress up against my body. This whole scenario was too mortifying. But how to salvage the situation? I'd need tips from a top escapologist to get out of this one. But the Derry Man did the work for me.

'Let's take a rain check. I think you're letting the martinis do the talking.'

My brain was too tired for this turn of events. The light had gone out of his eyes. My pupil's passion had cooled to the temperature of an Icelandic fjord. The door had slammed shut between us.

'You know what? You're right. It is just the martinis talking. A dog handler? What was I thinking?' I pulled the dress on over my head and yanked up the zip. 'I've turned down men a lot higher up the food chain than you.'

Sarcasm was gushing out of me now like an arterial wound. 'Don't get an inflated ego, Derry Man. Jabba the Hutt could have pulled me tonight. Shrek, Freddy Krueger, Tom Ripley... J.D. Vance, even.' Boozy bravado was fuelling my imprudence. 'I mean, look at you, with your side parting and white socks with black brogues. You're so anal. You probably used bullet points in your love letters to Bridget. Bullet point one: How do I love thee? Bullet point two: Let me count the ways... No wonder she dumped you.'

I couldn't believe what I'd said. It was just the embarrassment talking, but I could have sued my own mouth and yet my disobedient lips were still in gear.

'And don't take your dogs' admiration as conclusive proof that you're so friggin' fabulous, either. Dogs don't discriminate. If you weren't feeding this grave-robbing mutt, she'd take your balls off.'

My words hung in the air, like skywriting. They wouldn't disappear. When I clocked his stricken face, I wished I could suck them back in again.

The Derry Man's jacket, slung over the back of the kitchen chair, made a sudden, coughing sound, like a death rattle. A staticky voice then came over the police radio in his pocket. Suddenly, my kitchen had all the appeal and ambience of a crime scene. It was tempting to seal it off with tape and bring in some emotional forensic expert to analyse how I'd murdered the mood.

The Derry Man crossed to the kitchen sink, doused water over his face, then shook himself dry like a wet animal. He untied his huge pooch and strode down the hallway, his boots ringing on the naked floorboards. Was he really going to walk away, without grabbing me to say it was all some terrible mistake and could we try again? I rushed after him to the door.

'Hey!' I called out, his touch still reverberating in my body. He turned, looking pale under the frugal street lighting. 'Be honest, it's because you fancy my sister, isn't it?' I said, flippantly.

A gust of wintery wind blew my words back at me. I'd meant it as a kind of in-joke, but after urging the big dog to leap up into the passenger seat, he climbed into the van after her, speared the key into the lock, revved the engine and took off.

Oh God. What had Johnny done to me? I was ruined, broken. It wasn't just Maisie who needed to 'unlearn' some behaviours. Anger welled up, an anger bitter enough to taste. I felt a deep and desperate hunger for revenge. I was ravenous. Delirious. Greedy with it. London lay before me, a giant pincushion of lights. The city paused to stare, turned its back and didn't care.

THIRTY-FOUR

Sisters are supposed to act like tugs – letting each other know when you're off course then steering you in the right direction; that's what I told myself all the way to Verity's house in an Uber.

As I arrived uninvited at her door, Verity presumed I'd come to discuss our mother's impending marriage and career implosion, so immediately ushered me into the living room. I sat facing her on the sofa and placed my booby-trapped device of a phone on a coffee table artfully scattered with glossy style magazines and expensive art books. The martini buzz was wearing off. My tongue felt swollen in my mouth; my throat taut and dry. But I knew what I had to do. I picked up my phone, turned it towards her and pressed play. Verity looked at the screen with disorientated incredulity. Mesmerised, she just sat, gawping at the awful video. The moment felt frozen in time: Verity staring fixedly at the images in dismayed disgust, her mouth stretched open in horror.

Time split open and I could see myself exactly in her situation. Your man cheating on you affords all the joys of getting your arm caught in the food disposal unit, only it's much more disabling. After all, you'd eagerly give an arm and a leg to get back your peace of mind. You might as well be wearing a sign on your heart which reads 'In case of Emergency, Break'.

When the video finished, my sister gasped, shock gushing in like the sea pouring into a shipwrecked hull. A convulsive start shook her frame, from highlights to high heels. Her mouth was working wordlessly. Her jaw just kept flapping open and shut like a malfunctioning ventriloquist's dummy. She finally spat out some words. 'I feel sick to my stomach.' Then she gagged.

Clearly it was something she ate – as in, my wedding cake. I thought back to when Johnny left me. I'd always presumed that an unhappy marriage would creep up on you, like bad underwear. I thought you'd feel the love fading away, like the end of a pop song on the radio. But no. It had been a totally unexpected sucker punch. My body had immediately become a bumpy, sickening carnival ride. I vividly recalled once more the palpitations, sweats, nausea, hysterical laughter, uncontrollable sobbing, carpet-writhing, hand-wringing... And I could see that my sister was now boarding the same horrible roller-coaster. Did I feel a loin-flutter of schadenfreude? A soupçon of revenge? Nope. What I felt was unutterable sadness.

'Verity, I'm sorry. Just remember that love is curable in a way that, say, a close encounter with a great white shark is not. You will eventually get over him.' I left out the part that it had taken me five hard, horrible years, but hey.

Verity just sat, transfixed, staring at my phone. She put her lips through a series of rubbery contortions to hold back tears.

'While it's true that it once took me two years to get over

a bloke I'd never met – he was Jon Bon Jovi and I was pre-pubescent – I did recover,' I said, kindly, trying to take the sting out of it.

Her teeth started clicking like castanets. 'Where… where did… where did you get this?' Her voice was thick-lipped, juddering, broken.

'Off Johnny's phone. From his WhatsApp. Everything else he'd deleted. Apart from these most recent messages.'

I scrolled onto the incriminating missives, passing them to my sister to scan. 'Who? Who is s… s… she?' Verity stammered, thick-throated with repressed sobs.

'I don't know but she goes by the name of Minxy.' I handed her the bit of paper on which I'd scribbled the sender's number.

Verity's head moved in tight, quick, hard little shakes. She then stabbed the number into her phone. As expected, this 'Minxy's' phone was turned off.

'Start by making mental notes of all his misdemeanours then recite them like a mantra. Do this daily and I promise that you'll start to feel better. I also recommend you give up chocolate; you'll miss the chocolate so much, you won't miss him,' I suggested, feebly.

'You're enjoying this aren't you? Lobbing a grenade into my life.'

'No. I just thought you should know the truth.' It was one of the Sisterhood Rules: if her partner's gone straight from puberty to adultery, let her know he's cheating. 'Don't you want to know the truth?'

'The truth is that Johnny is the foundation of my happiness. And you've just kicked that out from under me.'

'Well, I certainly know what that feels like!'

There was a clatter of boots on the wooden stairs and Johnny appeared in the doorway, grinning cheekily, oozing regulation rock star come-to-bed brashness. 'Are you girls talkin' about me? Course you are. I mean, you're only human!'

A sombre-faced Verity stood up, turned the phone in his direction and pushed play. Johnny's head jerked back like a cobra surprised by a mirror.

'What the...? Where the... where the... hell did you get this?' His speech, usually so sure and strong, was muffled and hesitant, as if a hand was pressed over his mouth.

'Off your phone,' I said. 'Plus all those lovey-dovey messages too. Why don't you hand over your phone to your Significant Other so she can see for herself?'

He looked from my phone to me, to Verity and back again. He was reeling faster than a one-eyed man on a nudist beach. 'It's fake! Some kind of AI fakery crap.' He couldn't have been more on his toes if he was a principal dancer for the Bolshoi ballet. 'V, how can you honestly think that's really me in that video or that those messages are for real?' he stated, mulishly. 'I deserve a bloody apology.'

'Your birth certificate should be an apology letter – from the condom factory,' I replied, coldly.

'And how exactly did you allegedly get this mocked-up video off my phone?'

'I spiked your drink till you passed out, so I could get the evidence I needed to save my sister from your sordid shenanigans.'

'Wait. You spiked my drink?' Like a boxer, he rocked from one foot to another, almost stamping. 'Obviously that's when you put this doctored piece of shit and those other bullshit messages onto my phone. You're sick, do you know that, totally sick in the head.' He spat the words out, like poisonous darts from a blowpipe. 'You're settin' me up. Tryin' to destroy my relationship.' I saw something flash in his eyes... contempt. He put his seething, burgundy face up close to mine. 'It's some kind of warped revenge for me leavin' you.'

'I'm not mad because you left me. I'm mad because you're an asshole.'

I suddenly looked at him with fresh eyes. His ponytail sat on his head as though it had been taken hostage from a younger man. And surely he was dyeing it? I noted for the first time the flecks of grey at his temples.

He strutted around me now, stiff-legged, like a dog scenting a fight. 'You're in love with your anger. You're committed to it in sickness and in health, for as long as you can afford the shrink payments. No wonder you work such long hours and have no social life – you have a grudge to support!' He lit up a cigarette and puffed on it furiously.

Verity squeaked. That's the best way to describe it. A strangled squeak of outrage. I thought her anger was meant for him, not least for smoking inside, but she now turned on me. 'How could you do this to me?' Under fizzing brows, her stare was splenetic. 'First you sent me those anonymous messages, making me paranoid and anxious. And now you bring me this AI-generated video nonsense. You're a monster.'

Accusations were suddenly bouncing around me like hailstones on gravel. 'Wait? What? You actually believe that two-timing worm over me?'

The atmosphere became electrically charged as a

domestic storm blew up around us: thunder, lightning and a torrential downpour of tears – mostly mine.

The parentheses around my sister's mouth now set like clamps. 'Johnny would never hurt me.'

'That's right, babe. The trouble with you, Izzy,' he blew smoke in my face, 'is that you never got over being second best.'

I wanted to make a sardonic quip or let fly with some caustic Shakespearean quote. Instead, I just gawped like a goldfish. 'I did not tamper with his phone!' I finally said to my sister. 'That video is real. What you should be asking is who exactly is this Minxy?'

Johnny uttered a little hiss of amusement. 'Nobody believes your scaremongerin', Isabella.' Smugness was coming off him in waves.

My sister regarded me with slant-eyed hostility. I felt I'd entered a parallel universe. Johnny bared his teeth in a smile – the way a crocodile smiles. My loathing for him was so strong, I could taste its sour potency on my tongue.

'Clearly you need help, Isabella. This is bloody entrapment. It's libellous too. You've tried to frame me. Enough with your world-class hatin'... or there'll be consequences,' he said in his most sinister, smooth tones. There was a self-righteous note of certainty in his voice, tinged with menace. But the man held no power over me now.

'Wow. That's quite a feat, being able to lie out of both corners of your mouth at the same time... I'm only trying to protect my sister.'

'That would be a first!' Verity said, brusquely.

'How dare you try to destroy my beloved baby girl!' Johnny put a protective arm around Verity's shoulders.

'Johnny, show my sister out, will you?' I could hear hysteria bubbling beneath the surface of her words. 'And I think it best if you never darken our door again.'

'Oh, Verity! Switch on your misogyny monitor! He's playing you.'

'Out.' Johnny pointed to the door.

'You're such a wanker. Although, in fact, you're not even good at that. Otherwise why were you always asking me to do it for you?'

It was the equivalent of a kamikaze mission. I hit the ejector button before one or both of them decked me. It was teeming outside, but better to be lashed by the rain than my sister's tongue.

Well, I thought, climbing into an Uber ten minutes later, soggy and visibly shaking. That went well. Perhaps it was time I considered a career in hostage negotiation or international diplomacy. Drawing on my fine command of English, I put my head into my hands and groaned, 'Faaaarrkkk!'

THIRTY-FIVE

When I got home my daughter was rescuing a waffle from the jaws of the toaster while sipping a banana smoothie.

She hugged me. 'Want some?... Hey, you look a bit rough, Mum. Are you okay?'

'Oh fine... Just ignore the wavy line on the terminal by my bed as it fades to black.'

'Ohh-kayy.' She slathered her waffle in butter. 'What's happened?'

'Let's just say that I'm having a few days where fate seems to be holding a stick and I am the piñata.'

She passed her buttery waffle towards me. I waved it away. 'First, I had a fight with your dad ... That man is to women what myxomatosis is to rabbits.'

My daughter gave me a chastening look. Sensitive to the fact that the first rule of divorce is to never put down a child's father in front of them, no matter how big a bastard, I discreetly declined to point out that Johnny was clearly a founding member of Devil-Worshippers R Us – and moved on with alacrity.

'...And then I told my sister a few home truths... There were certain things I just had to say...'

'Have you ever thought of not saying things, Mum? I really think it's an option we should explore,' my daughter sighed, slicing open an avocado.

As I couldn't vent my ex-husband fury, I now veered towards my other big frustration. 'Plus I had words with your grandma. The life she's leading is ridiculous.'

Chrissie shrugged. 'I dunno, Mum. At least she is – having a life, I mean. Maybe you should start living too. It's better than being, well, just bitter.'

'Bitter?' I snapped. 'I'm not bloody bitter! Why do people keep saying that?!'

'Yeah… right… even though now you're bitter that I called you bitter.' My daughter's delicate face became a knot of opinion. 'Let Grandma live her life the way she wants. Why so judgey?'

'It's your inheritance she's wasting on that waster, Chrissie.'

My daughter sat down at the kitchen table among her scattered music scores. 'But Gran is so happy.' She started spooning avocado onto her waffle. 'I told her to go for it.'

'Maybe we should explore *you* not saying things! You really shouldn't encourage her, darling. She's quite bad enough already.'

'Gran told me that she wishes you'd take her as your inspiration… And you know what, Mum? I love you to bits and don't want to hurt your feelings, but I'd rather Gran as my role model than you right now.'

Her words stung me. 'I think you should put more faith in the life skills that I can teach you – like, never trusting a man. They're as slippery and treacherous as this.' I picked up the glove of banana peel she'd left on the table and tossed it into the compost bin. 'Get this gap year out of your system and then take up that music scholarship.'

'Oh, about that... I've decided to just concentrate on my band.'

I wheeled towards her. 'You certainly are not.'

My daughter stared at me with sullen intensity. 'Why not? At my age you were out in the world on your own.' She smashed the avocado into her waffle.

'Why does your generation have to smash everything? Avocados, potatoes, burgers, mothers' hopes and dreams... It's an epidemic of smashed things. Can't we just keep them whole?'

'Oh, like the way you keep our family together? You're the one who smashes everything, Mum.'

I shrank from her words as if they were blows. 'Oh, if only I were young enough to know everything,' I retorted, sarcastically.

'You know, the only reason old people blame everything on the younger generation is that there is only one other choice,' she lobbed back at me.

'One day you'll wish you listened to me about life, career, relationships...'

'Really? No offence but what do you know about relationships, as you never have any?' She pushed up from the table. 'So, honestly, why should I listen to you?'

'Well, why don't you listen to me occasionally and find out?'

My daughter gave me a flat, measuring look. 'You have to let people live their own lives and make their own mistakes... Just like you did.' She jammed her hands deep into her pockets. 'Stop living vicariously through me. Go get your own life!'

Chrissie gangled in the kitchen doorway, all legs and elbows, then turned for the front door.

'Where are you going?'

'Out.'

'Out where?'

'Just out.'

I checked my watch. It was 10 p.m. 'The only thing you can get into at this hour is trouble... Chrissie. Chrissie?'

The loose hall floorboard twanged and hummed and then fell silent as she banged out of the front door and down the steps. I looked out of the window to see her bare legs flashing like knife blades in the darkness as she jogged down the road. Then I saw her coat on the back of the chair. It was cold out. I grabbed it and ran after her. 'Chrissie! Chrissie?'

But she was gone. The stillness of the night felt as if an audience had quieted for a performance. I stood on the doorstep, arms raised, as though on a conductor's podium. Beneath the hush I could hear the rustle of small animals, the snap of a twig. The moon swam palely in the inky sky. I hit Chrissie's number on speed dial but she didn't answer. I was tempted to try again but stopped myself. My darling daughter was right – at her age I was out in the world on my own. I had to cut the psychological umbilical cord.

Back inside, I picked up my guitar and took comfort from Bach's perfect musical phrasing. I played through five of my favourite preludes and gradually calmed down enough to then improvise my way over a few jazz standards.

On the way to bed I passed my daughter's room and saw the cuddly toys, beanie babies and stuffed unicorns on the shelves and couldn't resist trying her mobile once more. When there was still no answer I texted a few of her friends – no, nobody had seen her, which meant that she must be with my mother. I rang Mum – no answer. I even tried Johnny – no response. Ditto Verity. I was clearly persona non grata.

Just when I was starting to worry, my daughter texted to say she was fine and to stop calling. That was it, that was all. Ignoring her entreaty, I rang back but her phone was now switched off. I suddenly felt weirdly homesick. But for what? I'd clearly been exiled. Well, self-exiled, which is the cruellest of aches. Okay, I rationalised, I might have a mild case of social frostbite, but I wasn't quite ready to utter my Captain Oats-esque 'I may be some time' wandering-off-into-the-wilderness speech. Yes, at the moment my family was making Macbeth look like Winnie-the-Pooh, but by the calm light of morning, they'd all realise that I was right. And that I'd done the right thing telling my sister about Johnny's sexual kleptomania. Then all would be well again.

THIRTY-SIX

Morning came, rapid and stark, like a hangover. The aftershock of the previous day's revelations reverberated through me like a tuning fork. I needed to restore some harmony. First off, I sent a text to the Derry Man.

> My shoes were drunk, not me, and they clearly led me astray... Sorry for my libido attack and whatever stupid stuff I said. I'm considering an emergency operation to have my voice box removed.

I could see from the green tick that he'd read the text, but reply came there none.

When I walked downstairs for coffee and realised that Chrissie hadn't come home, I didn't panic; she had her own room at my mum's place and always kept clothes, books and toiletries there. But I felt bad about our spat and sent her a voicemail.

'Being a mother requires the combined skills of a magician, chef, tightrope walker, psychologist, bouncer and entertainments officer on a cruise ship... Sometimes we get it wrong. I'm sorry, darling. Let's talk. Love you so much. Call me.'

Next I tried my own mother's phone. Zip. Then Verity's – zilch. I even tried Johnny's phone again – nada. Still, the whole shunning experience was proving quite educational; at least I now knew what it must have felt like to be a leper during the Dark Ages. After mainlining a macchiato or two, I drove to Mum's house, only to find it all closed up... I then motored over to Verity's place in Primrose Hill, but that too was silent and shuttered. I rang Melissa to confer, but she also declined to pick up. I called her office but it was only 7 a.m. and nobody was in yet. After sourcing Mel's address in my phone emails, I turned my wheezing jalopy towards the grittier end of fashionable east London.

The city lay before me on the right, impassive, hardboiled, stark, durable. The layers of London history, with its great sooty sweep of twisting, Dickensian laneways as dark as a debtors' prison, its murky Jack the Ripper backstreets, ancient Roman roads, Elizabethan cobbled courtyards, and post-war, grim, grimy prefab tower blocks, restored a sense of proportion. Watching the passing parade of pedestrians and finding narratives and mysteries and melodramas in every face, the magnitude of my own drama dwindled.

Houses began to tread on each other's heels as the satnav directed me further east. Impatient to get there, I found it infuriatingly difficult to stick to the erratic speed limits: twenty for one block, thirty for the next, forty for the stretch after that, then oh back to twenty again. I selected some slow and smoky Miles Davis on Spotify to help keep my foot off the accelerator until I finally pulled up outside a sweet Georgian terrace in a cobbled cul-de-sac in Dalston. I pressed the bell and was relieved when a bright sounding voice shouted 'Coming!' and the front door swung wide.

It wasn't Mel who greeted me but a young woman with iridescent green eyeshadow. She introduced herself as an oboist called Faduma who was also Melissa's cat minder. When I explained who I was, she ushered me in out of the cold wind. It quickly transpired that Mel had left for the airport to fly to Northern Ireland earlier that morning.

I checked my phone diary. The alpine horn concert. Oh God. And the wedding! Caught up in my own psychodrama, I'd forgotten all about both and, as my family was currently not talking to me, hadn't been included in any plans. Chrissie must have gone to Mum's place last night and then on to Northern Ireland with her this morning. As I stabbed at their phone numbers once more, Mel's cat shimmied under the sill, announcing her arrival with a noise that sounded like a rusty hinge. While Faduma went to the kitchen to make tea, the cat performed a little gavotte around my legs.

I caught sight of my wild, windswept hair in the mirror above the mantelpiece and reached into my pocket for a hair tie. My fingers were so numb with cold that I dropped it. The cat picked it up in its mouth and shimmied off into the nearest room. I'm not a pet person but had a strong suspicion that a swallowed elasticated furry hair tie might not be ideal, nutrition-wise, for a frisky feline. When I gave chase into what was clearly Melissa's bedroom, my heart stopped with a queer jerk. The surface of my skin tingled, registering a threat. Something was not right. In fact, from the way my hair follicles prickled, I knew that something very, very wrong had happened here.

I took in the rococo furniture and brocade wallpaper, the ornately carved bedhead and, wait... I'd seen this room before. I touched the linen – noting the fine thread count. I'd seen this linen before too.

I stood, rooted in disbelief, my mind rejecting what my brain so clearly deciphered. As I took in the carved bedhead inlaid with mock gold leaf depicting ornate asymmetrical designs and elaborate carvings, gildings and motifs of shells and floral patterns, the room pitched around me like a rolling ship. I felt a vertiginous sensation and lost my equilibrium. The floor undulated once more but when I finally forced the furniture and walls to stop moving, it was to see the snow globe knick-knacks I'd gawped at on Johnny's adulterous video. I instinctively threw back the bed covers and scanned the sheets for sperm stains, like an R-rated Miss Marple.

Right then, it seemed to me that the worst words in the English language, besides 'we need to discuss your test results', must be 'Melissa, what the hell are my sister's boyfriend's boxer shorts doing at the bottom of your bed?'

I retrieved the designer underwear – Sea Island cotton Turnbull and Asser – with pincered fingers and dropped them into my bag. At about a hundred quid per pant, only my sister would indulge a man so.

Johnny was having an affair with Melissa? My mother's manager? The woman who hashtags every Insta post with #pride and #lesbianvisibility?

I felt like an air traffic controller, I had so much incoming. It was total discombobulation; reminiscent of the first time I ever saw advanced algebra.

And then Faduma was in the living room calling, 'Minxy! Minxy! Here, kitty.' The cat shimmied back out to the kitchen for a feed.

Minxy? I felt as though I'd been spun around in a tornado and deposited in a place beyond my understanding. Beyond logic. Minxy was the pseudonym of the woman who'd been sending Johnny their sordid sex videos. Johnny and Melissa? The absurdity of the notion struck me and I doubled up in a paroxysm of nervous mirth, as unexpected as it was alarming. And then, just as suddenly, my mind became miraculously clear.

I started to rummage through Melissa's bedroom drawers, tossing aside clothes, books, make-up... And there, buried in the bottom drawer, behind the socks, I found them. Two burner phones. I looked up Melissa's birthday on Facebook and took a stab at a combination of the numbers until hitting on her phone code. Bingo. One phone was full of videos and text messages to Johnny. The other? The anonymous messages sent to Verity revealing her husband's infidelity. But why? It could only be to break them up. For what purpose? Was she really in love with that sly, rascally rocker? At that moment it would have been easier for me to spontaneously grasp quantum string theory. In fact, if I'd been a nuclear reactor, I'd have been going into meltdown.

Melissa? I had totally underestimated my mother's manager. She wasn't a candle-sniffing, aura-cleansing, validation mantra-making millennial after all. No. She was a piranha in a paddling pool.

'Tea?' Faduma, now cradling the Persian cat, poked her head around the bedroom door.

'Ah, no thanks. Sorry. I was just looking for my hair tie. The cat ran in here with it.' I tried to say more but my lips seemed suddenly full of Novocain. I couldn't stand to be in this place much longer otherwise I might burst inward, like those deep-sea mini submarines which can't take the pressure and implode. My thoughts were so slow, as if being piped down to me from the mother ship above, like dribbles of oxygen.

I made my mumbled apologies, surreptitiously stuffed the burner phones and a snow globe into my bag, then slammed out of the house. When the door thunked shut behind me, I leant against it as though a pack of werewolves was after me.

Next stop – Derry.

THIRTY-SEVEN

The Irish Sea, lying flat as sheet metal far below, soon gave way to billiard-table green fields scrawled with sinuous silver rivers. The sun was sparkling but the words I knew I had to utter felt heavy and sour within me.

The first thing after touchdown was to check my phone – still no word from the Derry Man; nor anyone else for that matter. As the plane taxied to the stand, I texted him once more to apologise. 'Please forgive my meltdown...Obviously I'm typing this on my padded cell phone.' Still nothing. Walking through Derry airport, I noted that the lounge was named after Amelia Earhart, which didn't exactly do much to alleviate my feeling of gloom and doom.

I caught a cab into the historic city of Derry and alighted at the ornate and stately Guildhall. Pushing inside the big wooden doors in search of my family, I accosted an anxious-looking young woman with a clipboard, who informed me that my mother was on stage rehearsing with the orchestra and Gawain, the alpine horn soloist; while her agent, Melissa, was backstage 'with some fella'.

I gave a half-hearted wave to Gawain in response to his exuberant cry from the wings of 'Your mother is a goddess!', then went to hunt down the duplicitous agent. With any luck I'd catch her in the sweaty clutches of my sister's cheating husband. The red sandstone, neo-Gothic building, with its elegant stained glass and impressive clock tower, presented so grandly to the world, but backstage boasted the usual glamour of a patterned nylon carpet pockmarked by cigarette burns, a fridge which hummed too loudly, an emphysemic radiator... oh, and a couple having loud sex in a tiny room. From behind a dressing-room door came the intimate murmur of endearments and lurid moans of pleasure.

I moved slowly forward as if drawn by the inexorable pull of a thread, dreading but also needing to see Johnny and Melissa together. Throwing open the door, I surveyed the scene before me with astonished eyes: my sister's legs wrapped around my ex-husband's waist, his face buried between her breasts. Oh God. How many years of therapy would I need to get over this? I wanted to wrench out my retinas right there and then and rinse them in disinfectant.

There was a dervish thrashing of arms and legs as they scrambled their clothes back into place.

'Oh Christ, not you again. The drink spiker and phone hacker!' Johnny spoke in a weary sing-song. 'What poison have you come to spread this time? Not that any of it will work. Verity and me, well we're gettin' on better than ever,' he bragged, with an acidic chuckle.

'That's right. Your lies and manoeuvrings and evil manipulations have only succeeded in bringing us closer.' My sister's words left her mouth like bullets.

'Verity... I need to tell you something...' I reached out a hand to touch her shoulder but she drew back from me as if I were radioactive. If only I had an emotional airbag to cushion the blow. 'I know who sent you those anonymous messages.'

'Oh, for Chrissake. Not this bullshit again.' Johnny poured himself a slug of Irish whiskey from a bottle on the table. My eyes locked on to the tail of a snake that writhed across the back of his shirt.

'Recognise this?' I pulled the purloined snow globe from my bag and held it aloft.

'Can you just cut the psycho crap? You'll be boilin' bunnies next.' He turned and the head of the snake moved towards me, threateningly.

My sister sucked in her lips, then sprayed out her words as if from a submachine gun. 'Johnny's right. I think the time has come for you to get professional help, Isabella.'

'Do you recognise this snow globe, Verity? From the sex video Johnny said I fabricated? Well, guess where I got it from? The very same bedroom featured in your little porno film, Johnny. Oh, and look what I found in the bed?' I threw the Sea Island cotton, Turnbull and Asser boxer shorts at his head. 'I believe these are yours. A gift from your very generous Significant Other, no doubt. So, are you going to tell Verity whose bed I found them in, or am I?'

Johnny cradled his whiskey glass and drank from it morosely and without pleasure. He then took a slow look at me, as if memorising my features so he could identify me in the morgue.

'And here's the burner phone used to send those anonymous messages to you, V.' I extracted it from my bag. 'Which I also found in the same bedroom.'

'What?' Johnny's eyes glinted, hard as metal. I saw the pallor of his face fade to a whiter shade of pale – his favourite Procol Harum song. I'd caught him off guard. Clearly Johnny had no idea that the anonymous messages alerting Verity to his cheating were being sent by his very own mistress.

His nostrils flared – an expression I'd heard many times but had never actually seen come to life before. Johnny then travelled towards me as if on cross-country skis. Making gigantic strides, his hand shot out like a tentacle to snatch the burner phone.

I lashed out with my free hand, scratching his arm, and he reared back.

'Minxy – the name of the woman who sent Johnny those videos of them fucking – is Melissa.'

My sister took a moment, then guffawed. 'Melissa?! It clearly is time for a straitjacket, Isabella!'

I understood her shock. This infidelity drama had all the hallmarks of a five-star blockbuster – betrayal, dramatic family break-ups in the rain, messages from an anonymous informer, incriminating naked sex videos with a mystery woman, denials, accusations, a totally unexpected adulteress... I could have sold it to Netflix. It took me a while to realise that the continuous death rattle I could hear wasn't my sister's life disintegrating, but the ancient radiator.

'There's photos of Johnny on here kissing Melissa, too.' I turned the other phone towards Verity, scrolling through a sordid selfie selection of Johnny and Melissa with their lips locked.

The vein on Johnny's temple was throbbing like an amplifier at an Ibiza disco. 'AI fakery. AI fakery,' he kept repeating like a Dalek. 'I have never kissed Melissa!'

'Oh, really? What are you doing then?' I pointed to a particularly passionate snog. 'Flossing her teeth with your tongue?'

'AI fakery. AI fakery,' the Dalek droned, his muscley arm now striated with bleeding claw marks.

'If it's a fake then how did I film myself in Melissa's bedroom?' I flashed the phone footage I'd taken the day before of me in situ. 'You can see her clothes and framed photos... Christ, there's even a photo of our mother conducting the New York Phil. When none of you would answer my phone calls, I drove to Melissa's place in Dalston...'

Verity looked up at me then. 'Dalston?'

'Yes.'

She glared at her partner. 'You've had so many parking tickets in Dalston.' Her face had gone the colour of fog.

'I chased Melissa's cat, called, coincidentally, Minxy, into her bedroom. That's when I realised it was the same room as the one featured on the sex video. So, I ransacked her drawers and found the burner phones, one with all the anonymous messages telling you that your beloved Johnny was having an affair... and the other full of details of their rendezvous and videos of their liaisons.'

The room held its breath. We stood facing each other, silent as tombstones. I threw open the big wooden shutters on the window and the room was suddenly seared with light. The adulterer squinted like a card shark stage villain. 'Why don't you try telling the truth, Johnny? I know it's a novelty, but you're never too old to grow up.'

My sister looked up at him with wide, dismayed eyes. 'What's going on, Jonathan?'

Anyone who thinks the art of conversation is dead just needs to accuse her partner of having an affair. Denials began to pour out of him. It was the best acting I'd seen outside of the Oscars night when the camera zooms in on the runners-up.

Verity, meanwhile, began rocking back and forth, like a Sufi in a trance. I handed her the burner phones. Studying the incriminating evidence, she began to gasp for air, like a cat coughing up a furball.

Johnny's remonstrations became more like one of those wartime broadcasts, fading in and out. Fear began to ooze from my ex-husband in globs of rancid sweat.

As she scrolled on through the photos and messages Verity's mouth became loose and her eyes unfocused. As she started to cry something cracked open in her and I could see straight through to her broken heart. My twin dropped all attitude and metamorphosed back into the girl I had grown up with, shared a bedroom with and loved with all my being.

I recognised her grief too, that inner homelessness, of no longer belonging, her foundations smashed. I knew exactly how she ached, body and soul. My own betrayal lost some of its tragic grandeur, suddenly. Turned out it was just like any other run-of-the-mill bit of ratbag male behaviour. Johnny had ruptured both our lives and destroyed us equally.

My perfect sister was now merely a limp and yawling ball of snot.

I'd expected this to be a vindicatory moment but, much to my surprise, compassion flowed through me. I felt the weight of a fleeting melancholy tinged with pity. I extended my hand across the gulf which separated us. She looked at it for a moment – then grasped it, hard.

'It's over, Verity. It was nothin' more than a one-night stand. A piss in the dark,' he said in the flat, lifeless voice of a man who can see that the writing on the wall probably includes his name.

Verity started reading out loud the dates on the incriminating videos and photos, which stretched out over a six-month period – including the selfie snaps of them hugging and kissing at the country hotel in Blenheim, the very night he was supposed to be checking out a venue gig in Brighton. She was crying without any noise now, just shuddering.

'It meant nothin'. I broke it off with her.' Johnny then lapsed almost parodically into the rote, textbook Cheating Lover routine. It was a midlife crisis. A lapse. She threw herself at him. The woman's mad... Clichés oozed out of him.

'Melissa's like one of those alligators on the bank of a river, ready to strike...'

'So you're the innocent prey?' I snorted, derisively. 'Poor you.'

'I tried to break it off. Many times. But she threatened to tell you, Verity. And I couldn't stand to hurt you.'

'That makes no sense,' I interrupted. 'Melissa takes a percentage of our mother's earnings. She wouldn't jeopardise her livelihood. No, she wanted Verity to throw you out of her own accord, so she could then pretend to pick you up on the rebound. That's why she sent the anonymous messages. To hurry things along. It's all there on the phone. You telling her how much you love her. That you want a life together... Read on, Verity. The truth is, Johnny, you're the top-order predator.'

THE SISTERHOOD RULES

Johnny smiled, but his eyes were dancing on hot coals, darting and flinching. 'You know how much I love you, V. You're the only woman for me... Melissa seduced me... She got me drunk and took advantage of me... It's shitty behaviour, I know. But you always say I'm a musical genius, and it's well known that all geniuses are bastards at times. Look at Elvis Presley... Picasso... Einstein... Chairman Mao...'

'Genius?! Oh, gimme a break!' I laughed. 'Your ego is so big it casts its own shadow. Oh gosh! That's what's blocking out the sun!'

My sister stopped scrolling through the evidence and threw both phones at him. 'Jonathan.' Her quiet lucidity startled him. 'How many other women have there been?'

'None! Like I said, it was just a midlife crisis. It meant nothin'. We can work it out!' His voice was jittery with dread.

Love blurs your vision, but after it recedes, you can see more clearly than ever. Once more I felt as though the tide had gone out, revealing broken bottles, rusty shopping trolleys, punctured car tyres... We both looked at him now and saw the man for what he was – weak and gutted, a netted eel. But I was not washed off the rocks and drowned out at sea. And nor was my sister.

'I want you out of my house by tomorrow.' Verity's eyes were pink and watery, like a laboratory rabbit's. 'Get your things and get out.'

'But... but you're the love of my life. In fact, in the last few days, I've fallen more in love with you than ever.' He moved towards her but I intercepted, standing between them, feet planted, arms crossed.

'A gazillion sperm sprinting for the finishing line and you got there first? Mind-boggling. The others must have been disqualified for doping.'

'You bitch.' I could feel a spray of his saliva on my face. His voice then became querulous in complaint. 'Look, everythin' happens for a reason, right? Sometimes it just got too much, you know? Havin' to be perfect! No shoes inside! No nail clippin's by the bed! No drinks without a coaster...'

Oh yes. Misdemeanours on a par with Pol Pot. I wanted to kill him then. All I needed were a few short-range missiles.

'It's not all my fault!' Johnny did a little light clutching at straws. 'I mean, those anonymous messages – you can see how twisted she is! The woman's mad. She's clearly entrapped me!'

Yes, Melissa was Iago in high heels and a diamanté thong. But she wasn't the guiltiest party. And my sister knew this too. To my surprise, she was now remarkably calm and cool. 'My mother's friend Helen left bits of her body to medical science when she died. I hope you'll donate your heart, Johnny, as it's clearly never been used.'

I seconded the emotion. 'You know what, Johnny? I hope you end up rotting in a prison dungeon overcrowded with sex maniac psychopaths. Ones especially chosen for their syphilitic ulcers, open sores and explosive dysentery... But otherwise, I wish you well.' I threw his coat at him. 'Just get out.'

'At least my daughter loves me. I'm takin' her jammin' at one of the pubs on Waterloo Street later... She's checkin' the joints out right now to find her favourite. And we'll be on the road together all the time now she's givin' up her scholarship.' He hunched into his leather jacket.

'Where is Chrissie?' I asked, urgently.

Verity suddenly sobered. 'She's with Melissa... Who left in a huff. A huff I couldn't work out, till now.'

Seeing Johnny making up with Verity must have been a terrible kick in the guts. But what kind of revenge was she planning? I spasmed with fear. Sending anonymous messages to her lover's partner in the pathetic hope she'd chuck him out was a clear sign that the woman was unhinged. Not in a gun-toting, school-shooting way, but possibly in an 'oops, I accidentally pushed my bastard boyfriend's daughter into the River Foyle' kind of way.

I suddenly felt as though I was back riding on that whirl-'n'-puke roller-coaster – and had forgotten to strap in. This was definitely the day that just kept on giving. And I had no doubt that there was more in store.

THIRTY-EIGHT

When feeling the need to drown your sorrows the best thing about the island of Ireland is that it's always beer o'clock. My sister and I stuck our heads into at least ten pubs on Waterloo Street – the Harp, Peadar O'Donnell's, Bound for Boston, the Rocking Chair, the Gweedore – all serving up lashings of traditional Irish music and velvety Guinness, before we finally found my darling daughter.

Heart jackhammering in my chest, I clickety-clacked over the cobblestones pumiced smooth by generations of footsteps, down into a dimly lit watering hole that was noisy with the roar of laughter and tapping of toes. I took in the cosy snugs, flagstone floors, wood-panelled walls, scratched stools and bar cluttered with bodhrans and squeeze boxes and other musical paraphernalia. And there she was, near the crackling turf hearth, playing an energetic slip jig on a borrowed guitar, surrounded by an assortment of grizzled old musos on tin whistles and Irish harps. But the main soundtrack was one of conspiratorial chuckles accompanied by a chorus of 'one for the road's. There were eager, young musicians playing along too on fiddles and guitars. They clearly took the trad music as seriously as the pints, shushing anyone who yabbered on too loudly during a heartfelt song.

Noting the proper order, proper pints and pure local charm on tap, I waited for a pause in the music, then flitted over to hug my daughter. 'Chrissie... I'm so sorry we fought. And you're right. I need to let you go your own way in life.'

She beamed. 'No, I'm sorry, Mum. I shouldn't have disappeared like that.'

'I can let you go your own way as long as you answer your bloody phone so I know where your own way has taken you... and whether or not I need to post bail.'

'Forgot my charger. Sorry.'

I glanced around at her new, young friends and realised that they all declined their stereotype by not displaying a single mobile phone between them.

Chatter thrummed and trilled around me, all those lovely lilting Irish accents sweeping up and down. Between songs, there was a symphony of talk, a performance of anecdotes, folklore, quips, gossip, leg-pulling, tale-telling and teasing, all flowing as easily as the beer.

A gnarly old bloke who made Jason Statham look wimpy offered me his seat.

'Oh thanks but I'm fine... So random musos just meet up here to play whenever the mood takes them?' I asked him, enchanted.

'Northern Ireland is a place where the inevitable never happens, but the unexpected often occurs.' He winked. 'Grateful customers usually pay us in pints, mind.'

'Oh right! Of course. What would you like? A Guinness, no doubt?' I fished into my bag for my credit card.

'Aye, a pint of the black stuff. It's Irish penicillin.' He drained the creamy dregs of his previous pint and licked his lips. 'I, for one, could get an entry in the Record Book of Guinness.'

One eye was oystered up with a recent bruise. There was bark off his nose. And the hair on his head resembled a bit of roadkill that had been dead for some time. But his twinkle was irresistible.

'I'll get the drinks, Mum.' Chrissie smiled, slipping the credit card from my fingers.

'You're an excellent fiddle player,' I said to the man.

He shrugged. 'Musical talent is what's left over from your ancestors after their land has been seized,' he said, before getting caught up in the craic with his chums.

I checked my watch. Now that I'd ascertained my daughter was safe, it was time to confront Melissa. 'Where's Mel?' I asked when Chrissie returned with the drinks.

'Said she had to pick up a few things at the pharmacy. No doubt Valium, to get her through the concert! But I think it's going to be great. Gran wouldn't be doing it otherwise. Speaking of which... Listen up.' She clapped her hands to get the attention of the assorted locals. 'My grandma's conducting at the Guildhall tonight. Nicole Nightingale. Maybe you've heard of her? She's debuting an alpine horn concerto. And she's awesome. You should all come along.'

This prompted a brief, bemused raising of eyebrows and a flurry of jokes.

'What's the definition of perfect pitch? When you throw an alpine horn in the bin and it lands on an accordion,' one old-timer said.

'Aye, and what's the difference between an alpine horn and an onion? No one cries when you cut up an alpine horn.'

More Guinness arrived, sent by some grateful American tourists beguiled by the soulful ambience. And then all banter subsided in reverence to a mournful ballad taking root among the musicians.

'I'll see you there later,' Chrissie mouthed to me, picking up a spare guitar and joining in with expert ease. I kissed the top of her head. She was luminous with happiness and totally in her element.

My sister was waiting by the pub door with all the patience of a grenade with the pin pulled out. She seized my arm and marched me back onto the cobbled lane to confront her nemesis.

Above us, seabirds wailed like cats. Up on Derry's historic walls, kids' kites were being torn to shreds by the boiling winds. But a bigger tempest was brewing. When we spotted Melissa, she was coming out of the pharmacy, her blonde hair blown out into an extravagant bouffant. It puffed up around her head like a cobra's hood.

'Oh hi!' Her voice was light and falsely cheery, like a breakfast TV weather girl. She smiled, showing perfect teeth between coral-coloured lips.

When I handed back her snow globe, shock flowed down her face from her widened eyes to an O-shaped mouth. 'Where did you get that? I have one just like it. It's actually a collector's item.' Her laugh vibrated on a high, metallic note.

'I thought you were a committed vegetarian, Mel?' I said to her, tightly. 'But it turns out you're a carnivorous man-eater.'

'So much for your model dairy farm based on ancient Indian Vedic principles of doing no harm,' Verity added, savagely.

'Exactly. I think it's safe to say that your whole milk-of-human-kindness trope has kinda curdled.'

My sister opened her phone, then read aloud from the anonymous messages she'd been sent revealing Johnny's affair. '"*The woman looked in her mid-twenties, slim, well dressed...*" You're not slim, well dressed or attractive, you narcissist. Nor are you in your mid-fucking-twenties!'

'I found both burner phones, by the way. In your sock drawer.' I extracted them from my handbag to wave in Melissa's face.

'All that woo-woo manifesting, affirmation candle crap,' Verity spat. 'I didn't realise what you were manifesting was my man!'

'And my ex... Ownership's debatable,' I muttered. 'Although neither of us wants him now.'

Melissa looked stricken for a moment, then her face hardened. 'Okay. Well. The truth is, Johnny's been lying to you. He's probably still lying to you. I sent the anonymous messages to bring the affair to a head. I felt sure you'd throw him out, Verity.'

I recalled then her exact advice when we'd confided in her about the alleged affair. Treat him like toxic waste – dump him. 'What?' I asked, appalled. 'So that you could scoop him up on the rebound?'

'You're so famously uncompromising, Verity. I felt sure that once you knew the truth you'd kick Johnny to the kerb... And soon after, I could simply take up with him. If you hadn't broken into my home, nobody would ever have known exactly when our affair began. And nobody would get hurt.'

The woman was taking so many flights of fancy she really should contact air traffic control to lodge flight plans.

'I didn't want to lose Nicole as a client, but of course, now she's thrown her career away, it no longer matters.'

'But you don't like men!' my sister exclaimed, confounded. 'You always say they're only good for mowing the lawn and filling in tax forms and that capable lesbians can do that for yourselves.'

'Yes, but I can't make a baby on my own, can I?'

My sister and I opened our mouths in pantomime astonishment.

'I mean, Johnny's handsome, talented, sexy... I'm actually non-binary as you know... Plus he's a proven great baby-maker. I mean, look at Chrissie... And who wouldn't want Chrissie as a big sister?'

My own sister began to make a whimpering, squeaking noise, like a stuck drawer. Verity had always been perfect in every way; she was the Swiss watch of women – but she seemed to have stopped ticking and her springs, wheels, cogs and coils were exploding in all directions: *boing!*

Drawing on my fine command of English, I then said eloquently, 'What the fuck?'

Melissa patted the paper bag in her hand. 'I have the pregnancy testing kit right here.'

Verity and I reeled to face each other with the exact precision of the synchronised swimming teams we'd mimicked in the Bondi Icebergs pool, as kids.

'But you said you never wanted children.' Verity's voice was small and shell-shocked.

I thought back to Melissa's visualisation board, full of images of all the things she wanted to manifest – a British classical music award, a holiday home in the south of France, four Persian cats, a red sports car, a penthouse on the river, a baby... 'You said your clients are your babies.'

She shrugged. 'They were. Well, still are. But this other craving just kicked in. I resisted it at first. I loathe the sexist discourse around child-free women. We're either pathetic sad sacks... Or selfish bitches... Or murderous psychopaths like Miss Havisham, Miss Trunchbull or Cruella de Vil... But then my ovaries just started throbbing... And Johnny told me your sex life was over long ago, Verity... And the man has such appetites...' Her smile was as sharp and sweet as icing. It set my teeth on edge.

My sister gave Melissa a narrow look of contempt. 'I did wonder why he'd doubled his Viagra order. Viagra I pay for, by the way.'

Melissa gave Verity a sympathetic look, like a nurse about to switch off the life support machine. 'Johnny doesn't need any little blue pills when he's with me.' She smiled beatifically, like the Madonna in a kid's biblical colouring book. 'Love is the ultimate aphrodisiac. Oh, the love songs he composes for me... The poetry of his letters! I'm his grand passion, he says... I'm sorry you had to find out this way. And no, as a feminist, I'm not proud of my behaviour.' Melissa's round, creamy breasts, nestled in low-cut, pale-pink silky ruffles, resembled some exotic fruit in a posh upmarket food hall. They heaved now with emotion. 'But the heart wants what the heart wants. That's what Johnny says.'

'Yeah well, I think it's actually another part of his anatomy speaking there,' I muttered.

Verity let out a groan of shock and pain. 'That's... that's... precisely what he said to me. And all those songs and poems... he love-bombed me in exactly the same way. It's how he won my heart.'

Melissa shrugged. She seemed to be made of marble and yet I was the one who felt cold suddenly. My body clenched and something icy rippled up my spine. All those years I'd avoided my sister as though she were an infectious disease, when all the time Johnny was the contaminator. He'd made me believe that Verity seduced him. But he'd clearly beguiled her – the way a hook beguiles the gills of a fish.

Melissa checked her watch. 'Enough. We mustn't be late. My client is about to conduct the world premiere of an alpine horn concerto! God help us.'

'You don't honestly think Mum will keep you on as her agent when she finds out how you've stabbed her daughter in the back... and the front... and the sides?' I asked, astounded.

'We just signed a new five-year contract.' And with that she strode off down the hill towards the Guildhall, her denim bell-bottoms flapping arrogantly in the breeze. I willed one of the billowing flares to wrap around the other ankle and bring her crashing to the ground, so we could leave her there, marooned and writhing on the pavement like some kind of demented, denim mermaid.

What the hell was happening? Were we actually in some grisly reality TV show? Was one of us about to be voted off? And if so, who?

As Verity and I followed after Melissa, I had the distinct impression that we were about to jump over a yawning chasm – but in two leaps.

THIRTY-NINE

Derry is famous for its political murals. You'll find Bernadette Devlin, the Hunger Strikers and Father Edward Daly depicted in the nationalist Bogside area; and then in the unionist Fountain enclave, the Apprentice Boys, Union Jacks and King William. But as we traipsed in shocked silence down to the Guildhall, I saw signs, literally, that the troubled past, although not forgotten, was being left behind; mostly evidenced by the newest mural to grace the city walls – a colourful portrayal of the Derry Girls, in all their cheeky charm.

But there was no sign of peace in our fraught procession. Smoke spurting in grey burps from passing taxi exhaust pipes added to the leaden atmosphere. The weather had grown as melodramatic as our lives, with gusts of wind whipping up and down the street and grey clouds gathering.

When we entered the backstage area, the musicians were spilling out into the square for a fag or a quick bite. Our mother had popped out to the pub for a fortifying fry-up, we were told. Melissa moved against the human tide, working her elbows like oars, then disappeared into the toilets, clutching her paper bag.

Verity and I walked in a zombie trance to the green room. My punch-drunk sister slumped onto a wonky couch and gazed at the eczema-ridden walls beneath a bare light bulb. Wasn't this what I'd always wanted? For her to feel the pain she'd put me through five years ago? And yet, I didn't feel any sense of triumph; nor the urge for a little light gloating. All I felt was sympathy. I handed her a plastic goblet of cheap wine, which she sculled.

Johnny poked his head around the door and smiled coyly. 'Okay, I'm a worm... but a glow-worm, surely,' he simpered, his big, brown puppy dog eyes set to Cute. 'That woman pursued me. And then, one drunken night, well, I succumbed... That was my first stupid mistake. Then she threatened to tell you everythin' unless I kept on seein' her...' Johnny began to speak faster, like a skater on thinning ice, accelerating to save himself from drowning. 'I couldn't see a way out. It was blackmail. I had no choice but to play along!'

'Oh no, there's always a choice, Johnny,' I interrupted. 'You've always got a choice whether or not to be a complete and utter twat.'

'I'll break it off right now. That woman just got inside my head. You can see how manipulative she is! Sending those anonymous text messages to you. I mean, how bloody underhanded is that! Melissa just entrapped me... I was clearly out of my depth... I need help. I'll go for therapy... Or on a sex addict course... I can change. I promise.'

I rolled my eyes. It was classic behaviour of a bloke who's been caught: promising to go on some sort of redemption arc and get therapy so as to recast himself as a good person. But Johnny would need to be reincarnated, after a Hindu funeral pyre ritual, to achieve that level of transformation.

Melissa entered now and Johnny wheeled around to face her, a sheen across his face. Her lip gloss had worn off, leaving only an emphatic outline of red pencil. Her thick blonde hair had been centre-parted by the wind. It curved inward beneath her chin, like a pair of parentheses containing some gratuitous aside – which is exactly what she was, basically, I thought to myself: a little bit on the aside.

And yet, there was no fear or guilt in her expression, just complacent smugness. She was like a bomber, watching and waiting for the device she's planted to go off. She took a swig from her ludicrously huge water bottle.

'Always with the water drinking! You're nothing more than a virtue-signalling hydration bore!' my sister hissed.

'Well, the thing is, I'm drinking for two, now.'

Kapow! And with that Melissa pressed down on the detonator switch.

My sister's face flickered and tensed. This must be what it feels like to wake up mid surgery, I thought. But then Verity laughed. It was a shrill, nervous sound I didn't recognise.

'You're really pregnant?' I asked, appalled. 'Are you sure it's yours? I mean, you've lied so, so much.'

Johnny's head jerked around like a lassoed bull. 'W... w... what?'

I flanked my sister, so we could face Melissa together. 'So tell us, do you have any pregnancy cravings... Like for a backbone? A conscience? Some integrity? A bit of morality maybe?'

'What the fuck's goin' on?' Johnny demanded.

'Apparently, you're going to be a father – again,' Verity said flatly to her Significant Other. 'Congratulations.' My sister never blushed but her face reddened now. It looked as hot and angry as sunburn. 'How could you be so fucking stupid?' she seethed. 'Why didn't you use protection?'

Johnny's tanned face had gone the colour of curdled milk. 'She said she was on the pill.' He swivelled to confront Melissa. 'You told me that.'

Melissa zapped a smile in his direction – the kind of smile that burns three layers of skin off your face.

'And you didn't consider her age? She's nearly forty... The now-or-never baby years,' my sister said, icily. 'Why do you think she was like a bloodhound sniffing at your crotch?'

'God, Johnny. You're so stupid,' I sighed. 'If you had to take a pregnancy test you'd no doubt write the answers on your hand. But you know what? A pregnancy test is the one test you can't cheat on.'

'But... but you're not going to keep it!' Johnny addressed Melissa in a voice suppurating with panic.

I laughed at this. Couldn't he hear her ovaries throbbing? They were thrumming like a jet engine coming in over Heathrow.

Melissa's silk top rustled like a snake. 'I most certainly am.'

'It's a mistake. It's a fantasy. You'll hate it. In fact, it's the only time in life you'll wish you were a year older,' Johnny gushed, desperately. 'And oh Christ, the agony of childbirth, gettin' split right open...'

'That's true enough,' I agreed. 'If pregnancy were an opera... they'd cut the last act.'

Melissa calmly reapplied her make-up in the green-room mirror. 'But you're the very reason I decided I wanted a baby, Izzy,' she purred, her mouth lipsticked bright red with bravado once more. 'I've watched you and Chrissie...

Oh, all that unconditional love. I want to feel the intense raptures of motherly love, the blind beautiful devotions which only a mother's heart can know...'

I turned to my sister so that our eye-rolls could synchronise to emphasise our abhorrence of Melissa's Hallmark card sentimentality, but Verity had bowed her head, vanishing from sight under her conniving fringe. I didn't need to see her face to feel the anguish radiating out from her in waves.

'What... the... fuck... Melissa?' Johnny's voice was staccato, as though he'd used a jackhammer as a suppository. 'I... can't... believe... you... sent... the... anonymous... messages... to...Verity...' He stared at her, as unblinking as a lizard. 'Is... that... true?'

'Well, you kept swearing undying love, but kept going back to her. It killed me every time you left. I wondered if maybe it was possible to love two women at once? But you'd told me you'd stopped having sex years ago, so I figured you were just too cowardly to confess. So I took charge. That's what agents do.'

Johnny started making the noise of a sink backing up.

'You told Melissa that we were no longer making love?' Verity asked him in a small, sad voice. She swayed like a heroine from a Greek tragedy. I had to wrap my arm around her waist in order to keep her upright.

I regarded my ex with slant-eyed hostility. 'This is a fuck-up on a grand scale – even for you.'

'It's the opposite of a fuck-up, sweetie,' Melissa insisted. 'You'll be joining the ranks of hot old dads – Rod Stewart, Robert De Niro, Mel Gibson...' She counted off the sad old farts on her fingers with an air of drilled belligerence.

'...Eddie Murphy, Boris Johnson, Keith Richards... all boasting about the power of their seed...' Her small, tight smile was now sharp as a razor. 'Forget weightlifting or cold-water swimming or upgrading your motorbike into some huge metal growling monster. A baby is the ultimate proof of alpha status.'

'Oh-kaaaay... when you put it that way...' Johnny's voice dropped down to a deeper level, like wet mud slipping down a gully. 'It's never too late, right?'

'It is for me,' my sister said quietly. 'You didn't want any more children. And I acquiesced.'

Rage, humiliation, rejection – these are the emotions left when everything else has been scoured away by infidelity. But the ache of childlessness, I'd been spared that suffering. Quashing your desire to be a mother, for a man – a man who had no use-by-date on his fertility? That would indeed give you something to brood over. The last thing my sister wanted, I suspected, was sympathy, but I squeezed her hand anyway.

'You know he has no money,' Verity said with sour satisfaction. 'Blew all our savings on Bitcoin. I've remortgaged the house.'

'And do you have any idea how much it costs to raise a child in the UK?' I told her. 'A quarter of a million, I read the other day. Manifest that, motherfucker!'

But Melissa just shrugged once more. 'All the more reason to bring your own fucking mother to her senses. Nicole needs to ditch Gawain and go back to work for the sake of her family.'

'She'll kill you, the minute she hears about your treachery,' my sister fumed.

A nonchalant lifting of her eyebrows this time. 'Not when I'm carrying her granddaughter's sibling. Besides, she'll be far too busy working to help Verity pay Johnny's palimony.' Melissa's voice rattled like a wasp in a jar.

'Just nod and smile benignly,' I said to my sister. 'I heard somewhere that it's best to humour the insane.'

Musicians were returning now. People were boiling around the backstage area. There was a buzz as my mother appeared. Emulation was in the air like desire – everybody wanted to be like the famous, fabulous and formidable Nicole Nightingale.

'Oh, darlings!' She seated herself, orchestrating her tailcoat out behind her. 'So pleased you're all here to support Gawain and me... not just musically and creatively, but also in our happiness...' She looked towards the alpine horn player and beamed. 'We've changed wedding plans. Rather than having a small ceremony in the registry office here in Derry, we've opted for a big, beautiful marriage in September. Back with family in Sydney. We'll cover all hotel bills and air fares.' My mother smiled broadly. 'And you're included too, Mel. Of course.'

Gawain beamed back at her. 'Oh, I just can't wait to marry into majesty!'

My mother laughed, excitedly. It took her a moment to clock the aching, torniqueted atmosphere, which she mistook for disapproval of her plans.

'Can you believe I cleaned their faces with my own spit on a hanky?' she laughingly told her fiancé. 'Girls,' my mother teased us. 'Can we just be friends?... I'd like to start seeing other offspring now.'

We remained standing or sitting in awkward silence. It was like a hospital visit.

'I'm starting to realise why mothers die in childbirth... Because it's preferable to this endless judgemental behaviour.' Mum gave a bemused lift of her shoulders. 'It's such a myth, darlings, that labour ends in the birthing room.'

When we still said nothing, she added, good-naturedly, 'I wish I believed in smacking children.' Then, to us, 'Is it too late to ground you both?'

Gawain, in his new black suede jacket and pale charcoal shirt, took a formal bow. 'There are some species who would die for love. Dogs and dolphins, apparently. And a besotted Swiss alpine horn composer! I cannot believe what your mother has done for me. This is the greatest act of love, agreeing to conduct my little concerto. Picking up her baton again, just for me. It's the ultimate act of devotion. And it means the world to me – as does she. This is the biggest night of my life. All the critics have come, because of you, Nicky darling. And they'll get to hear my music! I'm overwhelmed.' Gawain's eyes shone like small blue stones. 'And the fact that she's agreed to take my humble hand in marriage... well, I am so deeply moved.'

My mother waved away his compliments with a fluttering of her fingers, engagement ring gleaming. Outside the green room, the stage manager was shooing musicians towards the stage as if they were chickens. In the auditorium the air was filling with other people's buzz, their conversation, their breath, their tingling anticipation. A delightful throb of expectation lit up Gawain's eyes – the concert was about to begin. He kissed my mother's hand and her face flushed with happiness. But then, all of a sudden, her expression froze.

I turned to follow her gaze. There in the door stood the old grizzly muso from the pub with the oystered eye and scrape of bark off his nose. He looked very much like the sort of fella who could hot-wire engines and break a steering lock.

My mother and the stranger faced each other for a silent eternity: ten seconds, twenty years – hard to tell. She was surveying him with optometric attention to detail.

'Sorry, mate,' Johnny broke the stillness. 'But who the hell are you, exactly?'

'This is Derry, "mate"… And Derry men say nothin'.' The old guy spoke from lips no more than a crack between nose and chin. And then he gave a wink and crunched Johnny's fingers in a chiropractic handshake. 'Rory. Rory Rattigan.'

The stage manager was at the door now. She gave Rory a severe look; a look which said loud and clear that she was collecting CCTV footage to send to the police so he'd better not make any trouble. 'Fifteen minute call, Maestro.'

'Have a crackin' gig, Nic. Of course, as you know, I've brought the roof down here before.' The stranger winked. 'Blew it up in the seventies,' he explained to the rest of us. 'In retaliation for the British gerrymandering which was orchestrated from here… Made sure nobody got hurt, mind. Still on the run for it… Allegedly.' Playing up to the Bad Boy image, he tapped his nose to indicate that this was top-secret information.

'I'm sorry… but what's your connection with my mother?' I asked, bewildered.

'Mother, can you please elucidate?' my sister demanded.

'Isabella, Verity…' my mother finally said in a tiny voice I didn't recognise, 'meet your father.'

FORTY

'Rory?' my mother said in a piercing whisper. Her smile was held stiffly in place as if for an invisible photographer.

'You're Rory?' Gawain asked, amazed.

'All day, every day.'

Touchy-feely Gawain moved towards the stranger for a hug.

'What the fuck...? Get off me!' Rory repelled Gawain with a flick of his powerful wrist. 'Me da only hugged me once, and that was on his deathbed. Wise the fuck up, you eejit! So, what's the craic here?' he asked in a granulated voice, before shaking Gawain's hand with debilitating enthusiasm.

'You know who this man is?' Verity quizzed the alpine horn player.

'Mum?' I turned to her for an explanation. Her eyes had gone dark and glassy like those of a doll. 'What the hell's going on?'

'Nic...' The collar of the mysterious stranger's battered leather jacket was turned up in a kind of Graham Greene-ish spy novel way. 'Can't believe I'm seein' you again after all these years.'

'I thought you were in America.' My mother's voice had a peculiar ventriloquial quality.

'Yep. Boston. Lyin' low. Only just came back... Never stopped thinkin' about you though, darlin'... Not ever.'

My sister stood next to me. We looked like painted skittles waiting for fate to bowl us over. 'Wait. Is this actually our father?' Verity squeaked.

My mother bit her lip. She nervously twisted the baton in her hand. And then she nodded. Suddenly, the air in the room was too thick, too hot, like stew.

'You're our father?' I felt like some intrepid explorer who for years has read of the existence of pangolins or poltergeists but never expected to be this near to one.

'...and I never stopped thinkin' about my darlin' girls either.' He opened his arms, inviting us in for a hug.

'Wait! What? You knew about us?' Verity asked, astounded, standing firm.

'Raised you for the first two years of your lives...' He lowered his arms. 'The miracle and majesty of it, the marvel of you two perfect creatures... I only left when things got too dangerous.'

Verity's face gorged red with anger. 'You knew who our father was and where he was, and you never told us?' she implored our mother. 'You lied to your own daughters?'

The room was swooping up and down, swaying side to side. I had to hold the wall so as not to fall over.

'I'm so, so sorry, girls.' Mum's eyes filled with tears.

A lifelong mastery over tipsy triangle players and sauced-up saxophonists had given our mother an air of magisterial authority. The sudden discomposure of her strong, resolute features shocked me to my core.

'Meaning your role as martyred single mother was totally self-inflicted?' my sister pressed on.

'Christ almighty, can you bloody believe it?' Johnny scoffed, slapping his thigh. 'Here's my haughty mother-in-law, all hoity and toity, mountin' her high horse, lookin' down on me, when all the time... Mind you, funny, ain't it, that the very same bloke who wasn't good enough to marry your daughter can be the father of the smartest girl in the world, while you turn out to be the dumbest mother.'

'You're Chrissie's da?' Rory asked, suspiciously. He squeezed Johnny's hand again, just hard enough to show that he could break his arm if he chose to and grunted out a 'How's it goin'? What a little darlin'. It was only when the wee girl started talkin' about her gran, the great conductor Nicole Nightingale, that I realised you were in town, Nic. I mean, Derry. Of all places. Who'd have thought it?'

I could only agree. This whole scene was way too discombobulating. I sniffed at my glass of water. Had someone put gin in there? The high drama going on in the green room was smoking people out of their backstage nooks like wasps. Musicians gaggled in the hallway, craning their necks to see the Jacobean theatrics playing out backstage. All that was missing were the codpieces and ruffs.

'If you loved us, then why did you disappear without trace?' my sister interrogated.

'Aye, well, your ma's so overprotective I can't believe she ever let you out... out of her womb, that is!' He gave a small, caustic laugh. 'I was involved, politically... in various activities,' he said euphemistically. 'Against her wishes. There was talk of reprisals. She said if I continued, I could never see her or you wee girls again. I didn't listen and then, shortly after that, I had to go on the run and ended up in the States.'

'So, what's brought you back to Londonderry after all this time?' Johnny pried.

The man claiming to be our father gave Johnny the look of a mugger who's just spotted a tourist who hasn't realised they've wandered into a really bad neighbourhood. 'It's Derry, you prick.'

'Oh, don't mind Johnny. He's just a bit befuddled because he's only just found out that the woman he's been having an affair with for the last six months, my mother's agent, Melissa' – Verity jabbed a talon towards her nemesis – 'who we thought was basically gay, is having his baby.' My sister spoke without conviction, waiting for Melissa's denial; even hoping for it.

'What did you just say?!' my mother gasped, grasping instinctively for her daughter's hand.

'For fuck's sake,' Johnny moaned. 'It's so much goddamned easier being female, ya know that? For starters, youse don't have to worry about gettin' some random woman up the duff.'

'Some random woman?!' Melissa's chewed lips stretched taut over tailored teeth. 'I thought you loved me!' she said thickly, tears in her voice.

'Clearly he loves the trying-to-get-pregnant part... Just not too sure about the parenthood bit,' I clarified.

'And of course, it's too late for me to be a parent... A joy you denied me,' Verity said to Johnny in a voice sharp enough to cut sinew from bone.

'Johnny left me for my sister.' I added for Rory's edification, 'We're still not really talking to each other.'

Johnny shrugged. 'Yeah well, that's rock'n'roll, Izzy, babe. If you wanted to tame me, you should have adopted me, not married me.'

'Adoption's a good idea, as you're such a bloody child,' Verity spat.

'I think to commit adultery, you actually have to be an adult first!' It was my turn to yell at Johnny now, which I did at full volume.

Verity turned to Rory once more, keen to lay all our bizarre cards on the table. 'And our mother, the famous conductor, has been far too preoccupied reinventing the Kama Sutra with a Swiss conman half her age to be of any help to her disintegrating family,' she concluded, bitterly.

Gawain, who'd been standing mute and unregarded in the shadows, now spoke. 'A small reminder – you're all adults! Why can't you just let your adult mother lead her adult life?' He placed a protective arm around my mother's waist.

'Christ.' Rory ran a hand through his thick silver hair. 'And I thought my life was fraught with danger.'

A noisy whirlpool of musicians moving towards the stage drowned Rory out for a moment. He then laid a hand on my mother's shoulder, flexing one heavy forearm. 'You're the love of my life, Nic.'

'And mine.' Gawain pulled my mother away into an embrace.

'And who are you, exactly?' Rory's tone was one you'd use to address an unwanted cat that has strayed into a yard. He walked towards Gawain, slow and deliberate, like a gunslinger at the O.K. Corral.

'Nicole's fiancé,' Gawain announced, proudly.

'What? You're gettin' hitched to this numb nuts? Don't make me laugh, Nic.'

My mother looked from one man to the other, befogged and bedevilled. All her eye make-up had washed away from crying. Surprised into acquiescence, she'd become as docile as a child.

'Five-minute call,' a crackling voice announced over the tannoy. The stage manager's head shot through our door. 'Maestro, are you ready?'

My favourite tempo in every symphony is the presto or vivace. But things were moving too fast now, even for me.

With the skill and ease of a racing car driver, my mother shifted gears. She moved with such speed out of the green room that if she had actually been racing a car, a Grand Prix trophy would be in the offing. Within seconds she was gliding towards the stage, an anxious Gawain in tow.

A row of empty chairs were lined up against the green-room wall like a firing squad. Johnny kicked one over. 'This whole fuckin' family's insane!'

'Shut it…' Rory seethed at him, which I took to be Irish for 'Warning, brain pulverisation imminent'.

Johnny must have got the same impression, as he scuttled away. A moment later, I saw him slide through the auditorium door, like an eel into a rock, Melissa beside him.

My sister and I stood still, our dazed eyes locked, our new-found father leaning up against the wall behind us.

'What, are we just going to pretend like he isn't here?' Verity finally asked me.

'Why not? I'm busy pretending I'm not here.'

'Pub?' asked the stranger. 'I reckon it's the only option.'

'Hmm, I'm not sure,' I said, sarcastically. 'I just can't

handle any more drama. My timetable is full. My next nervous breakdown isn't scheduled till later this week.'

'Right, well, I'd better not tell you about your eighty-five first cousins, then.'

Christ. We'd suddenly inherited a whole flock. All we could do was follow the man, as meekly as sheep.

FORTY-ONE

'So, I won't believe everythin' I've heard about you, if you don't believe everythin' you've heard about me,' Rory said with a lopsided grin and a sidelong glance as he strolled, hands in pockets, towards the pub.

'We've heard nothing about you,' Verity said, bluntly. 'I only knew you as a kind of crude outline filled in with one or two colours...'

'Basically that you're Irish, a bit of a muso and like Guinness. Which is pretty much a tautology as far as I can see and doesn't exactly narrow the fathering field,' I added, uncertainly.

Rory laughed, well, chuckled really. He was more of a chuckle kind of guy. He lit his roll-up, inhaled luxuriously, leant back and bloomed smoke. When we reached the nearest pub, republican Rory rolled inside like an old rocker on a comeback tour. There was a general doffing of caps and muffled offers of free beer. The cheery tavern with its open fire, wooden nooks and convivial chat was another thrumming terminus of Celtic charm and traditional music. But the sweet tunes were hard to hear because blood was thudding so loudly in my ears. I was about to have a drink with – my father.

As Rory slid into the wooden nook and sat back on the pew opposite, I examined him more closely. He was a strong, robust man, hardly reduced by toil and time. His shirt stuck like a denim skin to his chiselled chest and broad shoulders. The years, however, had not bypassed his world-weary face. They had, in fact, trampled it. I wondered whether his splayed nose was the original edition or had been flattened. I presumed the latter. That and his scars indicated that this was a man who barrelled against every challenge. He looked a lot like a character out of an unpublished novel by James Joyce.

But I could see a genetic echo in him too. It was as if our features had been rearranged and misaligned on his face somehow; re-carved by a slightly tipsy sculptor. There was an audible grin in his voice and he spoke with a gruff, Brendan Gleeson, rough-and-ready charm. Americanisms like 'Whatever, kiddo' and 'Yeah, well, you're dreamin'' and 'Here's lookin' at you, kid' also punctuated his speech patterns.

Three pints of Guinness magically materialised on the wooden table. Rory nodded at someone across the bar, then turned back to us. 'Here's lookin' at you, kids.' He winked. 'Sláinte!' Then he took a long, appreciative drink.

'Do you have anything stronger? Like maybe, I dunno... heroin?' I suggested. 'Or crack or amphetamines? It's been quite the day.'

'Oh, girls. My darlin' girls. It's your da.'

'Dada, you mean, 'cause this is surreal,' I muttered.

'If you try to blame your ma, well, you're dreamin'. Nic made me an ultimatum. It was our family or the fight... And, well, I was young an' invincible and, well, I chose the Cause.'

Even though the man who was now calling himself our father looked like the kind of bloke you'd see on a Wanted Poster, his eyes were soft grey, a laugh lingered on his lips, and a Seamus Heaney poetry book stuck out of his back pocket.

And when he then went on to talk so eloquently about the days when local jobs were advertised as 'Catholics must not apply', he wouldn't have looked out of place on stage at a literary festival at Hay-on-Wye.

He told us how the city haemorrhages history, much of it soaked in sadness, from the 1689 Siege of Derry to the 1972 massacre of unarmed civilians at Bloody Sunday, the majority of whom were seventeen. 'They all died with their hands in the air.'

He quoted quite a bit of Yeats and some John Hume. What I gleaned is that in the North-West it's perfectly acceptable to quote poetry about flowers, salmon, hedgerow and fields in the same breath as war cries about resistance and the struggle.

'Gob-na-sgeal,' he said, 'do youse know the word? It means the mouth of the storyteller, hence the slang "gob"... And I've got a hell of a gob on me. So shut me up if I go on too long.' He was darkly funny too. 'There are upsides to growing up in the Troubles, you know,' he said, drolly. 'When I go to my school reunion, I've got the entire buffet to myself.'

Amusing anecdotes poured out of him as the Guinness poured in. Pausing to take another long drink, he then smacked his lips and sighed. 'But look at the orchestra tonight. Catholic and Protestant musicians... which is symbolic of how much things have changed here for the better. We Irish are the only people in the world who are actually nostalgic about the future,' he quipped. 'Anyways, after I blew up the Guildhall, I skipped town. Mostly 'cause I kinda liked my facial features in their current configuration, ya know?'

There was a fair amount of throat clearing and clothes straightening going on at this point. I couldn't think of anything to say, but luckily Verity located her vocal chords.

'Nobody was hurt, I hope.' She frowned.

He looked affronted. 'That's not the way I operate. But what I was doin' was dangerous. I couldn't jeopardise Nic or you two... So I took off for the States. Continued to fight for the Republican cause, givin' talks, raisin' money... And look at me! Still goin' strong...'

'Must be those regular doses of Irish penicillin,' I suggested, taking a tentative sip of the dark thick drink before me. More free drinks arrived; although Guinness isn't so much a drink as a meal.

Rory blew the froth off his medicine. 'I attribute my long life to the fact that I never touched booze, drugs or guns, till I was the ripe old age of... seven.' He winked once more. 'But I obviously gave up a lot... too much. And it was my loss, clearly.' He looked from one of us to the other. 'I've missed your whole lives. One thing's for sure. If I'd been around neither of you would have hooked up with that maggoty prick. Please tell me you're not still into that gobshite.'

'Oh, I'll always love him... It's just his life philosophy, infidelity, rotten, rat-fink, dirty-dingo lying I can't tolerate...' I explained.

Rory squeezed out another chuckle, then took another restorative sip. 'And yourself, Verity?'

'I will also always cherish the initial misconceptions I had about Johnny... the two-faced worm.' My sister slumped into her seat and took a deep breath, like a diver going under.

'Why don't we auction him on eBay?' I joked, defaulting into caustic commentary. 'For Sale: One Husband. Has had only two careful lady owners.'

Rory lowered his voice to a sinister level. 'Do youse want me to sort him out?'

Guinness spilled down my shirt front. 'NO!' I choked. 'He is still the father of my child! And children need their father.'

This prompted another awkward moment of throat clearing and clothes straightening but this time from our mysterious and unmapped paterfamilias.

'Why didn't you get in touch with us?' Verity demanded, crossly. 'You made no effort.'

'Yes. An occasional Christmas card would have been nice,' I added, crisply.

'Didn't wanna bring trouble to your door. And it was up to your ma. I'd already put her through so much shite. But still, j'know the difference between an adventure and an ordeal, girls? Attitude. I want to make it up to youse both. In whatever way I can. And to your mammy too. Let's drink to that, eh? Sláinte.'

We tentatively talked, trying to get to know each other a little, until it was time for the concert to wrap up. On the way back to the Guildhall, Rory took a detour, steering us towards the river. As we walked onto the undulating Peace Bridge in the moonlight, he explained how the bridge links the Protestant Waterside of the Foyle river with the

Catholic cityside. He pointed up towards the twin towers. 'Imagine each spire represents the hand of a Catholic and Protestant, respectively. As you walk by, an optical illusion makes it appear that the two spires merge,' he explained. 'This means that, from the right perspective, our hands can come together and we can walk toward a united future.'

It sounded as though he was standing for parliament, even perhaps making his maiden speech in Stormont. But it also had me wondering if that kind of rapprochement and unity would ever be possible for two warring sisters. And with a certain dog-handler I knew. I quickly checked my messages – but still no word from Fiachra on my 'padded cell phone'.

'You okay?' Verity asked, as we turned back towards the hall.

'I'm beginning to wish I had an emotional hazmat suit.'

'Oh God. Me too,' she said, quietly. 'If I'd wanted to be maimed spiritually, physically and emotionally, I'd have gone to a war zone and made a day of it.'

FORTY-TWO

The first thing I noticed as we sneaked into the back of the Guildhall was that the audience was coughing and nose blowing in a restless, bored way. It was unsettling because usually my mother's concerts commanded a respectful, overawed silence. But as we slunk into some seats in the back row, I immediately realised why. What was supposed to be a concertante concerto in a neo-romantic style had become cacophonic chaos. The tempo was all over the place. Cadences were botched. Cues were missed. The playing was lifeless and lacklustre. And it wasn't so much the composition; it was the conducting. Mum was conducting like a rheumatic sign language interpreter at an incontinence conference. Gawain's eyes were popping as though a rodent had taken a wrong turn and run up his alpine horn, where it was now trampolining on his tonsils. Astonished disappointment seeped forth from the auditorium and the orchestra pit.

When my mother finally put down her baton, there was half-hearted applause, no calls for an encore nor the traditional cry for the composer and soloist to take a bow. Patrons normally lingered after my mother's performances, even British audiences, who always seem to want to get away from concerts more urgently than they want to get into them. I was used to fans lining up at the stage door for autographs as though waiting for the Queen. Not tonight, though. Tonight's audience members fled the scene as if from an outbreak of malaria.

The atmosphere backstage was funereal. We gathered in the green room as though at a morgue – and what lay dead? The cold corpse of Gawain's alpine horn concerto along with my mother's reputation.

'I'm sorry, Gawain. I totally ruined your premiere. My conducting was horrendous.'

'Conductin'?' Johnny laughed, cruelly. 'Is that what you were doin'? I thought you were an air traffic controller tryin' to land a jumbo.'

'Crash land, that is,' Melissa added, bitingly.

The Swiss alpine horn composer looked as though he wanted to beat himself to death with a giant Toblerone. He bent his red face over his phone and began to scroll furiously. 'Twitter reviews are scathing. It's official. My compositional debut is an unmitigated disaster.'

'Well, what do you know? I'm not the only one who's bombed here,' Rory jibed.

My mother turned pale. 'I'm so, so sorry, Gawain. I just couldn't concentrate... Seeing Rory again, well, it was like seeing a ghost... My girls meeting their father for the first time...' She chewed her lip, looking totally discombobulated. 'Melissa pregnant! It's totally beyond me why any woman is attracted to that man.' She pointed at Johnny. 'His brain is powered by oxen.'

'You can talk! After that shit show!' he retorted, sharply.

'I take it this Johnny fella graduated from the university of life… but all he got on his test paper is mayonnaise, am I right?' Rory said. 'Or maybe a wee dab of mustard.'

Johnny went to speak but, at the sound of Rory cracking his knuckles, thought better of it and slunk out of the room, Melissa in tow.

My mother chewed her lip again. 'Up there on the podium all I could think about was how the hell I've managed to give birth to such a soap opera.'

'There's an operatic grandeur to it all, Mum, that's for sure.' I, too, was exhausted by the casual cruelties and heart-stopping revelations of the past few days. All that was missing were the surtitles, a fat lady singing, a bit of stabbing and a curtain call.

My sister screwed up her face. 'How could you have lied to us, Mother? All that single-mother martyrdom,' she reiterated, 'when all the time you knew who and where our father was.'

'I've let you all down. I'm sorry.' My mother's voice was clipped and stoic, like that of a brave bride in a black-and-white Second World War movie. 'I'm going back to London. Alone. Please don't try to contact me. Any of you. I need some time to think.' Her lips stiffened with the effort to say no more.

'No way, Nic. Fate has brought us back together. And now that I've found you, I'm not lettin' you go so easily this time.' Rory reached out a hand and wrapped it around her elbow. 'I'm comin' with you.'

Gawain knocked Rory's hand away. 'Leave her alone. Your relationship clearly has a DNR slapped on it… Do Not Resuscitate.'

'Wind your neck in, punk. Or better still, just go fuck the Pope sideways.'

'Ah, I may not be au fait with the minutiae of theological thought but considering your Catholic faith, wouldn't sexual intercourse with the pontiff count as a vague sin in some way?' Gawain condescended.

The two men bristled, invisible antlers locked.

'Enough!' My mother's voice rang out so harshly it echoed around the room. 'Do not follow me. Any of you.' She pointed her baton like a wizard's wand, willing us all to disappear in a puff of smoke. 'I need to be alone.' She Greta Garboed towards the door, wrenching it open fast enough to make the hinges wince. She took one last look, then closed the door on us all, majestically.

There was a brief scuffle as both Rory and Gawain fought each other to see who could get out the door first but by the time they'd both burst into the corridor, Mum was gone. We pushed outside into the cobbled forecourt but the only person we could see was Chrissie, sashaying towards us, a handsome Irish lad on her arm.

'Mum, this is Sean. He's from Muff. Can you believe there's a town called Muff?"

I could indeed. Clearly it was genetic, this family attraction to the Oirish charm.

"It's just over the border in Donegal... a county which is in the south, but north of Derry. It's just so deliciously Irish that the most northern part of the mainland, Malin Head, is actually in the south.' She laughed. 'And guess what? Muff has a diving shop. I'm not kidding. Plus they have this tall-ship festival and the sign reads "Clippers Come to Muff!" Oh, and a Muff Festival.' She craned upwards to kiss the young man's cheek. He was blushing madly. 'I'm not sure what I found more astounding. The ringed fort he took me to—'

'Grianán of Aileach,' the young man said, softly.

'—which dates back to 1700 BC. Can you believe it? Or that the sun was shining when we got there. And do you know what Sean said?' She beamed at me. 'That the weather is fierce mild. Oxymoronic but so charming! Anyway, I'm sorry I'm late. So, did I miss anything?'

PART FIVE

Sisterhood Rule
Never Let A Penis Come Between Us.
Men come and go, but the sisterhood stays
faithful forever.

FORTY-THREE

'Mum's missing.'

My blood ran cold, like some heroine in a Dracula movie. Déjà-bloody-vu. For ironic effect, I playfully repeated word for word my opening remark from my sister's first call eleven months earlier. 'I should have guessed it was you. The sky went dark and all the neighbourhood pets are running around in circles.'

Verity picked up my satirical drift, repeating her own phrase from that initial conversation which had broken our long, sad silence. 'I wouldn't have rung if it wasn't an emergency.' She then went on to report that when Gawain got back to Hampstead from Derry, Mum's house was empty and some of her clothes were gone.

I was still fucktose intolerant – the condition of being completely unable to tolerate other people's fuckwittery. It continued to be the phrase I lived by, even if I hadn't yet got around to needlepointing it onto my throw pillows. But my twin sister was no longer in that category. Mainly because I understood only too well the exact kind of excruciating anguish she was going through.

'Breaking up is a romantic Code Blue… but not as hard

as staying with a lying cheat,' I reminded her, in an effort to be kind.

She sighed down the phone, a quiver in her voice. 'I can't talk about that right now. It's Mother I'm worried about. She's not answering my calls.'

'Nor mine... There's a joke in there somewhere about the orchestral conductor who didn't leave a note.'

'Well, let's just leave it in there, shall we?' she said, but there was a fragile, friendly tone to her voice. 'What about Rory?'

'I um-ed and ah-ed but finally gave him Mum's number and he's also been texting her non-stop. But no reply.'

'Is Rory... I just can't call him "our father"... Is he still at your place?'

'Yep. I put him in Chrissie's room. She stayed on in Ireland with Sean, discovering the Wild Atlantic Way.'

'I bet that's not all she's discovering.'

I squeezed my eyes shut tight. Mother Info Overload. It was bad enough trying to cope with Mum's R-rated exploits.

'Anyway, can you ask Fiachra to help us track Mother down? Can he trace her credit card or utilise face ID on CCTV or one of those detective-type things they do on cop shows all the time... Tell him to meet us at Nicole's place in an hour.'

'The Derry Man's not taking any of my calls. He's also cancelled all future lessons.'

There was a pause. 'Izzy, do you think it's time we invested in a self-help book for social lepers? What do you make of him? Rory, I mean; our rebel father?' she probed.

I glanced over my shoulder into the kitchen and watched the heavy-breathing and heavy-drinking veteran of war, and who knew how many women, hunched over his roll-your-own, smoking like a 1950's film star. When he clocked me, his face slashed open with the wide wound of his grin. 'Do that outside!' I yelled at him, then to my sister, said, 'He's quite a beguiling old bugger, actually. And incredibly well-read. He's constantly quoting Joyce, Yeats, Flann O'Brien, Brendan Behan, Edna O'Brien... And reading between his own lines, he's totally besotted with our mother.'

'Bring him with you to Hampstead. Happy families and all that,' my sister said, with a huge dollop of sarcasm.

After a preparatory convulsion, my emphysemic car kick-started and rounded the corner onto Kilburn High Street under protest. Twenty minutes later my battered banger was moaning its way up Haverstock Hill through the sleet and into the leafy streets of Hampstead with Rory riding shotgun.

We arrived to find Gawain at the kitchen table, slumped over the broadsheet reviews of his concert. We gathered around the newspapers as if at a graveside. Verity started reading them aloud.

'*What has happened to this once brilliant conductor? An orangutan in oven mitts, brandishing a pair of barbecue tongs could have done a better job with this alpine horn concerto than Nicole Nightingale,*' read the *Guardian* review.

'*This was a feel-good concert only in the fact that you feel so much better when it's over and you're racing home to your warm cocoa,*' read *The Times*.

Gawain, winded by the body blows, buried his head on his folded arms.

'Harsh,' Verity said, matter-of-factly. 'But pretty much what I would have said. Still, I've never been on the receiving end before. Hurtful, huh,' she marvelled, as she watched Gawain wince in pain.

'Try not to be too upset.' I put a comforting hand on his shoulder. 'People think cage-fighting is brutal but it's child's play compared to classical music reviewing.'

Gawain turned on Rory, who was leaning against the door frame, smirking. 'It's not Nicky's fault. If you hadn't turned up and sabotaged everything, the concert would have been a triumph.'

Rory guffawed at this notion. 'After hearing that piece, pal, I'm penalising you eight points on your artistic licence.'

As the men started to argue, I went to check Mum's study. There was no indication on her desk of where she might be, but her passport was still in the top drawer. Wandering back through the sitting room, I hauled the cover off the grand piano, opened the lid and placed my hands on the keyboard, which sounded with a mournful sadness. The strains of Chopin's Prelude in B minor echoed dismally around the house. Every note I played seemed to ask the same plaintive question – where is my mother?

Verity summoned me back into the kitchen, where Rory was cross-examining Gawain as to our mother's possible whereabouts. His head was tilted in that hyperalert way that says nothing in the room will get past him. I had little doubt that he could kneecap someone using only a butterknife.

'If I knew where she was,' Gawain seethed, 'I'd be there.'

Rory craned his head inquisitively, like a sea turtle on a David Attenborough documentary. 'And what makes you think Nic would want to be with you, pal? You're like the least charismatic coffin salesman in a funeral parlour from butt-fuck nowhere.'

'And what makes you think she'd want to be with you? You're the oldest living thing on earth that's not a member of the Rolling Stones. Or a giant redwood, maybe... or possibly Uluru.'

'You've got a lot of gall saying that to me. You weren't even around when the Stones were great... You probably think "The Stones" refers to sharing a spliff with your stoner, drop-out mates.'

'Nobody calls it "sharing a spliff" now, you old fossil.'

'Fossil? Listen, you little knobstacle, maybe it's time I knocked the daylights out of you, one bulb at a time.'

My sister, who was boiling the kettle, turned to me. 'This is unedifying.'

'Really?' I spooned tea leaves into the pot. 'I'm rather enjoying it. Especially "knobstacle" – a knob who's constantly in the way. I'll be using that one on various school principals.'

But my sister was in no mood to be amused. I noted the bags under her eyes and the dab of lipstick on her tooth. Her hair looked bedraggled and lank and her pencil skirt wasn't ironed. But a chair being scraped across the kitchen tiles drew my attention away from her to the two men, who were on their feet now, squaring up to each other.

'Nic is the love of my life,' Rory stated in a voice that God could have used to part the Dead Sea.

'Nicky is the love of my life,' Gawain retaliated at equal volume. 'She's the most cultured, gifted woman I have ever met. We share an intellectual appreciation of music that an uneducated man like you could never fathom.'

'I see you've confused what you learnt in school with your actual education,' Rory said in a thick voice, cracking gnarly knuckles. 'If you went to a mind reader, pal, you'd get half feckin' price.'

'Okay, boys,' I interrupted. 'As entertaining as it is watching Neanderthals arm-wrestle, it's getting us nowhere. Why don't we split up to try to find Mum? Her passport's still in place so she can't have gone far. Let's check in with friends, musicians, orchestra members, favourite haunts, hotels...'

There was a general agreement that finding Mum was our only priority. Mum had sent a text saying how sorry she was for lying to us and not to worry about her. But we were worried. Over the next week, in between lessons and teaching assignments, I contacted everybody in Mum's address book. But I was also busy doing a little light Rory-wrangling. When Rory had fully understood the level of emotional havoc Johnny had caused his newly discovered daughters, our father was so furious that he couldn't talk; an unusual condition for an Irishman. He just walked back and forth across my kitchen, punching one fist into the other palm.

'Come on, now. Fair play. Let me cut his brake cables,' he fumed. 'Just picture that eejit crashing straight through the pub wall.'

'Yes, that way Johnny would be very, very dead, but also beautifully on time for a gig for once,' I replied, sardonically. 'But no! I don't wish Johnny ill... Well, maybe just a little light dragging behind an armoured tank over enemy lines by his scrotum, but you can't kill him! We may detest the man but he's still Chrissie's dad. And dads can be assholes,' I said pointedly, 'disappearing out of your life, for example, and not coming back for forty-seven years.'

Rory, who had started spreading marmalade onto a slice of bread, gave a guilty nod, then wielded his knife like a dagger. 'Yeah, but it'd be so satisfying to castrate the gnarly hole.'

'Forget about it! Johnny's way too old to sing in the Vienna Boys' Choir.'

Eyes glinting like metal, Rory amended his offer. 'At least let me kick him in that shrivelled raisin he calls a nut sack.'

'Absolutely not.'

'Or just impale your man on his own feckin' drumstick.'

'Good idea. Except, being dead, he won't appreciate the piquancy of the gesture,' I posited. 'Anyway, Johnny loves himself so much, he'd probably get a kick out of dying in his own arms.'

'Aye, well, I'd be happy to make that happen for him.'

'Aren't you a little too old for this vigilante routine? Maybe it's time you hung up your balaclava?'

'Jay-sus, why? When I clearly have a face made for modelling ski masks,' he joked, self-deprecatingly. 'And anyway, I'm not sure that pruning roses is a sufficient retirement occupation for a fella like me.'

I thought that was the end of it but then a few days later Johnny barged into my music room in the middle of a lesson.

'Weird shit's happenin'!' he said by way of hello.

'What's on your mind? If you can pardon the exaggeration.'

'First of all, my car got scratched. Then my tyres got slashed. Then a rock got thrown through Mel's window... I'm livin' there, as you probably know...'

But not very happily, I deduced by the dishevelled state of his clothes and his rumpled, crumpled hair. He'd lost weight and now had the hungry, predatory look of a neglected greyhound.

'And then, that fucker cut the brake cable on my mountain bike. Luckily I was comin' down an incline that wasn't too steep. But brakin' locked me into this rapid skid. All I could do was steer towards a grassy verge and dive head first over the handlebars. I'm okay but it scared the hell out of me.'

I quickly wrapped up the lesson with my intrigued Grade 8 student and followed Johnny to the living room, where he immediately helped himself to a whisky – necking it, neat. 'And what the hell did I ever do to him? I like the Irish! All I did was call his home town Londonderry, which he apparently heard as "Toodle-pip, old chap. I'm William of Orange. Prepare to be hung, drawn and quartered, ya Fenian scum."'

'Okay. I'll tell him to back off.'

'You'd better, because if that maniac father of yours doesn't stop playin' silly buggers I'm gonna rat him out to the cops. That bloke could scare hot piss out of an igloo,' he confided, nervously.

Johnny slammed out of the house just as Verity pulled up in a gleaming sports car. I'd forgotten that she was collecting Rory to drive around to some of our mother's favourite haunts to enquire if anyone had seen her. The electronic window whooshed downwards and she peered at her unfaithful partner over designer shades. 'My lawyer will be in touch,' she said, coldly. 'Not only are we not married, but as you lost most of our savings on Bitcoin, without consulting me, the courts will definitely find in my favour, so don't expect a cent. Oh, and I've sold the guitars and cars

I bought you and traded in my own wheels for this little beauty. Finally, my very own Shaguar.'

Whipped-cream clouds sailed overhead. The trees were sprinkled with a shiny confetti of new leaves. Dappled sunlight flickered through the branches, casting a mosaic of light and shadow onto Johnny's handsome face. He gave Verity his most adorable doe-eyed look – it was a look I knew well; a look that could melt a woman at a hundred paces. 'I could just die from shame and guilt, my love. I'm mortified by what I've done to you. If you hate me, imagine how much I loathe myself? Please forgive me? I just wanna come home, sweetheart.'

He seemed so genuinely repentant, then I remembered something the Derry Man had told me about dogs not feeling guilt, no matter how many cutesy Instagram photos you see of cringing, big-eyed pooches next to half-eaten legs of lamb. It's not guilt, he'd explained, but submission because they want to get back into your good books. But I could see my sister wavering, especially when Johnny added, plaintively, 'Oh, Verity, my sweet, beautiful woman, where did our love go?'

I stepped between them, protectively. 'To the charity shop, with the rest of your stuff.' It was a Sisterhood Rule – to always take her side in a break-up. Suggested supportive phrases, 'How do you get rid of cockroaches? Tell them you want a long-term relationship' or 'He's about as useful as a solar-powered vibrator on a rainy day', ran through my head – as did running him through with a carving knife.

'For Chrissake. How do I even know the kid's mine?' he said in a low plangent voice. 'Melissa was on the hunt for a baby daddy. What about that music exec from Sony who took her to Glastonbury? And that Danish tenor who whisked her to Glyndebourne?"

'Play stupid games, win stupid prizes,' my sister said, in a flat, frosty voice.

A hunching, ursine shape suddenly stepped out of the shadowy lane that ran beside the house. This triangular hunk of leather-jacketed muscle jabbed Johnny hard in the chest with a tobacco-stained finger. 'What the feck are you doin' here?' A book bulged in Rory's top pocket like a gun – at least I hoped it was a book. 'Not that fond of your testicles, I take it? If you were any more inbred you'd be a feckin' sandwich!'

Johnny kick-started his motorbike and sped off at warp factor speed.

'Rory, I told you to leave Johnny alone, and then you go and cut his brake cables!'

'That langer would rob the milk from your tea, then come back for the sugar. But as much as I'd like to take credit for cutting his brake cables, kiddo,' Rory flashed a wolfish grin, 'that wasn't me.'

'Yeah, right. Spoken by a wanted criminal on the run for blowing up a building. You're a blast from the past. Literally,' I said flippantly.

'Well, I'm certainly not the culprit,' Verity said. 'As tempting as it is. But Rory, Izzy's right. Back off. Johnny is Chrissie's father, after all. And fathers are precious.'

Rory gave a sheepish grin and contorted himself into the passenger seat of her new car, as docile as a lamb. After they'd glided off down the street I checked on Chrissie, who'd taken to sending voice messages from Ireland on what she was now calling her 'Aye Phone'.

'Oh, Mum. I love it here. The countryside is just so exquisitely beautiful. Every day various members of Sean's huge family drive me through rolling, green fields to mountain lakes or wild empty beaches. It's stunning.'

I rang her back on FaceTime. 'Oh, Mum, it's too funny. Sean's brought me to that town I told you about called Muff and look!' Her camera swivelled towards a hair salon called Muff Barbers. 'I actually do need a haircut and am tempted to pop inside, although I'm slightly worried which quiff will get a coiff. Gotta go!'

I'd just finished washing up when I got another text. 'Oh and the music! The marvellous music! Why would anyone ever leave Ireland?'

'Potato famine?' I texted back.

'And best of all,' she replied, 'it's been so sunny. I'm writing a song about it. The chorus is going to be about how the warm rays of the sun reach your upturned face like kisses.'

With a poignant pang I realised that my darling daughter was falling in love. I remembered then being just as high on happiness and hormones and pheromones. Oh, how I ached for that feeling now. How wrong I'd been to cut myself off from love. Here was my sixty-nine-year-old mother with two men fighting over her. The passion she inspired was awe-inspiring. Dear Chrissie was flying the nest; hell, she was nearly fledged. And here I was, all alone, as withered as Liz Truss's lettuce.

'Life is wondrous!' is how Chrissie captioned her final selfie for the day, cocooned in the arms of her new boyfriend. She was beaming, radiating joy. 'Don't break up with life, Mum.'

It struck me then like a bolt of lightning that I was lonely. With a jarring jolt I realised that Mum was right: my life had sneaked past me so stealthily it might as well have been dressed in combat fatigues and camouflage make-up.

I picked up a pen and scrawled a message on the notepad by the fridge.

Dear Life, I'm sorry we broke up. I want you back. Love Izzy.

FORTY-FOUR

'Can I bother you?' I asked, tentatively.
'Highly likely.' The Derry Man was so surprised to see me in his favourite watering hole that he sprang up like a ninja. Maisie also leapt to attention and gave me her usual friendly, fang-bared, spittle-soaked growl. He'd often told me about this old Irish pub, the Fiddler's Elbow, and how he liked to watch the brown tidal Thames rushing on by past the untidy skyscrapers of Canary Wharf, which jostled, cheek by architectural jowl, with ancient castellated buildings dating back through a hotchpotch of centuries. Maisie gave another anxious, angry bark. He patted her head, absent-mindedly, muttering soothing words.

'Mum's missing.'

'Is that why you came to see me?'

He must have been away on a holiday somewhere, as his normal, milk-bottle-white complexion now had a honey-gold glow that looked good enough to lick. His hair brushed his collar and was no longer severely side parted.

'Yes… and to say that I've missed you coming for lessons.'

He re-straddled his bar stool. 'Lost the desire.'

Silence lay between us like a bruise. 'Sorry I've been out

of touch. It's been crazy on the firefighting front but I'm hoping to soon rise from the ashtray.'

The Derry Man gave a half-hearted shrug. 'Aye well, the next time your ma runs off with a Swiss gold-digger, why don't you just go sort her out yourself and I'll just stay at home poking myself in the eye with a blunt pencil. Much less painful.'

'Read me my rights, officer. Guilty as charged. I took your help for granted. Hell, I took you for granted.'

His mouth twitched into a grimace. That was when I understood the depth of the pain I'd inflicted. 'How long have I been having lessons with you? Year and a half? And you still can't even pronounce my name… Fear, Far-quoir, Fear-queer…'

'It's Fiachra.' I pronounced it perfectly. 'Fiachra O'Flaherty. And you like to fish in the Faughan.'

He ran a hand through his unruly hair and eyed me suspiciously.

'Remember that time we pretend-flirted?… Well, I wasn't completely pretending… But I shouldn't have jumped you like a sex-starved boa constrictor.'

'Till dawn us do part… So romantic.' He took a big draught of his beer. 'I was off duty that night and not obliged to do a full-body cavity search.'

'Look, I had a bad case of being in love with my ex, but it turned out to be benign.'

I sat on the bar stool next to him. Outside, the sky was as broody and cloudy as the eyes of the man who hadn't asked me to join him.

'I'm sorry for anything cruel or unkind I said. I contemplated emigration to the Outer Hebrides right after that. Or possibly Mars.' The air in the pub was musty and heavy; I could feel the pressure of it against my eyes. The old Georgian joint thronged with ghosts. 'The Macarena', playing jauntily from the jukebox, was at odds with the eerie, brooding atmosphere.

Maisie circled my stool menacingly and gave another agitated bark. Fiachra placed a comforting hand on her head and she sat back down. 'You'd think in my line of work, I'd know better. You can't disrespect an animal's genetic disposition. Don't be surprised if a Border collie continually wants to herd things. Expect a Labrador to retrieve stuff. If you buy an American pit bull, bred for fighting, don't be surprised if it wants to gnaw the leg off strangers. You have to accept a creature's nature and admit that some natures are just not compatible.'

'Whatever happened to "love conquers all"? You swore by that, only a little while ago.'

'Aye, well, I'm a lot older and wiser now...'

'Gosh, you Irish lads sure do grow up fast!' I joshed. 'But you're wrong. People can change their nature.' I stretched out a tentative hand and patted his drooling beast on its hot, furry head. 'See?'

Fiachra gave another half-shrug. 'The more I see of humans, the more I admire canines.'

Emboldened by the fact that the panting, salivating creature hadn't bitten my hand off, I then ventured to give it a nervous scratch under the chin. 'Nice dog,' I said, hopefully.

'She is a nice dog. A real survivor. But I'll be leaving her soon to work with one of the most advanced canine breeding programmes in the world – guide dogs.'

The clouds parted and the whole river suddenly shimmered with rainbow fragments of light. It was time to reinvent; to become a more confident, positive person. 'Ah, you got the job? That's great. Then maybe you can help me too because I've been so bloody blind.'

His silence was as deep as a shout in a cave, his face shuttered.

'Oh, and guess what? I like dogs now, I really do. The sausage dog – a top fave. Those teeny-tiny little Charlie Chaplin legs! And Scottie dogs, with their big jowly moustaches and that nonchalant air. They look positively under-dressed without a smoking jacket and a whisky. And collies, bounding about like your mad mate who's on a coke high… Even Rottweilers. You've got to admire that rolling walk, like a 'roid-addled bouncer. And… um. Greyhounds! How about the old greyhound! Outrunning its own body. And poodles, of course. Ah, poodles. Clever. But brought low by their bad perms. I always stop to pat a poodle. Plus they're all named after cancan dancers, Fifi or Trixie or Tinkerbell. What's not to love about that? And who couldn't adore a British bulldog? Like Churchill reincarnated. Except with an excess of saliva… And not to forget the Chihuahua… Is it a dog or an accessory? Possibly just a brooch that barks…'

Eager to impress, I confidently took Maisie's lead from Fiachra's hand. But sensing my nervousness, the huge, hearty dog immediately dragged me off my stool and out of the pub door towards the park opposite. Yanked along at speed like that, I must have looked like some kind of amateur pavement water-skier. The big Alsatian then started to bark hysterically at some random woman who had dared to walk past us wearing a baseball cap. The woman screamed. Maisie yelped louder. Other dogs then joined in the canine cacophony, causing Fiachra's trainee pooch to tug me at breakneck speed round and round in circles chasing all the other dogs, till I overbalanced and crashed into a metallic bike stand. My shin throbbed like some kind of malignant tuning fork. Now I was the one yelping.

Fiachra, arms folded, stood watching from the sidelines, a quarter-smile on his lips. I was just getting a teeny bit hysterical when he took the lead from my hand. 'Aye. You're a natural dog lover now, I can see that,' he said, way too amused for my liking.

'Clearly I've been given my brain for nothing. Just a spinal column would have done... Fiachra, can we talk?'

'Actually, I'm meeting someone.'

'Oh yes?'

'Bridget.'

'Oh.'

'Aye, she's over for a conference. Big hitter in the finance world now. And suddenly single.'

'Oh,' I said, once more dazzling him with my spectacular vocabulary.

'Aye, well, good luck, Izzy. Have a nice life. I hope you actually start living yours.'

'Fiachra,' my voice was plaintive with defeat, 'wait, won't Maisie be upset? When you leave her?"

But the Derry Man had disappeared around a corner. The rainbow prisms had evaporated and the clouds scudding down the river were now bloated with rain. I knew just how they felt. I hobbled after him, clutching my sore shin, my heart full of everything I'd never said.

'Remember when you told me how you were teaching Maisie to "unlearn" some instinctive behaviours?' I called out. 'You said it was hard work but worth it!' But my words were lost on the wind, which had started to pat me down like I owed it money.

And that was when I saw her. Tall, willowy, with swishy, honey-gold hair and no doubt a puff of expensive perfume and peppermint breath. She wafted towards Fiachra with a tinkling little laugh. Bridget. She knelt down and Maisie leapt up into her arms. She lovingly nuzzled the big dog, completely at ease. It was like a meet-cute in a romcom.

Are you there, self-sabotage? It's me – Izzy.

Sure, I could learn to become a more confident, positive person – as soon as Maisie learnt to do the Macarena. I turned for home, my tail between my legs.

FORTY-FIVE

The long, wet, undulating street was running molten red and green as the traffic lights changed. A kind, caring, gentle, honest, sensitive, solvent, cake-cooking, dishwasher-stacking, musical man with a sense of humour. What an incredibly exotic species. I should have contacted David Attenborough to make a documentary. If only I'd realised Fiachra's rarity and not let him escape back into the wild. Reality was a wet thick thing alive in my guts.

As the engine died outside my house, the windscreen wipers made one last sluggish arc before collapsing, exhausted, like a couple of octogenarian athletes in a veterans' marathon.

I had a stranglehold on the steering wheel now and it only got tighter as I tried to fathom why women are drawn to bad boys. Even a super-duper clever woman like Verity could fall for a rogue like Johnny. Who to blame? It had to be that bloody trio of nineteenth-century virgins – Jane Austen, and Charlotte and Emily Brontë. They set the template for what kind of man is knicker-wettingly lustworthy – Heathcliff, Darcy and Rochester; all macho, unobtainable, cruel, brooding and borderline dangerous. How much more lovable is the passionate, poetic and heartbroken Captain Wentworth in *Persuasion*? Or the gentle, idealistic Will

Ladislaw in *Middlemarch*? And why had it taken me forty-nine years to work that out?

Bridget had clearly realised before I did the value of a man with emotional bandwidth. A man who will listen without trying to fix you. Who doesn't flinch when you say you're sad or anxious. A man who's soft but not weak; secure but not controlling; gentle but strong. A man's who's cool under fire, but also warm – and not just because of his daggy cardigan; a cardigan he'll wrap around your shoulders without being asked when it starts to get chilly.

Trudging inside, my spirits were as saggy as an old hippy's hammock. I was like a balloon with all the air leaked out. I lay on the couch and stared at the ceiling for a while, before half-heartedly eyeballing some American cop show I had no interest in. Channel-hopping, I then endured ten minutes of a reality show about ugly naked bodies, which at least reminded me that there are people out there even more pathetic than yours truly. Although that wasn't true because all those contestants clearly had way more courage and grit than Loser Girl here.

The front door wheezed open and Rory barrelled in, just back from his latest Nicole search, this time around London's concert halls. 'So much for the luck of the Irish… Still nothin'. How are you doin'?'

'Great.' Apart from a DIY lobotomy, I thought. The feeling that I was partly responsible for my mother's misery had begun to cling to me, like a chill. Mum had dared to shoot for happiness – and I had shot her down. Clearly my brain had logged me out, due to inactivity, and I couldn't remember my password.

Rory then handed me a huge bunch of sunflowers. 'Happy birthday, darlin'. I'm just so sorry I missed all the others.'

I realised with a dull thud that it was my fiftieth birthday. In all the anxiety about our missing mother, I'd forgotten all about it – as had my sister. I switched my phone back on. There were missed calls and messages from a few footy girlfriends and some favourite pupils, plus my music teacher mates. Best of all, there were so many messages from Chrissie. 'Happy birthday, Mum. Why aren't you answering your phone? You're probably out partying. I hope so. Let's celebrate when I get back. Life is wonderous! Don't break up with life, Mum, Love Chrissie.'

Too late, Chrissie, darling. Life had broken up with me. And who could blame it? I ran a bath and lay beneath the bubbles, ruminating on my many, many inadequacies. What a self-absorbed, whiny, wimpy, bitter bore I'd become. Just as well I'd given up singing because if I were practising my scales, it would come out as Do, Re, Mi, Me, Me, Me, Me, ME! If my life was being reviewed by critics, their unanimous verdict would be, 'Is there no beginning to her talents?'

I felt as though I was playing Scrabble with fate, only all the vowels were missing. My mother had disappeared again; my estranged sister was heartbroken; I'd wasted five years pining for a man who turned out to have love bites on his mirror; my darling, fledging daughter would soon find out that her father was a philanderer whose lover was up the duff; I was perimenopausal during an HRT shortage; and I'd thrown away the most lovely man imaginable. Meeting Fiachra was like stubbing my toe on a diamond in the dust. But, by the time I realised what a gem I'd stumbled upon, he no longer sparkled for me.

Another treasure I'd buried was Verity. She'd tried to reach out to me so many times. Your twin is supposed to be a mirror, shining back at you with a world of possibilities – but I'd just kept on shattering her glass. I reached for my phone and texted her a Happy Birthday missive – only to drop the bloody thing into the bath before pressing send.

Cursing, I groped through the bubbles for the phone and dried it on the bath mat. I then dunked my head under the water, like a diver adrift. I might as well have been dropping down into the Mariana Trench, such was the pressure crushing my spirits.

I floated there until the bathwater went cold. Towelling dry, I felt suddenly unsteady, as if buffeted by gale-force winds coming in all directions simultaneously. Throwing on a dressing gown, I trudged downstairs to put my phone into a bowl of rice. A few minutes later I was stretched out on my bed. I buried my head in the pillow, waiting for the heartache to pass, like a brief storm. But my daughter's words kept running into each other like raindrops down a windowpane. 'Life is wonderous! Don't break up with life, Mum.'

In the last five years, I'd stopped playing footy and let my friendships slip. I mostly had imaginary friends now, and even they didn't want to play with me any more. Understandably. My life had turned into a country-and-western song. If only I could play it backwards, like the old joke… I tried to remember it. Oh yes. Your lover returns to you, your dog comes back to life, you stop being alcoholic and get out of prison.

But all I wanted was the chance to be loved again.

The world was in such turmoil, wars, famines, traumas and catastrophes dominated the news on a daily basis, and yet all I could think about were my own puny problems.

I was clearly taking Pathetic Pills. I gave myself a pep talk to stop being so self-absorbed, but the tonnage of emotion waiting just behind my tonsils erupted, like a dam bursting. I wanted a refund under the Lost Half-Decade Fund. I was still fucktose intolerant – only now that meant an inability to tolerate my own fuckwittery. Great heaving sobs rose up out of my core. I cried like a toddler, with gulping, shaking and hiccups... And then suddenly I was thumping and pummelling my pillow – bam! bam! bam! What I'd learnt about life of late is that when fate closes one door... it slams the next one right in your face.

Emotionally exhausted, I finally, eventually, lay still, until darkness toppled down and pulverised me.

FORTY-SIX

The next morning, after resuscitating my phone, I rang Johnny. In between digging grains of rice out of my ear, I set up a meeting. Chrissie was coming back from Ireland and we needed to break the news of her father's affair and soon-to-be sibling. It would be quite the homecoming. We agreed to meet at the Horny Toad – so appropriately named under his philandering circumstances – where he was playing that night. But the scene that met my eyes as I entered the pub in Kentish Town was so surprising, so bizarre, so outrageous that it might have been a tableau in a Grand Guignol, deliberately contrived to astonish and horrify.

It was the kind of incident that really required silent movie piano accompaniment. Picture it – in the middle of a vigorous, cymbal-crashing solo, a drummer leaps to his feet with flames shooting out of his arse. He then flails around the stage, jumping from one foot to the other, while band members try to put him out with beer.

I'd always thought my ex was smoking hot, but not in this way. I just gawped at Johnny in a wide-eyed parody of disbelief. He was in a paroxysm of shocked fury, kicking and screaming at the top of his lungs, his face distorted into a red gargoyle mask. His hair had taken the worst of the charge and his eyebrows were smouldering. Bits of his drum kit were blown all over the stage. The air was acrid with smoke. I clamoured over the debris, each ragged breath like inhaling fire.

'Johnny! Are you okay? What's happened?'

'Fffmiminak!' Johnny said. What he lacked in clarity he made up for by bleeding heavily from where he'd fallen face first over the bass drum and crashed hard onto the stage floor.

I tried to comfort him as we waited for the ambulance. As I was busy mopping Johnny's singed brow, the roadie, Dave, informed us that he suspected foul play.

'I used heaps of gaffer tape, as usual. Your thumper was secure. I figured it must have been tampered with, so took a closer look.'

'His *what* was tampered with?' I asked, perplexed.

'His throne thumper... It's a way for the drummer to feel more of the bass drum when he's working in a controlled volume situation. It's powered by electricity...' the tech-head nerded on. 'I checked inside and it looks like some joker's wired a stun-gun-style pulse circuit into the butt-kicker's mount set to release a low voltage fuse. Looks like the same nut job put a small heating coil right under the throne's central cushion to deliver a sharp thermal burst right through the metal plate under the seat. That's what really packed the punch! Not exactly attempted murder, mate, but definitely GBH.'

'Grievous bodily harm,' I decoded. The brutal legal vocabulary sent a hair-raising jolt through me this time. My fingers reached instinctively for my phone to call Fiachra.

When he didn't answer, I texted. 'Emergency. Please call urgently.'

He was too nice a person to ignore an SOS, no matter how peeved. My phone buzzed a moment later. 'What's the craic?'

'It's Johnny. He's had a kind of… premature cremation.'

As anecdotes go, I didn't think this would make it onto Graham Norton's chat show sofa but it definitely sent a seismic shock through Fiachra, who agreed to meet me at the hospital.

There was clearly only one suspect. Radical, battle-hardened Rory knew how to take aim and shoot; and not just with a witty one-liner like his daughters, but with an actual rifle with real bullets. He knew how to blow things up too. On the way to the hospital I rang my recently discovered father from the car. 'Rory! You electrocuted Johnny!' I blurted. 'Clearly a one-way trip to Australia is not the deterrent it once was!'

But Rory pleaded his innocence. 'There's no denying that I'd read his obituary with feckin' relish, but not me, I swear!'

As I turned towards Euston Road, the summer sun began to sink in a gloriously vulgar, murderous display of blood red and orange. But Rory had an alibi; he'd caught the train to Heathrow to surprise Chrissie (as if "hi, I'm your granddad" hadn't been surprise enough in Derry!) and also, no doubt, to do a bit of a background check on this new Irish boyfriend of hers. They'd only just got home. Lowering his voice, conspiratorially, he said, 'I can't blame you for wanting revenge on the low-life, darlin'.'

'Yeah, well, revenge is a minor occupation of mine which

I rank just above, you know, breathing... But I don't want to maim the man. As I keep saying to you, he's the father of my kid, for God's sake.'

I stepped outside myself then and watched my reaction. Why wasn't I more upset? Johnny just had no impact on me now. He was like an old T-shirt from a band nobody listened to any more. I pressed Verity's number on speakerphone to explain the surreal scenario I'd walked in on at the pub, hastily reassuring her that Johnny was only slightly chargrilled.

The hospital waiting area was crowded. Overhead spotlights sunk into the ceiling made everybody resemble a decaying corpse. I'd only just sat down in a plastic bucket chair when the 'pshsssss' of the hospital doors announced the simultaneous arrival of Rory, Chrissie and Fiachra – all looking equally ghoulish in the grey light. While Chrissie rushed straight to her father's side, I introduced the two men. Rory gripped my ex-pupil with his customary wrestler's handshake, a grip that left most blokes pleading for a chiropractor.

But Fiachra didn't even wince. 'How's it goin'?' he merely said.

'You're from Northern Ireland,' Rory remarked.

'Aye. Derry.'

'Ah good man, yourself.' Rory slapped him on the back.

'Rory is our long-lost father by the way."

Fiachra's eyebrows scrunched up in surprise.

'But don't go in for a manly hug,' I warned him. 'Rory doesn't hug men. Even with a best buddy, anything less than three seconds is technically fine – if it's an emergency, like your leg's just been blown off... but any hug longer than that he considers foreplay.'

'Aye, too right,' Fiachra agreed. I searched his face for the faintest reassuring flicker of a smile. How I longed for the miraculous comfort of his arms. But Fiachra went straight into professional mode, trying to establish everybody's whereabouts at the time of the accident. Chrissie reappeared and we turned as one to face her.

'How is he?' I asked gently, circling my arms around her.

She gave a huge sigh of relief. 'Only first-degree burns. The nurses are applying the bandages now. He's pretty drugged up, but making jokes, so that's a good sign. He introduced me to the nursing staff as his daughter with a typical bad Dad joke. "What did the drummer call his daughters? Anna One, Anna Two, Anna Three." I suggested they put him out of his misery. Oh!' Her phone was ringing. 'That's Sean. Hi,' she said, turning away from us.

My anxiety dissolved, evaporating like aspirin in a glass. Verity strode into the hospital waiting area then. Her hair was strangled back into a tight bun. Her skin was bone white, her lips a slash of glossy carmine. Despite the brightness of the fluorescent lights, it felt cold in the room suddenly, as though winter had come again.

'How bad is he?' she asked between thin, pinched lips.

'Bit singed in the nether regions. Thanks to the butt-kicker thumper thingo he was sitting on," I explained, 'but he'll live.'

'Singed nether regions… how appropriate,' my devastated sister muttered.

'Poetic justice,' I agreed.

'So, this explosive device was set to a timer, meaning it could have been put in place at any time. If Johnny calls in the police, forensics will narrow it down,' Fiachra explained.

'They'll also want to verify everybody's movements leading up to the time of the accident. Verity, I'm sorry to ask this, but where were you this afternoon?'

We went through our various alibis. Verity had been at work at the *Sunday Times*. I'd been teaching up in Hampstead at a girls' school. Melissa was on a business trip to New York – at least we thought she was; Fiachra said he'd look into it. Just how mad was she about Johnny calling her "some random woman", I wondered?

'Rory?' he asked next.

'I have a name for cheating husbands: organ donors... Especially those who hurt my darlin' daughters. But I was at the airport.'

'Hold on, Sean,' Chrissie muted her phone, 'that's true. Grandad was with me.'

Grandad. I still couldn't get used to it. Fiachra steered me out of the way of a passing stretcher, his warm hand at the small of my back. Oh, how I longed for him to keep it there.

'And what about your ma?' Fiachra asked. 'Where is she?'

'If only we knew,' Verity tsk-ed. 'We haven't been able to find her for over a week.'

'Grandma?' Chrissie said, hanging up. 'I know where she is. We follow each other on a location app. She likes to know when I get home safely.'

We all stared at my daughter. Ten anxious days – all for nothing.

'So, where is she right now?' I asked, tentatively.

'Anna One...?' the nurse called out to Chrissie, playfully, indicating that Johnny's bandages had now been applied.

'Ha ha. Boom, tish!' My daughter joked, then checked

the Find My app on her phone as she moved back towards her father's room. 'A place called Diddy's, in Marylebone.'

'Diddy's?!' Rory said. 'Well I'll be damned.'

'Do you know it?' Chrissie asked over her shoulder.

Did he ever.

FORTY-SEVEN

A sad, wilted thing of skin and bones pretending to be my mother was slumped in the far corner of the beer garden wrapped around a whisky glass. Deep red blotches had appeared around her eyes and the rest of her face looked mouldy under a pale green awning. For the first time I noticed the tiny fjords at the sides of her mouth. The contact lenses were gone, replaced by her old thick, black frames, and her hair was wild once more. The leopard-skin-print, diamanté kaftans had also bitten the sartorial dust. She'd reverted to her standard, all-black, mannish attire.

A flood tide of relief washed over me. 'Mum! Thank God you're okay!'

She glanced up at me. Her eyes were tiny crescents. Lost in her own private torment it took her a moment to place me. I could feel misery rising like steam when she spoke at last in a voice thick with self-loathing.

'Oh, so you found me. This is the last place I thought you'd look.'

She gave a cheerless smile, painful in its transparency. Her shoulders were up around her ears. She shifted in her chair, sighed, looked about, fluttered her hands aimlessly, then drummed her fingers on the wooden table.

I'd rung Gawain en route and he arrived now, shouldering us aside to hug his fiancée, laughing so loudly and deeply that he sprayed her face with his happiness. 'It doesn't matter about the concert. It wasn't your fault.' He glared hard at Rory then, who harrumphed in reply. 'None of that matters. All that matters is you and me.'

My mother reached up as if to touch his face, but ruffled the primulas instead. Petals tumbled down like dandruff. She then unclasped Helen's Gift of Life pendant and laid it on the table.

'I was deluding myself. Women can't have a sensational second act.' She shook her head emphatically. My mother's confidence level and general spirits were so low, I'd need a deep-sea pressurised mini sub to locate them. 'I'm officially retiring, by the way. I'm going to issue a press statement.'

'Don't be ridiculous, Mother! You live for music,' Verity stated, brusquely.

'Music is your heartbeat, Mum,' I added, more gently.

'Music is my curse, you mean! It's led me down all the wrong roads in life, from meeting you, Rory, right here in Diddy's, that fateful night... To prioritising my orchestral work over my daughters... I'm sorry, girls.' Her wind-tangled hair blurred around her face. 'I'll never forgive myself for missing your year-eight swimming gala.'

'Mother, it was one gala!' Verity placated.

'And we don't even like swimming!' I added.

'I should never have uprooted you both from Australia and brought you back to live in Britain, far from family and friends... Because of music I also missed my dear parents' dotage...' She ran a fractious hand through her bird's-nest but it couldn't be tamed. 'Music is to blame for finding myself beguiled by a young alpine horn player too – a ridiculous state of affairs at my age. What was I thinking? You girls have been right all along.' Her voice seesawed with emotion. 'Older women cannot reinvent ourselves. What a pathetic idea.' She slipped off her engagement ring and placed it next to the pendant. 'It's over.'

Verity and I immediately fell over ourselves to sing her mothering praises. Gawain and Rory were also trying to speak, but Nicole silenced us all with a hand.

'If motherhood is such a natural phenomenon, how come there are so many manuals and TV programmes teaching women how to do it? And I got it spectacularly wrong, obviously, because look at the terrible man both of you chose.' She clawed at her breasts as if scorched by a red-hot bra. 'I should have protected you both from that mongrel.' She scowled like Beethoven. 'I should have been more vociferous in my objections. You were only attracted to him because you had no fun in your teens. All those endless bloody music exams...' Her voice became steely with disgust. 'But electrocuting him on his own drum kit did at least put new meaning into Sex Cymbal!'

Her laugh was like a saucepan dropped on a hard stone floor; the burst of it startled me. I felt trapped between a hug and a scream.

'What the...? Wait! *You* electrocuted the eejit!' I could hear a laugh beginning to surface in Rory's voice. 'Jaysus. Well, good for you,' he chortled. 'The little shit-weasel deserved it.'

'What can I say? A thirst for revenge came over me. And no wonder, given all that he's done to my beautiful girls.' Mum seemed on the brink of flying apart like a supernova.

'Mother, can we just be clear on this?' Verity asked, astounded. 'Are you actually saying you electrocuted your own ex-son-in-law?'

From somewhere far away I heard a great cackling like some Victorian asylum inmate at the bars of her cage. It took a while to register that the deranged noise was coming from my own mother.

'Mum! Couldn't you have just slapped his face? I mean, did you have to flambé his nether regions with a hot-wired throne thumper?' Clearly not a sentence I ever thought I'd utter.

'Well, if you're going to break the law, one should at least do it in a way that's enjoyable, don't you think?'

'And the car scratch, tyre slash, cut brake cable and rock through Mel's window?' I asked, aghast.

'Yes, it has been a bit of a busy week.' Mum drained her whisky glass.

'So, lemme get this right.' Rory scratched his forehead. 'Johnny's butt-kicker. It's mounted directly under his standard drummer's seat?'

'Yes. It's basically an integrated amplifier with two hundred watts,' my mother explained, calmly. 'It makes the seat vibrate in sync with the bass frequencies of the drums.'

'And you rewired it to short-circuit during his solo?' Fiachra asked, amazed.

'Well, yes.'

Rory gave an appreciative whistle. Gawain was also pretty damn impressed.

'Mum, I'm so staying on your good side,' I told her.

'Jay-sus. Can you hear that dog barking?' Fiachra asked me, cupping a hand to his ear. I shook my head, bemused. 'Aye. It's so loud I couldn't hear anything incriminating your ma might just have said, as, obviously, I'd have to act on any knowledge of criminality.'

'Oh yes, I hear it now,' I twigged. 'Cacophonous! A Hound of the Baskervilles.' I sent a conspiratorial smile his way. A small flicker of one came back; not really an olive branch but perhaps just one small olive?

'Mother, how on earth do you know how to rewire and sabotage a drum kit?' Verity probed, intrigued.

Nicole shrugged. 'I'm a single mum. There's not much I can't do. Needs must.'

This was true. While we were growing up, when Nicole wasn't dragging a drunken bassoonist who'd gone AWOL from a brothel, she was clutching a tool belt, Allen keys or cement mixer. My main image from our childhood was Mum racing from school sports day to orthodontic check-ups to concerts as if in some kind of maternal decathlon, a wire stripper in one hand and a baton in the other.

Fiachra's phone pinged. He checked it. 'It's the hospital. I asked a paramedic pal to let me speak to Johnny… but he told them that I'm just a dog handler, expert in bitches, which, and I quote, "are the female of the dog, and vice versa".'

'Charming,' my sister sighed. I noticed now how puffy her face looked, the eyes slitted closed from too much crying, plus she hadn't dyed her roots. There was a racoon stripe down her centre parting. Her nails were also uncharacteristically chipped.

'Is that arse threatening to go to the cops?' Rory demanded.

Fiachra scrolled down through his phone messages. Seconds plodded by, each separated from the next by an eternity. 'Aye,' he finally said.

My mother's eyes, glazed with the dull impassivity of fate, were fixed way beyond us, no doubt onto a dank and dreary prison cell.

On an impulse, Gawain stepped forward, lifted my mother's hand and kissed it with grave tenderness. 'I will take the blame, my beloved. I've been to jail before. It doesn't terrify me.'

I glanced at my sister. Her eyes were as wide as mine with amazement. Was the alpine horn player's devotion to our mother sincere, after all? I felt as if I was pushing against something; a pressure was on me, like trying to open a submarine hatch underwater. It was guilt. That's what it was. A ton of the stuff.

'You would do that for our mother?' There was a note of stern admiration in my sister's voice.

'Yeah well, if any mug's gonna take the rap, it's gonna be me,' Rory stated nobly. 'After all, I'm the one who let Nic down all those years ago. And you girls.'

Once more, Verity and I locked eyes. Our sixty-nine-year-old mother had electrocuted her ex-son-in-law on his own drum kit and now, in a glorious moment for older women everywhere, two men were prepared to go to prison on her behalf.

'You wouldn't survive a second in jail here, mate... I don't think they serve gluten-free organic oatmilk skimmed lattes in Pentonville, mucker.'

'Oh, and what do you live on? At your age, probably oatmeal. You no doubt mainline Viagra too, meaning you don't know if you're coming or going.'

It was like seeing a bear antagonised by a wasp. 'Keep that up, pal, and I'll put you through that window – in instalments. But Nic, I mean it, I should never have chosen politics over family. Going to jail on your behalf is a fitting penance. As you get older, you get wiser and—'

'You must be a genius then…' Gawain interrupted.

Rory cracked his knuckles, menacingly.

'Gawain, um, I think you're a bit out of your league here,' Verity interjected, warily. 'If it comes to a fist fight with Rory, I don't think you'll cut the mustard.'

'Hey, at least I can open the jar.' Gawain was on a roll, showing off for Mum's benefit.

'You know the best thing about gettin' older?' Rory grumbled.

'Carpet slippers?' Gawain suggested.

'No, you little snot weasel, it's not givin' a toss about weedy wee fuckers like you.' Rory drew back his fist, prompting our mother to bang her hand down on the tabletop so hard her empty whisky glass jumped.

'Stop it,' she ordered in dismay. 'Nobody is taking the blame for what I did. I planned the electric shock. And executed it. Not enough to kill, but enough to send him a message. One thing I did teach my girls is to take responsibility for their actions. I did not raise them single-handedly and forge a big career in a patriarchal world to now be rescued by a man,' she said stoutly. 'Girls, I'm just so sorry you had to find out about your father like this. It's just another way I've let you down. The truth is, I've let everybody down. I don't deserve any of you.'

And with that, as if responding to some invisible conductor's baton, she stood up and moved towards the door. 'And do not try to follow me.' It was a bold exit speech, but I noted that one of her shoes was sighing sadly as she walked.

FORTY-EIGHT

A match flared and *voom!* Up went a pile of my wedding photos in flames in the charcoal-filled disposable barbecue grill tray I'd bought from the supermarket specifically for this purpose. I picked up two serrated carving knives and handed one to my sister. A moment later we were both stabbing a huge, tiered wedding cake to death in a shower of crumbs. Gloria Gaynor's 'I Will Survive' was blaring from my iPhone. The framed wedding photo of me in Vegas, beaming, besotted, at Johnny, I sent hurtling into the stone wall beneath Tower Bridge. I then handed Verity a framed photo of her cuddled up with Johnny on a beach in Tahiti, which I'd swiped from her house that morning.

'Go on.'

The sound as the glass shards cascaded onto the flagstones proved deeply satisfying.

I'd dyed two wedding veils black for the occasion and attached one to Verity's hair before donning my own. The dead groom cake-topper, which I'd positioned face down in a pool of blood-red icing, was now upended in the wreckage of the smashed wedding cake. I placed the tiny plastic corpse into a small paper coffin, along with my wedding ring. There was room for Verity's promise ring too.

She hesitated for a moment, then with solemn ceremony laid Johnny's gift next to mine.

'This is our first step to healing,' I told my sister as we pushed the improvised coffin out into the current. I felt some formal words were needed and extracted a piece of paper from my jeans pocket, scribbled with words I'd crafted earlier.

'When Johnny left me, I went for a medal in the Women's Long-Distance Cross-Bearing. But no more sobbing into self-help books entitled *Why Men Leave You and Why It's All Your Fault, You Fat, Middle-Aged Frump*. No. What we're going to do is remind each other of all the positive aspects to a Johnny-ectomy.' I started to list them on my fingers. 'No more snoring or boring... Never again will you have to pretend to laugh at his inane anecdotes... Plus you can now do whatever the hell you want...'

'I'm going to buy an exotic pet,' my sister interrupted, 'tint my hair electric blue and wear nothing but cerise.'

I topped up our champagne, pouring it into crystal glasses – a belated wedding present from my disappointed mother. We both took a long, satisfied swig, saying, in unison, 'Disgusting habit,' then continued watching the cursed rings Johnny had given us bobbing away on the tide.

'Now, in my experience, when traded in by a bloke all women make a misguided lunge for the wine bottle,' I read on, from my testimony. 'Next will be the peroxide bottle. Just don't get them confused. Don't drink and drive either. Believe me, no police officer is going to be moved by the fact that you feel the need to keep your car with you at all times so that it won't leave you for a younger owner.'

'Well, no male officer,' my sister clarified.

'True. I've been in recovery for longer than you, so here.' I handed her the champagne bottle. 'Finish it. Besides, I've got to keep sober enough to stop you from dancing naked on a tabletop or going to work topless.' It was a Sisterhood Rule – after a bad break-up, be her wingwoman.

My sister laughed but the laugh quickly turned into a heart-wrenching sob. She sank onto the flagstones and buried her face in her hands. I abandoned my speech and sat down beside her. The loss, the devastation, it just swept all away in its terrible wake. I knew this desolate terrain only too well.

'I... just... can't... stop... crying.'

'Perfectly normal. There will be bouts of this for months. Years even. And terrible sick feelings as bits of the puzzle fall into place – the lies he's told you, the alibis, the excuses, the whole flocks of wool pulled over your eyes...'

'I just feel like such a total fucking fool that I didn't see it. Why wasn't I more attentive? How could I not have noticed? I want to go around there and rip her heart out.'

'But it's his heart you need to rip out. Yes, Melissa has behaved appallingly. Underneath all that woo-woo, new age niceness, she's nothing but a Mean Girl, after all. But he's the one who really betrayed you. I blamed you when Johnny left but accept now that he pursued you, the way he pursued her... Johnny's as slippery as a banana skin soaked in baby oil. But of course, ironically, Melissa trapped him, in the end.'

'Oh, Izzy, I tried to stay away – but the man's magnetic. Well, you know that only too well. Then, after Chrissie was born, he told me he was out of love with you, that you were sleeping separately and that he'd always adored me. And then came the avalanche of love songs...' She tried to go on but became thick-throated with sobs.

I stroked her hair back from her forehead, which was hot and wet. I didn't know how to make her feel better except to keep talking. 'Oh, and heads up. You may give up eating, too. Or rather, eating will give up you. Alternatively, you may require speed bumps in the kitchen to slow down your progress to the fridge. When heartbroken it's important not to skip a meal... even if it's four or five courses an hour.'

Before us, the nonchalant river rolled forward, unconcerned by the many dramas playing out along its ancient banks.

'So, on the positive side then, I might lose weight?' Verity asked, rallying a little.

'Not that you need to but, yes, for sure. Your only workout will be a daily three-hour worry about where your relationship went wrong. It's a mental and emotional marathon. Of course, there are always two sides to every relationship breakdown: yours, and that arsehole's.'

Verity laughed then. We both did. And then we looked at each other, not sure what we were now if we weren't adversaries.

'The point is,' I concluded, 'my husband ran away with my sister... and I miss her.'

'It's karma, isn't it? Because of what I did to you. I deserve it. But oh, Izzy, I had no idea the level of pain. Oh, what I've put you through...' Her lips were puffy from crying.

'Heartbreak is like motherhood or death: you can't hire someone to go through it for you. But V, I think Johnny not letting you have a child is punishment enough.'

She hung her head. 'I've been so jealous of you, Izzy, marooned as I am in my vacuous life. Oh, to be lost in that labyrinth of motherly love, with all its twists and turns and captivating joys…'

Her turn of phrase was elaborate; well, she was a bestselling author. But the sentiment was spot on. 'Chrissie is the light of my life. And do you know the lesson I'm passing on to my darling daughter? That husbands come and go, but sisters are forever… Be they girlfriends in the sisterhood, or real sisters… Which should be the same thing, really.'

Big, fat tears rolled down my sister's face then. 'I'm also just so upset that we were so mean to our mother.'

'Christ! I know. We've been so bloody judgemental! We're guilty of the exact same ageist sexism we've railed against in our own lives. Can you believe that? Why shouldn't a younger man love our mother? She's amazing!'

'Dynamic!'

'Inspiring.'

'And who were we to judge Gawain's youthful indiscretions? Dear God, we had at least one of our own! A shared one.'

The photo was burnt up now except for the charred remains of Johnny's face. She poked it with the toe of her shoe into the little pile of embers still glowing red in the disposable barbecue dish. Johnny's once cherished features evaporated with a sizzle.

'An alibi. That's what Mum needs. We're just going to have to concoct one.' I stood up and started pacing around a bit. 'Yes, your honour, I swear that this is the Truth, the Whole Truth… the Varnished Truth.'

My sister immediately stopped crying and got back on her feet. Now that our mother was in trouble, we swung into action like a precision drill team of Viennese Lipizzaners from the Spanish Riding School. And Mum was in trouble. This was actually the biggest understatement since the captain of the *Hindenburg* said to his crew, 'Is it getting hot in here?' The police had confirmed that there were suspicious circumstances, as in, deliberate sabotage. If our mother was implicated and Johnny pressed charges, this could mean jail time. As it could for us too, if we fabricated alibis. Perverting the course of justice would have us all banged up faster than you could say 'pepper spray', 'invasive pat downs' and 'mystery meat meals'. But we vowed to do it, for our marvellous matriarch.

'Or... maybe we should just kill him?' my sister suggested, necking the Moët straight from the bottle. 'Our newly discovered father has offered... Did you know that for three dayssss after death, your hair and fingernailsssss keep growing?' she slurred, the Lady Medicine taking effect.

'Yes, but your dinner party invitations tend to peter out... Of course we can't take out a hit on Johnny! He's Chrissie's father, for Chrissake, in case you've forgotten.'

'Have you ever thought about how you'd like to die?' my tipsy sister asked me, swaying slightly. 'I'd like to drown in a jacuzzi of champagne with George Clooney.'

'Or in a tub of tiramisu with Jamie Dornan... No, wait, Pedro Pascal.'

'What about Idris Elba? Ryan Reynolds... And don't forget Chris Hemsworth...'

I sighed, happily. Her cure had begun. 'But one thing's for sure,' I said, grasping her arm to stop her from toppling over into the Thames. 'Our new pact?' I picked up my own crystal flute and raised a toast: 'To never let a penis come between us.'

'I'll drink to that,' my sister said, clinking the bottle up against my glass. 'The most important Sisterhood Rule!' We sang Irving Berlin all the way home. Sisters, sisters...

When we got back to my place, Chrissie was getting ready to go to rehearsals. 'Mum,' she babbled, excitedly, clicking her guitar case closed. 'We've got the most brilliant gig. In a week's time. The Fiddler's Elbow, near St Katharine's Dock. Will you come? And will you bring Grandma? She's nagging me about going to music college in September, but she hasn't even heard the band. I want her to sample my new songs. I know she'll agree to another gap year then... And maybe even a gap life!'

Out of the corner of my eye, I saw Verity curling up into a tight little ball on the sofa. I suddenly couldn't remember if I was the good sister or the evil sister. 'Darling,' I whispered, 'do me a favour. Can you go hug your auntie?'

'What?! I thought that was not allowed. On pain of death.'

'Not any more.'

'Oh that's great, Mum. I'm proud of you.' Chrissie kissed my cheek, then bounced across the room and threw her arms around my startled sister's neck. Verity clung on to my darling daughter as if she were a lifebuoy in big seas. And then she started to really sob. Not the polite crying of a perfectly poised music critic and style guru, but big, snotty, gulpy, gaspy, unhinged howls. The agony of not having a daughter of her own or the brutal realisation of all the anguish she'd caused me? Possibly a mix of both. Either way, all I felt was a tsunami surge of sisterly compassion.

'At the worst time of my life, when you stole my husband…' I started to say.

'Stop! Please! Can you promise never to say that again?' my soggy sister begged.

'Okay… But do you know what got me through?'

'Lady Petrol?'

'Yes, and realising that the grass isn't always greener on the other side… It's just Astroturf.'

FORTY-NINE

Talking of Astroturf, trying to make contact with my mother was the equivalent of watching grass grow. In fact, Astroturf might have grown faster. Nobody could get through to her.

'Why won't she take my calls?' Gawain's voice was parched, his throat on fire with misery. 'Or let me up to her hotel room. She's holed up above that pub, Diddy's, and won't come home.' He paused to drain his teacup to the dregs. 'All night I toss and turn, plagued by nightmares.'

I topped up his Darjeeling, then watched him worry the spoon around the cup.

'There's no more money, you know,' I lied. 'Mum's given it all to charity.'

Gawain paced around my mother's music room. His shoulders hitched upwards near his ears then slumped. 'What does that matter? Or the concert. All that matters is being with my beloved.' He then proceeded to drone on for approximately, oh, eternity, rhapsodising about my mother's many wonderful attributes until I wished he came with a mute button.

Rory was pining as well, moping about my kitchen like a wet weekend listening exclusively to miserable songs about drunks, mostly by Tom Waits. 'There's so much I need to say to the woman – she's my *anam cara* – the pulse of my heart,' he decoded. 'But she won't take me on.' His face was so wrinkled with worry it looked as though he'd fallen asleep face down on a corduroy jacket.

'Maybe if I organised a birthday party?' I texted both men. 'It's her seventieth next weekend. She'd have to turn up for that.'

I immediately started nagging Mum by voicemail about her approaching Big Birthday. She finally texted back to say that she didn't count candles any more. 'After all, there's nothing to celebrate. Although if I do end up in jail, feel free to bake me a cake with a file.'

My nerves shrieked like the unoiled hinges of a door in the wind. This whole catastrophe felt like my fault. I'd need a Nepalese Sherpa to carry the amount of baggage for this guilt trip. If only Mum would see me to talk it all through. But she steadfastly refused to meet any of us. A trap was the only solution. I recruited Chrissie to beg her gran to give an expert opinion on her all-girl band. 'Tell Mum I'll pick her up next Saturday, at eight. Promise her that if you're no good, you'll go to music college, as planned.' I felt pretty confident that this ruse would lure Mum out of her hermit's cave.

Meanwhile, my mother may not want to talk to any of us, but the police certainly did. We needed to concoct an alibi and fast.

'Think!' I urged my sister. 'What would Emmeline Pankhurst do?'

'Forget Emmeline. Sylvia should be our role model right now – the vigilante Pankhurst.'

And luckily, we just happened to have a vigilante on tap.

*

Johnny was lying in a white, backless hospital gown in a narrow steel bed, his hands and feet wrapped in gauze; a bulging bandage over his flambéed groin.

'Your fuckin' family!' he erupted as we entered. 'The throne-thumper wires? Turns out they were tampered with! The police checked the CCTV footage. And guess who was seen enterin' the pub while we were out on our dinner break before the gig and nobody was around? Your friggin' mother! What the actual fuck!?'

'Clearly a case of son-in-law-icide,' I scoffed. 'Revenge for placing both her daughters not on but under a pedestal.'

My sister and I flanked the patient's head, either side of his pillow. His furious eyes swivelled from one of us to the other.

I kissed his furrowed brow. 'Oh, Johnny! Look!' I pointed at his cranium. 'Your hair was burnt off right at the top of your head. Must have been where the electrical charge left your body. Although wait.' I leant in. 'That patch? It's not actually singed. I think it's just where you're going bald. Now I look more closely, your hairline's clearly receding, too.'

'Fuck off! I am not goin' bald,' he seethed.

'Are you sure?' Verity added, thoughtfully. 'I had noticed that it was taking you a lot longer to wash your forehead.'

'And you will be fifty-two next birthday. A tricky age for a rock star. Too young for chair aerobics... too old for crack at a whipped-cream orgy,' I reminded him.

'Quit the bullshit! You were no doubt your mother's bloody accomplices. Your whole fuckin' family's goin' down.'

The atmosphere thickened, turning malevolent. Then he

started laughing. Not a nice laugh. But a gleeful, spiteful sneer of a thing. And that was Rory's cue to enter. In one swift movement, he'd gagged Johnny with one hand and started squeezing on his charred nethers with the other.

Johnny tried to punch him, but as both hands were bandaged it was like being savaged by a soufflé.

'So, where would you like your ashes scattered, mucker? Or would you like me to surprise you?' Rory chuckled, menacingly.

Johnny's eyes grew wide with alarm. They darted back and forth to the little window in the door, desperate to grab the attention of a passing nurse.

'Let's compose your epitaph, shall we?' Rory riffed. 'He led a wonderful life and never suffered... Oh, unless I wanted him to... ' Rory squeezed the wound again and beads of sweat broke out on Johnny's forehead. 'Of course, if you tell the police to drop the case, your recovery's guaranteed.'

Verity mopped Johnny's brow once more. 'Yes, that's definitely taking me so much longer to mop. You might consider a hair transplant... if you live long enough.'

Johnny's eyes popped out even further but he shook his head with fury, like some obstinate infant.

'You're such a cartoonish character, Johnny,' I said. 'I can't believe all those little thought balloons don't crush your head.'

'So, girls, if Lover Boy here won't drop the charges, what would you like me to do with the little gobshite? Or, rather, your main *squeeze*?'

Rory squeezed again and Johnny writhed about in pain, his pathetic backless hospital gown twisting itself around him into a tight, white cocoon.

'Hmmm... we could redeploy his penis as a novelty hat peg, perhaps?' I suggested.

'Excellent idea,' my sister agreed. 'Sorry. What did you say, Johnny? Our ex is clearly the strong and silent type. If you shoot him, Rory, you won't even need to use a silencer,' she joked. 'Oh and by the way, Johnny, I'm citing irreconcilable differences in our separation proceedings, especially when it comes to dental hygiene. Apparently you seem to think it's okay to put random women's genitals into your mouth.'

'I should have got our marriage annulled. I mean there was no way I ever agreed to a vow that read "Till death us do part... or till my hotter sister comes along".'

'Oh, that's a sweet thing to say, Izzy, but you're much hotter than me.'

'It's called a hot flush, Verity. And I'm having one right now.'

'Me too. And it's making me want to do the most craaazzzzy things.'

'And of course, as we're being taken hostage by our hormones, we can't be held responsible for our actions.'

'Exactly. It just wouldn't stand up in a court of law... And nor will that,' Verity said now, crushing Johnny's injured todger.

A few more squeezes and Johnny was persuaded not to pursue the matter, nodding in agreement to all Rory's demands.

'It's the least you can do, you feckin' eejit,' Rory concluded. 'After ruinin' the lives of both my darlin' daughters.'

'You and the duplicitous, malicious Melissa deserve each other.' My sister was using her most supercilious voice. 'Although will she want you any more? Now that you're balding, broke and unable to play your drums?' Her vowels were more perfectly formed than those of a sequestered duchess; yep, she was really enjoying this.

As soon as Rory ungagged him, Johnny hissed, 'I'm not scared of you maniacs. I'm only not pressin' charges because it's Chrissie's grandma. And I don't want to upset my darlin' daughter. Now, get out! The Nightingale Sisters. Christ! For some insane reason, I really did love you both, once. But now? Well, now I'm fresh out of fucks left to give about either of you!'

'So eloquent,' my sister said. As we made for the door she turned back to take one last long look at him. 'How should we remember you?'

'As the man we've already forgotten,' I suggested.

'But you should remember something, Johnny,' Verity said. 'That I have a sister and I'm not afraid to use her.'

'Exactly. My sister has an awesome sister – and vice versa.'

And we laughed all the way down the hospital corridor.

FIFTY

When Mum saw Verity, Gawain and Rory lying in wait by the stage, the scorching flame-thrower glower she sent my way nearly set my hair on fire. She swivelled on a haughty heel to walk out but Chrissie's voice suddenly soared above the band – clear, strong, sweet and true.

Femifesto, although playing with enthusiasm, were not up to Chrissie's virtuosic level of excellence. The drummer missed a few beats, the keyboard player was half a heartbeat behind and the bass wasn't sitting well.

My mother instinctively started moving her arms to steady the rhythm. She snatched a multicoloured swizzle stick from a passing cocktail as an impromptu baton and moved towards the stage. Up, down, up, down – my mother's graceful hands drew the focus of the band and soon the music was pulsing in harmonic synchronicity. My daughter beamed at my mother, a smile warm enough to melt a glacier.

Chrissie's voice grew richer with each verse, dirty and angelic all at once – a voice that reminded me so much of my own, all that time ago, when it was me up there centre stage.

There were instruments lying around, propped up against speakers – a guitar, a fiddle, a saxophone… My legs were mounting the stage steps before my brain registered what was happening. It was pure muscle memory. The guitar strap slid over my shoulder so naturally. Music began to flow from my fingertips, thickening out the band's sound. Chrissie sent me another sunbeam of a smile. 'Sing along,' she mouthed. My singing voice had seized up when Johnny left me. I didn't even sing in the shower. But I'd heard Chrissie practising this song a million times, so just opened my mouth and let the music pour out. My voice was a little thin and scratchy at first but the harmonies came easily, as did being back on stage – the first time in over fourteen years.

The sweet strains of a violin swooped down over us now like drops of golden honey. I half turned to see Verity drawing her bow across the strings, improvising a solo. And all the time, our mother's swizzle stick kept us right on the beat. It was just like old times – the Nightingale Girls, playing together, weaving a spell over the audience, embroidering musical magic onto the warm summer air. We just slipped into the moment like a hot bath.

As we played I felt a great resonance chime through my whole being. A part of me that had been missing for so long simply fell back into place. I was in my natural habitat once more. We played seven songs in all, our mother leading us through the whole set with panache and aplomb. This was what we'd done all our lives, playing together; from the cradle on, ours had been a musical household. Inveterate musical omnivores, we chewed on all forms Renaissance, baroque, romantic, the Great American Songbook – jamming, rehearsing, improvising, performing. It was how we communicated. It was how we showed love. It was how we'd always found harmony after discord.

When the band took a break to loud applause and cries of 'more' and 'encore', my sister and I stood at the front of the stage, facing our beloved mother. Mum's face was flushed with some elusive emotion – could it be joy? I jumped off the stage and seized her hand. Verity made a more ladylike exit down the stairs, then grasped my mother's other hand in hers.

'Mum, at the worst time of my life when Verity—'

'If you say "stole my husband" one more time I'll hit you over the head with this violin,' my sister said, raising her instrument in a mock threat.

'I was not going to stay "stole my husband" because I told you I wouldn't mention it again…'

'Okay, then,' Verity backed off, 'I'm sorry I snapped.'

'At the worst time of my life,' I continued, 'when Verity requisitioned a male who didn't belong to her…'

My sister brandished the violin as if to whack me once more but my mother eyeballed us both. 'Girls, behave!' she chastened, in a voice straight from our childhood.

'What I'm trying to say, Mum, is that it was music that got me through the worst time in my life. And you gave that gift to me. I hear and feel you in my playing every day.'

'And you gifted music to me too, Mother. The greatest gift,' Verity added. 'A gift you've also bequeathed to your granddaughter. Chrissie's a phenomenal musician.'

'What we're trying to say is that you didn't take a wrong road, Mum. Music is your road. And ours. We've been so out of tune as a family, for so long. V and I should never have judged you for falling in love with Gawain.'

My mother sighed. 'You've both been vile. Your children are supposed to be a great comfort in your old age… but they sure as hell make you get there faster too,' she declared, with gruff affection.

'If you love Gawain, then please go enjoy your amorous duet...' I insisted. 'If it's Rory you love most, then play your hit tunes together in a romantic musical revival.'

'And if you want to play solo – that's an option too,' Verity added. 'But you must never, ever fall out of love with music.'

'Oh, and happy birthday.' I dug into my dress pocket and fished out the Gift of Life keyring disc Mum had ripped off days before and left on the table at Diddy's bar. The cheap lacquer had flaked off, but it glittered there, in the lights. Mum took it from my hands, rubbed it affectionately, then held it up to her lips. She looked at us both for a moment, then opened her arms. My sister and I fell into her embrace. I hugged her with a relief so intense that it was almost painful. And then Chrissie piled on and hugged us harder still. The entire world, I thought, needs comforting right now. A hug for humanity. But this was a good start.

'The family that plays together, stays together,' I said, cornily.

'Jesus Christ. Who are we all of a sudden? The fucking Partridge Family?' my sister whinged. But in truth, neither of us could have been any happier; nor did we break out of the warm embrace.

Our little moment of familial harmony was eventually interrupted by the long forlorn call of an alpine horn. I'd never rated the instrument before, but the sound that silenced the pub was velvety, melancholic and deeply profound. The instrument was so long, at least thirteen feet, that the whole audience strained to locate the player.

Gawain was so far back on the stage he was practically in Oxfordshire. But the haunting tune was of such longing and loss that all chatter ceased. Which in an Irish pub is nothing short of a miracle. And while Gawain played his heart out, he gazed devotedly at my mother. She gracefully lifted her swizzle-stick baton to mark the beats, never taking her eyes from his face.

As the beautiful, aching melody concluded and the last long note shimmered there in the air, an electronic chord twanged. The audience swivelled as one to see Rory, riffing on the electric guitar from the other side of the stage. It was a rebel song; a call to arms; a song of love and loyalty, passion and promise. While squeezing, wrenching really, the achingly poignant notes from the Gibson guitar, he too gazed at my mother, who laughingly smiled back.

At the bar afterwards, Rory was the first to make his play. 'Nic, you're the love of my life. My *anam cara*. My soulmate. Let's pick up where we left off.'

'You can't turn back the clock,' Gawain interrupted, abruptly, placing his arm around my mother's waist.

'Aye, but you can wind it up again,' Rory retorted, holding my mother's elbow.

'Nobody winds up clocks any more, old-timer.'

Rory's eyes narrowed, dangerously.

I exchanged a nervous glance with my sister. This was not going to end well. I knew from Olympic Games' coverage that the Swiss enjoy a sport known as the biathlon, which involves skiing, pausing, shooting a target, then skiing on again. For Rory, that was just a typical day out in Derry.

'Keep calm,' I chastened the Irishman, under my breath.

Rory cracked his knuckles but refrained from throwing

a punch. 'Aye, you Swiss twerp. Sure, I've been around the block… Christ, every time I turn around that once-in-a-lifetime super-moon eclipse is feckin' back again… But I'm young at heart, and that counts for everything, don't you reckon, Nic?'

Gawain scoffed, then addressed my mother. 'He gets symptoms… I get urges.'

'I'm gettin' the urge to put you in a box, that's for feckin' sure!' Rory flexed his huge biceps, each one bigger than Gawain's head.

'Okay,' Gawain admitted. 'You're a big muscle man. Mother Nature may have given you a lot, but Father Time sure as hell is taking it away. You're ageing faster than the pop songs you play.'

He might as well have flung acid in Rory's face. 'They're not pop, you eejit! They're rock. Rebellious, subversive, political… Not that you'd understand that. I betcha the only political party you belong to is the "We Love Lederhosen; Keep Every Other Bastard off our Pristine Mountain" brigade…'

'Nicky, my darling, this ruffian is on the run from the law. What do you think your future together would be?'

'Short,' Rory shot back. 'Which is why I want to enjoy every minute of it, with the most beautiful woman in the world.'

I glanced at my mother, expecting a disapproving, or even embarrassed, scowl, but she was wearing a cat-that-got-the-cream beam.

'Oh boys, boys.' She now laughed. 'First off, Rory, get over yourself. The only beautiful woman you've ever had on your arm is a tattoo… And as for you, Gawain, Rory's right. There's not a political bone in your body. The Swiss motto? Climb every mountain, ford every income stream!... But go on, the two of you. Tell me more!'

She was positively basking in all the attention. My seventy-year-old mum had two men in love with her, whereas I couldn't even keep one. It was time I changed my tune.

FIFTY-ONE

I'd invited Fiachra by text to my mother's impromptu, secret birthday bash. Even though it was his favourite pub, now that Bridget was back in his life I was pretty sure he wouldn't turn up. And I had treated him so badly. The man was from Derry; kindness may be his default position, but fuck off was his wingman. Nanoseconds ground by as I ran my eyes around and around the room in search of the wag of a dog's tail or a glimpse of his dear face.

I'd more or less resigned myself to a life of celibacy atop a snow-capped Nepalese peak when, on my way back from the bar, my ears were snagged by the most mellifluous melody. I followed the musical trail, Hansel and Gretel–like, outside onto a small balcony perched precariously above the rushing river. The heaving black surge of the Thames was quicksilvered with reflections of light from boats and buildings but the dark, secluded balcony was lit only by stars.

Eyes half closed, head tipped back in a light trance; his fingers danced across the strings, engrossed, entranced, transported. I could almost see the music as it left his guitar, lifting into the air like smoke.

As my eyes adjusted to the gloaming, I watched the muscles in his arms tense then relax as he played. I drank him in, as if for the first time. His skin was smooth and pale in the moonlight, his thick, curly gold hair flecked with silver. His cheekbones were sharp enough to shave Parmesan; his sea-green eyes warm and deep enough to swim laps.

After the final flourish of Albéniz's 'Asturias', I clapped my hands together with delight. 'Your fingering was excellent, the rhythm stirring...' I said on an impulse.

'Well, I had a pretty good teacher,' he said with a speculative smile.

'But don't they say that the pupil eventually becomes the master?' I gave him a look which I hoped was sexy and tender. He returned me the ghost of a smile. I also hoped he realised that I was actually flirting, for real this time. A tiny flicker in his eyes told me he did... Plus the fact that he glanced down at my nipples, which had become so hard they were poking up against the cotton of my backless, strapless dress, like little torpedoes.

I clocked a sly smile, then an eye twinkle. 'Why don't you be the judge? Which of my fingering techniques do you like best?'

He stood up and ran one hand along my arm to the nape of my neck, then caressed me there with steady, strong strokes. I moaned a little, which was his cue to put down the guitar. Then he leant me back against the wall, bunching my curls into his hand, his hard body pressed into mine.

'If you kiss my neck, I'm not responsible for what happens next...' I warned. His touch was running through me all the way from my nipples to my knees, loitering in lots of soft, velvety places in between.

'Isabella.' He nuzzled the word into my ear, savouring my neck and throat with hot, gentle kisses. And then his lips were on mine. I wanted to vanish inside the kiss. I wanted the heat to extinguish me.

And then, ever so slowly, dizzyingly slowly, he ran his hand up my leg, up my thigh and under the lacy elastic. He started to stroke me, never breaking his rhythm. He dipped his fingers inside, gently at first, then pressing more firmly, moving at the same tempo as his tongue, which had now found my breast. My pulse beat with pleasure. His strokes became bolder, more confident and assured, slowly working their way up to a crescendo.

I recognised every stroke technique as he moved through his repertoire.

'*Rasqueado*,' I said, identifying the intense flamenco-type strumming I had taught him. Then a moment later, 'Tremelo' – the continuous melody repeated rapidly with right-hand fingers. Oh and now, *étouffée*, from the French *étouffer* meaning to stifle, where the note is damped immediately after being played. '*Pizzicato*...' I whispered then, as he now mimicked the right hand muting the strings while the left hand played. After a few gasps from me, he then moved on. '*Campanella*...' I identified. 'Crossing strings to create a bell-like continuous sound.' And I was making a lot of sounds by now, groans, moans and whimpers of pleasure as he rang my bell over and over and over. After a while he moved on to the rest stroke I'd taught him. '*Apoyando*,' I murmured into his neck, and then, 'Free stroke – a *tirando* used... used... for... arp... arpeggios,' I whimpered, a slave to the rhythm.

'And now some improvisation,' he joked. 'The clit-tickly-ando.' The calluses on the fingertips of his left hand formed by all those glissandos up and down the fretboard added a delicious frisson to the eroticism. And that was when I reverberated body, heart and soul.

And there, on the dim, dark balcony, cantilevered out over the rushing river, my body became pure energy; solidified light. I sparkled, effervescent, phosphorescent. There in the shadows, the only illumination a feeble light from the porthole of the odd passing boat, I caught his eye. He was looking at me in the same way I'd seen him look at his favourite dogs. Okay, not a girl's favourite analogy, but from a dog man – no greater compliment. And then there were no other words needed. I ran my hand down the xylophone of his spine. I could feel his backbone tense, strung to breaking. Suddenly I wanted him with every cell of my being.

'Those jeans look great on you,' I murmured.

'Really? Even though they're ironed?' He gave a slow, honeyed smirk.

'Yes... but they'd look so much better on the ground.' I moved my hand down to his hips and unbuttoned his jeans, very, very slowly.

'So you're ready for an encore...?' he panted hotly into my neck.

'Well, with that standing ovation, who could say no?'

The look he gave me now was sexy, amused and tender. 'Isabella.' He said my name in the most velvety way. 'Bella... Izzy...'

I wanted to reply but none of my favourite writers had invented the word I needed to describe how I felt right now, not Shakespeare or Austen or Wilde or any one of those many Brontës, so I had to make do with a gurgle and grunt of lust before lunging for his lips.

'But wait. What about Bridget?' An electric current was running from my tonsils to my toes and back again.

'I never told you what her last words to me were at the altar…'

'Tell me.' The warmth of his body was now radiating into mine.

'You're just not good enough for me.'

'Harsh. And now?' My skin was made of thousands of fine silk threads, all of them pulled tight.

'Well, since we reconnected, I've realised that she's not good enough… Because, well, she's not you.'

And then we were slipping off each other's clothes, him slowly edging down my lacy knickers, me easing off his jeans, revealing boxers patterned in four-leaf clovers – 'A gift from my ma,' he muttered – but I couldn't have cared if they were thermal tweed long johns at this stage…

He knelt down and tasted me – salted caramel, he said. While he tasted of nutmeg and cinnamon. Oblivious to the world, we spun a cocoon of breath around each other, out there on the tiny, forgotten balcony. And then, as he pulled me down on to his lap and entered me, there was nothing to do but call out his ludicrously unpronounceable Gaelic name – 'Fiachra… Fiachra!… Fiachra!!!!'

FIFTY-TWO

By the time we slunk back into the pub, the place was rocking. On stage, Chrissie's all-girl band were twirling, trilling and sliding velvet, lusciously eyelined glances at their captive audience. Chrissie's sweet, honeyed voice, now a little tired and frayed around the edges, had taken on the smoky, sexy sound of a rusty clarinet. Everywhere I looked, people were dancing, prancing, gyrating, laughing, hugging, chug-a-lugging the black gold and jamming away, or 'having a ding-dong' as Rory called this kind of improvised mischief.

Rory and Gawain, busy vying for my mother's affections, were locked in some kind of musical duel. They took it in turns to serenade Nicole, Rory with rock ballads, Gawain with alpine folk ballads, while the other musos riffed around these competitive compositions.

'Call that a tune? That chorus is so simple it could be learnt by a toddler, or even an advanced sloth,' was Gawain's verdict on Rory's R & B love song.

'Well, your feckin' ditty's more complicated than advanced algebra. Who could ever croon along to that atonal clusterfuck?' Rory retorted. 'I think the time has come to get out my bouzouki.'

There was some confusion as to whether this was a guitar or a gun – but Rory then proceeded to uncase a long-necked lute with a round body and a fretted fingerboard. Gawain's response was to unpack his folkloric hammered dulcimer and offer up a yodel. To say that Mum was relishing the attention is a little like saying that Lauren Sánchez is only slightly botoxed or the Earth just a little bit round.

'Gosh, girls, how to choose between these two men?' Mum thrilled, the moment Verity and I slid onto the banquette of her chosen nook. She'd summoned us both with an urgent curl of her finger. 'What do you advise?'

'No, no, no!' Verity raised her hand as if stopping traffic. 'Who are we to judge your emotional trajectory, Mother? Our denigration of your union with a younger man, well, it was nothing more than blatant ageist sexism. You must make up your own mind.'

'V and I behaved like spoiled brats, Mum. And I'm so sorry. Whomever you choose, we'll support you.'

Mum cut us all off a big slab of the chocolate birthday cake Verity had baked. 'That's good because my birth certificate may be saying "settle the hell down", but my spirit is saying – "request fucking denied!"'

I forked a delicious bit of cake into my mouth. Much to my amazement, so did Verity. It was the first time I'd seen her eat carbs since the eighties. Next time we got our nails done, she might even let me eat the complimentary doughnuts – and not just the air in the hole.

My daughter squeezed into the booth too then, her arms warm around my neck. She smelled of vanilla and lemon and carefree happiness. My mother turned to her.

'What do you think, Chrissie darling? Which man do you like best? Gawain rocks my world, sexually and creatively, but Rory's a soulmate. My feelings for the rascally rebel are clearly unresolved and run deep. Plus we share the same sense of humour and cultural references and, of course, these two!' She hooked a thumb in our direction. 'My emotional metronome moves to Rory's beat... and then swings back to Gawain's. Chrissie darling, what do you advise? You're worldly. In your short life, you've been through quite a lot...'

That was true enough. As I cut Chrissie a slice of cake, I ran through a mental checklist. Chrissie's father had an affair with her auntie and then abandoned us; her aunt, a leper for five years, was no longer contagious and in need of a lot of hugging; she had a half-sibling on the way and a brand-new grandfather who may or may not be a wanted felon. Oh, and her grandma currently had two lovers – a former freedom fighter on the run and a Swiss toy boy with a phallic instrument.

'So...' My mother took Chrissie's hands in hers. 'Who should I choose, darling girl? One has a future and the other – a past. What do you suggest?'

My daughter shrugged. 'A throuple.'

At this unexpected reply our eyebrows raised as one; the brow version of the corps de ballet.

'Although I tried to get both men to play together and look what ensued. Some kind of duet duel.' Mum nodded towards the stage, where Gawain and Rory were still engaged in their musical one-upmanship.

My daughter gave an exasperated eye-roll. 'This kind of macho male behaviour is why I've gone gay.'

Cue the hairy corps de ballet once more. 'You're gay?!' my mum, sister and I chorused.

'What about Irish Sean?' I asked, perplexed.

'Oh, he's lovely. But I'm too young to get bogged down. Which is quite funny, as he's from the Bogside! Look, I'm not exclusively gay, but I want to experiment. I'm currently dating my bass player, Clementine, plus a law student called Larry, Garry from Greenpeace a Palestinian film maker, a Jewish podcaster, a guy who's at clown school in Paris, oh, and my current favourite, Sadie, a trombonist who is a non-binary celibate.'

'Oh, right... Okay!' I said, taking on board the fact that my daughter's current favourite suitor was lust-agnostic with homoerotic overtones. 'So, you're basically offering something for everyone, like a Royal Variety Show.'

'Ah... that's one way of putting it, Mum.' She laughed and the laugh was so blissful that we all joined in – our gravelly guffaws rattling like shingle on a beach in big seas. 'I'm basically keeping all options open.'

'Me too, darling,' my mother said. 'Oh and just so you know, I identify as a post-menopausal woman. My pronouns are Try Me.'

I grinned at Mum then. Her pronouns were actually hee/hee as she was back to being her funny, feisty self.

Up on stage, the makeshift band now segued into a slower tune. It was in a minor key but achingly sweet and full of promise. I felt a hot, wet tongue on my hand and turned to see Maisie. I braced myself, ready to lose a limb or two in her snarling gnashers. But she didn't seem poised to drag me into the underworld as usual. In fact, the big attack dog was panting happily up at me, ears twitching, rivulets of drool drenching my arm. Fiachra paused by our nook and winked. I squeezed past the big dog, floated towards him and melted into his chest. As we glided off around the dance floor, this time it was me who prompted the eyebrow corps de ballet. Chrissie gave me an enthusiastic thumbs up.

A few songs later I saw Verity and my daughter smiling and joking, basking in their new-found friendship, taking it in turns to rub Maisie's big belly. Gawain and Rory, meanwhile, continued to tussle musically over my mother, who beamed, Cheshire cat–like, at their shenanigans. But it was her daughters' melodious reunion Mum most relished. She kept looking from one to the other of us, delighted by the congruence and resolution in our family. I realised then that our symphony had reached the scherzo, the most joyous and frolicsome of musical movements.

In true Gaelic tradition, the jubilant, surprising, spontaneous night rolled on. Revellers played and sang along together, quipping and quaffing. Nor did I care that my over-exuberant Mum-manoeuvres, circa 1982, were giving me a bad case of MARDI (Middle-Age Related Dance Injuries) and meant I'd soon be in need of a Zimmer frame. There was even time for another balcony encounter. 'Read me my rights, officer,' I sighed into Fiachra's sweaty neck at about 3 a.m. 'I clearly need a full strip search.'

Eventually, after another furious bout of singing, dancing and random toasts to Taliesin, Dagda, Angus Og and the many, many other Celtic gods of music, my liver started to fly a white flag of surrender. I staggered off the dance floor to the bar to beg for coffee.

'So, what time does this joint close?' I asked, as the barman poured me a steaming cup from a giant cafetière.

'Oh, about four hours ago.' He twinkled. A lovely warm aroma of bacon began to waft from the kitchen. 'It's a lock-in. Hold tight. Bacon and egg rolls are on the way.'

My sister materialised beside me.

'I'll take one for my sister too,' I called out to him. 'She's a very brilliant woman... Obviously we're twins.'

'This woman is not just my sister,' Verity elaborated for his benefit, 'we're the best of friends – for example, she thinks I'm a natural brunette and I think she's too skinny.'

Oh, how I'd missed this kind of comedic camaraderie, when we'd call each other to discuss a new approach to a situation we'd already discussed six hundred times, then ring each other again five minutes later to reiterate. Sisterhood is built on a solid foundation of such shared minutiae, plus, of course, a soupçon of sarcasm and chicanery.

'In truth,' Verity told the busy barman, who was very kindly pretending to listen, 'it's our contrasting characters that make us stronger. Together, our various fortes combine to make up one pretty formidable female.'

'Exactly.' I smiled.

And then we clung together in a slumped embrace, like exhausted boxers at the end of a long bout – wrung out and strung out, but still bloody well standing.

FIFTY-THREE

We took our coffee and bacon rolls and climbed the rickety wooden stairs to the rooftop of the old riverside pub, a once favoured haunt of pirates and parvenus. After a hefty heave, a grimy window opened out onto a little flat roof which overlooked the river. We put our shoulders to the frame, hoisted it upwards then climbed through and sat down, our backs propped against the wall.

The rising sun looked like a knob of butter in a red hot skillet, sizzling and caramelising into golden butterscotch. It was a greeting-card sunrise of the life-goal-messages kind.

'I feel as though I should be feng-shui-ing my chakra or something,' I said, through a mouthful of bacon butty.

Verity snorted. 'Really? After all Melissa's madness, I have a third-eye infection.' All our rough edges were gone, replaced by smoothness, like those sand-scoured pieces of glass we found as girls on a beach once when Mum had a concert in County Durham.

Growing up, my sister had always lifted me two octaves on the happiness scale without even realising she was doing so. Our laughter would effervesce in us like champagne as we danced to female torch songs until the wee hours.

Sisters, especially twins, instinctively understand each other. If under attack, the wagons circle. Wagons? Who am I kidding. Having a formidable sister on your side is like having a bombproof, flame-retardant armoured vehicle on hand for quick getaways.

'Oh, happy birthday, by the way,' I toasted Verity with my coffee cup. 'In all the kerfuffle of Mum going missing we forgot to celebrate turning fifty. Can you bloody believe it? Time to make our bucket list. Here's to having a sensational second act. Just like Mum.'

'Hear, hear.' She clinked her cup up against mine. 'Although I prefer to call it a Fuck-It List. Number one? That we spend a lot more time together. Thank you for forgiving me, Izzy,' she said, cautiously.

'People make mistakes. Nobody's perfect, I've realised that. The truth is, despite everything, I would take a bullet for you. And not just a light graze either, but a full-on Peaky Blinders-type machine-gun body strafe.'

'Really? Well, I might take a light graze for you, maybe, on the upper arm... Seriously though, I just can't believe that, after all I put you through, somehow, miraculously, you still love me... I keep waiting for the hallucinatory drugs to wear off, but no.'

'I won't love you for much longer if you keep hogging the rolls. You rat! I can't believe you ate the last piece of bacon!'

'Huh! Whatever happened to nobody's perfect, everyone makes mistakes, just, like, four seconds ago?'

A leg suddenly jutted through the open window, followed by a familiar torso and there was Mum, clambering out over the sill.

'Oh, girls, I've been looking everywhere for you!'

'Well, that makes a change,' I said, sarcastically.

'Yes, now you know what it's like!'

She laughed. 'Sorry I've been so elusive. God, it just fills me with joy to see you together again. Sisterly love isn't just the icing on the cake – it is the cake,' she told us. 'Believe me, by my age, I've learnt a lot...'

'Yes, but can you remember it?' I teased.

My mother biffed me good-naturedly across the top of my head, before lowering herself into the space between us, Verity and I wiggling sideways to fit her in. Then we all three gazed out at the dawn.

'Mother, I just wanted to thank you for giving me the best gift imaginable... a truly sensational sister,' Verity said, drawing us both into a clumsy embrace full of awkward elbows and bumping knees.

'You just want my bone marrow!' I teased, to cut through the treacle. 'In which case you'd better be much, much nicer to me!'

Mum pulled the Gift of Life pendant up from under her shirt. It glittered there in the morning sunbeams. She rubbed it affectionately and held it up to her lips. 'Ah... the gift of life,' she sighed, sadly. 'What dear Helen's death taught me is that our time on earth is short. So, don't age with grace. Age with mischief, audacity, sass and a scintillating tale to tell. Do or say something outrageous every day. And get horizontal as often as possible. Basically, live so that if your life was turned into a book, Florida would ban it. Now, go forth and be fabulous!'

I clung to my mother even harder now, paralysed by love.

'So, you and Fiachra....' my mother enquired, happily.

'Yes, I didn't notice it at first, but he really is a

gorgeous-looking man,' my sister said. 'I quite fancy him myself, actually...'

My stomach dropped for a nauseating nanosecond before I realised she was joking. 'I wouldn't put it past you, you sexual kleptomaniac!' I really did hit her then.

'Girls, behave! Looks as though I got you just the right present.' Mum began to rummage through her coat pockets. 'Scored you some drugs to celebrate your birthdays.' For a disorientating moment I worried she'd become addicted to Gawain's enamel pill pot of weed gummies and micro-dosing pipette. Then laughed as she handed each of us a packet of HRT patches. 'Believe me, my loves, it's rocket fuel! Oh and another thing,' she sidebarred, 'I've been asked to conduct a new work at the Sydney Opera House. It's about Aussie suffragettes, who got the vote long before the rest of the world... It's a huge, musical celebration of the sisterhood. I've said yes, on the proviso that you girls come with me.'

'What about the dreaded Melissa?' I asked, concerned.

'Sacked. Breach of contract. All she's got left in the world are some burnt offerings.'

The audacity of what our mother had done to Johnny to avenge us plus our follow-up badass gangsta behaviour in the hospital had us detonating into hoots of astonished laughter. Our irreverent chortling was only curtailed by the sound of my favourite voice.

'What have I missed?!' I turned to see Chrissie now popping her head and then her legs through the wonky window. She gave me a look fizzing with joy, happiness spilling from her eyes.

'Basically, Mum is telling us to live every day as though our pubes are on fire,' I told her.

Verity slapped my wrist. 'The wisdom your grandma would like to impart, Chrissie, is that the world throbs with pleasures and treasures and that we should try them all.'

'Except for crystal meth…' my mother clarified.

'And bungee jumping,' I added.

'And a Trump rally,' my sister instructed, firmly. Chrissie nestled amongst us and handed out hot fresh bacon butties.

'Basically, darlings, when I finally kick the bucket, I want it to be a champagne bucket,' Mum clarified. 'And I want that bucket to be nestled beside the hammock swinging gently outside my Byron Bay beach house, where I've been celebrating my hundredth birthday with you three and for my latest boyfriend to be so upset he has to abandon his iron man triathlon to race home to give me the kiss of life.'

That set us off on a comedic riff, itemising all we wanted to do in life – a list that soon had us putting hands over each other's mouths to muffle our snorts and chortles, in a feeble attempt not to wake the neighbours; although of course in the quiet, pre-dawn stillness we must have sounded like elephants doing karaoke.

I felt a tingling happiness along my veins. Nothing was needed to enhance this mood of utter contentment. And so we sat, side by side, my mum, my sister, my daughter and I, the sisterhood of our family, watching the sun set the big, old city alight, the usually manic Thames strangely, magically still as the tide turned. We were like Orion's Belt: always there, lined up alongside each other. Whenever I felt lost and couldn't find my place in life, these three people were my bookmark. As I was for them too – all of us on the same page, the same page of the most magical score.

I was reminded then of the closing moments of fugue

in which all the complex, difficult, nuanced, challenging themes of our long journey were picked up again: a poignant vignette followed by a tease; an apology by a self-deprecating aside; a heartfelt emotion by a witty wisecrack.

And so we greeted the day, glugging down hot coffee, ripping into juicy bacon butties and laughing like kookaburras – kookaburras which have just heard a side-splitting anecdote from some even funnier kookaburras – euphoric with love and ravenous for life.

THE END.

ACKNOWLEDGEMENTS

To my beloved, Brian O'Doherty, thank you, darling, for all the love and laughter.

To my dearest sisters, Jenny, Liz and Cara, a medal to each of you for wading through my first draft. Greater love hath no sisters! You light up my life, every day, in every way. You are the greatest gift our mother could ever give me. Oh, and thanks, Mum. You, of course, are the most inspiring, accomplished and adored matriarch imaginable.

Thanks also to all the many friends who helped me with obscure details. My drummer pals, Ian Paice, Nick Mason, Monti, Kram and Alon Ilsar for helping me work out how to singe a drummer's buttocks. (Not a sentence I ever thought I'd write!) Tommy Bodmer, thanks for Swiss tips. Thanks to Elsa and Lily Hall for teen-speak checks. For police dog handling info, thanks to Carol Davison, who brought my prose to heel. And for top undercover surveillance tips, I hope I'm allowed to mention you, Will Gedes, or will you now have to kill me?

To my perspicacious editor, Vicki Mellor, your guiding editorial hand is deeply appreciated. To my dynamic agent, David Headley, thanks for all the cheerleading. To Amanda Ross, your steadfast literary support is so uplifting. To the teams at Head of Zeus and Bloomsbury, especially Kathryn Colwell, Yasmeen Doogue-Khan, Holly Humphreys, Jo Liddiard, Shannon Hewitt and Hermione Davis – thanks for all the TLC. And to Cathy Odusanya, thanks for keeping my crazy show on the road.

To my darling Jules and Georgie, thanks for all your unconditional love and for not resenting the many long hours your deranged mum has spent slaving over a hot manuscript.

To Giovanni Groppoli, thanks for supporting Palestinian health workers by bidding at an auction to be mentioned in this book. It was a last minute request so I hope being a failed Eurovision song contestant didn't hit a bum note!

To sisters everywhere, how lucky we are to have each other!

And to the sisterhood, my wonderful, witty, warm, wise and generous readers – thanks for coming on this long, literary, funny, feminist ride with me for the last fifty years. I hope I've offered some comedic comfort through all the trials and tribulations of adolescence, dating, broken hearts, marriage, pregnancy, child-rearing, neurodiversity, divorce, menopause, sexist ageism and beyond. I trust I've encouraged you all to have a sensational second act. Now all you have to do is to go forth and be fabulous. All my love, Kathy x

ABOUT THE AUTHOR

Kathy lette first achieved a *succès de scandale* as a teenager with the novel *Puberty Blues*, which was made into a major film and a TV mini-series. She has written twenty books, which have variously been translated into nineteen languages and adapted into movies, TV series and an opera. Kathy has two children and divides her time between Sydney and London. Kathy is an autodidact (a word she taught herself) but has three honorary doctorates. She is a TV presenter, newspaper and magazine columnist and also an ambassador for Their World, the National Autistic Society and Ambitious About Autism. Kathy recently completed a tour of her one-woman show, 'Girls Night Out', and is pleased to report that she didn't fall out with the cast.

Visit her website at www.kathylette.com and find her on X @KathyLette, Facebook/KathyLetteAuthor and Instagram @kathy.lette

Thanks for reading!

Want to receive exclusive author content, news on the latest Aria books and updates on offers and giveaways?

Follow us on X @AriaFiction and on Facebook and Instagram @HeadofZeus, and join our mailing list.